# 'Nine Yarns'
-
# Introducing Private Eye David Moss

© Neal Hardin 2024

All rights reserved.

First Edition

Neal Hardin has asserted his rights under the Copyright, Designs and patents act 1988 to be identified as the author of this book.

No part of this book may be reproduced or used, or transmitted in any form, without the prior written permission of the author. For permissions requests, contact the author.

**This is a work of fiction**. Names, characters, businesses, places, events, and incidents are either the products of the author's imagination or used in a fictitious manner. Any resemblance to actual persons, living or dead, or actual events is purely coincidental.

ISBN 9798322278382

*~~~~~~~~~~~~~~~*

*In memory to my friend*

*Steve Western.*

*5th April 1955 to 29th February 2024*

*~~~~~~~~~~~~~~~*

# Contents

Book I:      Novel:   The Hong Kong Brief.

Book II:     8 short stories:
             The Dark Web.
             Going Dutch.
             Little Sister.
             In a New York Minute.
             The Wayward Genius.
             Old Soap.
             Five Angry Men.
             The Gingerbread Man.

*With thanks to Leo Batt, and Alison Henesey for your advice, guidance, corrections, and suggestions.*

# Book I

## The Hong Kong Brief

London, April 2017

Chapter One

The melodic sound of the busker's guitar echoed against the low, tiled ceiling of the pedestrian walkway. The artist was serenading the swarm of commuters buzzing through the cross tunnels in Oxford Circus tube station. She sang... *'But February made me shiver...With every paper I'd deliver...Bad news on the doorstep...'*

Dave Moss, his head down, his thoughts elsewhere, didn't register that she was singing the second stanza of 'Bye-Bye Miss American Pie' which just happened to be one of his favourite pieces of music. She had arranged it in a jaunty tempo that sounded more up-beat than the Don McLean original. But the words still recalled the memories of years gone and the tragic death of Buddy Holly and his music.

Moss was aiming for the strip of light at the top of the stairs and some much-needed fresh air after the stale tainted humidity on the underground train.

As he emerged into the opening at the summit he drew in a breath. The sharp, cold, icy breeze whipping along Regent Street caught him by surprise. He let out an audible 'brrrr', then shivered as the chill hit his senses. In response, he pulled the collar of his coat up and hunched his shoulders like a man who was about to be drenched by a bucketful of cold water. Despite the watery sunshine, London was still in the grip of the back end of a week-long cold snap that had left the early April days feeling more like the first week of January. The pavement was slippery under foot. He slipped his hands into the deep recess of the coat pockets and made a tight fist. The sounds of the city clamped around him and gave him an increased jolt of energy. After all, he was in the centre of one of the world's truly great cities, for this part of central London, situated right in the middle of the bustling West End, was a busy backdrop of people going about their business.

He walked along Regent Street for a couple of hundred yards then took a left and ventured into a maze of narrow, tight thoroughfares that marked the beginning of Soho. An area full of eateries, hotspot pubs, small niche shops and the home of many micro-businesses.

His office wasn't too far away. Once he was inside and he had a cup of hot, steaming coffee in his hands he would feel much better and warmer.

Dave Moss was a proverbial one-man band. He had been in the private investigator business for two years short of a decade. His office was in a cramped, two-room space on the first floor of a building above a pastry shop on Broadwick Street. He wasn't exactly the Sam Spade or the Philip Marlowe of London town. His list of cases didn't consist of assignments in which he had to use his wit and charm to get out of sticky situations, neither were they glamorous or demanding. His work load usually concerned the surveillance of errant company employees or a suspicious husband wanting to keep tabs on his wife who he suspected – mostly incorrectly – was involved with the local Casanova. The guy who couldn't keep his pecker in his pants. The private investigation business wasn't like that portrayed in the movies, in which some character who resembled a modern-day Humphrey Bogart was assigned to follow a stunning blonde to an exotic beach side location. Or on the other side of the coin, a criminal to some desolate former industrial site that was now a rust strewn carcass of decay. Nor was he paid thousands of pounds to crack some high-end jewellery theft.

His assignments tended to involve the more hum-drum things in life, that sadly, for him, didn't involve the former scenario. Still it paid okay, and he had a reasonably good standard of living, though – for the record – being a private detective in modern day Britain wasn't all it was cracked up to be. It was a hard slog and he was in a dog-eat-dog kind of industry that involved things that in some cases were close to being unethical.

He made it to his office within five minutes of leaving the underground station. His priority was to fill the kettle, then turn on the heating and open the post. The office had a desk, a PC, and several metal cabinets full of files suspended on plastic runners. There were diplomas attached to the walls, a thin rug on the floor, dust on top of the cabinets and a lack of sumptuous decoration. The plaster walls were a shade of mint paint. As very few clients ever visited his office, he never had much need to worry about the look of the place. He preferred to conduct business by email or face-to-face meetings in mutually agreed locations, sometimes in full view of witnesses, other times in private.

Behind his desk was a six-pane single sheet window that allowed light in and provided him with a view onto the narrow width of the street below. The diplomas hanging on the wall inside thin narrow wood frames, blu-tacked to the wall, were genuine. A couple contained photographs of classic Hollywood produced PIs, like the late, great Humphrey Bogart in his industry defining portrayal of Sam Spade. The other was Paul Newman, as Ross MacDonald's insouciant private detective, Lew Harper. Moss loved private-eye movies. His all-time favourite was one of the best movies ever made, Chinatown. He just loved the character Jake Gittes, played so wonderfully by Jack Nicholson.

In truth, he didn't know why he bothered to display the diplomas because very few clients ventured into here. In these days of rapid, modern technology, Skype and Zoom and all the rest of it, business tended to be carried out by face-time meetings. Or perversely in mutually agreed locations, such as public houses and eateries scattered far and wide across the city.

As a former Met police detective, Dave Moss knew the score and had the wherewithal to be good at what he did. He would confess that he didn't have a selection of one-liners and the laconic charisma of those aforementioned fictional characters. Still, he knew the ins and outs of the game. He had divorced both his wife, Jenny, and the Met police at the age of thirty-eight. That was getting on for eight years now. At forty-six years of age, he viewed life from a philosophical plateau of whatever-will-be-will-be. He dealt with everything modern day life could sling at him to eke out a decent existence. He resided in a small flat in a 1950s building on a stretch of Knightsbridge, therefore he was literally a couple of hundred yards from the beating heart of the city.

On this day, he was sitting at his desk for ten to ten, scanning through the pages of a morning red top newspaper, when he was distracted by the flashing, red light on the telephone on his desk.

He closed the newspaper, then pressed the loudspeaker button. "Dave Moss Private Investigator," he said. "How can I help you today?" This was his normal opening patter for the question asked at the end invited the caller to indulge in shared conversation.

There was no instant reply, so he asked the question for a second time. He waited for an answer with his finger poised over the terminate button. He could just make out the sound of a breath on the other end of the line.

"Hello," came a hushed voice from down the line.

"Good morning. How can I help you today?" Moss asked again.

"It is my daughter-in-law," came the reply in precisely worded English. Hearing the speaker's accent, for the first time, suggested that English wasn't the one he used for day-to-day communication.

"What about your daughter-in-law?" he asked.

"She is…" the caller paused in mid-sentence and seemed to lose the will to continue.

"She is what?"

"Missing."

The caller was hesitant. His accent sounded oriental, Chinese, or Korean or somewhere from that part of the world. Moss reached for a pen and a notepad.

"What is the name of your daughter-in-law?" he asked.

"Lily Fung," he replied.

"Lily? L-I-L-Y? Fung? F-U-N-G?" Moss asked.

"Yes."

"How long has she been missing?"

"Two to three weeks," came the reply.

The caller was definitely not a young man. There was a throaty edge to his voice which suggested he was in his late sixties or early seventies. Moss saw the face of an elderly Chinese man appear in his mind's eye. Almond shape eyes, a yellow tint to his skin and short grey wiry hair.

"How old is Lily?" he asked as he scribbled the name, LILY FUNG onto the note-pad.

"Twenty-eight," came the reply.

"Do you want me to help you find your daughter-in-law?" Moss asked.

"Yes. She leave home three weeks ago. Nobody see her since."

"Where's home?" Moss asked.

"Kensington," came the reply. Moss wrote: RICH and CHINESE on the notepad in upper case letters, next to the name of LILY FUNG. He was instantly intrigued.

"Do you know where she has gone?" he asked.

"Yes."

"Where?"

"Hong Kong," came the reply.
"Hong Kong!" Moss asked seeking confirmation.
"Yes."
"Do you know where in Hong Kong?"
"I think so."
"What would you like me to do if I find her?" Moss asked.
"Find her and bring her back to London," the caller said.
"What if she doesn't want to come back?"
"You tell her to come back," said the caller with a hint of command in the tone.
"Okay. Is she in Hong Kong with anyone?"
"Yes."
"Who?"
"The man who take her away from my son."
"A male friend?" Moss asked cagily and warily.
"But she already married to my son. Hue."
"Why doesn't your son go to Hong Kong to ask her to come back?" Moss asked.
"He can't," replied the caller.

Moss was about to ask why his son couldn't go to Hong Kong to find his wife, but thought better of it. An image of a family in dispute or in some kind of marital crisis filled his mind. It was too early to jump to such a conclusion. Maybe there was a sound, legitimate reason why his son couldn't go to Hong Kong to bring his wife back to London. Did he have some connections to the troubles in that part of the world? Or was it for other reasons that weren't immediately obvious?

"Do you know her whereabouts in Hong Kong?" he asked.
"Yes."
"And you'd like me to go over there and persuade her, because that's all I can do, to come back?"
"Yes."

Moss quickly summarised the task and considered his options. He refrained from asking the caller any more probing questions at this time.

"Okay," he said. "What I suggest is that we meet to discuss the brief face-to-face. Is that agreeable with you?" he asked.

"That is agree," the caller replied.

"If you require me to go to Hong Kong to find your daughter-in-law this is something I can do. Is that okay?" There was no immediate response to the question. "Would you like to meet with me to discuss the job?"

"Yes. That is acceptable to me," said the chap, breaking the word 'acceptable' into its four syllables.

"We can meet in my office or a place of your choice. It's completely up to you."

"You come to my home," said the caller.

"That's fine. Can I ask your name?" Moss asked.

"My name is Ho Fung."

"Where is your home, Mr Fung?"

He provided Moss with an address on a street in the heart of Belgravia. One of London's most desirable and expensive locations to live in. Dave Moss was even more intrigued. He looked at the clock on the wall.

"What time would you like to meet?" he asked.

"Can you be here at two-thirty?"

"Today?"

"Yes."

"Yes. I can."

And with that Mr Fung terminated the conversation.

The time was ten-fifteen. A day that had started off quiet and cold was about to get a whole lot more interesting and a lot warmer.

Following the telephone conversation Moss got straight on-line and carried out some desk research. He typed 'Ho Fung' into Wikipedia to see if it had anything on that name. After a couple of clicks of the mouse he had a good stash of information to hand. He was ultimately surprised by what he discovered. If it was the same person. A man by the name of Ho Fung, had been a major industrialist in Hong Kong in the engineering and the ship building industry during the seventies and the eighties. He had amassed quite a fortune. His business interests had links to large multinationals based in China and elsewhere throughout South-East Asia. In a rather grainy black and white photograph taken a few years before there was an image of Ho Fung. He had typical Chinese features, a short nose, narrow eyes, and a pallor shade to his skin. According to his Wiki page he had two children, a son called Hue and a daughter called Mia, aged forty and thirty-six, respectively. Was he the same man? At this time, he had no way of knowing.

If it was Ho Fung's daughter-in-law and he accepted the job there was absolutely no guarantee he would be able to find her in the teeming hustle and bustle of Hong Kong. If he did, would he be able to persuade her to return to London with him? After all, he assumed she had left her husband to take up with someone else under her own free will.

What Moss later discovered through some more desk research was that Ho Fung had left Hong Kong in early 1997, three months before the Chinese takeover of the former British administrated territory. He brought his family and all his money to London, rather than take the journey to North America where many Hong Kong Chinese had headed before the handover and return to Chinese control. He and his family were now naturalised British citizens and European Union passport holders.

Chapter 2

The afternoon temperature was up a few degrees from the low of the morning chill. The sun was high in the sky and beginning to spread a vibrant orange glow over the streets of central London. Shadow from the row of buildings on the east side of Sloane Street was slowly progressing across the road like an incoming tide. Despite still being on the cool side it wasn't such a bad day for mid-April. The city wasn't yet swelled with tourists. As a result, Londoners could still get from A to B without too much hassle.

Moss made his way into Belgravia and walked through the streets, with their pristine smartness and up-market *savoir-vivre*. The Fung residence was the last but one house in a long row that was situated in a cul-de-sac at the end of Seaton Place. At the top of the street was an opening that led into a small square which was encased by tall poplar trees set aside a grassy area. All the properties were high, five storey, white-walled stucco houses, behind wrought iron black metal railings that lined the street. Similar balconies ran along the entire length of the first floor in front of high, floor to ceiling windows. All had steps leading to solid front doors and steps going down to a basement level.

He stepped off the pavement, up a step, onto a tiled porch and approached the front door that was under the shade of the overhead balcony. He pressed a door bell in an intercom and waited for a response. A quick glance at his wrist told him he was dead on time.

Within a few seconds of pressing the bell, the front door opened and a small middle-aged lady with oriental features appeared. She was wearing a kind of grey housemaid's uniform. She had a somewhat glum, unwelcoming expression on her face. Looking beyond her shoulder he could see onto a vestibule with a shining, marble floor and blanch walls. A black-carpeted staircase on the right-hand side led up to the first floor. A corridor straight ahead went into the back of the house. A scent from lavender incense sticks filled his nostrils.

The lady in the maid's uniform observed him, still unsmiling, then she nodded her head at him.

"Mr David Moss. Here to see Mr Fung," he said.

She didn't say a word, but opened the door wide and invited him inside with an inward wave of her hand. He stepped over the threshold, wiped his shoes on a thick brush door mat and entered the vestibule that was furnished with a Queen Anne style antique writing bureau and a matching chair. Both probably early nineteenth-century and French in origin. Several large, gold leaf traditional Chinese dragon statues were dotted here and there on the floor. A silk-thread embroidered picture of a young woman sitting on a tree branch playing a flute was attached to a wall. Close by was a Hong Kong British flag placed inside a gleaming glass case.

The maid came past him. "This way," she said in a faint voice. She led him into the hallway. He followed her for a few paces to an open door and she escorted him inside a formal reception room that faced the street. There was a curvy back sofa in a gold fabric covering and a single chair to a side. A multi-coloured rug covered the floor. A large mahogany desk with intricate carvings was placed by the back wall. Light was streaming in through a pair of narrow, high windows that were covered with open venetian blinds. The room was spotlessly clean and tidy.

The high ceiling had a central rose from where a cut-glass chandelier was hanging. An open fireplace and ornate tiled fire surround were the dominant features in the room. Above that was a gold and silver twine wallcovering of a Chinese landscape scene with rolling hills in the backdrop and a lake in the foreground.

She pointed to the sofa, but remained mute. Moss nodded his head. He stepped to the sofa, plumped down, sat back and crossed his legs. She immediately backed out of the room to leave him alone and closed the door behind her. The

Fung family were obviously very wealthy. Wealthier than the average Joe and far wealthier than the average Hong Kong Chinese family. Moss adjusted his tie to make sure the knot was tight into the shirt collar.

Five minutes passed with no one coming to see him. It was as if they were waiting to see if he would become impatient and leave. Maybe they were testing him. Of course, he wouldn't leave until someone asked him to do so.

He was beginning to feel like the forgotten man when the door opened, and a man stepped into the room. He was alone.

Moss got to his feet and offered him his open hand. "Mr Fung?" he asked, assuming he was the client. The man gave him a solemn nod of his head. "Nice to meet you. My name is David Moss of Moss Private Investigation services." It was the standard patter.

The man didn't smile. He was in his late sixties to early seventies and had the common oriental features. His head was lined with thick, short cropped wiry, grey hair. His skin had a pallid yellow tint. He had small liver spots around his eyes. He did resemble the man in the Wiki photograph. He was a short chap, only about five feet two or three. Thin and gaunt. His waist wouldn't have measured more than thirty-two. But dignified looking. As you would expect for a wealthy individual.

Fung looked at Moss then took his hand and they exchanged the briefest of handshakes. "Please be seated," he said. Moss reassumed his place on the sofa. Ho Fung went to the desk and sat in a black leather armchair. Moss noticed the liver spots on his face and how they were almost like for like down both sides of his cheeks. He had thin almond-shaped eyes behind loose lids.

He was wearing an everyday plain blue acrylic cardigan over a chequered shirt and grey trousers. The clasp of an expensive watch on his left wrist. He looked closely at Moss.

"Thank you for come to see me today," he said in a heartfelt tone. His English was good, though not word perfect. Moss nodded his head in a deferential manner. He wasn't going to say anything until he was asked a direct question.

"My daughter-in-law she go back to Hong Kong with her lover. I need someone to find her and bring her back here." Moss didn't respond and let him continue. "She leave her husband, my son, and bring dishonour to my family."

Moss uncrossed his legs. He was trying to assess Fung's integrity. He spoke in an even measured tone and hadn't displayed any residue anger. He appeared to be in full control of his emotions.

"She go with a play...boy. She fall for this man and leave her husband. Her husband, he is sad," he said. Moss kept his expression neutral and continued to listen with his eyes. Fung continued. "You go to Hong Kong and bring her back here," he instructed.

Moss considered his words for all of three seconds. "I'll have to see," he replied.

"What you need to see?" Fung asked. Perhaps he now realised this wasn't going to be as straight forward as it sounded.

"A few things," Moss replied. He dipped a hand into a side coat pocket and extracted a notepad with a pen clipped to it. "Can I ask you a few questions?" he asked.

Fung thought about it for a moment, then nodded his head.

"What's your daughter-in-law's name?"

"Lily Fung."

"How old is Lily?"

"She twenty-eight."

"What's her background?" he asked. Fung seemed confused by the question. "Does she have any business interests?" Moss asked.

"No."

"Do they have any children?"

"No."

"What's the name of the man she went with?"

"Leo Sinnott."

"Please can you spell that?"

Fung spelt out the name in clearly pronounced letters. "L-E-O…S-I-N-N-O-T-T."

Moss wrote it down onto the notepad. "What's the name of your son?" he asked.

"Hue."

"Why doesn't Hue want to go to Hong Kong to find her and bring her back?"

"He not want to go to Hong Kong." He didn't offer any explanation as to why this was the case. Maybe there was a legitimate reason why he didn't want to or couldn't return to Hong Kong. Though he didn't seem to want to elaborate.

"Okay. Do you know where she is right now?" Moss asked.

"He has a home in an apartment in the Leighton Hill area."

Moss wrote it down on his pad. He had spent some time in Hong Kong ten years ago, and recalled the name of the area. "How did she meet…," he paused to look at his notepad. "Leo Sinnott?" he hoped he had pronounced it correctly.

"He come to London on business. He seduce Lily and persuade her to go back with him."

"How long was he here in the UK?" Moss asked.

"Several weeks."

"What was he doing here? Do you know?"

"He is race horse trainer in Hong Kong. He visits some horse auction in England to buy racehorses for Hong Kong owners."

Moss wrote, 'horse racing trainer' on the pad. "Did he target her from the outset?" he asked.

Fung seemed fazed by the question. "What you mean?" he asked.

Moss had to think this through carefully and not put ideas into his head. "Do you think his intentions towards her were genuine?"

"I not know."

"Do you have the address?"

"Yes."

"And you think she could be there?"

"I think so."

"Why do you think so?"

"Because she told me."

"When did you last speak to her?"

"I not speak to her."

"How do you know where she is?" Moss asked.

"Because she writes to me."

"And she gave you an address?"

"Yes, that right."

Moss wasn't going to ask him why he wanted her back here. Maybe there was a good reason why she had left her husband, but this seemed to be of little interest to Fung. It could all be about family honour rather than anything untoward. "You go to Hong Kong to find her and bring her back?" Fung said in a raised tone. Again, expressing his desire that she had to return.

Moss's face displayed a neutral look. "I can go, but if I'm being truthful, I can't guarantee that I can bring her back. I can't force her to return," he said.

"You try?"

"Yes. I can try."

"Good. When can you go?"

Moss had already checked the times of the flights leaving London for Hong Kong. "There are a few seats left on a flight from Heathrow tomorrow afternoon at two. I can be on that flight."

Fung retained an impassive face. "Good," he said. "Be on flight. Do you know anyone in Hong Kong?" he asked.

Moss smiled. "I spent some time there about ten years ago."

"Doing what?"

"I was there on police business for several weeks. We were seeking to extradite a British man back to the UK to stand trial," Moss said.

"Do you know anyone there?"

"I know a couple of people. A guy called Laurie Sullivan was a detective in the Hong Kong force. He showed me around the city. We worked together on the case and he was my interpreter."

"Is he still there?"

"In Hong Kong?" Fung didn't reply. "Yes. As far as I know he's still lives in Kowloon. I still keep in contact with him from time to time. A card at Christmas. The occasional email. That kind of thing."

"This man. He might be useful to you?"

"Could be." Fung smiled at him for the first time. "Tell me about," Moss looked at his notes. "Leo Sinnott."

"He is race horse trainer at Happy Valley. He also a gigolo," he snarled. "He uses women," he snarled once again. He clearly had a genuine dislike for the man who had taken his daughter-in-law from his son.

"Can you give me his address?"

Fung opened a drawer in the desk and extracted two sheets of paper. He placed them on the desk top, then slid them towards Moss. He reached out of the seat to take them.

One was a folded piece of plain white paper from a pad; the other item was a glossy hardback photograph showing two people. A Chinese couple. He opened the folded paper and written there on the inside was an address in the Leighton Hill district of the city.

Fung sat back into the armchair and sighed out loud. It seemed as if a huge weight had been lifted from his shoulders. Moss did wonder why he had asked him to take on the job and not rely on a Hong Kong operative to contact Lily Fung and persuade her to return to London. Perhaps he didn't trust anyone out there. It crossed his mind to ask Mr Fung, but he refrained from doing so. He looked at Fung. He admired his style and character. He was akin to a wise Chinese philosopher from a bygone age who displayed great wisdom and foresight.

"Can we talk about my fees?" Moss asked. Fung nodded his head once. "I charge one thousand pounds a day, plus expenses, payable at the end of the job." Fung nodded his head once again. "One more question. Do you want me to contact you with progress?"

"No. I just want her back here. When she is back, I be happy man," Fung said.

Moss pursed his lips then nodded his head. He looked at the photograph. It was of a couple who were standing slightly apart. Like a married couple, who maybe didn't want to remain married for much longer. The man was on the right of the shot, the woman on the left. It looked as if it had been taken at a social event of some description because it was an internal location and they were both dressed in evening wear. He was in a dark lounge suit. She was in a long, dark dress. She was taller than her husband. "I assume this is your son and his wife?" Moss said.

"That is my son Hue and his wife Lily Fung," he replied.

She was an attractive woman with high cheek bones and a pretty face. Petite looking and very slim. She had long, straight black hair that reached the turn of her waist. She looked almost flat-chested as the slit in the dress revealed little in the way of cleavage. Hue Fung, her husband looked overweight and podgy. He wore thick black-framed spectacles over his eyes. His suit looked expensive Saville

Row. Definitely not off the peg from some cheap Oxford Street store. It reeked of top end tailoring.

"When was this taken?" Moss asked.

"Last year. At my seventy-fifth birthday party."

"May I keep it?"

"Yes, of course."

Moss carefully slipped the photograph into his inside coat pocket, along with the paper with the address on it. His brief was simple, in the extreme, he had to find Lily Fung and return her to London.

"When you leave for Hong Kong?" Fung asked.

"Tomorrow afternoon on a British Airways flight."

Fung got to his feet. Moss did likewise. Fung looked at him. "Thank you," he said.

He went to the closed door, opened it and led Moss out into the vestibule, across the floor and on towards the front door. Light was beaming through a window to spread its reflection over the marble floor. The gold leaf of the big dragon statues glinted in the light. The housemaid appeared. She opened the front door to let him out.

Moss was soon walking along the pavement and past the steps going down to a door leading into the basement. His first stop was a travel agent on Sloane Street. He would get himself a seat on the BA flight and pay for a room in a central hotel for five nights. If Fung was picking up the tab it would be a five-star hotel in the best part of Wanchai. That got him thinking about contacting Laurie Sullivan to tell him he was coming over to HK for a visit. Laurie Sullivan was a detective in the Hong Kong police force when the territory was under British control. He had stayed on following the handover in 1997 and remained in the HK police for a further twelve years or so until he retired in 2009. He still lived in Kowloon. Moss had met him when he went to HK to extradite a commodities dealer wanted in London for fraud. Sullivan was fluent in Cantonese.

When Moss came over Sullivan had shown him the ropes and the city. They got along fine. Although they hadn't met face-to-face for three years, when Sullivan came home for a short visit, Moss still sent him an email now and again to ask him how he was getting on and enjoying his retirement. Although he was now in his mid-sixties, Sullivan was an active guy in that he kept fit and his ear close to everything that was going on. Moss was more than pleased that he had kept in touch with him because he could be a big help. It was almost as if it was meant to be.

## Chapter 3

The following day, Tuesday, Moss made it onto the British Airways mid-afternoon flight to Hong Kong. He secured the last remaining seat in business class. He had paid for a room in a five-star hotel in the heart of the Wanchai district, the bustling epicentre of central Hong Kong island. He planned to stay for five nights.

He knew from his previous visit to Hong Kong that there are few places in this world to match the vibrancy and pace of Hong Kong. The place where the modern west meets a rapidly developing China. But in a setting where many traditional eastern customs and beliefs remain in a fusion of colour and neon and in a melting pot of culture. Sadly, for Moss he wouldn't be seeing many of the sights. He had a job to do, one that could be very tricky for he had no idea if he was going to be able to find Lily Fung, never mind persuade her to return to London. It had been ten years since he had last been on the island. A decade was a long time and a lot of things may have changed. Therefore, he would have to refamiliarise himself with the surroundings. This is where Laurie Sullivan might be of tremendous use to him.

Before leaving London, he emailed Sullivan to tell him he was coming over. He gave him the barest details of his brief, only telling him that he was on a *misper* case. *Misper* being short for missing person. Sullivan emailed him back within two hours to say that he would be able to meet him in a Wanchai pub called 'The Old Country' on Jaffe Road on Wednesday afternoon at two o'clock.

Following an overnight flight of twelve hours, Moss arrived on the other side of the globe at nine clock – Hong Kong time, the following morning. He cleared customs and immigration within the hour. Rather than take the train or bus onto Hong Kong island he took a red taxi from Chek Lap Kok airport and made it into the central district of Wanchai. He was checking into the Wanchai Mandarin Garden hotel all within one and a half hours of getting through immigration.

After a couple of hours of much needed rest, Moss was out of the hotel for one-forty in the afternoon to meet Laurie Sullivan. Despite the jet lag in his body he was determined not to waste a minute of time. He wasn't here for a sight-seeing trip; therefore, he was looking to get out and start his investigation as soon as possible. From what he could recall from his last visit, much had changed in the past decade. There were now several new high-rise buildings and more glitz, but the old commercialism was just as rampant. What hadn't changed at all was the fast pace of life and the sights, sounds and the smells of Hong Kong, the beating heart of the new assertive China on the south-east tip of the Chinese mainland.

'The Old Country' pub on Jaffe Road was a fifteen-minute stroll from his hotel, through the back-street markets of Wanchai. It was precisely two o'clock when he spotted a neon-lit sign advertising the pub, attached to the building above an entrance. He stepped off the pavement, through an opening, up a flight of steep stone stairs, through a second open door and into the bar area.

Despite being a Wednesday afternoon, the bar was full of young, business types in sharp suits, shiny shoes, and executive haircuts. Asian, European and North American voices filled the air. The talk was of business and money. Two pretty girls behind the bar were serving food and drinks to the patrons. A wide screen TV above the mirrored bar was displaying Hong Kong stock market movements. Whirling fans in the ceiling wafted a pleasant, cooling breeze throughout the interior.

Moss put his eyes on Laurie Sullivan the instant he stepped inside. It wasn't hard to see him. Sullivan was a man of good stature who, even at sixty-five-years-of-age, hadn't lost any of his size. He was standing adjacent to the bar with a bottle in one hand and a full glass in the other.

Sullivan was originally from the Salford area where he was a detective sergeant in the Manchester force for several years before transferring to the Hong Kong police service in the mid-1980s. He had a northerner's gruff approach to life and a no-nonsense approach to what was right and what was wrong. This may have been tainted by some misdemeanours from his past. Which is why, when the opportunity arose, he had gotten out of the North of England and transferred over here. Once here he had ascended the greasy pole rapidly to become a top detective in the island's police department. He was a copper's copper in the days when a good whack across the back of the head was all a 'scallywag' required to keep him on the straight and narrow.

Moss knew Sullivan had a reputation for being a detective who seldom played it by the book, but he was well-respected. When the British left Hong Kong in 1997, Sullivan decided to remain in post. The new police authorities thought it prudent to retain his services. He was still here twenty years later. He was, by now, fluent in Cantonese and Mandarin. At the time he was married to a local girl twenty years his junior. The marriage didn't last long. They divorced within three years. He lived in an up-market part of Kowloon, in a high-rise apartment block. Just like most of the locals.

It felt good for Moss to see him in the flesh after three years. From what he could tell Sullivan hadn't changed all that much. He had a shaven head three years before and still had one today so that hadn't changed. As a result, he wasn't grey. He was wearing a plain, white cotton shirt, open to the second button so he was displaying a line of chest hair and a pendant on a gold chain around his neck. His skin looked waxy and his face sported the tell-tale signs of ageing. Still he wasn't a bad-looking guy even at this age.

Sullivan observed Moss enter the bar. He had a wide smile on his face. As they met, he held out a meaty hand and they exchanged a firm handshake. "How are you?" he asked Moss. He hadn't lost any of his strength.

"Good," he replied, "and you?"

"Can't complain. If I did no one would take a blind bit of notice anyway."

Sullivan laughed out loud, raised the bottle to his lips and took a swig. In the time it took to lift the bottle to his lips Moss detected that his personality hadn't changed. He still retained a warm personality, a dry sense of humour, wit, and inkling of self-deprecation.

"So, what brings you to Honkers?" Sullivan asked.

"Long story."

"Okay." Sullivan smiled. "Care to fill me in?" he asked.

"Yeah. Can do. But first let me buy you a drink. What 'you having?"

Sullivan asked for a bottle of imported Danish lager. Moss asked the bar girl for two.

Once they had a drink in his hands Sullivan shepherded Moss across the room to a vacant table. They stepped into an area adjacent to an open window overlooking Jaffe Road. Across the way, clothes hanging on washing lines pulled across the balconies of a run-down tenement, were motionless in a non-existent breeze. The ceiling fans were spinning to send a delightful wave of cool air around the interior. They sat in a pair of wicker chairs at a pine topped table. Sullivan looked out of the window for a moment, then back on Moss.

"So, you've come all the way out here on business. What's the score?" he asked.

"I'm here to find a girl."

"Aren't we all?" said Sullivan, then chuckled to himself before taking a swig of his fresh beer. "Who is she?" he asked.

"Someone you might have heard of," Moss replied.

Sullivan looked interested. "Oh right. Like who?"

"The daughter-in-law of Ho Fung. Her name is Lily Fung."

"Ho Fung. The big business bloke. I know him," Sullivan said. "I did some work for him a few years ago. And he's called you to find her?" he asked, seemingly surprised by this revelation.

Moss didn't ask him what kind of work he had done for Ho Fung. Perhaps he would enquire later. He looked down onto the activity on the road. At the steam rising from the street side food vendors who were cooking rice and noodles to sell to the passing trade. The noise of the traffic and the sights and sounds of people on the pavement filtered their way through the open window. Moss noticed that Sullivan's brow was peppered with beads of sweat, though it wasn't a hot day in mid-town Hong Kong.

"That's right," said Moss responding to his question.

"What do you know about her?" Sullivan asked.

"Not a lot. I've got a photograph of her and her husband. He doesn't seem bothered about her. I picked up that vibe from the old man."

"Who doesn't seem bothered by what?"

"Her husband. Hue Fung doesn't appear to be bothered that she's gone."

"Let me see the photograph," Sullivan requested.

Moss extracted the photograph from a jacket pocket and handed it to him. Sullivan glanced at it fleetingly. "Pretty woman. How old?" he asked.

"According to the old man she's twenty-eight."

"Twenty-eight hey?"

Moss said nothing. He rubbed his tired eyes. He'd had several hours sleep, but the jet lag was still deeply imbedded in his head. He was suffering from a bout of Hong Kong haze and culture shock. It would take at least another twenty-four hours for it to work out of his system. He took a sip of the beer in the glass, then looked down onto the top of a double-decker tram trundling along Jaffe Road.

Sullivan handed the photograph back to him. "What did Fung tell you about her?" he asked.

"Not a great deal. Just that she's got into bed with this playboy type and returned here with him."

"Maybe the marriage was already on the rocks and she didn't need much persuasion to run off with this guy. What's his name?" Sullivan asked.

"According to Fung. He's called Leo Sinnott." Sullivan's eyebrows lifted on mention of the name. Moss saw his reaction. "You know him?" he asked.

"I don't know him. But sure, I've heard his name and heard about his reputation."

"What reputation?" Moss asked.

"Bit of a charismatic guy with matinee idol good looks. Rich. Well educated. Connected. Old money type. British father. Hong Kong Chinese mother. Born here in HK."

"He's a racehorse trainer," said Moss.

"Yeah, that's him. Have you got an address for him?" Sullivan asked.

Moss nipped his fingers into a pocket and extracted his notepad. He had written the address on the first page. He opened the notepad and looked at it. He read it out in a low voice. "Apartment 35A, Tower C, Leighton Hill, Hong Kong."

"Sounds about right. A location overlooking Happy Valley racecourse," said Sullivan. He took an intake of the beer in the bottle in his hand. "Where did he meet Lily Fung?" he asked.

"Not sure where exactly. Fung never said. All he said was that Sinnott was in England on horse racing business and met her somewhere. Swept her off her feet and persuaded her to come back here with him. Next thing she's in Hong Kong. But the old man wants her to return P.D.Q."

"P.D. what?" Sullivan asked.

"Pretty damn quick."

Sullivan chuckled. "He's got serious form of doing this kind of thing."

"Who?" Moss asked. "What kind of thing?" he added.

"Leo Sinnott," replied Sullivan. Moss immediately thought that Sullivan may have known Sinnott better than he was letting on. There was something in his tone and reaction that suggested he knew him well. He parked it at the back of his mind for the time-being. He looked at his notepad.

"This is the only address I've got for him. The one in Leighton Hill."

Sullivan edged forward. "I suggest you go there to see if she's there. If not, he may know where she is," he said. He took another sip of his beer and savoured the taste of the hops as they hit the back of his tongue. Then he wiped the back of his hand over his brow to dislodge the beads of sweat. His skin was glistening with perspiration and the oil on his bald head was reflecting the light.

"I think that sounds like a good suggestion. I'll start by contacting this guy to see if she's there or if he knows where she is. Thing is I might need backup. Would you watch my back?" Moss asked.

Sullivan considered the question for a few brief moments. "Yeah. Of course. Glad to assist in any way I can. Let's go. Do it now. Strike while the iron's hot. We'll take a taxi. If he's not there he'll be at the track this evening. Wednesday night is race night at the Valley."

"Okay," said Moss. It appeared as if Sullivan was more than happy to get involved right from the start. Moss could only think this was a positive development.

It was a further five minutes before they stepped out of the pub and went down the stairs to street level. The sound of the street-life and the traffic on Jaffe Road bounced off the walls in the tightly packed valley of tall buildings.

On the street, water was running in the gutter to sweep litter away. The surroundings were so different to those in London. Moss was still finding it difficult to grasp that he was in Hong Kong. It might take a few more hours for the location to really sink in.

Sullivan led the way to a taxi rank on the corner of the street. He spoke fluent Cantonese to the cab driver and asked him to take them to an address in Leighton Hill.

## Chapter 4

The taxi driver soon took them out of Wanchai and the two or three miles across town to Leighton Hill. The surrounding hilltops contained a semi-circular wall of eight apartment blocks that reach up forty floors to ring the valley and encase it in a spectacular backdrop.

The high towers were in an area overlooking the large oval-shaped segment of open land that was the magnificent Happy Valley racecourse.

The cabbie set them down outside the front of apartment tower C and by a garden area in front of the glass foyer area that led into the tower. As it was on high ground, Leighton Hill afforded a spectacular view out over the skyscrapers spread across the cityscape, the harbour and the top of Victoria peak.

They got out of the cab. Sullivan paid the fare on the path. He asked the driver to hang about for ten minutes just in case they needed him to take them back. Then they stepped through a well-tended manicured garden and on towards the glass entrance. Moss looked up the sheer face of the building soaring up forty floors with a majestic curve of its structure. In the wide balconies, turquoise-coloured blinds cascaded up like rows of perfectly-formed building blocks. Sunlight was reflecting in the windows and steel to splinter off in rays of sharp light.

Sullivan led the way through the glass sliding doors and into a foyer that had a polished marble floor. Cool air was wafting out of an air-conditioning duct. The interior was furnished with several items of artwork and fine decoration, such as several highly-decorative china vases and bottle green glass jardinières full of green leaf plants.

Across the floor was an opaque glass desk at which a man dressed in a pale blue security guard's uniform was sitting reading a newspaper. The sight of two westerners approaching the desk didn't appear to unsettle him as he continued to look at the newspaper until the men were virtually on top of him.

Sullivan gained his attention and said something in Cantonese which immediately attracted his interest. As he didn't understand one word of what was being said Moss could only watch and listen. He was aware of a jasmine fragrance in the cool air. Sullivan and the security guard continued their conversation and even exchanged a smile and a chuckle. The words pinged around the interior and bounced off the high ceiling. On the back wall were two sets of silver-metal doors that led into elevators. The illuminated number count above the doors - from forty to zero - was lit as two cars ventured up and down the huge building. One was stationary on the 10$^{th}$ floor, the other was moving from the 8$^{th}$ floor to the ground.

Sullivan said a few words then the security guard took a telephone, prodded a four-digit number in the pad and waited for a reply.

Sullivan looked to Moss. "He's calling Sinnott's apartment to see if he's home."

"Okay."

"He's only just come on duty," Sullivan said. He looked at his watch. "In the past fifteen minutes. He's no idea if he's at home or if he recently left."

"Did you ask him if he's recently been seen with a pretty woman?"

Sullivan smiled a toothy grin. "He's a playboy for crying out loud. He's had more women up there, than you've had hot dinners."

Twenty seconds passed. One set of the lift doors opened on the ground floor. An elderly Asian lady and a younger woman stepped out and made their way across the floor and out of the sliding-glass doors.

Before they had gone from view the security guard put the telephone down into the cradle. He looked at Sullivan and said something in Cantonese. Sullivan replied in kind and they exchanged a few more words in a pleasant manner.

"He's not here," said Sullivan, referring to Sinnott. "He said, he'll probably be at the stables at the racetrack. Tonight, is race night. He'll be at the track getting his horses prepared for the meeting."

"Okay," said Moss. He extracted the photograph from a coat pocket. "Ask him if he's seen him with her." He also took out a roll of fifty-dollar Hong Kong notes and let the man see the wad. He peeled off three notes which were about the value of fourteen pounds Sterling. "These should jog his memory." Sullivan smiled. He liked Moss's style.

He spoke to the chap. Moss handed him the photograph and wafted the three notes inches from his nose. The guy ran the tip of his tongue over his lips. He looked at Sullivan and spoke at a swift pace.

Sullivan translated: "Yeah, he's seen her, but not for two weeks at least. He said Sinnott brought her here, often, but he hasn't seen her for a while."

"Okay, thank him will you." Moss said. He dropped the notes onto the open pages of the newspaper. The guard instantly whipped them up and placed them in a pants pocket.

With that done, Sullivan and Moss walked out of the foyer, under the shade of the canopy and on towards the waiting taxi. "Let's see if he's at the track," said Moss.

Once they were back in the red cab Sullivan asked the driver to take them to the stables at the racetrack. If Sinnott was going to be anywhere, it would be there.

The racetrack was just down the hill in the valley at the foot of the steep decline, less than five hundred yards from the complex of towers at Leighton Hill.

As the taxi was about to bypass the entrance to the stables Sullivan asked the driver to pull over and drop them outside the gates. The driver set them down by a pair of open, high wrought-iron gates that led into the stable complex.

They got out of the cab. Sullivan paid the driver at the window.

A pair of seriously looking beefy guys were standing close to the entrance, preventing anyone without the requisite accreditation from getting into the courtyard. Inside the yard there was a path on the left-hand side snaking through a set of stables. The path must have led onto the racecourse proper. Several vehicles were parked in the courtyard along with a couple of horse boxes and vehicles which were plastered with the racecourse logo.

Sullivan and Moss approached the two men. "You no come in," said one of them in broken English.

Sullivan responded in Cantonese which immediately put the chaps at ease. In the yard a young man was leading a glistening chestnut thoroughbred racehorse out of a horse box. There was a sound of activity and the sight of someone hosing down a black stallion.

The other security man joined his companion at the other side of the gate and eyed the strangers. Sullivan looked to Moss. "Give them a hundred dollars each," he advised, "then they'll let us in. They think we're bookmakers' spies here to keep tabs on the horses. I've told them that we're just looking for Leo Sinnott. He's here okay. That's his silver Nissan parked over there," he pointed to it. Sure enough, there was a new-model Nissan Juke parked on one side of the courtyard in a line of vehicles. Moss slipped his hand into his pocket and withdrew the roll of notes. He peeled off four fifty-dollar notes and gave them two each. They stepped aside and allowed the Englishmen to enter. The way to the racetrack was along the path in between the patchwork of stables.

They stepped across the yard, then down a path. Moss could smell the fragrance of the turf in his nostrils, intermingled with the stench of fresh horse manure.

Sullivan led the way along the snaking path and in front of the stables in which horses were being attended to.

He seemed to know where he was going or maybe he had a good sense of direction. He led Moss down the path, by the side of the last set of stables, and they came out into a lawn area by the rails at the bottom end of the track. Over to the left, in the near distance, the huge arc of the grandstands, by the finishing line, loomed high above the track. It was a very impressive sight. The massive towers of the apartment blocks on the hills that ringed the track provided it with a spectacular backdrop that couldn't be matched by any other racecourse in the world.

Several racehorses were on the track, pounding the turf, galloping around the bend at breakneck speed. The jockeys were standing high in the stirrups, with their hands tightly clasped around the reins, as they drove the mounts over the lush turf. The hoofs, thudding into the turf, provided an authentic soundtrack. About one hundred yards away, two men were standing by the rail watching the horses fly by. One of them had a stopwatch in his hand, timing the horses as they covered a measured distance. Both men were dressed in light-coloured jodhpurs, green racing capes and both wore calf length leather jockey boots.

One of them turned his head to observe Sullivan and Moss coming their way. The horses were now just turning onto the straight leading to the finishing line. The two men parted company and one of them began to walk along the rail at a slow pace. His eyes were still on the stopwatch in his hand. The other one remained resting his arms on the top of the rail.

"Is that Leo Sinnott?" asked Moss to Sullivan.

"Don't know," he said. But maybe he did. There was something almost manufactured about this or maybe he had just got lucky. They strode across to the guy who looked to his right as another pair of thoroughbreds came hurtling by. Moss took the shades from his eyes. He had to blink several times then pause to let his eyes adjust to the bright colours and the power of the sunlight. Sullivan raised his voice and said something in Cantonese.

The man at the rail turned his head and looked at them.

"Hello," he said in English. He was a tall man. At least six feet in stature, slim, long-legged and barrel-chested. His jet-black hair was neatly arranged. Thick on top, less so down the sides. The fringe was pushed up in a modern style. He had a polished, sophisticated look. With mixed Caucasian and Oriental colouring and features, he resembled a handsome, glossy-magazine male model. He had the gold band of a Rolex on his right-hand wrist and a thin gold choker around his neck. He was wearing tortoise-shell frame shades over his eyes. He looked well turned out in a red-pink Polo shirt under the green cape that was closed at the neck.

"Are you Leo Sinnott?" Moss asked, pronouncing his surname: sin not. The man didn't respond immediately. "Mr Sinnott?" Moss asked again.

The expression on his face told Moss he had located Leo Sinnott. Sinnott's eyes went from Moss to Sullivan then back again. He looked slightly fearful as if he felt that something nasty was about to happen to him.

"Who are you gentlemen?" he asked.

"My name is David Moss. This is Laurie Sullivan." Sinnott's stony, inquisitive glare didn't change. "I've come from London on the request of my client Mister Ho Fung to find his daughter-in-law, Lily Fung," said Moss.

A mention of the name seemed to have an instant effect on Sinnott. He took a hesitant step back and the tense, stony look in his eyes intensified. His body language, which was already taut, became even more palsied.

"Do you know where she is?" Moss asked him.

"I haven't seen her for several weeks," Sinnott said.

"So, you do know her?" Moss asked.

"Yes. I know her. But I've not seen her for days."

"How long precisely?"

Sinnott looked at Moss, raised himself and cocked his head back as if to make himself taller and to seek an advantage over him, though he was already two inches taller than Moss. "Who are you?" he asked.

"Dave Moss. I'm a private investigator sent here by Mr Fung to find his daughter-in-law."

"I know her, but she left," Sinnott said.

"Where did she go?" Moss asked.

"I don't know," Sinnott clamped his lips together as if he wasn't going to say another word unless someone was going to make him talk.

"You don't know where she is?" Moss asked.

"She left my place. I haven't seen her since," Sinnott said after the briefest of pauses.

"Well, she's not back in London. So, she must still be here in Hong Kong," Moss said.

"As I say. She left my apartment with her possessions. I have no idea where she went."

"Why would she leave?" Moss asked.

Sinnott shrugged his shoulders. "We didn't hit it off," he replied in a blasé tone.

"Did you know she's Ho Fung's daughter-in-law?" Moss asked.

"Yes."

"So, you've no idea where she is?" Moss asked.

"No."

"Could she be with friends?"

"Might be." Sinnott said in a cold tone. He had quickly recovered his composure and seemed happy to engage in conversation.

"Do you know any of her friends?" Moss asked.

"No."

Moss immediately sensed that this case was going to get a whole lot more complex than he wanted it to. Simply finding her and asking her to accompany him back to

London, seemed a lot more unlikely than it did two hours before. "Did you have a falling out?" he asked.

"A what?" Sinnott asked.

"An argument. A fight of some description."

"No."

"You sure?"

"Of course."

"So why did she go?" Moss asked.

"That's what you'll need to ask her. She went on her own free will," said Sinnott.

"When?"

"On the night of the twenty-ninth of March."

"How do you know it was that night? How can you be so precise?" Moss asked.

"It was a race night," Sinnott replied.

"Today is the twelfth. So, she's being gone fourteen days."

"When I returned home that evening she had gone and taken her things with her," Sinnott said.

This seemed to tie in with what the security guard in the building had said. He said he hadn't seen her for two weeks.

"Okay," said Moss. "She's gone but do you know where?"

"No," Sinnott said unequivocally.

"How do I know she's not tied up in your apartment."

Sinnott gave him a bemused face and sought to chuckle, but pulled back from doing so. On first impressions, it looked as if he was on the level. "Why would I do that?" he asked.

"I don't know. Maybe it's something you do to pretty women." Moss said. Sinnott grinned. "What if we check your apartment to see if she's still there," Moss asked.

He had effectively backed Sinnott into a corner with no way out, other than to agree to take them to his home to let them look inside his apartment. Maybe Moss would find some evidence of her existence and where she might have gone. It was an outside chance, but one he wanted to take. Sinnott considered it for a few moments. "All right. First, I'll change," he said.

"Be my guest," said Moss.

Sinnott stepped around them. Sullivan and Moss followed him across the lawn and over to the stable block. Moss didn't know how this was going to pan out. There seemed to be a whole lot more to this missing person case then he had anticipated.

As they came into the yard there was a lot more activity than there had been ten minutes before. The number of horse boxes had increased two-fold and there were now more stable lads and lasses leading horses around the yard. Several stable girls in their colourful equestrian gear were carrying buckets of water towards the stables. Several men in jockey silks were standing close-by chatting. As this was a Wednesday it was race night at Happy Valley, clearly the activity in preparation of the first race at seven-thirty was in full swing.

Sinnott entered a block at the end of a row of stables and went out of sight. There was a sign which said: 更衣室, then the English translation saying: Changing Room.

Moss and Sullivan waited on the outside for him to emerge. Nothing was said. Moss had an awful, deflated feeling that this enquiry could quickly spiral out of control. For the first time, he seriously considered that it was likely he would be returning to London without Lily Fung.

## Chapter 5

After a wait of about ten minutes, Leo Sinnott emerged from the changing room. He had changed into a pair of chinos and had a pink cashmere jumper draped over his shoulders. He still had the tortoise-shell sunglasses over his eyes. He was carrying an expensive looking brown leather sports grip in his hand.

He looked at Moss and Sullivan. "We'll go in my car," he said. He led them to a top-of-the-range silver-grey Nissan 4x4, opened the driver's door and got in. Sullivan and Moss got into the back and immediately breathed in the fragrance of brand-new leather.

He started the engine, backed the vehicle into the yard, did a three-point turn and headed through the open gates and out onto the busy Wanchai Road. Nothing was said.

It didn't take Sinnott long to drive up the steep incline to the Leighton Hill tower complex and head along the same service road the taxi had taken. This time he took a turn off, drove around to the back of the towers then along another service road. After fifty yards or so he drove to the back of the huge tower looming high above, to a gated entrance that led into a ground-floor car park, under tower C.

Once there he pulled up, put the window down, reached out and punched a five-digit number into an electronic number-pad. The metal gate at the entrance began to wind up. When it was all the way up, he drove through the opening and into the car park. He drove to the far side, put the vehicle into an allocated parking spot and killed the engine.

He opened his door, Sullivan and Moss did likewise and they followed him across the smooth concrete floor to an elevator. It wasn't long before the lift arrived at the bottom floor. Sinnott directed it to the thirty-fifth floor of the forty-storey tower.

Once the lift was on the thirty-fifth floor, Sinnott turned right and led them onto a landing that was covered by a red and burgundy patterned carpet that ran from one side of the building to the other. Moss was aware of the same cool air and the scent of jasmine. The same smell in the foyer, thirty-five floors below. Sinnott's apartment was the last door on the left-hand side of the corridor.

He punched a number into a number-pad, opened the door and led them into his apartment. It opened straight into an open plan lounge. The first thing that struck Moss was the incredible view of the city from a high window that ran along the length of the lounge.

The interior was gorgeous. The furniture and fittings were of the highest quality. From the blanch-white leather, circular sofa in the centre of the lounge to the modern Kandinsky style artwork on the walls. Everything oozed wealth, class and good taste. All the light fittings were silver stainless steel. The apartment's key selling point was the view of the high-rise blocks and office buildings in the central district of the island. In the gaps between the skyscrapers, it was possible to see a stretch of water in Victoria harbour and beyond that the spread of Kowloon towards the Chinese mainland disappearing into the distance.

Moss took in the view. Behind the window was a balcony, an iron rail balustrade then a drop of thirty-four floors to the top of the entrance canopy roof on the ground level.

Sinnott put his sports bag on a side table aside of the sofa. He went to a telephone and pressed a button. It told him he had three new messages. He elected not to listen to any of them.

Moss looked around. Nothing was out of place. A huge widescreen TV was attached to the far wall. A set of six tall bulrushes were in a large earthenware glazed clay pot.

There was no evidence of a fight or anything remotely like that. Several doors led into rooms off the main living area.

"What do you want to see?" Sinnott asked.

"Everything," Moss replied.

"I've nothing to hide. She's not here." Moss could see there was no evidence that she was here. "You can tell Mr Fung. She's not here," Sinnott said in a calm tone.

"Okay. I'll do that once I'm satisfied," said Moss. "What's that room?" he asked thrusting his chin to a closed door.

Sinnott didn't reply. He went to the door and opened it. Moss followed him into a master bedroom that was furnished in a kind of seventies explosion of colour. Reds and crimsons, shades of apricot and pinks were dominant. The bed was king size. It was neatly made up. Half a dozen pillows were arranged across the bottom of a semi-circular head-board. There was a thick, fluffy carpet on the floor. A door led into an en-suite powder room.

Moss glanced around the room. She wasn't in there. Next Sinnott took him into the main apartment bathroom. It was decked out in black ceramic tiles, glass and chrome. There was a fancy heart-shaped bath with water jets inserted into the surface. A set of snow-white towels were arranged on a ten-bar high stainless-steel heated rail. Glass shelves were lined with several male-grooming products. Moss noticed the lack of female products. From the bathroom, Sinnott took him into a kitchen. It looked as if he didn't eat-in often because everything was spotlessly clean and looked virtually unused. It was a bachelor pad all right. Of course, Moss knew it didn't mean to say he wouldn't have another place elsewhere. Still, this was the address he had been given. There was absolutely no evidence of a female presence here.

Sinnott showed him the rest of the apartment. She wasn't here, nor was there any evidence to say she had. The security guard had said she was here for two weeks. Therefore, she had gone elsewhere.

Sinnott ushered Moss back into the lounge area where Sullivan was standing by the window, enjoying the magnificent view of the city. Down below the horseshoe shape racetrack, the stands and the stables were picture-postcard magnificent. On the balcony, the petals of a child's windmill were turning at a furious pace as the humid air, hit a high, at three o'clock in the afternoon.

"You can see she's not here," said Sinnott. "I don't know where she is." He sounded genuine. "She'd been here, but then she went." It would appear that the handsome, rich playboy, race-horse trainer was telling the truth.

"I believe you," said Moss, "and thanks for showing me around," he added.

Laurie Sullivan turned away from the window and came into the centre of the room.

"Let's go," he said looking at Moss.

Sullivan led the way to the main door of the apartment. Sinnott didn't move from the spot. Sullivan stepped out onto the landing and headed towards the elevator doors. Moss was a few paces behind him.

The fact that Sullivan seemed to know where he was going wasn't lost on Moss. It could have been down to his 'copper's nose' or maybe he had been in a similar building to this or in this very block in the past. After all, he was a detective in the Hong Kong police for longer than Moss had been a detective in the Met. He didn't think a great deal about it.

They were at the lift in a few moments. They rode down to the ground floor and out into the warmth of the mid-afternoon sunlight blazing into the foyer.

Sullivan spoke a few words to the guy at the reception desk. He asked him to call a taxi. The chap picked up a telephone and tapped in a number. A car to take them into central Wanchai arrived five minutes later.

## Chapter 6

The taxi driver dropped Moss right outside his hotel in Wanchai. Sullivan said he was going on to the Star ferry terminal for a leisurely boat ride across the harbour to Kowloon.

Moss entered the hotel and took the lift to his room on the twentieth floor. Unfortunately, the view from the room wasn't as stunning as the one Leo Sinnott enjoyed. The view from this one looked straight out onto the face of a dilapidated residential tower block. Once in his room he sat in a chair at a writing desk, relaxed and spent the following few minutes pondering his next move.

The last couple of hours had been somewhat of a whirlwind experience. Something wasn't right. Something was very wrong, but he couldn't put his finger on it. Here he was half way around the world, looking for someone who may not exist. Something in the back of his mind told him that it was too smooth, that it was all stage-managed. Moss had his doubts about Sullivan too, but didn't have a clear inkling why he was thinking like that. Maybe it was just his thought process in flux, putting two and two together and coming up with five.

What he did suspect was that Sinnott's apartment was too clean and sanitised. Almost too perfect to be true. No one could live in such a dust free space, but maybe he did. Maybe he didn't. Had someone been brought in to clean the apartment from top to bottom to remove all traces of Lily Fung? Had Sinnott been too accommodating and too insistent that she wasn't there. The sense of stage management was strong. Moss knew that he had to get Sinnott alone and interrogate him one-on-one. Perhaps his chance would come later that evening at the Happy Valley racetrack, for Wednesday night was race night. As he was a horse trainer, Sinnott would be meeting jockeys and others in the parade ring. This could be his one and only chance to meet him face-to-face in order to put some questions to him.

For now, he took a shower, slipped on a warm fluffy bathrobe, laid on the bed and took a nap. The residues of the long flight were still in his system and he was fighting the fatigue that had clamped tightly around his body, nulled his brain and put all kinds of weird stumbling thoughts into his head. His mind was still in kind of a daze, brought on by suffocating jet-lag.

At just after six-thirty on a pleasant Hong Kong evening Moss left the hotel. He took a taxi from a rank outside the hotel and asked the driver to take him to the Happy Valley racetrack.

Race night at Happy Valley was something to behold. The course was renowned for its atmosphere, fine dining, and the buzz of excitement as a dozen thoroughbred race horses came galloping down the final straight, under the glare of floodlights, with the roar of the crowd in the background.

Moss got to the track at seven o'clock and joined a queue at the ten dollars 'tourist' pay gate. Once inside he made his way into the spectator area and joined the crowd, most of whom were locals. If there is one thing that a lot of Hong Kong Chinese enjoy doing, then it's a flutter on a horse race at Happy Valley. In one night, literally millions of Hong Kong dollars are gambled on the outcomes of the eight-race card.

On a Wednesday night in April the arena was buzzing. The grandstands were already packed when the horses appeared on the track and came into the parade ring for the first race at seven-thirty. As darkness was falling the floodlights illuminating the track were at full strength to splash light over the verdant green of the turf. In the high-rise tower's lights were beaming out of the glass and metal blocks like pin-pricks of colour suspended in the dark sky.

Moss paid the two dollars for a race-card then joined the rest of the punters on a stretch of ground near to the finishing post. The majority of those on the terrace below the huge grandstands were consulting racing papers.

A huge TV on the other side of the track was showing the action from previous race meetings. The sound of commentaries was playing over the public address. Neon figures displaying the forecast betting patterns, on a huge board across on the other side of the track, were changing in the blink of an eye. In the betting halls, the spectators were putting their hard-earned cash onto their fancied mounts.

The first race was due off shortly. By the time Moss got to the parade ring the horses were being led round the circle by stable lads and lasses. Several of the jockeys, in their colourful racing silks, were already in the centre of the ring talking to trainers, owners, and the connections.

Moss consulted the race card. He wasn't into horse racing, so he didn't understand the terminology and the language. But he wasn't here to gamble on the races, therefore it wasn't a problem. He was here to find and speak to Leo Sinnott.

He slipped the race card into a jacket pocket, made his way through the crowd gathered close to the finishing line, and walked around the outside of the parade ring. The evening had turned warm, and the floodlights were giving off a residual heat. The fragrance of spicy food cooking in a mobile kitchen made his mouth water. The race announcer came over the public address and welcomed the spectators to the meeting. The atmosphere was building. Punters were coming out of the hospitality suites in the grandstands to watch the horses being led out of the ring and onto a cinder track to parade in front of the stands.

Moss stopped at the top of the parade ring and leaned against the rail. He looked at the race card, at the list of runners and riders for the first race. Like any other race card, the world over, it listed the name of the horse, its form over the past five races, the jockey, the trainer, and the owner's name, whether it be an individual owner, a family or a syndicate.

The first race was a six-furlong dash for two-year-old maidens. He carried on around the ring to a point where he could see the horses parading on the cinder track in front of the punters, then they turned onto the turf, picked up speed and trotted down to the starting stalls at the bottom of the long straight.

In the stand the number of spectators standing on the concrete steps of the terracing had increased so there were few free spaces.

When all the horses were in the stalls, a bell sounded, and the announcer declared, *they're off.* The big screen showed the action as the horses put on the turbo and came thundering up the finishing straight. The crowd roared as they approached the final furlong. The intensity of the sound of the hoofs thudding against the turf increased in velocity as the nags neared the finishing post. The sight of eight thoroughbred race horses galloping at full pace under the floodlights was magnificent. There wasn't another racetrack in the world to match the majestic Happy Valley.

The first of the eight races was over in no time at all. The winner, number three: 'Sacred Heart', prevailed by a short head.

The second race was due to get under way at eight o'clock. Moss looked at his watch; the time was twenty to the hour. The horses for the second race would be parading in the ring in ten minutes. He had some time to kill before the next race, so he did what most of the locals and tourists were doing and that was to visit one of the bars inside one of the track-side beer tents, for like the British, the Hong Kong Chinese loved a beer every now and again.

In contrast to the frenzy on the track-side the atmosphere inside the beer tent was tranquil. The dominant language was Cantonese although a few English accents could be heard.

Moss purchased a pint of amber nectar and jostled for a position at a table to put his beer down. He looked at the runners and riders for the second race, a one-mile sprint for three-year-old geldings. He ran his eyes down the list of horses. What caught his attention was horse number eight. A horse by the name of 'Steel Rapier'. Rider: Mike Fallon, Trainer: Leo Sinnott. What he read next made him gulp. The owner was 'Ho Fung Belgravia Racing Consortium.' *Oh, my word,* he said to himself. Here was a sign from above. It was like a thunderbolt hitting home. A tangible connection between the owner and the trainer. Though they were six thousand miles apart here was a connection that linked two of the key players in this affair; the trainer and the owner had a connection to each other.

It was standard practice for the owner of a horse or his or her representative to meet with the trainer before the race in the parade ring for the trainer to brief the connections. In this case Ho Fung wouldn't be here. Still Moss knew that he had a chance to meet with Sinnott, face-to-face and ask him some questions.

At a quarter to eight a bell sounded which told the punters that the horses were about to enter the ring. Moss stepped out of the beer tent and into the area in front of the ring. The horses were being led along the cinder track. This was one of the feature races of the evening, a group one race for thoroughbreds, with the first past the post picking up a purse of four hundred and seventy-five thousand Hong Kong dollars. A straight mile from the stalls at the bottom of the track to the finishing post in front of the stands.

Moss made it along the rail to the opening into the parade ring where two suited security guards were checking the credentials of those seeking to gain access. Some horse owners and their guests, or better known as the connections, were already in the ring talking to the jockeys and the trainers. He observed the scene for a few moments then a line of horses began to come through a gate at the cinder track and into the ring.

Moss watched the activity. Most of the people were in groups of five or six. There were eight horses in this race. Therefore, eight sets of connections. The jockeys emerged from the weighing room and made their way into the ring. Moss couldn't see Leo Sinnott from this spot, but then a group of people moved away, and he saw Sinnott, standing, talking to a group of four people.

Sinnott was in a sharp-cut suit, shirt, and tie. He was wearing his shades. He looked every inch the sophisticated lady-killer and playboy of Hong Kong society and the darling of the Happy Valley jet-set. Moss decided to take a chance. He dropped his head, looked at his race card and approached the gate where the connections were going through. The two men closed the gap, looked at him and searched for the purple badge attached to his jacket to indicate he had the necessary accreditation. He looked for all the world like a journalist and not an owner. Moss eyed them then looked at his race card.

"I'm the representative of the owner of Steel Rapier. Horse number eight," he said in a convincing manner. The two guys looked at each other, but didn't want to challenge him and ask him who he was. The more assertive-looking one stepped aside and allowed Moss to walk past him and enter the parade ring. He made straight across the lawn for Leo Sinnott who was standing in the centre watching his mount circling the ring. Moss was upon him in a couple of strides. Sinnott turned to see Moss coming towards him. At the same moment one of the jockeys came walking up to him. Sinnott's gaze didn't waver.

"Good evening," said Moss as cool as you like. Sinnott was shocked to see him this close and could only mutter something under his breath. "Ah, just a minute. I need to talk to my jockey," he said.

"Not a problem," replied Moss and stepped back a pace.

He could hear Sinnott and the jockey have a short conversation about the tactics for the race, then the jockey moved away from him to leave Sinnott and Moss alone. The group of four people, Sinnott was previously talking to, were drifting off to the exit to get to their seats high in the grandstand.

"What do you want?" Sinnott asked with an edge of irk in the tone.

"You know where she is. Don't you?"

Sinnott glanced from side to side as if looking for someone to come to his aid. He must have calculated that shouting out for help or causing a scene would only draw attention to himself. He wasn't going to make a song and dance in front of the people in the ring. He turned his body full on to Moss and fronted up. He whipped the shades off his eyes and fixed them on Moss with a stare.

"I don't," he replied bluntly to Moss's question.

"What don't you know?" Moss asked.

"Where she is," Sinnott replied.

"You must know Ho Fung well. He's a racehorse owner. He owns the horse you're training in this race."

"Yes. I know him. I never said I didn't," said Sinnott with a shrug of his shoulders.

"Did you meet him in London?" Moss asked. Sinnott rang a hand across his mouth and his eyes darted around the ring. He was ill at ease and his body language was tense. "Did you meet her in London?" Moss asked.

"Who?"

"Lily Fung?"

"Yes."

"Why?"

"Why what?"

"Why did you target her?"

Sinnott must have sensed that Moss was far more clued up than he had anticipated. "I was paid to," he replied.

"You were paid to bring her here?" Moss asked.

"Yes."

"By whom?"

"Ho Fung, of course," Sinnott said, as if Moss should have known the answer to the question.

"Why?" Moss asked.

Sinnott shrugged his shoulders. Then his eyes went to a horse as it suddenly reared up. The stable lad leading the animal was able to get it back under control.

A bell sounded, and the lads and lasses brought their horses into the centre of the ring.

"Just a minute," Sinnott said. With that he stepped away from Moss and went to the horse, where the jockey was now standing, checking the straps holding the saddle in place. The jockey presented his leg to Sinnott, who took it and gave him a leg-up. The jockey swung into the saddle, placed his feet into the stirrups and took the reins in both hands. Meanwhile, the numbers on the neon illuminated totaliser on the other side of the track were turning over at a rapid rate. Money was pouring onto the runners. The favoured bet appeared to be a dual forecast on horses three and seven.

The first of the horses left the parade ring and went out onto the cinder track to parade in front of the grandstand. A buzz of anticipation increased in velocity.

Moss watched Sinnott come back towards him. He looked very cool in his expensive suit and the shades. The revelation that Fung had paid him to bring his daughter-in-law back to Hong Kong, caught Moss by surprise. He had no idea why he would do that.

Sinnott was soon next to him. "I don't understand," Moss said.

"What?" Sinnott asked.

"Why would Fung ask me to find her if he paid you to bring her here?"

Sinnott shrugged his shoulders for a second time. "No idea," he replied.

"Is her marriage to his son on the rocks?"

"What do you mean?"

"Is their marriage in some sort of trouble?"

"How would I know?" he replied.

"Fung paid you to get her out of London?"

"Yes."

"Where is she now?" Moss asked.

"Pardon me."

"Where is she now?" he repeated forcefully.

"I don't know," Sinnott replied in a tiresome tone. He watched the first of the eight horses turn off the cinder track and canter down to the starting stalls at the bottom of the straight. The huge TV screen on the other side of the track monitored the horses going down to the start.

"How long was she with you?" Moss asked.

"As I said earlier. Two weeks at the most."

"Did she know Ho Fung had paid you to entice her away from London?"

Sinnott pursed his lips. "I don't think so."

"Did she leave a forwarding address anywhere?" Moss asked.

"I would have told you if she had."

"Why do you think Fung wanted her back here?"

"No idea," replied Sinnott.

"Okay," said Moss. He was even more puzzled now, though he knew he couldn't do much more than take Sinnott at his word. If Sinnott was telling the truth and he had little doubt that he wasn't, then her whereabouts was a mystery. "Does she have many friends here?" he asked.

"I don't know," Sinnott replied.

"What was her name before she married Hue Fung?"

Sinnott looked at him as if it was a trick question. "I don't know." Moss concluded he didn't know much about anything.

The race commentator came over the PA and became embroiled in a chit-chat with a colleague who went through the form-guide of the horses for the second race. 'Steel Rapier' was mentioned a couple of times, but it was low down in the list of fancied runners. The favourite was horse number three, 'Shanghai Knight', at odds of nine-to-two, with 'Court Jester', number seven, second favourite at five-to-one.

Moss could see that Sinnott was eager to get to the rail to watch the race, so he backed off. "Thanks for fronting up," he said.

"What's that mean?" Sinnott asked.

"Nothing," said Moss.

The commentator came over the public address to tell the crowd that the horses were about to be placed into the stalls for the second race.

"Thanks for your time," Moss said, but Sinnott didn't hear him above the clamour of sound coming from the crowd.

Not for the first-time Moss thought that the chances of leaving Hong Kong with Lily Fung on a plane bound for London were much less than fifty-fifty. His only hope was to ask Laurie Sullivan if he could ask some of his contacts in the HK police if they knew where she was residing.

Moss left the racecourse before the second race started. He took a cab back to Wanchai.

# Chapter 7

The streets of Wanchai were busy with activity on this Wednesday night. Since the 1997 changeover the area had lost most of its edgy character following a period of forced gentrification. There weren't half as many bars offering passers-by the opportunity to enter a hostess run establishment, as there once were. They were traps in which some naive victim would be charged large amounts of money for the cheapest of drinks.

As Moss entered into the glass entrance of his hotel and the wide-open floor of the foyer, he glanced towards the desk where several members of staff were standing. One of the senior clerks at the concierge desk saw him and immediately raised his hand and beckoned Moss towards the desk. He had a serious urgent look on his face.

Moss acknowledged him with a vague nod of the head then stepped across the floor towards the desk. He had no idea what he wanted. The chap was a medium build, nice-looking, slim middle-aged man in a freshly-pressed jacket with the hotel logo and emblem on the breast pocket.

There was a nervous smile on his face. He looked as if he was about to give Moss some bad news. No one back home knew he was here, therefore it wasn't likely to be a message to call home or anything like that.

"Mr Mosey," said the chap. "Please wait here for one moment."

Moss didn't reply. He could only do as asked as thoughts went through his mind. He wondered if his credit card had been rejected. The chap turned away, went along the back of the desk and through an open door. He emerged several moments later with an older, more senior hotel employee leading the way. He too wore a frown.

The older chap approached him alone and came towards the desk. He held his hand out. He was a short, mildly-overweight guy, wearing silver-rimmed spectacles.

His hair was grey and swept back to reveal a thinning patch on his forehead. Before Moss could take his hand, the chap took his glasses off. Moss took his hand. It was meaty and sweaty, and his body language was stiff, but his handshake was firm and strong.

"My name is Mr Lee. I'm the hotel security manager. I'm so sorry," he said.

Moss narrowed his eyes. "Sorry. About what?" he asked.

"Perhaps we should go into your room."

"Why? What's in my room?"

"Someone has broken in and looked through your things," the man said.

Moss was stunned. "Broken in!" he exclaimed incredulously.

"That's what it looks like," Mr Lee said.

"Oh, my word," was Moss's somewhat under-stated response.

"I will accompany you to your room. We will, of course, reimburse you for your trouble."

Moss didn't say anything. He was in a quandary. This was a five-star hotel. Things like this were only supposed to happen in budget hotels. The reality was that they could occur anywhere. Here was the proof.

Mr Lee stepped along the back of the counter, through a flap at the end and came onto the foyer. Moss followed him across the floor to the bank of lifts. There were a few people sitting in an arrangement of seats set around walnut topped circular tables near to a concessionary snack and beverage outlet. Some were chatting in conversation. Others reading newspapers or eating and drinking. A large screen TV was airing a twenty-four-hour English language news channel. It was standard in any large hotel anywhere in the world. Moss couldn't help but wonder if one of those sitting there was responsible for what he would find in his room. Then he wondered if the burglar had got access into the safe and stolen his money, passport and other valuables. He didn't want to think of the consequences if his possessions were no longer in the room.

Mr Lee led Moss into an elevator and they travelled up to the twentieth floor in silence.

As Moss emerged out of the car and stepped onto the long landing, he could see a hotel employee standing outside the door to his room, guarding it. The door was open. Mr Lee took Moss into the room. A second man, another hotel employee, was already inside the room, standing by the window with the view out to the high-rise tenement building across the way.

It was clear to see that someone had been in the room, emptied his clothes out of two bedside drawers and scattered most of them onto the mattress and over the floor. The bed clothes had been stripped off the mattress which was lying at an angle, half on - half off the bed frame. Whoever it was had clearly been looking for something under the mattress. Moss went to the wardrobe. The door was hanging open. When he looked down to the safe unit, he could see that the door was closed. He got down on his knees, took the handle and pulled on it. Thankfully, it was still locked. He let out a sigh of relief. The burglar hadn't been able to get into the safe, therefore his money, passport and other valuables were still inside. "At least they didn't get into here," he said.

"Pardon me. They?" said Mr Lee.

"He. She. It. They." Moss said in a barbed tone. He tried the flap again, just to make sure it was locked, then he tapped the four-digit code into the pad. The mechanism buzzed, and the door popped open. He put his hand inside and felt his possessions which were still in place. Maybe the burglar was disturbed before he could get into the safe. As it was bolted into the floor, it would have been near impossible to pull it free unless he had his hands on a drill of some description to unscrew the bolts.

Moss got to his feet. He was at a loss to explain why anyone would want to break into the room, but obviously someone had. Was it something to do with the assignment he was on? He didn't want to begin jumping to conclusions or speculate at this early stage. However, no one breaks into a hotel room without good reason, unless it was an opportunist thief. Perhaps a chancer had walked in off the street, tried his hand, and chose this room at random.

The other chap in the room was a hotel employee. He was perhaps a couple of years younger than Mr Lee. He was a small, shifty-looking guy with nicotine-stained fingers and slightly bulbous dark eyes which held a menacing quality. He picked up the discarded bed sheets then nudged the mattress back onto the frame.

Moss looked at the security manager. "Who found the room and when?" he asked.

"My colleague here," said Lee gesturing to the chap who was now picking up some of the discarded clothing from the floor. "At just after eight o'clock this evening." Moss looked at his watch. The time was eight-thirty. He had left the room close to two hours before. Just forty minutes before he was talking to Leo Sinnott at the track. Sinnott would have had plenty of time to call someone to tell him that Moss was there asking him questions. Maybe the burglary was a kind of warning.

Moss stepped to the main door and examined the lock. There was no evidence that the door had been forced open. Whoever had come in must have used a replica key-card to trigger the opening mechanism. The explanation was simple. The burglar was either looking for valuables or a specific item of interest, such as the photograph of Lily Fung and her husband.

"We are most sorry for this disturbance," said Mr Lee in an earnest tone. "We will of course move you to another room. Has anything been taken?" he asked.

Moss looked around. "Not that I can see," he replied.

"He's a chance burglar," said Lee.

"Has anyone else being targeted tonight or in the past few days?" Moss asked.

"Not that I am aware," Lee replied.

"I don't think it was a chance burglar then," said Moss.

"Why?" asked Lee.

Moss realised he was saying too much. "Just a hunch," he replied as if he was trying to lessen the implication of his suggestion.

Lee offered him a frown, then forced a meek grin. "We will provide you with a deluxe room," he looked out of the window to the side of the high-rise tenement block. "On an upper floor," he added.

Moss didn't reply. He was still trying to figure out the ramifications of coming back to the hotel to discover his room ransacked. He still had no way of knowing if it was in anyway connected to his investigation into the case of the *misper* Lily Fung, or if it was a pure coincidence. It was becoming almost too sinister for words.

Lee said something in Cantonese to the other fellow who had now picked up the items of clothing from the floor and had laid them all onto the mattress. Mr Lee looked at Moss.

"I will take you to your new room. When you are ready of course. I will be waiting outside."

Lee and the other chap stepped out of the room and left Moss to pack his suitcase, empty the safe, collect all his belongings and put them into his case. He felt like he should be checking out, rather than agreeing to remain here, but at least they had offered him another room. As he wasn't due to check out until Monday. He still had four nights to stay. Four nights to find Lily Fung, though he suspected he wouldn't find her.

Over the course of the following five minutes, he put all his clothing and items into his case and emptied the safe, then he left the room. Mr Lee was waiting for him on the landing. He took Moss to the lift and escorted him to a suite on the fortieth floor.

It wasn't so much as another room but a massive change. The suite had a separate sitting room, and a spacious bedroom twice the size of the one he had just left, a deluxe bathroom and a view of the city that could only be seen in the TV programmes of the lifestyles of the rich and famous.

Once settled in the room he raided the free mini-bar and had a couple of miniature bottles of whisky. At a time, just before midnight he put in a call to Laurie Sullivan and asked him to meet him the next day. They arranged to meet in 'The Old Country' pub on Jaffe Road at one o'clock in the afternoon. He didn't mention anything about the meeting with Leo Sinnott or the break-in to his room. He was certain he wouldn't be visited for a second time, still it was with a sense of heightened security that he settled down for the night. Out there, across the spread of the city and over the harbour, the neon and the lights of Kowloon blinked and twinkled on the water in the harbour well into the early hours of Thursday morning.

# Chapter 8

**M**oss woke up at eight o'clock to the sight of grey-leaden skies over Hong Kong. A stiff wind was splattering heavy raindrops against the window. Out over the harbour the backdrop of Kowloon was hidden behind a bank of mist and fog that might remain static for most of the day. The water in the harbour was so choppy white-capped waves were sent crashing against the harbour wall.

The previous night, the weather girl on the English language CNN TV channel had told the viewers that a twenty-four-hour storm would come over the entire southeast peninsula of the Chinese mainland. The storm should clear out by this time tomorrow. The coming weekend was going to be fine with the first day of higher temperatures coming in on Saturday. Still the storm was no-way as bad as some of the typhoons that the city had to endure during the monsoon season when the New Territories and the island went into virtual lockdown and very few people, other than the foolhardy, ventured out.

Moss had no intention of staying in the hotel. He was going out at one o'clock to visit the 'The Old Country' pub to meet with Laurie Sullivan. He showered then went into the restaurant for breakfast with the other several hundred guests. The ramifications of last night were still playing heavily on his mind. He couldn't help but think that one of the hotel staff had a duplicate key-card and used it to gain access to the room, searched through his belongings looking for something, couldn't find it, then raised the alarm. Maybe it was the other chap who had been in the room when he entered with Mr Lee. He just didn't know. If it was him, who had told him to do it? As he glanced around the restaurant at the other guests eating breakfast, he couldn't help but wonder if one of them had done the deed. He felt himself becoming suspicious of everyone, which in truth didn't help him to deal with it. The fact that the safe hadn't been opened, suggested to him that it wasn't anybody who had access to the rooms. Perhaps it was an opportunist thief who had walked in off the street, evaded the security measures and managed to get up to the twentieth floor unchallenged.

During the telephone conversation with Laurie Sullivan, he had purposely refrained from mentioning the break-in. Something in the back of his mind pointed to a connection. As a detective, his mind was trained to look for connections. Maybe there was a modicum of connectivity here, though he conceded it could be his inbuilt analytical thinking that encouraged an inquisitive retrospective review of all the variables. He knew that the majority of crimes had an element of causation link. All criminologists know that most crimes have linkage and are committed by a person known to the victim.

His breakfast consisted of little more than a small bowl of cereal, coffee, fruit and juice. He planned to have something more substantial at lunch time when he met with Sullivan in the pub on Jaffe Road.

By midday the skies were beginning to clear and the strength of the wind had dropped. The storm was downgraded from a force seven – moderate gale – to a force five – a fresh breeze.

Moss left the hotel at a few minutes to one. He decided to approach the pub from a different direction. He made his way onto Hennessey Road and to the long line of stores that are famed for selling gold and jewellery. He crossed the road at a busy crossing and came onto Jaffe Road, then along the pavement for fifty yards, then up the concrete steps to the first floor, through the open door and into the pub with its pine tables, wicker chairs and low-slung, leather sofas. The ceiling fans were spinning at a gentle rotation. The long glass mirror behind the counter and the lines of liquor bottles gleamed in the light.

The open windows were partially covered by fancy wooden shutters, so it was only just possible to hear the activity on the street below. The room was frequented by a dozen or so people. A few tourists, along with office workers from the nearby businesses. The smell and sight of chilli bubbling in a large cooking pot and chicken breasts rotating on skewers in an oven made Moss's mouth water.

Laurie Sullivan was sitting at the same table they had frequented the day before. His bald chrome doom was prominent. He was wearing a dark, zip-up jacket. He seemed a lot bulkier in dark, as if the shade emphasised his wide thick chest and barrel shape. Moss realised he hardly knew Sullivan. Something in the back of his mind told him he might have been somehow involved in all this. But what? He wasn't exactly sure, nevertheless something told him he could have had a hand in this somewhere along the line. There were tell-tale signs. Like the time when they had arrived at the stables. Sullivan had led the way along the path to the side of the racetrack. Maybe he had been there before, or was it that he just guessed which path to take.

As Moss entered the pub, Sullivan turned to look up at him, then he raised his hand that contained a glass with an amber liquid. Moss joined him at the table, so they were sat across the pine top. The waxy leaves of a rubber plant in a glass pot were gently wafting by the force of the draught from the ceiling fan.

Within moments of settling into the seat a pretty waitress was making her way to the table to hand Moss a menu for lunch and to take his order. A bowl of steaming hot onion soup with croutons wouldn't go amiss.

Sullivan had dark lines under his eyes as if he hadn't had much sleep the night before. He eyed Moss with a neutral expression etched on his face.

"How's it going?" he asked.

Moss sat back in the seat. "Not good," he replied as he continued to run his eyes over the menu. He asked the waitress for a bottle of lager, but changed his mind about the soup, ordering a chicken curry with rice, instead. She took his order then left them alone.

"What's not good?" Sullivan enquired as soon as she had gone.

"Someone breaking into my hotel room. That's not good," Moss said.

"Oh, my God," was Sullivan's somewhat over-played reply. He ran a hand over the top of his forehead as if he was patting down a non-existent hair piece. "What happened?"

"I returned to the hotel last night to discover someone had broken in and rifled through my things," Moss replied.

"Did they take anything?" he asked.

Moss was instantly aware that he had used the word 'they' as if he knew more than one person was involved. "Nothing," he replied. "The safe was still intact."

"Maybe they were disturbed," said Sullivan. There it was again. The word 'they'.

In the next moment, the waitress was at Moss's side with an open bottle of lager in one hand and a glass in the other. She placed the bottle and the glass onto the table top. "Your food will be two minute," she said, then stepped back towards the bar.

"What time was this?" Sullivan asked.

"About eight o'clock."

"Where'd you been?" Sullivan enquired.

Moss wondered why he wanted to know. "To the racetrack," he replied. Above him the speed of the fans suddenly increased so the waft of breeze became stronger.

"So, nothing was taken?" Sullivan asked.

"Nothing."

"They must have been opportunists."

Again, the plural rather than the singular. Moss poured the contents of the bottle into the glass. He looked at the label. It was a well-known imported brand. A bit like Sullivan. He had been in Hong Kong for much longer than the imported product. He knew a lot of prominent people from his days in the police department. He must have accumulated quite a few associates and friends in all his years on the island. In this time, he must have also accumulated quite a few people who disliked him.

Moss took the glass and drank a mouthful of the amber liquid. It had quite a bitter tangy taste that left a hit on the back of his throat, almost as if it had been in the bottle for too long. He looked at Sullivan who took a long sip of beer before raising his head and looking at him.

"Do you have any idea who broke into your room?" Sullivan asked.

"No."

"Strange isn't it that someone would want to break in. Maybe they were searching for something."

"Like what?" Moss asked.

"Tell me this."

"What?"

"Who knows you're here in HK?"

"Ho Fung, you and Leo Sinnott," Moss replied.

"Plus, the people in the hotel and the people you booked the trip with."

"That's true," said Moss. He took a good intake of the lager. A taste of bitter almond once again nipped the back of his tongue. He looked at the glass in his hand, then at Sullivan whose face began to contort and become almost like a gargoyle caricature. Moss tipped his head back as he tried to dislodge the image from in front of his eyes. He looked up to the ceiling and the blades of the fan turning above his head. Then he suddenly felt ill and with that feeling a misty haze seemed to fall in front of him and double vision played in his eyes. The four blades of the fan emerged and became one spinning arm. The strength of the chatter near to him came and went in decreasing then increasing echoing waves. His head suddenly began to feel heavy and he had a sensation of being on the edge of a precipice. The glass slipped from his hand and hit the table top, shattering into several pieces. The liquid spilled over the pine surface. Before he knew what was happening his whole body seemed to go into convulsions. His hands went into spasm. Noises in the distance seemed to echo and increase three-fold in decibels. He tried to focus his eyes on Sullivan's face and say 'what the fuck' but the words came out as a slurring undecipherable garble. Then a darkness fell, and he slumped forward onto the table head first as his lights went out.

Moss lifted his head. His neck felt stiff. He opened his eyes and cringed against a bright, brilliant yellow light beaming into his eyes. He felt as if his whole body was spinning like a Catherine wheel. He could taste the scent of vomit in his mouth. After a few moments of consciousness, he realised his wrists were secured to the arms of a chair by duct tape wrapped around his wrists. He was fixed to the arms of a chair.

Beyond, in the brilliant blinding light he could just about make out the dark shape of a figure sitting at the other end of a table. The air was stone cold and there was a dust filled, fusty smell in the air. The light was so blinding he couldn't keep his eyes open for a few seconds before he had to close them. He felt an ache in his stomach and the remaining scent of nausea in his throat. He tried to move his arms, but they were well and truly secured to the chair armrests. He could feel the rungs of the chair grating into his buttocks and the edge of the seat cutting into the back of his knees. The room was pitch black. He was aware for the first time that he was naked, but for his underwear.

"Moss," said a voice from in front of him. The sound pinged against the solid concrete walls of the cell or the dungeon. There were no windows or any outside light.

"Who sent you to Hong Kong?" the voice asked. The accent was oriental English.

"Ho Fung," he replied.

"Why?"

"Why? What?" Moss asked.

"Why you come here?"

"To find Lily Fung."

"Why does he want to find her?"

"I don't know."

"When you find her. What then?"

"I'm to take her back to London with me."

"Why does he want her to return?" the voice asked.

"I don't know. He never told me."

"How do you know she wants to go back with you?"

"I don't," said Moss. It dawned on him that the mysterious person before him may know where she was. "Where is she?" he asked.

The silhouette figure did not reply. Moss felt he was slowly returning to some form of normality, though he didn't recognise the voice of the interrogator. With the blinding white light, he couldn't see him, only the outline of his head. He could hear his voice. From the accent and tone, he guessed the man was Hong Kong Chinese and he was in his fifties or sixties. He tried to move his hands to loosen the tape around his wrists. It was a pointless exercise. He wasn't going to be able to free his hands anytime soon.

"You come here to find the wife of Hue Fung?" the voice asked. "And did you?"

"No."

"You know nothing. You mission, it failed," the man said and laughed out loud. The sound bounced against the thick side walls.

Moss was suddenly aware there was another person at his back. He looked over his left shoulder. The figure emerged out of the dark. He was a man, dressed from head to toe in black. He had black-lens sunglasses over his eyes and a black cap on his head. He stepped to Moss's left side and proceeded to tie a thin leather strap around his bicep, then pulled it tight. He held a syringe in his hand. The applicator was open and there was a colourless substance inside the transparent tube. The needle must have been six centimetres long and had a tip as sharp as a hat pin. The man twisted the strap. Under the pressure, a vein in his bicep popped up. The man prodded the tip of the needle into his flesh, punctured the skin, applied pressure to the applicator and emptied the content of the syringe into Moss's blood.

## Chapter 9

**W**eird dreams filled with spinning wheels, a kaleidoscope of assorted colours and shapes and a cacophony of different sounds filled Moss's brain. A dry ice mist swirled in front of his vision. He could see himself in a kind of outer body experience as he rolled and tumbled down a steep decline and into a dark pit of a concrete-lined bunker.

His eyes flickered open. He could make out a dark shape above him. He was in the land of the living, or maybe this was death, part of a dream sequence or a near death experience. Nonetheless, the first feelings of consciousness were returning to him and he calculated he was back in the real world, if such a thing existed.

As he returned to the here and now his eyes focused. The dark shape above him was a ceiling. During the course of the next ten seconds, he became aware of his surroundings. He was laid flat with a cushioned surface beneath him. He could taste the remnants of vomit in his mouth, feel a sticky salt like dryness in his throat and a fragrant smell at his nostrils. He lifted his right hand and rubbed it across his mouth. He could feel the thick bristle of stubble on his chin and along his jawline. A pain throbbed in his head and there was an ache in his legs. He felt as if he was in the eye of the worst alcohol-induced hangover he had ever experienced in his life. He closed his eyes, then opened them again and saw double vision that sent his head spinning like an out-of-control child's spinning top.

His head continued to throb, and a cloud of mist still remained in his eyes. He closed them then opened them again before managing to turn his head to observe a white lace curtain fluttering by an open window. He could feel the force of a light breeze blowing across his face. The backdrop of a blue sky was highlighted against the window frame. It took him a few seconds to realise he was laid on a mattress of a bed with a linen sheet beneath him. His head was deep in the softness of a sponge pillow. Above him was a timber panel roof that met in the centre directly above his head to form the apex of a structure.

He was totally naked. Then on his upper left arm he was aware of a weight pressing down on that side of the mattress. He instinctively turned his head in that direction in a series of robotic-like movements. When he came face-to-face with what was on the other side of the mattress it stunned him to the core of his soul. He found himself looking into the sickly pale blanched face of a woman. Her eyes were closed. She could have been sleeping, but there were no sounds coming from her. All sound had gone from her being. Her dry lips were a shade of cornflower blue. A wedge of dark hair had fallen across her forehead. She wore a pale mask of death.

He tried to pull himself up and summon the strength to lift the top half of his frame into an upright position. It took a huge amount of effort before he managed to raise his head off the pillow. Then a dizziness came over him and hurt his eyes. He had to lower himself back down into the softness of the pillow.

Several moments passed then he attempted to get up for a second time. Again, it took an enormous effort. On this occasion he was able to move his legs and swing them around ninety degrees, so he was sitting on the edge of the mattress. Out of the window the view was of a tree-lined terrace sweeping up a steep hillside possibly a mile or so into the distance. Buildings were perched on the hillside at varying levels. In the background the cry of a flock of seagulls was audible against the sound of the sea rolling in over a beach or rocks somewhere close by. As if to emphasise he was near to the sea he could taste salt particles on his lips. He remained sitting on the bed for a while to let his senses return to something resembling normal. He was still finding it difficult to focus his eyes and collect his thoughts into a coherent order. No matter, he knew he had to get out of this place. There was a dead woman lying on the other side of the mattress. Then he wondered if his captors were close by. He stayed perfectly still for the next thirty seconds and listened for any sounds. He couldn't hear anything except for the cry of the gulls and the swoosh of the waves lapping onto a near-by beach.

His clothing was scattered over the floor. As he had no memory he couldn't recall ever being in this room, then the scene in the cell with the piercing white light came back into his mind. He saw the darkened image of the guy injecting the contents of a syringe into his arm. He asked himself how long he had been out.

With a determined thrust from his thighs, he was able to get to his feet and stand erect. He moved forward a few paces to the window and peered out. He was raised up from the ground, maybe fifteen feet or so above a grassy terrain. Directly below was a narrow semi-rough track that led to a rocky beach approximately fifty yards away. He turned his head back to look at the mattress and the dead body. She was naked. Her legs were tightly clamped together. Then he saw the table at the other side of the bed and the items on it. He concentrated his sight on it. There was a glass bong, a thin leather strap, a large silver metal dessert spoon, tinfoil, a syringe, a cheap gas-filled cigarette lighter and a plate that had a heap of white powder on it. Everything a heroin addict needed to score.

He looked at the face of the woman. She looked familiar, but he didn't know where he had seen her before. It took him a good fifteen seconds to see it was the face of the woman in the photograph. Had he found Lily Fung?

He gingerly stepped over the rough wood floor to the other side of the bed frame, leaned over the body and looked at her. She had the same long raven hair, the same slim face. The same skinny slender frame. It was her. He had found her. Sadly, she wouldn't be going home with him.

He murmured the word *'fuck'* to himself. After a few moments he went to the other side of the bed, and picked up the items of his discarded clothing.

He still felt very dizzy, unsteady on his feet and in a kind of daze. Nonetheless, he was able to put his clothes on. His watch was in his jacket pocket along with some money. Maybe fifty dollars in notes and some loose change. The time on his watch said six-forty-five. He guessed it was the morning as the sun was low in the sky.

He dressed himself as best as he could, then went back to the body and examined it by checking her arms. There was a track of pinpricks in the fleshy part of her upper left arm. Someone must have injected her, or she had done it herself. She may have passed-away due to a heroin overdose. Though there was no telling. He guessed the white powder on the plate was heroin. He must have also been injected with the same chemical but couldn't be sure. Had he survived an overdose or hadn't been injected with enough to kill him. He didn't know. What he did know was that he had to get away from here as soon as possible. Despite feeling like death, he felt his cognizance returning to him in small doses. He went to the window and peered out again. He could just make out the roofs of a settlement perhaps a quarter of a mile away snaking up the side of the hillside with its jungle-like terrain. Out over the ocean a junk was drifting across the sea. There was nothing else to see except for the horizon which suggested to him he may have been on the remote side of Hong Kong Island. Maybe he was miles from Hong Kong. For all he knew he could be on the Chinese mainland.

He put the curtain to a side, put his head out of the window, sucked in a deep intake of fresh air, then ran a finger over his upper left arm. He could feel a sore welt on his flesh where a needle had penetrated the skin. It looked and felt red, almost like the aftermath of a bee sting. Maybe he was supposed to wake-up from the sleep and find her or maybe he wasn't supposed to survive so they would be found dead together, the result of a heroin overdose.

Her mouth was slightly ajar as if she had taken one last deep breath before she expired. The look on her face was one of peace and deliverance from evil.

He took a few steps across the floor towards a closed door. There was still a massive throb in his head and a pain in his temple. Despite the wobbling effect in his legs, he was able to grab the door handle, pull it and open the door. The opening led onto a landing then a dozen or so steep wooden steps of a flimsy stairway leading to a door at the bottom. The door had panes of frosted glass in it. He stepped onto the landing and took a firm hold of a rickety handrail. Before taking the first downward step he stalled to prick his ears and listen for any sound coming from inside the building. He couldn't hear a thing. After about twenty seconds he began the descent to the door at the bottom at a slow careful pace.

At the bottom of the stairs was a door on the right that might have led into a ground-floor space. He made it down the last few steps to the bottom, took a pace to his right, took the handle and pushed the door open. It opened into a shade-filled room that contained all sorts of junk like a rowing boat and various bits of fishing gear, such as nets, buoys, tarpaulin sheets, ropes and other gear. The building must have been a fisherman's store of some description. There was even a bicycle propped up against the side.

He gingerly moved inside the room and felt a thick layer of dust under his feet. It seemed as if no one had been in here for a very long time. A slant of sunlight was blazing through a crack running down the centre of a double wooden door to illuminate a cloud of dust particles. All was quiet and still. The sound of the sea rushing onto the shore just beyond the building was audible in the background. He knocked against a rusty oil can which fell to the floor and made a metallic clatter that rung in his ears like the chimes of a church bell.

He had clearly regained most of his senses, but he felt as if he was about to vomit at any time. He looked at the bicycle. It was perhaps thirty years old, but it still looked useable and roadworthy, although the tyres were flat to the rims. It might come in handy to help him balance so he took hold of the handlebar and manoeuvred it across the floor and out through the door.

Once at the outer door he took the handle, pushed on it and the door opened. As it did a wave of fresh air rushed inside and he breathed it in, then he coughed several times as a sheet of dust particles went up his nostrils and lay on his throat.

Taking a tight grip of the bicycle he bowled it out of the door, up a five feet wide incline and onto the dirt track. Overhead, he was aware of the warmth of the early morning and the sound of seagulls sitting on the roof of the building and calling out. He looked up the side to see the white cotton curtain billowing out of the window of the room he had just left. It still didn't seem like this was happening, almost as if he was stuck in some kind of never-ending dream or a scene in some weird arthouse movie. This was the real world.

He stayed motionless for a few moments and contemplated his next move. He had to discover where he was, then try and get back into the city. Then he realised he had to do something. He placed the bicycle on the ground then went back inside the building and climbed the stairs to the room. He went inside. First, he took the sheet on the mattress, pulled it out from underneath her body and laid it over her. He wanted to give her some dignity in death, then his eyes went to the white powder and the syringe. He decided to do something for a reason he wasn't sure. He took the spoon. There was a trace of powder in the base. The underside was blackened by the flame from the lighter. He put the spoon into the powder, scooped up a heaped level, then took the lighter, flicked on the flame and began to turn the powder into a liquid. Next, he took the syringe. There was a small amount of red liquid in the tube. It must have been blood. He pressed down on the applicator to eject it. Then he put the needle into the fresh liquid and drew it into the tube. He filled it half-full, then he put the syringe into the inside pocket of his jacket.

He had one last look around the room, then he went out onto the landing, down the steps, carefully one at a time, and out into the daylight.

Picking up the bicycle by the handlebars he pushed it up the slight incline and onto the dirt track. After walking for twenty yards towards a spread of buildings in the distance he paused to take a breather and look back to the ramshackle building he had left behind. Beyond, the flat, calm surface of the sea stretched away to the horizon. The vessel he had observed must have laid anchor as it didn't appear to be moving against the backdrop of the green and blue horizon.

He turned back and held the handlebars tightly to aid his balance. The feeling of sick in his throat had reduced and the foggy blurring of objects and the sensation of dizziness were going, but he still felt as if he was wading through treacle.

The whole episode he had just witnessed was like the component parts of a bad dream. What he didn't know was how the dream ended or for how long it lasted. By the feeling of the stubble on his face he had been out for at least two days. Could it be that he had lain on that bed for over forty hours or even longer? By the rumbling in his stomach the answer to that was probably yes.

He continued up the incline of the dirt track for about two hundred yards then came across a tarmac road that led towards the buildings in a small settlement. He didn't have a clue where he was. He doubted he was in mainland China. After all, there was a controlled border between the New Territories and Shenzhen he would have to cross. What he did know was that he had to get away from here. With every passing stride his thoughts were becoming a little bit more coherent.

## Chapter 10

After walking for five minutes, he was close to the end of the track and the nearest buildings came into sharper focus. Up ahead was a road, then a car appeared and swept by. By the fact that the vehicle was on the left-hand side of the road he knew he was still on Hong Kong Island.

On reaching the end of the track he turned onto the tarmac road. There was a road-sign further ahead which pointed in the direction of Stanley, therefore he knew he was on the south side of the island. As the atoll was thirty-four square miles in area it was only about four or five miles back to the area of Wanchai and the centre of the city.

As the warm air wafted over him, he could feel his body returning to some form of normality, though he still had a throbbing ache in his forehead and down both temples. He progressed along the road and edged towards the fringe of a tiny settlement of no more than a dozen structures. He still had hold of the handlebars of the bicycle. Up ahead were the high peaks of the hillsides that effectively split the island in two. He didn't intend to walk all the way back into town.

After another one hundred yards he was in the settlement of small, mostly modest, unassuming houses. Further along the road was a bus-stop and an adjoining shelter. He slowly made it up the road to the centre, then leant the bicycle against a brick-and-mortar wall and took a few steps to the bus-stop. A couple of local people: a youth and an elderly lady were standing inside the metal shelter waiting for a bus. They observed him. He smiled which didn't draw a reaction. He must have looked like a vagrant. His hair was dishevelled and the growth of bristles on his chin and jawline must have given him the appearance of someone who had been partying for too long.

He put his eyes on the youth. The chap was pleasantly dressed in jeans and a t-shirt under a tight denim jacket. He wore round-rimmed wire spectacles over his eyes and had the strap of a rucksack perched over one shoulder.

"Excuse me," said Moss. "Do you speak English?"

The guy's languid look appeared to stiffen. "I speak a little," he replied.

"Is there a bus which goes into Wanchai?"

"Wanchai?"

"Yes."

"The number *tree*," he said and looked up to the plate on top of the pole. "In ten minute from now," he said.

Moss thanked him. He took a step back and leaned against the Perspex sheet at the back of the hut. Feeling in his jacket pocket he took the few notes and the handful of loose change. At least he had the fare to get into Wanchai. He could also feel the weight of the syringe in his breast pocket.

A single-deck, blue and yellow Hong Kong transport mini-bus, arrived a minute or two after the scheduled leave time. Moss got on after the elderly lady and the youth, gave the driver some of the coins, and took a seat close to the front. There were only five people on the bus as it set off for the city. It wasn't long before it was grinding up the first of the hillsides that form the spectacular backbone of the island.

After a struggle it managed to ascend to the top of the peak, and the full eight-mile-long spread of the north side of the island appeared below in the valley that sloped down to the harbour. It was indeed one of the truly breath-taking sights with the multitude of skyscrapers and huge office towers reaching skyward and the spread of green topped hilltops disappearing into the distance.

The bus took the quick route into town along the main Wanchai road. Within twenty minutes of setting out the grandstands of Happy Valley racetrack and the line of apartment blocks in Leighton Hill came into view.

The morning sun was just beginning to slip behind some cloud, but the prospect of a warm day was on the cards.

The tops of the glass and steel in the tower blocks in the central district were already gleaming bright.

Moss wondered what to do. Whether to make the hotel his first port of call to take a shower and change his clothes. He didn't know if that was such a good idea. Maybe someone in the hotel was connected to this. Was Mr Lee a player? Could it have been Mr Lee, or his accomplice, who had entered his room to look for evidence of his mission. On that note he decided to hold-fire on returning to the hotel until much later in the day. Then he began to think about the sequence of events that had got him to this point in his investigation. Had he survived an attempt to kill him? Was he supposed to be found dead with Lily Fung in a conspiracy linked to her death? He didn't know the answer to either of those questions. It left him feeling tormented to a degree. He felt relatively okay in himself and relieved he was still breathing, but at the same time beaten and abused by those who had killed Lily and those who had possibly attempted to frame him for her murder.

As the bus came close to the racecourse it stopped at a bus stop to pick up several passengers. Moss had an idea. He knew he was fairly close to Leo Sinnott's home. Perhaps he should pay him a visit. He got up from his seat and stepped off the bus. From here he crossed the road and ambled along the pavement adjacent to the back of the racecourse grandstands. The area of Leighton Hill was perhaps half a mile away. He knew there was a long flight of stairs to climb then he would be on the hilltop overlooking the racetrack.
   As he walked, he ran his hand over his head. The heat of the sun was already beginning to make itself felt, though it wasn't much past eight o'clock. The traffic on the road wasn't heavy, therefore he assumed it was Saturday or Sunday morning. Had he really been out of it for more than forty hours? By the thickness of the bristles on his chin and

the smell of perspiration coming from him it may have been that long. The effect of the chemical in his bloodstream was giving him the occasional hot flush on his skin and a slight blurring of his vision. Still it wasn't as bad as it had been an hour before.

It took him the best part of the next thirty minutes to ascend a long concrete staircase to reach the top of the hill overlooking the racecourse and the spread of the city beyond. Above him the eight-tower complex of Leighton Hill loomed high. The green-turquoise sun blinds in the balcony windows beamed out from the face and resembled blocks of exotic jade stone. He had no idea if Sinnott would be at home or even in town. The only way to find out was to enter the tower, ride up to the thirtieth-fifth floor and knock on the door to his apartment. The only way he could gain entry to the building was through the gate leading into the ground floor car park.

    When he had arrived in Sinnott's vehicle, the first thing he noticed was the security camera by the left side of the gate, which meant there was a blind spot on the other side. If he could sneak through on the right side, as a vehicle entered or left the car park, then he might be able to gain access without been seen. It was in many ways trial and error. If he did gain entry and confront Leo it would be interesting to see how he reacted to his appearance. If he was involved in the murder of Lily Fung, he may choose to admit it. Or alternatively he could deny having anything to do with her death. Moss knew he would have to play it cute. He couldn't be one hundred per cent sure that the body was that of Lily Fung. He had to assume it was. The only other possibility was that it was someone who looked very much like her.

    On reflection, he wondered if he should have alerted the police or gone straight to his hotel to shower, rest, change into a fresh set of clothes and consider what his best strategy should be. Too late. He was close to the glass foyer entrance of tower C.

As there were a lot of apartments in the tower, he assumed it would only be a matter of time before a car approached and stopped at the gate.

He followed a path by the service road and came to the back of the tower. A wide wedge of shadow from the structure was projected out over the grassed area which was festooned with patches of flower beds and the occasional park bench. At a point where the block C began, he crossed the road and approached the gate in the wall.

There were several huge support columns that jutted out from the building, so he would be able to hide from view in the shadows. He couldn't see any other cameras attached to the structure.

He edged towards the turn off in the road that led to the gate. A white painted sign above the opening read: 'Car park entrance' and the equivalent in Cantonese characters. There was a continuous steel mesh fence that prevented anyone from gaining access into the car park. He was aware of the sound of a car inside the car park. He was just too late as the car appeared and came out of the opening. The heavy metal gate rolled down and closed over the entrance.

An opportunity missed. Never mind he would be patient and wait for the next opportunity.

He stayed out of view by standing in the shadows and hidden behind one of the columns. Though he was in the shadow if a car came along the road and slowed to turn, the driver would surely see him. Ten minutes passed. Ten minutes became twenty. No vehicles came along. A further ten minutes ticked by. He was starting to feel a little conspicuous, but still no one had spotted him. Standing in the shade he was beginning to feel chilly but couldn't do anything other than shiver and close the buttons on his jacket.

It wasn't too long before he heard an approaching car on the service road. The engine noise reduced as the speed decreased. The car turned into the short road leading to the roll-up gate. He set himself to dart behind the body as it pulled up by the gate. He chanced a quick glance at the car. It was a long, sleek black saloon. A single driver in the car. The vehicle went out of view. Nevertheless, he could hear a metal rattle of the gate lifting and the sound of the hydraulic motor echoing inside the cavernous area.

He edged forward to take a peek around the corner. The car was just about to drive under the rolled-up gate. In the same instant the sound of the motor ceased, and the car moved into the gap. Moss stepped out from the shadow, crouched down and got close to the back end of the car and slipped through the opening as the vehicle went inside the car park.

The car drove off into the interior and the screech of brakes echoed around the roof like the squeal of a frightened animal. Moss slipped by the inner wall and looked into the shade, at the parked cars, each in their own allocated bay. The block that contained the lifts was approximately forty yards away. After a moment to acclimatise, he made his way in between two cars, crossed the floor, and went to the lift doors.

He couldn't see any security cameras. He soon made it to the lift doors and pressed the call button. It was a minute before the car arrived at the floor. There was a ping as it reached the ground floor. The car wasn't empty. It contained two people, an elderly man and woman. They didn't look surprised to see him standing there. He smiled and said 'good morning' then stood aside to let them pass. He stepped into the car, faced the control panel, and pressed the button with the number 'thirty-five' on it.

From what he could recall from the visit with Sullivan there were no CCTV cameras on the landing. The lift quickly accelerated up the building. Within a matter of thirty seconds the car was slowing down as it neared the thirty-fifth floor.

As the door slid open, he peered out and onto the landing with its red and burgundy circular pattern carpet and mauve paint walls. The walls were lined with silver-framed picture frames, he hadn't noticed the first time, all at equal length along the corridor. He turned to the right and walked down the corridor at a relaxed pace. Each of the frames had a photograph of an iconic Hong Kong scene behind a sheet of thin glass. There was no one in the corridor and no sound; not even his feet as they sank into the lush pile.

# Chapter 11

**M**oss was soon outside the door to apartment 35A. He pressed the doorbell. After thirty seconds no one had come. He pressed the button for a second time. Maybe Sinnott wasn't at home. No problem. He would wait for him to return, but then he could hear a key turning and a bolt opening. The door opened to a narrow degree and a face appeared in the gap. It took him a few moments to see it was Leo Sinnott. The thick metal links of a security chain were stretched across the opening. Leo looked half sleep as if Moss had just got him out of bed. Behind him the light inside the apartment had him framed in a kind of halo effect. He rubbed his eyes and blinked several times. He recognised Moss.

"What you want?" he asked in a brusque tone.

"To talk."

"About what?" Sinnott asked.

"Why don't you open the door and let me in."

Sinnott could see Moss was about to put his shoulder to the door and ram it. Rather than have him barge his way in and damage the door, Sinnott wisely elected to unhook the chain and open the door wide.

He was wearing a knee length, blue, silk man's kimono. His feet and legs were bare and the thick cover of black hairs on his chest was visible. Moss had indeed got him out of bed. His hair was dishevelled, he was unshaven and there were sleep residues in his eyes. He didn't appear to be overly concerned by Moss's sudden and unannounced visit to his home.

Just then there was the sound of a female voice from inside the apartment, asking or saying something in Cantonese. Moss stepped in beyond the door and glanced to his right to see a pretty, long-legged girl appear in the doorway to the main bedroom. She was wearing a man's button-down shirt which came level to the centre of her thighs. She saw Moss, stared at him for a few fleeting moments, then turned into the bedroom and went out of view.

Leo said something in Cantonese, but remained calm and unperturbed. He tightened the sash around the kimono and pulled it tight to his waist.

"What you want?" he asked for a second time.

"I think you know."

Sinnott's face rippled into a quizzical frown. "Know what?" he asked.

"That Lily Fung is dead."

Sinnott took a step back. His expression changed from one of puzzlement to one of stunned surprise. "Lily?" he exclaimed. "How?"

"You tell me," Moss said.

"Tell you what?"

"How she died."

"I don't know," he said adamantly. Though it was early in the exchange his body language and reaction seemed to suggest he may have been telling the truth.

Moss moved into the centre of the lounge and looked out of the window to the spread of the undulating cityscape in the near distance. He put his eyes back on Sinnott who was patting his hair down, but hadn't moved from the spot close to the door. "She died from a drug overdose," Moss said and gauged Sinnott's reaction, which was closed. "Someone filled her blood with a chemical that popped her heart. They've tried to make it look like an overdose."

"Who are they?" Sinnott asked, seemingly dumfounded by the tragic turn of events. He was assuming that more than one person was involved. In this case he was probably on the money.

Moss looked at him. "I've no idea who *they* are," he said. "But you might."

Sinnott stared at him with a startled expression. "No way," he snapped. His use of slang made his denial sound slightly more authentic.

"What did she know?" Moss asked.

"About what?"

"Let's try the horse racing game for starters."

Sinnott looked perplexed and shook his head. "What're you getting at?" he asked, then took a few steps back across the hardwood floor in his bare feet.

"Did she know that Ho Fung was doping his race horses?"

"Doping horses?" he asked incredulously.

"Or is Fung using a performance enhancing cocktail. She knew this and threatened to reveal the practice." It was a theory Moss had considered, but he didn't have a shred of evidence if it was anywhere near the truth.

Sinnott looked genuinely stunned by the allegation. "I've no idea what you're talking about," he replied in a stiff tone.

Moss took a step to a side and put his hands on the edge of the circular sofa. Sinnott remained standing in a defensive posture with his legs wide and his arms down by his side. He looked less tall and much less flash in bedroom attire.

"Is Fung using performance-enhancing steroids?" Moss asked. "Did she know and threatened to tell? Therefore, he paid you to seduce her to bring her back here, so he could have her silenced. Then he sent me to look for her to act all innocent."

Sinnott took in his words and the underlining theory. "That's crazy," he said.

"It's a possibility," said Moss.

"But it's not true."

"How are you so sure?"

Sinnott didn't answer. There was a period of silence that lasted twenty seconds while they both took stock of the situation. "How are you absolutely sure she's dead?" Sinnott asked, voicing a modicum of concern in the tone.

"I've seen her body," Moss replied.

"Where?"

"In a place on the other side of the island."

"Whereabouts?"

"In a small abandoned hut, near to Stanley," replied Moss. He looked to the window as the sun appeared at the edge of a dark cloud to produce an array of golden sunrays that spread far and wide over the city like a blast of power from several klieg spotlights.

"Take me to the place," Sinnott said.

"Why?"

"I want to see her."

"It's not a pretty sight."

"I need to know she's dead and it's her."

Moss wondered why he was so adamant. Maybe he had a genuine desire to see her with his own eyes. "Why would you want to do that?" he asked.

"I feel as if I'm guilty for her death," said Sinnott. "I need to know you're telling me the truth," he added.

"Okay. Fine. If you insist. Let's go. I'll take you to where she is," Moss said. He was in effect calling his bluff. Maybe Sinnott had no idea Lily Fung was dead or perhaps he was wiser than he acted. Moss knew he wasn't to take him lightly. Sinnott was shrewd. He had to keep his guard all the time.

Sinnott asked to be excused for a minute. He stepped into the bedroom; through the door the girl had emerged from. Moss could hear them talking in a hushed tone. He remained by the edge of the sofa, listening to the conversation, but he couldn't understand a word. The effect of the drug in his system had all but gone from his body. Climbing the steep concrete staircase from the base of the valley to the garden in front of the apartment block could have sweated out most of the residues of the chemical. He could feel damp under his armpits and in the nooks and crannies all over his body. He looked at his clothing, then felt the bristles above his top lip and along his jawline. He must have resembled a vagabond, but that was the least of his worries.

Sinnott came out of the bedroom. He was clipping the steel strap of a watch over his right wrist. He had changed into a pair of black gym trousers and a round neck red t-shirt which had a well-known designer's logo splashed across it. He had clearly dressed in haste. It appeared that he was keen for Moss to take him to see the body of Lily Fung.

Moss looked at him. "Tell me this?" he said.

"Tell you what?" asked Sinnott.

"What day is it today?"

Sinnott looked at him, bemused by the question. "It's Saturday," he replied.

"Geez. I've been out for nearly two days," Moss said under his breath.

"Out of where?"

"My head...I was drugged for two whole days." Sinnott didn't reply. "Can I use your bathroom?" he asked.

Sinnott looked towards the door to the room. "Of course," he replied.

Moss stepped through the door and inside the room with the black wall tiles, the sleek fittings and the gleaming white porcelain washbasin. The face that greeted him in the mirror was like that of a stranger. He hardly recognised himself. He looked like death warmed up. His face was thin and gaunt. His eyes looked like saucers stirring out of pale grey flesh. He hadn't eaten anything substantial for nearly two days. He hadn't shaved for three mornings so his face was beginning to develop a kind of hound-dog appearance. His clothing was dishevelled and dirty. His jacket and shirt were stained with sweat and dirt. He looked like a man who had slept rough for the past two days.

He slipped off the jacket and shirt, then ran hot water into the basin and washed his hands and face. Never in a million years had the effect of warm water hitting his skin felt so good.

Sinnott appeared in the frame of the door behind him. He had put on a casual zip-up sports jacket over the t-shirt. Moss dried himself, slipped back into his shirt and jacket, then stepped into the lounge area to where Sinnott was standing by the long balcony window looking out over the spread of the city. Down below in the valley, Wanchai Road snaked around the racecourse and off into the distance. The huge grandstands and the oval area of open land in which the track stood were like a green oasis in a sea of concrete. Ironic, perhaps that Moss assumed this whole affair might have had something to do with the doping of racehorses Ho Fung owned. Maybe it wasn't the correct assumption, but it was still one that resonated in his mind. There was one other person who may have known a great deal more about the why's and the what's of this affair and that was Laurie Sullivan. Moss had to catch up with him.

As he came close to Sinnott he turned to face him. He had his car keys in his hand. "We go now?" he said as if he was eager to get out.

"Yeah."

Either he was playing a clever game, or he was on the level. Either way Moss had to keep his wits about him. He followed Sinnott across the lounge and they went out through the front door. The time was a shade after ten o'clock.

Once out on the corridor they went to the lift. No words were exchanged.

Within a matter of four minutes of leaving the apartment they were driving out of the ground floor car park in Sinnott's top-of-the-range 4x4.

He took the turn onto Wanchai Road and headed in a southerly direction. Moss remained mute. He was eager to see if the playboy, race horse trainer would lead him to the ramshackle building without been given directions of where to go.

It was the reverse route the bus had taken slightly more than an hour before. Nothing was said. Sinnott concentrated on driving and drove at a reasonable pace towards the area near to Aberdeen harbour. Moss wondered if he would drive straight to the fisherman's hut and therefore reveal he knew far more about the location than he was letting on. He decided to enact some conversation and seek to get more information out of him.

"You still have no idea why Ho Fung wanted her to return to England?" he asked Sinnott.

"No," His one-word answer was given in a blunt tone.

"And you've no idea where she may have been staying after she left your place?"

"No," he replied again. He had his eyes fixed on the road. They were now on a stretch of road several miles from Leighton Hill going down a narrow road that contained several blind corners and sharp bends that required full concentration. A line of vehicles was coming up the hill in the opposite direction. "When I accepted Fung's request to bring her to Hong Kong, I didn't know why. I didn't think it could lead to this," Sinnott volunteered.

"Lead to what?" Moss asked.

"Her going missing."

"You were acting on his orders?"

"Yes."

"How much did he pay you?"

"Ten thousand pounds."

"Did you receive the money?"

"It was transferred into my London bank account."

"Ten thousand. Just to bring her here?"

"That's correct."

"Not a bad sum."

Sinnott didn't reply. He had his eyes on the road where it turned at a downhill corkscrew bend. "Now he desperately wants her back in London. I wonder why?" Moss asked.

"No. I don't know," said Sinnott.

Moss believed he was telling the truth. In a strange way he didn't think Sinnott was a bad person. Perhaps out of his depth. He was caught between a rock and a hard place. Moss stayed silent and let him concentrate on driving.

# Chapter 12

**W**ithin twenty minutes of setting out they were close to the turn off towards the town of Stanley with a view across the South China Sea where a scattering of tiny islands was spread out into the sea for as far as the eye could see. Aberdeen was on the western side, Stanley to the east. As they drove down the gradual decline from Violet Hill, they had a great view of the thick green-lined terraced hillsides, the flat calm of the sea and the armada of small fishing vessels close to the shoreline.

At the bottom of the hill the road forked off into two directions. Repulse Bay Road to the right and a stretch of road known locally as Island Road to the left.

"Which way is it?" Sinnott asked. Perhaps he sensed that Moss was waiting for him to make a fatal mistake and lead him straight into the small town, then down the dirt track to the hut. Was he being cute? Moss had no idea.

"Keep left," he replied.

"Island Road then," said Sinnott. Moss didn't reply.

After another two minutes they were in the small town from where Moss had caught the bus. The beach area and the turn off onto the dirt track was only another couple of hundred yards further along.

Sinnott slowed down as he went past the bus stop. The old rickety bicycle was still propped against the wall where Moss had left it.

"Which way?" he asked.

"Drive on for another two hundred yards. There's a turn off on the right onto a dirt track that leads to a rocky cove and beach area."

Sinnott went through the town and down the incline. The turn off to the dirt track was only a matter of yards further on.

"There," said Moss, pointing out the turn onto the track.

Sinnott reduced speed, waited for a car to pass on the other side of the road, then turned the wheels of the vehicle off the tarmac and swung the Nissan onto the rocky uneven terrain of the track. He manoeuvred slowly down the dirt road towards the beach area at the bottom of the hill.

The wooden structure was only a matter of two hundred yards further along the track. There were no other vehicles in sight and all appeared to be quiet. The road was so bumpy the chassis of the 4x4 rocked from side to side. It was on an incline that didn't seem to be this steep when he walked up it with the bike to help him keep his balance.

After another few yards the structure came into full view where the track levelled out and the land flattened to a narrow stretch of beach just beyond. The building was little more than a single, two storey structure that must have been an abandoned fisherman's store. As they came to it Moss looked at the building. Something was missing, something didn't look right, but he couldn't put his finger on it for the moment.

"Is this the place?" Sinnott asked.

"This is the place," Moss said. "Stop here."

"Here!" said Sinnott, as if he was crazy. "It's just an old storage hut for fishermen. No one will use it now," he said, as if he knew what he was talking about.

He pulled up outside and looked to the door with the glass panes in it.

"You certain?" he asked.

"Yeah," Moss replied.

Moss got out of the passenger side. He looked up to the side and noticed that the shutters over the open window were now closed. When he left, they were open. He stepped to the door and tried the handle. The door was still unlocked so he opened it and went inside where he was met by the stairway with the loose hand rail to a side. Sinnott was a couple of paces behind him.

The door to the ground floor storage room from where he had taken the bicycle was closed. Moss could have sworn blind he had left it open when he had departed. He took the first step on the stairs and ascended up towards the room on the upper floor.

When he reached the landing at the top of the stairs, he looked into the room expecting to see the mattress and the body of Lily Fung covered with the white sheet. When he looked inside there was nothing. The room was completely empty.

The bed frame and the mattress were no longer there. There was nothing. No white sheet, no side table with the bong and the other drug-related items on it, no body of a naked female.

Moss was stunned into silence. He turned back to see Sinnott enter the room and cast his eyes around the empty space.

"She was here, I tell you. In this room. Right there." He pointed to the spot where the bed had been. "She was lying on a bed right there. There was a table to the side, just there."

Sinnott raised his head and looked up into the roof to see speckles of light beaming through the tiny slits in the surface. "She's not here now," he said. "Perhaps you dreamt it all," he added in a what's-going-on tone.

"I tell you. She was..." Moss's words tailed off. "Here I tell you," he said almost in a hush. He was at a loss to explain what had happened. In truth, there wasn't a lot to explain. Someone had come in, removed the body and took away the furniture and the other items.

Maybe she wasn't dead. Maybe he had dreamt it all. But then something caught his eye. He went to the shutter over the window. Something was moving in the draught. A piece of the lace curtain, several centimetres long, had become snagged on the end of a rusty nail. Whoever had removed the curtain had left a tiny ripped section remaining.

"Here. Look at this," Moss said.

"What?"

"A piece of the curtain that was over the window."

Sinnott moved towards him and looked at what he was pointing at. "So?" he said.

"So, there was someone here. I haven't dreamt anything," snapped Moss.

Just then there was a sound of the door at the bottom of the stairs coming open. This was instantly followed by the sound of feet on the stairs. In the next moment a figure appeared at the open door.

It was a man who looked to be in his mid to late fifties. He had the wizened face of a local fisherman. He was wearing a dirty sweatshirt with a faded motif on the front, baggy pants and a stained thin, red windcheater jacket. He had a plain baseball cap on his head with the peak pushed back so it was high on his head. Moss noticed his hands were covered with dirt as if he had been clearing out items of furniture and the like.

As he came onto the landing, the man paused to eye the strangers inside the room, paying particular attention to Moss. He glared at them in a disapproving fashion then said something to Sinnott in a volley of Cantonese.

"What's he saying?" Moss asked.

Sinnott didn't reply. The two of them, Sinnott and the man, began to hold an animated conversation which quickly became heated.

"What's he saying?" Moss asked again.

Sinnott looked at Moss, then suddenly in the blink of an eye his manner changed to a more assertive volatile one. He jumped towards Moss and seemed to be reaching for something inside his jacket. Within an instant, he had extracted a shiny metal object which he held in a menacing fashion and assumed an offensive stance. He didn't say a word, then thrust his hand towards Moss.

Moss hardly had any time to comprehend what he had said or done. He reacted by taking a step backwards. In the same instant Sinnott raised his right-hand level with his shoulder and took another swing at him. A flash of steel in the form of the pointed end of a blade swished by him. Moss managed to pull himself back at the moment of impact and narrowly avoided been stabbed high up on the chest. Meanwhile, the other fellow was moving on him from the other side in a coordinated harassing manoeuvre. Moss instinctively assumed a defensive stance and raised his hands. He was trained in the art of self-defence, during his police training, therefore he wasn't going to be easily beaten into submission.

He sprang onto his tiptoes and stood there at a forty-five-degree angle, Sinnott to his right, the other guy on the left. A kind of standoff ensued with neither of them moving for a good five seconds. Moss could feel adrenalin pumping into his veins. His whole body was now on high alert. It was then that he felt the weight of the syringe in his breast pocket. In the next second Sinnott moved a step forward and swung his hand again. Moss anticipated the attack. He was able to use his right hand to block the move, but also grab hold of his arm at a point close to his elbow, then bring his left hand around and chop down onto his exposed wrist. Sinnott lost his balance for a brief second. His clenched fist came open and a dagger fell from his hand. It hit the floor with a solid thud. Moss retained a grip of his wrist. He was able to make a fist of his left hand and bring it arching around and punch Sinnott on the jaw, all within a time frame no longer than a couple of seconds.

The force of the punch snapped Sinnott's head back. He was jerked backwards for one step. In the same movement Moss kicked the dagger and sent it spinning across the wood planks to the other side of the room.

The other fellow now moved closer towards Moss, but he had apprehension glued to his face. This was going to be harder than he had anticipated. Moss turned slightly towards him, and aimed a kick. The sharp end of his foot caught him high up on the thigh and close to the groin. He was instantly doubled up with pain and shock. Reaching inside his breast pocket Moss got hold of the syringe in his left hand. Sinnott looked dazed by the punch he had taken to the jaw, but he came back at Moss. It was now one against one, fist against fist. The other one having sustained a kick was in no fit state to continue the fight.

Sinnott lunged at Moss and attempted to grab hold of his front, but his movement was mistimed. He partly stumbled – partly hesitated in his approach. This allowed Moss to swing his left arm in a circular motion and thrust his hand towards the aggressor. He stabbed Sinnott with the needle of the syringe. The tip went deep into the right side of his neck at a point in or close to his carotid vein. Sinnott's immediate reaction was to put his hands to his neck and try to pull the needle out. But it was well and truly inserted into a bulging artery. In the act of swinging the syringe Moss had pressed down on the applicator and injected most of the content into Sinnott.

His reaction was almost instantaneous. His eyes seemed to go cross-eyed and lose focus. His expression was one of dumfounded shock. Then his legs gave away and he fell to the floor with a thump. The needle still stuck into his neck.

On seeing that Sinnott was no longer able to fight, the other one attempted to leg it out of the room. Moss ran after him and caught up with him on top of the landing. The fellow was about to take the first step down when Moss got behind him. He raised his left foot, put it against his back, kicked out and sent him tumbling down the steps like a bag of bones turning over and over. He hit his head against the bottom of the bannister. Moss took the handrail and went down the steps two at a time. The fellow wasn't moving, and neither was he saying anything. He was knocked out cold. There was a gash several inches wide on the top of his head from which blood was pouring.

Moss turned back and went back up the stairs two at a time. Inside the room Sinnott was stretched across the floor. He was either dead, dying or in a drug-induced sleep. Moss reached down, took his wrist and felt for a pulse. It was hardly registering. His heart may have already gone into cardiac arrest. His skin had taken on an almost blue-grey tinge. His limbs appeared to be limp. Moss reached down, took the syringe and yanked it out of his neck. As he did a spurt of blood came out and splattered across the floor. The needle had gone straight into his carotid vein.

The milky-white colour of the heroin inside the tube had been replaced by a quantity of Sinnott's blood. Carefully and without touching the needle Moss slipped the syringe back into his jacket breast pocket. He searched in Sinnott's jacket and found a wallet and the keys to his vehicle which he took into his possession.

With the car keys in his grip, he left the room and went down the steps. He stepped over the crumpled heap of the guy at the bottom of the stairs, then went outside. He went to the 4x4, opened the door, climbed inside, got the motor running, put it into drive and drove along the dirt track and away from the wooden structure.

# Chapter 13

Thirty minutes after setting out from the beach on the south side of the island, Moss was driving along Wanchai Road and heading into the built-up area of central Hong Kong. He contemplated his next move. He toyed with the idea of heading to his hotel to pack his bag and get the hell out of Hong Kong. But was that such a good idea? His sudden reappearance at the hotel would reveal he was very much alive.

He had no idea if Sinnott and company had intended to kill him or just frighten him by knocking him out and leaving him next to a dead body. Could it be they sought to implicate him in the murder of the woman he was looking for. He had seen with his own eyes that Lily Fung was dead. Now he could give the sad news to Ho Fung. He asked himself if it was all part of a Fung family dispute. Like a lot of questions, he didn't know any of the answers. If it wasn't anything to do with a horse doping swindle, then it had to be something else.

Laurie Sullivan had to be involved in the affair in one capacity or another. After all, he must have been a willing player in drugging him with a form of Rohypnol, stripping him, then taking him to some place for interrogation before he was injected with heroin or whatever was in the syringe.

He had Sullivan's address from the last time he had been in Hong Kong. His landline telephone number hadn't changed therefore it was safe to assume he was still at the same address in Kowloon.

Sullivan's home was close to a sports stadium and in an area of Kowloon famed for its flower market. The last time he had been there was ten years ago. He didn't know how close it was for sure. After considering his options he decided to dump the vehicle somewhere in Central then take the Star Ferry across the harbour to Kowloon then a cab to the flower market area and find Sullivan's home.

He drove the 4x4 along the busy Hennessey Road, deep in the Central district and into an area that was in a valley of skyscrapers. The traffic was moving at a slow pace. After driving east for half a mile or so he saw the sign for a multi-story car park in a high-rise office and shopping complex. He drove off the main road, up a ramp and into a car park. He drove up several exterior circular ramps for five levels or so before he came across an empty space on the sixth floor of eight.

He parked the car. Before leaving he made sure to wipe his fingerprints off the steering wheel and the door handles. From here he made his way down six flights of stairs to the ground level and out onto the busy street. It took him five minutes to walk into the tightly packed business quarter, through an open-air clothes market and on towards the harbour front. On the way, he deposited the Nissan keys and Sinnott's wallet into a rubbish bin.

His plan was to take a Star ferry over to the Kowloon side of the harbour and seek out Laurie Sullivan's residence. He knew he lived in an address on Prince Edward Road. He vaguely recalled visiting his home. It was a tiny five room flat in a high-rise apartment block that must have been thirty years old even back then.

He soon made it to the harbour and the Star ferry terminal. It cost less than one pound to cross the iconic harbour to Shim Tsa Tsui on the Kowloon side. The quay area by the ferry terminal was close to the huge steel and glass structure of the Hong Kong convention centre. It was teeming with people, both locals and tourists alike. Each day seventy thousand people would cross the half mile wide harbour between the island and the land that was official termed as the 'New Territories'. It was perhaps one of the most sought-after short ferry trips on many people's bucket-list.

Moss purchased a ticket from a coin-operated machine and boarded the next ferry along with several dozen passengers who were evenly spread between the upper deck and the lower deck. The boat soon set off over the choppy waters of the harbour for the ten-minute crossing to Shim Tsa Tsui.

On the Kowloon side of the harbour, adjacent to the famous Canton-Kowloon Railway clock tower, was an ornamental pond and garden. Tourists could purchase drinks from a number of vendors and linger to take photographs of the famous Hong Kong skyline from advantage points next to the promenade railings.

Moss made straight for a nearby taxi rank. He had to wait five minutes for the next available cab. He asked the driver to take him to Prince Edward Road and the area near to the flower market. Luckily for him the driver knew where he wanted to go. The taxi set off into the heart of bustling Kowloon with its busy streets, narrow pavements, and with its vast array of business signs. Air conditioning units hung out of windows in the almost never-ending stretch of tenement blocks set behind the street market stalls that line the length of Nathan Road.

After a journey of twenty minutes, they were on a stretch of Prince Edward Road close to Mong Kok Stadium. Sullivan lived on the fifteenth floor of an apartment building near to the flower market and street side stall holders selling fruit and vegetables. Moss recalled visiting him at home and admiring the excellent views over the stadium to the hillsides in the distance that marked the boundary between the New Territories and the beginning of the Chinese mainland. The city of Shenzhen skyline was visible in the haze.

## Chapter 14

It wasn't that long before the taxi was in an area Moss recognised. From memory he recalled the apartment block had a kind of narrow curved frontage with red paint edging to the stone of the façade. Eighteen floors high. He soon came across it on the western end of the road and close to the stadium.

Unlike ten years before, it was now hemmed in and dwarfed by a new slender condominium that was tightly squeezed in on one side. At ground level there was a long row of stores and stalls selling bushes, fledging trees and everything else associated with the horticulture trade. Roadside hawkers were stopping traffic on Prince Edward Road to sell posies of flowers to passing motorists.

Moss asked the driver to stop on the corner where some steps went down to a concourse that led to turnstiles going into the stadium. He paid the fare, then got out and was immediately aware of the smell of freshly cut flowers and the sounds of this part of Kowloon. On the other side of the street, behind a line of shrubs was a chain link fence and the side of one of the stands of the sports stadium. Moss wasn't sure which sports were played there. It may have been football, baseball, or rugby, or all three.

Before making a move, he watched the taxi pull away and disappear up the street, then he turned to walk the fifty yards to the front of the apartment block. There were four apartments on each floor – two at the front, two at the rear – making seventy-two in total. Each one had a small balcony. Air conditioning units were installed in the windows. Several of the balconies were festooned with tall plants. There was a sign on the front in Cantonese characters. The window frames looked in urgent need of replacement.

He was conscious of the need to find Sullivan quickly, but had no way of knowing if he was at home. He made his way across the path, up a step, through an open entrance and into a tight entrance. Flaking red and yellow masonry paint was peeling off the walls. The bottom half was red, the top was yellow. A notice in traditional Chinese characters and English asked the residents to ensure the front door was locked after nine at night. There was a stone clad stairwell doubling as a fire escape should the building catch fire. Straight ahead was a single lift shaft that served the entire building. He recalled using the lift when he had visited Sullivan all those years ago. From what he remembered his apartment was a compact space of five rooms that contained all the essentials for living. There wasn't a great deal of space, and very little in the way of storage, which wasn't uncommon in Kowloon. A balcony with the view across the border to Shenzhen was a bonus.

After a few moments to get his bearings, he pressed the button to call the lift. The car came down from the third floor. He got in and pressed the button for the fourteenth floor. He would take the stairs for the final flight to the next floor.

The car was slow and rattled all the way up fourteen floors. Once there, he got out, opened a door to the stairwell and the stone steps serving the building. The stairwell was cold. A single pane window at the half-way turn allowed a shadowy insipid light to illuminate the otherwise dingy backdrop. He could feel his cold breath on his face. The sound of his feet against the stone chamber made a pinging echo.

When he reached the top of the stairs and the door that opened onto the fifteenth floor, he paused for a moment to listen for any sound. He couldn't hear anything except for the beat of his heart. He felt tense and jumpy. He gently opened the door, peered through then moved onto the corridor. A landing ran from one side of the building to the other, along a bare tile surface. There were two doors to flats across the corridor and opposite each other. Taking a step forward he gently closed the door, then moved onto the landing.

It was dim. Natural light was at a premium. Dull, and dusty bulbs attached to the ceiling provided the light, therefore the ends of the landing were bathed in permanent shadow. The space was narrow with hardly enough room for two people to pass. Sullivan's place was on the left, the last door facing the front of the building. He ventured forward. He could hear the sound of a voice from inside one of the flats or maybe it was from a television. He couldn't tell. This being Saturday afternoon, he assumed that many of the residents would be at work or in one of the public parks that dot this part of Kowloon. He made it down to the last door on the left-hand side. And there, attached to the door was a kind of decorative porcelain plate with the name of the flat owner: 'Laurie Sullivan,' engraved into it in dark paint letters.

He waited for a moment to collect his thoughts, steady himself, then he tapped on the door. He patted the breast pocket of his jacket to feel the shape of the syringe. No one came so he knocked for a second time, this time louder.

In the next moment he heard a chain being released from the door frame, then the sound of a bolt opening. As the door opened wider escaping sunlight raced across the landing. Moss recognised Sullivan immediately. He was wearing jogging pants and an off-white sports type of string vest. Before Sullivan could utter a word, Moss lunged at him and got the first punch in, hitting him plumb in the face. Sullivan staggered back through the doorway. Moss followed him inside, stepped into an alcove and pushed Sullivan with a shove. He staggered back, fell through a metal ball-bearing curtain hanging from a door frame at the end of the alcove, and hit the deck with an almighty clatter. Moss was soon upon him, wrapped his left hand around the vest to take a firm hold, and pummelled him in the face with a second punch.

Moss stepped through the metal curtain and went into the living space. The room was tightly packed and scruffy. It must have been ten feet by twelve feet wide at most. There was a two-seater sofa on one side and a coffee table which was covered with several glossy, English-language magazines. A rug covered a plain tile floor. A paper lantern hung from the ceiling. The furniture was old and cheap. A kind of mix of Chinese reproductions and old country. On one wall were a couple of Monet prints of Westminster Bridge scenes at twilight or dusk. A retro, 1960s Manchester United football shirt was hanging on a coat hanger attached to a picture rail. A single door led onto the balcony with dusty looking windows allowing the daylight to illuminate the room. Behind the thin net curtain, it was just possible to make out the spread of rainbow-coloured seats in the stadium across the road.

Sullivan was on his back, but managed to get onto his haunches. He wasn't a young man and neither was he fit, but he was still a size and therefore a threat so Moss was prepared to defend himself if Sullivan chose to come at him.

Sullivan shook his head as if he was trying to get the shock of the assault out of his system. He didn't utter a word, but he managed to spring to his feet and come swinging. Moss anticipated an incoming punch, telegraphed it, and was able to duck out of the way. As Sullivan lunged his body Moss twisted his knee and sent it slamming into his midriff. The blow propelled him back against the door leading onto the balcony. He fell to a side and onto the edge of the table which tipped over and sent the magazines flying into the air then spilling across the floor. It was only then that Moss saw that a television was on. Sullivan had been watching a football game. The volume was so low it was hardly audible. He groaned out loud, managed to right himself and was about to get onto his feet when Moss aimed a kick that hit him on the chin. The force propelled him against the upturned table. Now in a more aggressive manner Moss grabbed him by his throat and delivered a third punch which smacked against his jaw. Sullivan fell to the floor, face first. Moss knew he had rendered him defenceless. He was aware that he needed to keep the sounds low just in case the neighbours had heard the initial confrontation. He found the remote control to the TV and adjusted the level of volume, so the roar of the crowd and commentator were increased, but not loud enough to cause offence to the neighbours. He was done with violence for the time being. He looked around the room and saw a sit up straight-backed wooden chair. He went to it, took hold of it by the top and placed it down in the centre of the room. Then he went to Sullivan, slipped his arms under his armpits and hauled him up. Sullivan was half conscious and half out of it.

Manoeuvring him onto his feet Moss put him in a headlock that threatened to cut off the oxygen to his brain. He managed to turn him one hundred and eighty degrees and force his backside down onto the chair. There was a rivulet of thin almost colourless blood coming out of one nostril and there was reddening on his face from the punch. His shaven pink head was pale but shining with a layer of oil. The old tattoos on his arms had long before lost their colour and were partly hidden by the wrinkles of the skin and by the thick cover of body hair.

Just then the volume coming out of the television increased as the commentator became excited by something happening on the pitch. Sullivan was taking in long breaths of air as if the beating he had taken had expelled the air out of his lungs. With Sullivan in the seat, Moss grabbed hold of the ball-bearing curtain and yanked it off the door frame. Taking it, he went to the chair and proceeded to wrap the long metal strings around Sullivan and the back of the chair. He worked quickly and soon had him secure with his arms tied tight. Once he was satisfied, Sullivan wouldn't be moving any time soon he turned away and stepped through a door and into a tiny kitchen. He opened a head high cupboard and found what he was looking for – a container of some description – which happened to be a copper pan. He placed the pan under the cold water tap and filled it until it was three-quarters full. Taking the pan handle he stepped back into the room and emptied half of the contents over Sullivan's head. The effect of the cold water, hitting him, quickly had the desired effect. He came alive and gasped out loud. The water drenched his vest. A combination of mucus and blood coming from his nose dripped down his chin.

Moss then tipped the remaining water over him. Sullivan tried to shake himself free, but the metal strips were tightly wrapped around the back of the chair and his arms, so he couldn't get any leverage to prise them off.

Moss stood over him. "Okay. You fuck. You left me there to die. Didn't you?" He smacked Sullivan across his cheek with an open palm slap. The force was enough to jolt his head and the sound of the blow made a dull thud.

On the TV, advertisements were now playing over a merry jingle. Out through the dust-covered window the spread of the multi-coloured rainbow seats in the football stadium were now in shade. Moss was trembling, not with fear, but with a desire to hurt Sullivan all he could, but without making him scream. "You left me to die. Didn't you?" he repeated.

Sullivan raised his head and stared at him through his dark eyes. "You don't understand," he said in a tone of voice that contained an acknowledgement of wrong doing.

"Understand what? All I know is that someone drugged me, and you let it happen," said Moss.

"No. Not me."

"I woke up in a fucking dungeon, strapped to a chair with a bright white light blinding me. Like a fucking spy in an interrogation cell. Then some cunt injected me with a chemical and left me to die. And what were you doing all the time this was going on?" He nipped his fingers into his jacket breast pocket, took the end of the syringe, extracted it and put the needle close to Sullivan's eyes. "I swear to God. If I don't get answers. I'll inject you with this deadly shit in here." Sullivan's eyes focused on the combination of milky white liquid and the red of blood inside the tube. Moss placed the tip of the needle against the flesh on the right-hand side of his neck and gently inserted the tip into his skin. Sullivan tried to free himself. His efforts to snap the chains intensified so he had the chair rocking. Moss grasped him by the shoulders and pressed down to stop him. He soon gave up the fight.

"What's it going to be? It's down to you."

"Okay. Okay. I'll tell you everything," Sullivan said.

"Talk."

"What do you want to know?"

"What's your connection with Ho Fung?"

"We knew each other when he was in Hong Kong."

"In what sense did you know each other? Were you drinking buddies or summat? Or were you, his snitch?" The word 'snitch' was a very emotive word to use. Accusing a police detective of being a snitch was code for a bent copper who fed information to someone who paid for it.

"I was his protector," he revealed.

"Okay. I'm impressed. From what? From who?" Moss asked.

"I worked for his operation. He used the information I gave him to spy on and get information about some British officials and other high-ranking people in the HK administration at the time."

Moss had no idea of the structure of the local government or the legislative arm of the authorities in the old British run Hong Kong so couldn't hazard a guess at how high it went. "What else?" he asked.

"Keeping tabs on political enemies," Sullivan said.

"What political enemies?"

"Those working for the pro-democracy movement."

"Where?"

"Here in Hong Kong."

"Explain," said Moss.

"The Beijing government used him to disrupt the pro-democracy movement before the handover in ninety-seven," Sullivan said.

"Surely Ho Fung was pro-democracy, which is why he got out and went to live in London."

"The reverse," said Sullivan.

"So, what's he doing in London?" Moss asked.

"I guess he's working for the Beijing government."

"Doing what?"

"Spying on Chinese dissidents. Spying on the British. The Yanks. Who knows? Anyone who could do harm to the Chinese communist party. He's using his influence to lobby on behalf of the Chinese community but spying on them at the same time."

On the television, the second half of the football game was just getting underway. A goal was scored in the first few seconds of the game resuming. The commentator raised his tone of delivery to an increased level of excitement.

"Tell me this," said Moss. "Did you tell Ho Fung to contact me?"

"Yes."

"Why?"

"He wanted someone who would accept the job without asking too many questions."

"You suggested me?"

"Of course."

"So, I accepted the job. Where does Leo Sinnott come into it? Did Fung pay him to seduce Lily Fung to get her back here from London?"

"Yes."

"Why?" Moss asked.

"It's simple."

"Is it?"

"Yes."

"What's simple?"

"She was supporting Chinese pro-democracy groups in London."

"What kind of support?"

"Financial mainly. She was using his son's money for Christ's sake. Her brother Lee Wang is a leading figure in the pro-democracy movement here," Sullivan said.

"So, she's giving them money against her father-in-law's wishes. Did her husband know?" Moss asked.

"Probably not, but I'm not sure. Going against Ho Fung is a big no-no. That's a major issue."

"What happened when he found out?" Moss asked.

"I guess he told her to stop. I guess she refused."

"Go on," Moss encouraged.

"So, they planned to entice her back here using Leo Sinnott as a love interest. In a honey trap," said Sullivan.

"It worked."

"Yeah."

Sullivan took in a deep breath through his mouth. The blood in his nostrils had become a thin rivulet. His right eye was puffy where Moss had punched him. His vest was drenched with a combination of water and blood that had turned the white material a pink and crimson shade.

"What happened when she got back here with Sinnott?" Moss asked.

"She went to his place and stayed with him," Sullivan replied.

"Then what?"

"She was snatched by a gang."

"Then?"

"Then…? They killed her," said Sullivan.

"Why?"

"To send out a message."

"To who?" Moss asked.

"To the pro-democracy hot heads."

"Why?"

"To show them that the Hong Kong government has the power to eliminate any threat to the natural order of things."

"Did they need to go to those lengths?"

"I don't know, but I guess they did."

"Stop guessing for fuck's sake." Moss warned.

"They wanted her dead to send a message to not only the Hong Kong dissidents, but those inside Britain as well."

"Geez. This is heavy stuff."

"It's politics. Hong Kong politics. Chinese politics," Sullivan said.

"But why use me?" Moss asked.

"I guess they wanted to put you in the frame."

"Why me?"

"If she was found dead with a Brit, it might cause a diplomatic incident and discredit the British government, who are poking their nose into Chinese affairs. That's the trouble with the Brits, they never know when to leave things alone."

"But I've got nothing to do with the British government."

"You and I know that. But the implication would be that you're a British agent," said Sullivan.

Moss was flummoxed by what Sullivan was telling him, but assumed he was telling the truth. "How come you know so much about this?" he asked.

Sullivan didn't reply for a few moments as if he was choosing his words carefully. "I still work for Ho Fung," he confessed.

"You must know him well?"

"He pays for this place and gives me a monthly salary." Sullivan admitted. He looked at Moss, then at the ball bearing chains wrapped around him. "Are you going to free me from this?" he asked.

"No. I can't say that I am."

"Why? I've told you what I know. That's the deal," he protested.

"No deal."

"Why?" Sullivan asked.

"Because you left me to die in that place." Moss said.

He put the business end of the needle tight against the flesh of his neck.

"No please," shouted Sullivan. His cry for mercy was partly lost above the sound coming from the television.

"I hope you enjoy the trip," said Moss. He put his finger on the applicator and dug the needle deep into his neck, then pushed down to deliver the content of the tube into his blood. Reaching down he took hold of the metal pan, brought it level, and whacked him in the face with the heavy base. The blow shattered his chin and teeth. His head was jolted back. The blow propelled Sullivan into the middle of next week.

Before he left the flat, Moss decided to do a search to see if he could find anything of interest. He opened the top drawer of a bureau and rummaged inside. Hidden under some papers there was a thick wad of US one hundred-dollar bills, British pounds, Japanese Yen, and a thick stack of five hundred-dollar Hong Kong notes. He stuffed most of the wads of cash into his trouser and jacket pockets. Then he stepped to the front door, opened it and peered out onto the landing. There was no one about. Before he stepped out, he looked back to see Sullivan. He wasn't moving. His head was bent back. Sullivan was either out cold or dead. Moss had little feeling in his heart. He was oblivious to the possibility he may have killed Sullivan. In truth, he didn't care that much.

He closed the door on the latch then set off along the corridor. Rather than take the lift he opted to walk down the fifteen flights of stairs to the ground floor.

As he stepped off the last step and down into the foyer, he looked at his watch. The time was fast approaching three o'clock. Where had the time gone? He asked himself. He knew there was a British Airways flight leaving Chek Lap Kok airport bound for London at nine-forty that evening. He intended to be on the flight come what may.

Once on the street he walked for several hundred yards towards a busy junction where he came across a line of stationary red taxis at a rank. He got into the first cab and asked the driver to take him to the nearest Metro station from where he could take a subway train across the harbour to the main island.

The taxi driver dropped him close to Jordan metro station.

When the metro train arrived at Wanchai station the time was getting on for four o'clock. He had three hours to get to his hotel, go into his room, pack his things then go to the airport. If he couldn't get on the nine-forty flight, there was another London bound flight leaving at five to midnight.

Once in Wanchai he didn't dawdle. He made it into the front lobby of the hotel. He felt somewhat conspicuous. He still had a pass card so that didn't present a problem to get into his room. He took the lift to the fortieth floor. Once inside the room he had a very quick wash, shaved off the two days of growth on his chin, then changed into a fresh set of clothes. He didn't intend to hang about. There could be people looking for him, so it was wise to get out of there as soon as possible. He swiftly emptied the safe then packed his suitcase. He was in two minds about taking the content of the mini-bar, but decided against it.

As soon as he was ready, he left the room and closed the door for the final time. Rather than take the lift he decided to take the emergency exit stairs. It took him ten minutes to walk down the forty flights.

As he finally reached the ground floor, he opened a door that opened onto the lobby. There was a large number of people milling around the desks and sitting in the seats close to the concessionary drinks and snack bar. After a few moments he opened the door, aimed for the wall of light at the glass entrance and stepped around the people, through the hub-hub of sound and towards the exit. He didn't intend to check out. Still anyone observing him would see his suitcase. He moved from the centre of the floor, made it to the wide glass entrance, out the sliding doors and onto the street. He increased his pace and spirited away into the line of pedestrians ambling by the front of the hotel. Once he was out of the range of the hotel, he crossed a busy road, walked by the entrance to a shopping arcade and on towards the nearest taxi rank where two taxis were standing, waiting for passengers.

He opened the door, of the first cab in line, and slid onto the rear seat.

"Where you go?" the driver asked.

"The airport," he replied. He had a plane to catch. The bad news was that in the height of the late afternoon rush hour it could take one hour to get to the airport, the good news was that he still had several hours to make the nine-forty flight. If the plane was full, along with the later London flight he intended to take the next one to any destination in western Europe. Paris or Amsterdam or even Frankfurt would suffice. He just wanted to get out of Hong Kong as swiftly as possible.

As he was being driven through the streets of Hong Kong to the airport, he took time to reflect on everything that had happened to him in the past eighty hours. The sheer madness of it all! He was still hounded by the sight of waking up next to the body of someone who he believed to be Lily Fung. It was a memory that would stay with him for a very long time. The explanation Sullivan had given him still left a lot of unanswered questions. Had Ho Fung really gone to those lengths to dispose of his troublesome daughter-in-law? Perhaps the only way to find out was to ask him.

Once in the airport Moss went straight to the British Airways desk. It was his lucky day. He purchased the last remaining ticket for the nine-forty departure to Heathrow. He had to settle for economy over business, but he wasn't bothered. He got the last ticket. He was pleased to be on a flight heading out of Hong Kong with his life still intact.

## Chapter 15

The flight was full of Brits going home after trips to Australia and New Zealand, and some expats returning home on business, along with tourists to the UK from mainland China. There wasn't a spare place to be had. Moss settled down into an aisle seat. He couldn't do a lot but grin and bear it. It was cramped and noisy, so he had to suck it in, but he was very relieved to be on his way home after an eventful four days. The in-flight meal was the best airplane food he had ever eaten. Boy was he hungry and thirsty!

The twelve-hour flight time seemed to drag. He spent most of the time watching movie after movie. Most of them instantly forgettable. He did sleep for some of the time but in small periods.

Eleven hours after setting out, the outline of the east coast of England appeared on the monitor screen imbedded into the back of the seat in front of him. He was as good as back home after what was a nightmare of a trip to the Far-East. But it wasn't over. He knew he had to go back to visit Ho Fung in Belgravia to present him with his report and his invoice.

On touchdown in Heathrow, he cleared immigration and customs in less than one hour. Rather than take public transport into the centre of the city, he grabbed a taxi from outside Terminal Five to his flat in an apartment building opposite the British Army barracks on Knightsbridge. It felt good to be back in Blighty and on the familiar streets of London. The temperature in the capital was down a good ten degrees from what it had been on the other side of the planet. He was greeted with an overcast sky and drizzle in the air. Still, these were his streets. The place he called home.

Once back in the familiar surroundings of his flat he took a long, hot shower, then went to bed and slept like a baby for the next fourteen hours. It was good to be in the safety of his home. There were a few messages on his answerphone and a couple of emails he had to deal with, but there was nothing to be alarmed about.

He didn't emerge from his bed until late on Monday morning, nearly exactly one week since he had received the telephone call from Ho Fung. Now he had to plan his next move. He had to return to see Mr Fung to inform him that as far as he was concerned the job was over, but it was highly likely that his daughter-in-law was dead.

He had to consider where he went with this. He couldn't very well go to the authorities to tell them the tale for several reasons. He could have killed Leo Sinnott and Laurie Sullivan and going to the police would be breaching client confidentially. Yes, he was home, back in London, but it didn't mean to say this was over by a long way.

If Sullivan was telling the truth and it was all about quelling the anti-Chinese, pro-democracy group in London it could all turn very nasty for him. He didn't want any of that. On a more ethical scale he had to think about the client. There was an unwritten and unspoken code of practice that private investigators don't reveal the content of discussions with clients or reveal the assignments they are on. The only task he was determined to do was to visit the home of Ho Fung and inform him of his findings and to tell him that in his opinion Lily Fung was likely to be dead. Perhaps he already knew this. Maybe he was just seeking confirmation. Moss didn't know for certain. He wasn't sure of anything anymore.

What was clear was that Ho Fung had known Laurie Sullivan for many years. When Fung had hit on the plan of using a gigolo called Leo Sinnott to entice his daughter-in-law to Hong Kong, he had sought Sullivan's assistance. Sullivan knew of David Moss from way back when. He knew Moss was now a private detective working out of an office on Borthwick Street in Soho. Had Sullivan set up the entire operation? There was a chance he had. He had calculated Moss would be likely to contact him for assistance. The objective of the whole operation was to get Lily Fung back to Hong Kong to kill her and end the alleged funding of a pro-democracy movement of which her brother Lee Wang was a leading member. From here the scenario went down one of two different routes: One, they wanted him to see with his own eyes that Lily Fung was dead, Or, two: they intended to murder him and put him in a position whereby he would be implicated in her death in order to create a kind of diplomatic incident. When they – the bad guys – discovered he wasn't dead and had in effect escaped they removed her body to another location and hid all the evidence. When he returned to the dilapidated fishing hut with Leo Sinnott they intended to try and kill him there and then.

# Chapter 16

Two days passed. It was now midday on Wednesday. Moss had by-and-large recovered from the jet lag. He had spent the previous evening counting the money he had taken from Sullivan's flat. It amounted to quite a tidy sum. There was £2,000 in US dollars. £3,000 in Japanese Yen. £7,000 in Hong Kong dollars, and £6,000 in pounds' sterling. A total of £18,000. A sum of money he would put through his books as money earned from legitimate case work. From Wednesday afternoon onwards, he wondered how long he should wait before visiting the home of Ho Fung to present him with his end of assignment report and invoice.

A further day passed. He had heard nothing. No emails. No post. No messages on his business answerphone. He had received an offer of a job from a company who wanted him to spy on a finance manager who they thought was cooking the books and stealing money from them. There was nothing connected to the Ho Fung job.

To put a closure on it he decided to pay a visit to the Belgravia home of Mr Fung on Saturday to seek a meeting with the man who had given him the task.

Saturday afternoon was cool and a little breezy. The days of April were about to become the first days of May. A shower had just dropped its contents over the centre of London, leaving the central streets with a wet sheen and puddles which were now glistening in the sunlight breaking through the clouds. Saturdays in these parts were usually quiet with many of the residents away for the weekend. Therefore, there was little traffic on the roads.

In Belgravia there wasn't a lot happening. The cars parked tight into the side of Seaton Place told of fine taste and few money concerns. The facades of the homes with their white walls, metal grills, first-floor balconies, and colonnade porches, gave the appearance of a classy, highly sophisticated London neighbourhood. Which it very much was.

Moss walked along the pavement. He was dressed in a dark suit. He held a document holder wedged under his arm. He hadn't made an appointment, but guessed there was an even chance that Mr Fung would be at home. If he was it would be interesting to see how he greeted him.

He was soon at the front of the four-storey house with the step up to the front door and the steps down to the basement. A quick glance over the ground floor rails and down the concrete steps revealed a door at the bottom of the stairs.

He moved onto the raised step and took the several short paces to the front door with its stout, gold-plate decorative knocker, gold plate letterbox and door button in the intercom unit under the shade of the overhead balcony. He pressed the door button.

Thirty seconds passed with no one answering his call, so he hit the button again. Then he heard a voice coming out of the intercom enquiring: "Who is it?" Asked by someone with an oriental sounding accent.

"It's David Moss, of Moss Private Investigations, here to see Mr Fung," he replied.

Silence. One minute passed. Moss was beginning to think the door would remain closed to him, when he heard the sound of the lock opening. The solid slab of polished wood moved inward to a narrow degree and the eyes of a male with Chinese features appeared in the opening.

"Yes. I help you?" he asked in faltering English.

"It's Mr Moss to see Mr Fung," he replied.

"What your business?"

"I've got a report for Mr Fung," said Moss and held the document holder in front of his midriff.

The door opened slightly wider. The fellow on the other side looked to be in his mid-thirties. He was wearing a pinstriped jacket, matching waistcoat and trousers combination, a white shirt and a dark tie which had a large knot tucked into the neck. He looked at the document holder then at Moss and gave him an up and down inspection.

"Mr Fung. He is expecting you? Yes," he asked.

"No," replied Moss. "He's not expecting me."

"So, what your business?"

"I have the report Mr Fung requested," Moss replied.

The chap looked at him with a combination of uncertainty and confusion forming a squint in his eyes and a pout along his lips. "He knows you coming?" he asked.

"No. As I said, I want to give him a report."

"What report?"

"My final report and invoice on the search for Lily Fung."

The chap didn't reply for a long moment and continued to look at Moss with a pinched-eye expression of puzzlement and uncertainty. "One moment," he said and promptly closed the door on him.

Moss waited. A minute passed. He turned towards the path and took a couple of steps back and moved out from under the shade of the balcony. As he stepped back, the door opened and an imposing looking guy with a wide girth, thick chest and a Charlie Chan type of moustache appeared in the doorway and stood in the frame in a wide-legged stance. The guy in the pinstriped jacket, waistcoat and trouser combo was standing at his side.

"Come in," said the larger man and took a sideways step.

Moss nodded his head to him, then took a few steps and entered through the door and into the white marble vestibule room with its authentic Hong Kong British flag in the glass case attached to the wall and the gleaming gold leaf dragon statues. There was a smell of burning incense sticks in the air.

The bigger guy was at least six feet tall and he must have weighed twenty stone. He looked at Moss. "I search you?" he asked.

"Sure."

Moss put the document holder down and rested it in between his ankles, then he raised his arms and held them level with his shoulders. He had expected to be greeted by the housemaid. Not two men. This was a surprise. The chap patted him down in a professional manner which seemed to suggest he had done this on many occasions before. Then his eyes went to the document holder and he gestured to it. Moss took the holder and passed it into his hand. He opened the zip and looked inside for any concealed weapons or anything of a suspicious nature. When he was satisfied it was clean, he gave it back to him.

Just then Moss was aware of a man in his seventies gingerly coming down the staircase in a slow careful ascent. He was wearing a cashmere mustard coloured cardigan over a plain, button-down shirt, and grey flannel trousers.

He stepped off the last stair and came to join the three men assembled close to the front door. The other two stepped to a side to let him take the central position. Moss had never seen him before in his life, but he looked strikingly similar to the man in the grainy photograph of Ho Fung, he had viewed online, and remarkedly similar to the man he had met previously.

"Yes. Who are you?" he asked directly to Moss.

"I'm here to give Mr Fung my report," Moss said.

The chap had heavy-lidded brown eyes, and a slim, slightly pugged nose. His teeth were the same colour as his olive skin.

"I am Mr Fung," he said stiffly and looked at Moss through inquisitive eyes.

He wasn't the Mr Fung; Moss had spoken to twelve days before. He looked at him and smiled.

"No, Mr Ho Fung."

"But I am Mr Ho Fung," he repeated bluntly and glanced at the two men at his side.

"I was here on Monday. Not the Monday just gone," said Moss losing his train of thought for a moment ... "the week before. I spoke to a man who said he was Ho Fung."

"I wasn't here, last week," said the elderly chap. The other two men didn't say a word. Both had edged closer to the older man. Not for the first time in the last few days Moss wondered if he had dreamt all this, or if it was part of a new dream? Or something far sinister.

"But the man asked me to go to Hong Kong to find his daughter-in-law, Lily Fung. Locate her and bring her back to London. Here look at this...." he unzipped the document holder, reached inside and withdrew the photograph Ho Fung had given him.

He offered it to the man who seemed reluctant to take it, but he relented. He took the photograph from him and looked at the figures for a few fleetingly moments. His eyes gave nothing away. He handed the photograph back to Moss.

"I know no-one in this," he replied stiffly.

The guy in the pinstriped jacket said something in a language Moss couldn't understand. The older man replied in short shrift. "What's this about?" he asked Moss.

Moss narrowed his eyes. "I received a telephone call from a man who called himself Ho Fung a week last Monday. He asked me to come to this house..." He looked around to take in the wood panelled door leading into the reception room where the meeting had taken place. "We talked in there," he thrust his chin in the direction of the room, just a few feet away... "about his daughter-in-law called Lily Fung and that he wanted me to go to Hong Kong to find her then bring her back to London."

"Lily is at home in Kensington with her husband. My son Hue," the chap replied.

"So, who did I find *dead* on the bed?" Moss asked.

The mention of the word *'dead'*, caused the other two men to look at each other. Something was very amiss here. If the man he had spoken to previously wasn't Ho Fung then who the hell was he? Moss was plunged into a deep chasm of uncertainty. Not for the first time he had to ask himself what in God's name was going on.

He looked at the tip of his shoes then raised his head and looked into the eyes of the man who had said he was Ho Fung.

"Do you know an ex-police officer in the Hong Kong police called Laurie Sullivan?" he asked.

The man considered the question for the briefest of moments, then he shook his head, but didn't say a word.

"Do you know a racehorse trainer called Leo Sinnott?" asked Moss. He observed his eyes to see if his pupils diluted to reveal he did know the name or they closed to reveal the opposite. The man shook his head for a second time. His pupils remained pretty much the same size. Something completely and utterly off the wall was going on. Moss considered for the first time that the man in front of him was an imposter, or that the man in front of him was the real Ho Fung and that someone else had given him the brief to go to Hong Kong to find someone who was apparently alive and well and living in Kensington. If that was the case, what the hell was going on?

Was one of the men at his side responsible for the set-up? If so, what was his goal? Or was the man in front of him, the one who said he was Ho Fung, somebody else. If so, what was his objective? The two men who said they were Ho Fung did have similarities. They were the same age. The same stature and physical dimensions. They had the same, thick spikey grey hair. The same facial features. One of them was the real Ho Fung. The other was an imposter. But who was the real one? Moss had no idea. According to Sullivan, he and Fung knew each other well, consequently this guy must have been lying. He also knew Leo Sinnott because he trained his racehorses. He had lied again. Moss looked at the three men, then sought to wriggle out of this.

"Sorry, I must be mistaken," he said. "I'm so sorry to have bothered you with this. I have the wrong Mr Fung. Please accept my sincere apology."

None of the three men replied. They watched as Moss took a step back and edged to the door whilst keeping his eyes on the three of them. He turned, one-eighty, opened the front door and moved out under the overhanging porch. The man, in the pinstriped suit, who had opened the door stepped forward, followed him to the end of the porch then paused and watched him walk away along the path. Moss carried on, walked by the wrought iron fence and the gate leading onto the stairs that led down to the basement, then away from the house.

He wondered what his next move should be. Should he forget about the whole thing or should he continue the investigation? More than one person was deceased, therefore maybe he should continue to try and discover what it was all about. He simply couldn't forget about it. With this thought going through his head, he pondered on how he could gain access to the house. The short flight of eight steps going down to the basement could be a way to get inside.

He soon made it to the street off Sloane Square where he had parked his car on a meter. He was back in Seaton Place within twenty-five minutes of leaving the house. The time was edging close to three o'clock. He managed to find a parking space about one hundred yards from the front of the house. He knew he couldn't stay here for too long. The parking wardens in this neck of Chelsea and Kensington were known to be keen. They would slap a ticket on a non-resident's vehicle in the blink of an eye. He knew that he had to find another way of obtaining answers. It was at this point he considered asking for assistance from a chap called Bob Ambrose.

Ambrose owed him a favour from six months before, when Moss had done some surveillance work for him. It was now time for Ambrose to pay his debt.

He had known Ambrose for several years. Ambrose worked for himself as a designer and installer of high-tech surveillance systems, security detectors and eavesdropping equipment. He was in a similar line of work to Moss. He had been in the Met police at the same time as Moss, therefore they knew each other well. Ambrose just happened to be a good break-in-and-enter exponent. They hadn't spoken to each other for about a year. Moss had him on speed dial on his phone. He called him from his car. Ambrose picked it up on the fifth ring.

"Bob Ambrose Security systems," he said.

"It's Dave Moss. Long-time no see. I need a favour doing."

Ambrose had a reputation for being laconic, serious and deadpan. "Such has?" he enquired.

"A B and E on a house in Belgravia."

"Reason."

"A job."

"Fire away."

"You won't believe me if I told you."

"Try me."

Moss told Ambrose the full story of how he had gone to Hong Kong to try and find the daughter-in-law of a rich Chinese man and everything that had occurred to him. It was true, Ambrose didn't believe him. He was finding it hard to believe what sounded like the scenario of some far-fetched movie. Moss tended to agree with him.

"What do you want me to do?" Ambrose asked.

"Help me break into the house to see who and what I can discover," Moss replied.

"When and what time?" Ambrose asked.

"Tomorrow morning at one o'clock."

"Where?" Ambrose asked.

"Seaton Place."

Ambrose said nothing for a long moment. As if he was considering the request. Moss stayed silent.

"Okay," said Ambrose without further question or debate. He must have known Moss would call him one day and ask him to repay the debt in time and energy. That day had come.

# Chapter 17

At one o'clock on a Sunday morning, Belgravia was quiet. Nothing much stirred along Seaton Place. The low glow of lights in several of the homes were visible behind drawn curtains. The good people of Belgravia were settling down for the night. The streetlights bathed the roadway in a patchy splash of illumination. As there were a few embassies in this part of town, the area was well-policed. This did give Moss plenty of concern about this operation. If he was going to gain access to the house, then he might have to take a few chances. His car was parked on the street in a spot three hundred yards from the front of the Fung residence.

At the bottom of the street the dark shape of the inlet leading to the tree-lined grassy square was just visible at the end of the cul-de-sac.

Moss's mobile phone rang. It was Bob Ambrose telling him that he was just about to enter the street. With the area they were in and the relatively early hour of the day, it was a tricky situation to put it mildly. It would have been better if it was a weekday and perhaps later in the morning, but this is what it was. If they managed to break-in into the house, they just might be able to get in without setting off an alarm. This is where Ambrose's expertise would come in handy. The notice about a neighbourhood watch scheme pinned to several lamp-posts may have been a ruse to put off any potential opportunist burglars. Ambrose said he would come prepared with the tricks of the trade, such as a bunch of skeleton keys, a can of quick expanding foam to knock out any alarm boxes and reflective metal strips to place over any motion sensors.

The most obvious point of entry to the Fung house was down the stairs to the door leading into the basement, rather than through the back garden which was probably secured by a high barb-wire topped fence and security lights that would come on when activated by movement. If they did gain entry via the basement door, they may be able to gain access to the rest of the house, but there was no guarantee of success.

It had just turned five past one when Ambrose pulled up in a space behind Moss's BMW. He killed the engine and turned the headlights off. Then he got out of his car, opening and closing the door with the least sound possible. He slipped into Moss's car and sat on the back seat. He was carrying a canvas bag in his hand.

Bob Ambrose was taller than the average bloke. A slim, good looking fifty-year-old. He had been in the Serious Crime squad in the Met police before a purge of the ranks got rid of him and several other guys. He had used his detective skills and contacts to turn in a new direction. He went into the security game. He worked for several companies and organisations as a freelance. He even supplied security expertise for several embassies in the city and organisations, then branched out into the service sector. It was the best thing he ever did, so he said.

His hair, which was plentiful, was now almost grey-white. The moustache and goatee beard combo suited his quirky nature. He was wearing black jeans and a black sweatshirt under a zip-up jacket, also in a shade of black.

"What's the score?" he asked.

Moss filled him in again. The details hadn't changed since the last time he had spoken to him on the telephone at ten o'clock.

Moss looked up the street. "The target house is in complete dark. It's the last but one at the end of the row on the left."

Ambrose looked up the street, while Moss continued to update him. "Lights were on in a first-floor room at the front until about eleven-thirty, then lights in a second and third floor windows came on."

Ambrose looked at his watch. "Let's give them to one-thirty," he requested.

"Okay. I'm in no rush," replied Moss.

Moss looked to a side to observe an urban fox, which must have come from the tree-lined area at the bottom of the road, nonchalantly wander along the path. It stopped then looked at their car as if it had detected a sound from inside. Moss wondered if this was an omen, either good or bad. Ambrose also saw the fox, but didn't comment.

Neither of them said anything for a few minutes, then it was Ambrose who broke the silence. "What do you know about the inside of the house?" he enquired.

"Not a great deal," Moss replied. "Plenty of rooms as you would expect in a property of that size. Inside on the ground floor is a staircase going up to the first floor."

"Any internal lift?" Ambrose asked.

"Probably," Moss replied.

"How about the back?"

"Not sure."

"What about an alarm system?"

"I never saw evidence of any. But I wasn't looking for one," Moss said.

"So, you didn't see any motion detectors? CCTV cameras or anything like that?"

"No. There's not any that I know of."

"There's bound to be something. I've got some bits and pieces in my bag. How about any people?"

"Three men when I came this afternoon."

"Age ranges?" Ambrose asked.

"Two guys in their thirties, another older guy in his seventies."

"Guards?"

"May have been."

"Size?"

"One large. The other no size," Moss said.

"Okay."

Ambrose looked at his watch again. "Mind if I smoke?"

"Feel free," Moss said.

Ambrose took a pack of cigarettes from his jacket pocket, took one out and lit it with a lighter. The car was soon full of the aroma of tobacco and mist of blue-grey fumes.

Twenty-five minutes of silence passed. There was no movement on the street. Several of the lights in the houses were now out. Residents were retiring for the night.

It was exactly one-thirty when they got out of the car with the least sound possible. Once out they quickly crossed over to the other side of the road and walked up the pathway at a quick pace. Within a matter of twenty seconds or so they were at the front of the house. The noise of a living city played out its cacophony of background sound. There was no breeze to speak of. The air was still and in no way chilly. There were lights on in some of the homes, but the majority were in dark.

On reaching the Fung residence Ambrose took hold of the metal gate in the wrought iron fence and opened it. Luckily the hinges didn't squeak. He stepped down the eight steep steps to the area in front of the door that led into the basement. Moss closed the gate behind him, then followed Ambrose down the steps. Under the shade of the front of the house above them, the door was hardly visible. It was a plain door with nine glass panes in the top half and a hardwood panel beneath.

Ambrose tried the handle. It was locked. He tried it again and this time he put extra leverage behind his shoulder. When he forced it, it soon became obvious that it wasn't bolted from the inside. Ambrose put the canvas bag on the floor, opened it and reached inside. The first thing he extracted was a pencil torch, then a bunch of long keys with different shaped serrated edges. He turned the torch on then aimed the beam at the keyhole. The light reflected in the glass panes in the door. He delved into the bag again, felt inside and extracted a thin section of rolled metal six inches long. It had a flat surface at one end. The second item he extracted from the bag was a roll of something that looked like a child's plasticine. He ripped some off in his fingers and placed it onto the flat end surface of the bar, then flattened it with his thumb and forefinger. He threaded the end of the metal into the keyhole. The plasticine would take an imprint of the internal lock.

He withdrew the implement from the lock and put the torch light onto the plasticine to see the imprint the lock made. Then he quickly looked through the bunch of keys until he found one that just about matched the imprint. He then took the key off the ring, inserted it into the lock and flicked his wrist to turn the key. He didn't say a word. He reached into his inside jacket pocket and took out a slim, sharp pointed piece of metal that resembled a nail file. He fitted this into the lock, with the key still inside. Using both hands he wriggled the tools. In the next instant, the door bolt snapped open.

Before doing another thing, he put the tools into the bag, then took hold of the door handle and turned it. The door opened to reveal the pitch-black inside. He took the torch and aimed the beam in and ran it along the door frame.

"Seems okay," he whispered.

"What's okay?" Moss asked.

"Doesn't appear that there are any wires or detectors in here. We could be in. Follow me. Do as I do."

Ambrose got down onto his hands and knees then shuffled forward and over the raised threshold running across the opening. Moss got down on his knees, then on to his stomach and followed Ambrose as he crawled on all fours into a corridor and into the pitch-black inside of the basement. Underneath them was a bare concrete floor. The air tasted cold and fusty as if the basement hadn't been used for some time.

Ambrose lifted the torch and spread the beam along the length of a corridor. There were a set of five steps at the bottom end that led up to an internal door. Ambrose concentrated the beam on the surrounds of the door, looking for some form of detection device. He couldn't see one, so he got to his feet. Moss did likewise. There were two closed doors along the length of the corridor that led into rooms on each side. Ambrose put the light on the flights of stairs then onto the lock in the door.

"This must lead to the ground floor," he said.

Moss had already guessed that. Ambrose took the lead. He picked up the tool bag, took a few steps to the bottom of the steps, then up them to the second door. He gave Moss the torch and asked him to put the beam on the lock. Ambrose got hold of the door handle and forced it down. The door was locked. He delved into bag again and withdrew the skeleton keys and the secondary device. He repeated the same procedure, found the required key and threaded it into the lock. He gave it a twist. The door partly opened so he took the nail file and slid the hooked end into the keyhole and manipulated it. The bolt opened. He took the handle, turned it and the door popped open.

It opened onto a dimly-lit area with the smooth marble surface. Ambrose asked Moss for the torch, took it from him, and immediately wafted the light along the corridor. He took the final step and moved off the last step, through the door and onto the ground floor. Moss was a few feet behind him. The light, from a fixed wall lamp on a dimmer switch, left a reflection on the floor. A few feet to one side was a single silver-metal door. Moss had guessed right. The house did have a lift. The call button was embedded in a silver aluminium plate.

Moss moved past Ambrose, stepped by the lift door then came to the end of the corridor and into the vestibule. So far, so good. They were in the house and hadn't come across any detection devices. The front door was just across the shiny marble surface. The window at the side looked out onto the street. The gold-leaf cover on the dragon statues caught the streetlight. A corridor led to a second door that must have led into the back of the house.

Moss turned to look at Ambrose. "There's the stairs," he whispered.

"Which way?" asked Ambrose.

Moss glanced to the door that must have led into the back section of the ground floor. "Let's see where this goes." He pointed at the door.

He took the lead, grasped hold of the handle and opened the door. It led into a large glass roof conservatory which was full of large glass plant pots, containing an assortment of huge flowers and shrubs. The smell was like a garden. The light of the moon was raining through the glass roof, so everything was bathed in light and shade. A pair of French windows led out onto the garden that was bathed in moonlight.

Moss turned back. "Let's go back and up to the first floor," he suggested.

They crept back along the corridor and into the area by the front door and the carpeted staircase. Moss looked up the stairs to see a lamp light on the landing and an antique painting attached to the wall at the summit.

This was now becoming scary. If the two men he had met this afternoon appeared, there was bound to be a kerfuffle. Hopefully, there were no more than two of them.

Moss moved onto the first step and ascended the stairs; Ambrose was a few steps behind him. At the top of the stairs, Moss turned onto the first-floor landing. There was a corridor leading into the back of the house and doors to rooms along the length. There was no sound. The deep pile of the carpet beneath their feet effectively cushioned the sound of their movement. A clock, with a gold plate face, high on the wall, was a few minutes fast.

Moss made it along the landing to the door that led into a room at the front of the house. The one that opened onto the first-floor balcony. He opened it gently and poked his head around the frame. A lamp light was on low. It was a lounge room that went across the width of the front. There was a large sofa in the centre and an assortment of furniture. Art on the walls and various other artefacts like expensive looking pots and vases dotted here and there. Some of them no doubt genuine Ming-dynasty. Floor to ceiling shiny gold fabric curtains were closed over the high windows.

Moss backed out and closed the door behind him, again with the least sound possible. He pointed up to the next floor. Ambrose nodded his head.

Moss took the first step up to the second floor. He was conscious there were two more floors. The house was huge, twenty plus rooms without a doubt. They made it up the stairs onto the second floor, then along the landing to the door of the room above the lounge on the first floor. This must have been a bedroom.

Moss tried it, but it was locked. Bob Ambrose, had it open in less than half a minute. Moss carefully opened the door. Inside, a low pink light was shining from a lamp to illuminate the room in a kind of subdued half-light. It illuminated the figure of a woman who was laid flat on a mattress. She was dressed in night attire, but the most striking thing was that her wrists and ankles were tied by a restraint. Moss didn't recognise her immediately. It took him several long moments to see it was the housemaid who had shown him into the house when he visited on the first occasion.

It was as strange as it was bizarre. What had she done that had resulted in someone wanting to tie her up? Moss looked at Ambrose and they shared a face. There was clearly some skulduggery going on in here. Moss couldn't smell anything. There was no whiff of alcohol or drugs. The room was just like an average, everyday standard bedroom: a bed, a storage unit, an in-built wardrobe unit on one side and several chests of drawers, plus a fancy armoire. Lacy curtains were drawn closed over the window.

The figure on the bed suddenly moved and let out a snore. In the next instant, she opened her eyes and saw the strangers in the room. Moss immediately put a finger to his lips.

"Shhhh," he said. Ambrose stepped into the room and closed the door behind him. Just then there was a sound of feet on the stairs coming down from the third floor.

A few moments passed then the door opened and the smaller of the two men, Moss had met earlier that day, entered the room. He clapped his eyes on the two intruders and immediately sought to get out. He was wearing a plain white singlet and boxer type dark underwear. Before he could shout out or move, Moss grabbed him around the head and clamped his hand over his mouth. He fought with him for a few moments to get control. It was only then that Moss saw the black object in the grip of his right hand. He whacked him on the wrist with his fist which caused him to drop a firearm to the floor. Ambrose swiftly retrieved the gun, then clubbed the chap with a punch that buckled his legs. Moss let go of him and the chap fell to the floor like a tree felled by a single strike of an axe. He was out stone cold.

Moss didn't know if the lady spoke English. "Where is Ho Fung?" he asked slowly. The sight of the gun had spooked him.

She looked up at the ceiling. "On the next floor," she replied, her words were heavily distorted by an accent.

"Is he okay?" She didn't reply immediately. She looked stunned that there were two strangers in the room who had come to help her. "Where is Ho Fung?" Moss asked again. "Is he okay?"

"He's been held prisoner. Like me," she said quickly.

Moss set about the task of untying her and soon had her wrists and ankles free of the restraints. He took her by the arms and pulled her upright, then put her down so she was sitting on the edge of the mattress. He put a pillow behind her back to help to prop her up. She rubbed her wrists. Moss threw the restraints, two pieces of platted, twisted cord to Ambrose.

"Use these to tie him up," he advised.

Ambrose took the cord and did as he was requested. He put the semi-conscious man onto his front, pulled his arms back, tied his wrists together and extended it to tie his ankles with the same length of cord.

Moss looked at the lady. She looked none the worse for the ordeal she was going through. "How many of them are there?" he asked.

She hesitated for a moment as if she didn't understand the question. "Three," she responded after a few seconds.

"Is Ho Fung being guarded?" he asked.

She looked confused, before she understood the question. "Yes," she replied.

"We'll be back in a moment," said Moss. He looked to Ambrose. "Fung's upstairs. The other one is guarding him."

He turned back to the lady. "Is someone pretending to be Ho Fung?" he asked her.

Again, she was a little slow understanding the question. Then she nodded her head. "Yes. Yes. That is right," she replied.

"Okay. We'll try to free him," said Moss. He looked to Ambrose who was examining the handgun. "Let's go and get the other two."

Ambrose suddenly looked put out by what was happening. "Eh. I didn't sign up for this," he uttered. It was getting too heavy for him.

"Neither did I, but we're here now," said Moss. "Ho Fung is super rich. You'll be well rewarded. I can guarantee that," he added.

The suggestion of impending financial reward seemed to end Ambrose's desire to back out. He didn't say a word. He followed Moss out of the room. Just as they were stepping onto the landing the thick-set guy with the Charlie Chan set of whiskers was coming down the stairs at a pace. He seemed keen to tackle Moss, but when he saw there were two of them, he hesitated.

Ambrose raised the semi-automatic handgun and levelled it at him. "Down you come," he ordered.

The man turned and set off to run back up the stairs, but he was a large, ungainly fellow. He didn't have the turn of pace. Moss reached out, grabbed his ankles, yanked his legs back and brought him down to the ground. He fell face first onto the edge of the stairs. Moss took his feet and pulled him down the final six stairs. His chin banged against the edge of each stair. As he turned his head Moss punched him in the face. He screamed out loud once before Moss was able to clap his hand over his mouth. The guy tried to bite him. Moss managed to pull his hand away from his mouth. "Find something to tie him with," Moss said to Ambrose while he continued to hold the fellow down.

Ambrose went into bedroom. He came out twenty seconds later with a sash cord from a curtain. He handed it to Moss who used it to tie the man's hands behind his back. Once the man was well and truly secure, they hoisted him up and manoeuvred him into the second-floor bedroom and put him down alongside the other one.

Then Moss and Ambrose went out of the room and took the stairs to the third floor. On the landing, Moss approached the front room at the bottom of the corridor. If the lady was correct, Ho Fung was in this room.

Moss looked to Ambrose. "Cover me," he said. He waited for a moment. When he felt his adrenalin peak, he flew at the door, took the handle and pushed on it. The door was locked. This time Moss didn't wait for Ambrose to open it with his tools. He lifted his foot, aimed it against the door and kicked against the panel. The bolt snapped, and the door flew open.

Moss pushed the door open and stepped inside. The room was illuminated by the light from a single lamp. The man who Moss knew to be Ho Fung was lying on a king-size bed. His head resting on a pillow. Then Moss could see Fung's hands were tied in front of him. Moss went to him. He was wearing a towel like robe over a vest and plain pyjama bottoms.

In order not to frighten him, Moss took him gently by the shoulders and gave him a light shake. "Mr Fung. Mr Fung. Can you hear me?" he asked. Fung opened his eyes and looked up to see Moss leaning over him. "It's me, David Moss," he said. "Are you okay?" he asked.

"I know you," Fung said in a hesitant, confused manner. "You're the man who came to the house."

"That's right. Who tied you up?" Moss asked.

"What?"

"Who tied you?" Moss repeated.

"They did."

"Why?"

"Why!" He hesitated. "Because they want you to believe that he is the real me."

"Who?"

"The man you saw today."

"You know I was here today, trying to see you?" Moss asked.

"He tell me."

"Who told you?"

"The man who is pretending to be me."

"Who is he?" Moss asked.

"A man called Wan Jok."

"What is he to you?"

"He was my assistant," replied Fung.

"I thought that was the case," said Moss. He untied Fung's hands, then helped him to sit on the edge of the mattress and to get him to his feet. After a few moments to get over the shock and sudden movement, Moss led Fung out of the room, along the landing and down the stairs to the second-floor.

In the second-floor bedroom the lady was still sitting on the edge of the mattress. Both the kidnappers were lying tied-up on the floor.

Ambrose followed Fung into the room. He looked at Moss. "What you gonna do?" he asked.

"Get them out of here."

"I thought you said there were three of them."

"The other guy must be elsewhere."

Moss escorted the lady and Mr Fung all the way down the stairs to the ground floor. Moss had freed both Mr Fung and the housemaid. Perhaps the smart thing to do would be to get them out of the house and call the police for assistance and to report a case of unlawful abduction and kidnap.

"I'll take them out through the basement, then I'll call the police," Moss said to Ambrose.

"I don't want anything to do with the *police*," said Ambrose concerned that the word *police* had been used.

"That's okay. I won't mention your involvement or your name," said Moss.

"Okay. But there's one thing."

"What?"

"Remember it was me who helped. Won't you?" he said looking at Mr Fung and thinking about his riches.

"Of course, I will," said Moss.

Ambrose led the way along the corridor, around the corner, then through the open door leading into the basement, down the steps, along the corridor, then out and into the cool of the early morning.

The four of them, Moss, Mr Fung, the housemaid, and Ambrose walked up the steps, out of the gate, along the pavement and away from the house.

Moss went to his car, opened the back door, and shepherded both Fung and the lady onto the rear passenger seat. He closed the door, then he climbed into the driver's seat, took his smart phone, and tapped 9-9-9 into the number pad. Meanwhile, Ambrose got into his car, started the engine, pulled away from the kerb, drove up the street and disappeared around the corner. He didn't want anything to do with the police and who could blame him? This incident still had legs and it wasn't over by a long way.

## Chapter 18

The 9-9-9 call was answered within five rings. Moss asked for the police. He was transferred to a civilian controlled communication unit. A female operator asked him what was the nature of his call.

"I want to report a break-in at number eighty-six Seaton Place in Belgravia," he said.

"What's your name?" she asked.

"David Moss."

"Where are you calling from?"

"Right outside the house on the street."

"How do you know there's been a break in?" she asked.

"I broke in," he replied.

The operator suspected it was a crank call. "Why would you break in?"

"Because I had to find if Mr Fung was alive and well."

"Who is Mr Fung?"

"My client."

"How did you break in?"

"Through a door and into the basement."

"The basement?"

"That's right." Moss suspected that the operator was trying to keep him talking to put a trace on the call.

"What did you find in the house?"

"The housemaid and Mr Fung have been abducted by three men, tied up and held against their will."

"By whom?"

"The other men," he replied.

"Where are they?" she asked.

"Who?"

"The three men!" she said with the hint of a question mark in her tone.

"In the house. I tackled two of them."

"By yourself?"
"With help."
"From whom?" she asked.
"A friend…Look are the police on their way?"
"Where is the other one?"
"What other one?"
"You said there are three men."
"He's still inside the house someplace or somewhere else."
"Where are you calling from?"
"My car."
"Wait there."
"Are the police on their way?" Moss asked.
"I've despatched a car to the address."
"Thanks," said Moss then hung up before she could utter another word.

He turned to face Mr Fung and the lady who were both sitting close together for comfort and warmth. They had just escaped from a traumatic experience. After all, being trussed up and held captive in your own home couldn't have been much fun. He didn't want to carry out an interview in his car, but had no other option.

He looked at Mr Fung. The streetlight was slanting across his face to highlight the lines and the wrinkles by his eyes. His skin had a pale-yellow tint and the pigment marks were like brown gravy spots. His hair was sticking up and unkempt. He didn't look as polished as he had done the other day. In the robe, over the pyjamas, he had the appearance of a rich, eccentric aristocrat who walked around all day in his nightwear and couldn't be bothered to dress himself.

"I've got some bad news for you," Moss announced.

"Did you find her?" Fung asked, perhaps guessing that he was referring to Lily Fung.

"I found your daughter-in-law. I'm sorry to say it's not good news."

"Is she…" he didn't want to utter the dreaded word that was on the tip of his tongue. He could guess by the mournful expression on Moss's face that she was dead. He held out a thick curved hand to the lady, she took it and tenderly cradled his fingers.

"Will you level with me?" Moss asked. Fung didn't reply. "Did you pay Leo Sinnott to romance her and whisk her to Hong Kong?"

"No. Her brother did that," he replied softly.

"Why would he do that?" Moss asked.

"The government in Hong Kong knew she was using the family wealth to fund a pro-independence movement. They had a spy in their number. Lee Wang."

"Her brother?" Moss asked for clarification.

"That is right" Fung said. "He pay Leo Sinnott to come here to take her to Hong Kong so that they could threaten her to stop her funding the group. But they kill her."

Moss tried to make some sense of the confusion and the underlying connections. He was finding it extremely difficult to grasp them. The lady released Fung's hand. He ran the tips of his fingers through his hair.

"How do you know she dead?" Fung asked.

"I was drugged with a shot of something. I woke up a few days later and found myself in a semi-derelict building by a beach on the south side of the island. I was probably not supposed to survive, but I did. Then I saw the dead body next to me. I'm sorry to say it was your daughter-in-law, Lily Fung."

Fung put his flat palms to his face to cover his eyes. Moss gave him a few seconds to regain some of his composure. "Why would her brother want to set her up?" Moss asked.

"The Hong Kong government must have promised him big job for helping them. They would make him an important man on the council body. That would make him popular in Beijing."

"Let me get this right," said Moss, still unconvinced by his explanation. "Her brother contacted Leo and paid him to come to London to begin an affair with her?" Fung didn't respond. "He has to be a pretty lowlife character to do that to his own sister." Moss thought it didn't stack up. It didn't seem quite right, but maybe, in this crazy scenario it had some semblance of truth.

Moss turned back to Mr Fung. "Do you know an Englishman by the name of Laurie Sullivan?" he asked.

"Yes."

"What is your connection to him?"

"Laurie Sullivan work for me in Hong Kong. He was a police officer in the Hong Kong force."

"What did he do for you?" Moss asked.

"He gave me information on criminals' activities."

"He was a paid informer?"

"Yes."

"Why?"

"So, I know what is going on all the time and what those who could hurt my business are doing," Fung replied.

"Who does he work for now?"

"I not know."

"How did you know to contact me?"

"I remember him telling me that you are a private investigator in London. When I wanted someone to try and find Lily, I remember you."

Moss assumed it was a total coincidence that he had sought Sullivan's assistance. The smart money told him the old man knew of the connection between the two of them and used it as a way of finding his daughter-in-law.

"So, you don't work for the Beijing government as a spy?"

Fung looked genuinely aghast at such a suggestion. "Who say that?" he asked in a piqued tone.

"Laurie Sullivan."

"He lie," said Fung adamantly.

Moss sighed then turned to face the windscreen and look up the street. He had no idea how he was going to explain all this to the police when they arrived.

It wasn't too long before a saloon car appeared on the street and drove past at a fast pace.

# Chapter 19

Moss watched the vehicle go up the street towards the backdrop of trees at the end of the cul-de-sac. It came to a halt directly opposite number eighty-six. Moss looked at his watch. The time was fast approaching two-fifteen.

He turned back to Fung. "I'll be ten minutes. Fifteen max," he said. "There's something I have to do." He got out of his car, leaving Mr Fung and the housemaid sitting on the rear seat. He crossed the road and walked up the pavement to the house. He was aware of another car coming up behind him and turned to see a marked Metropolitan Police vehicle go by. It pulled up close to the unmarked car. Two uniformed police officers got out of the police car, looked up at the front of eighty-six, then approached the unmarked car.

Moss quickened his pace and was soon at the front of the house. The two uniformed cops observed him. Then the front doors of the unmarked car opened and two guys in civilian clothes got out and joined their uniformed colleagues on the pavement outside the door to number eighty-six.

One of the cops in uniform clocked Moss. "Who are you?" he called out to him.

"I'm the guy who called you. Dave Moss," he replied.

"Moss," said one of the plain clothes cops in a raised voice. Moss immediately knew who he was. He was a former Serious Crime squad member by the name of Peter Randall.

DCI Peter Randall was a long serving cop in that unit. Moss had known him for a few years, though he hadn't seen him or spoken to him since the day he left the service. He knew that Randall was now a senior officer in the Diplomatic Protection Service. Perhaps he had gone back to the Serious Crime Unit in the recent past.

The streetlight was reflecting on Randall's bald pate. He wore what remained of his hair in a short close to the bone fashion. At fifty-five years of age, he maybe only had a couple of years to go before he hung up his raincoat and handed in his warrant card.

Moss had no idea who his partner was. He was a younger guy. Mid-thirties. Bright eyed and bushy tailed. Much leaner and fitter than Randall. They were both wearing thigh length raincoats in a neat, casual style. Randall didn't look as imposing as he had in the past. Still at just one inch short of six feet tall he was still a decent size.

DCI Randall and his colleague approached Moss. "What brings you here?" Randall asked.

"Long story," Moss replied.

"Did you call it in?" asked the other cop.

"Yeah," Moss replied.

"What's the score?" asked Randall in a less-than-thrilled manner.

"There's three men in the house. Two are tied up. The other is an imposter."

The cops soaked up the information, but didn't immediately reply. It was a few moments before Randall spoke. "An imposter of whom?" he asked.

"Ho Fung."

"The businessman?" Randall asked.

"Yeah. Do you know him?" Moss asked.

"I've seen him around."

"He's in my car recovering from an ordeal," said Moss.

"Okay," said Randall and glanced up the street to the line of cars parked in the kerb. "Who are the guys in the house then?" he asked.

"No idea," said Moss.

Several lights in the surroundings houses were coming on. Clearly the voices and the sight of a police car on the street had alerted some of the neighbours that there was police activity on the street.

"Can we get into the house?" Randall asked.

"Through the basement," Moss replied.

"Let's go," said Randall. He paused for the briefest of moments. "This is my partner DI Tony Crocker." The younger detective nodded his head in Moss's direction.

Both Randall and Crocker, followed by the two cops in uniform, made their way across the pavement. Moss led them down the basement steps, along the corridor, up the steps and into the area by the lift door, then around the corner and into the vestibule.

Randall and Crocker took in the surroundings of the gold-leaf dragon statues and the bright colours of the old colonial Hong Kong flag in the glass frame attached to the wall.

"Where are the men you apprehended?" Randall asked.

"In a second-floor bedroom."

Randall looked at the two uniformed coppers. "One of you stay in here and guard the front door. If one of you comes with us, we'll see what we can find up here." He looked to Moss. "You'd better lead the way," he requested.

Moss led the way up the staircase to the first floor, along the landing, then up the second flight of stairs. Randall and Crocker closely followed him. A cop in uniform brought up the rear. His radio unit crackled and the alien sounding voice of a controller came over the air waves.

Just then the door of a room opened and a man who looked half asleep came onto the landing. He was dressed in a long silk robe that was hanging open over shiny deep crimson silk pyjamas. He rubbed sleep out of his eyes. It was the elderly man who had told Moss he was Ho Fung.

Randall's eyes went to the man. He seemed to know him or recognise him. "You're Mr Ho Fung, aren't you?" he asked.

"Of course," said the chap. He took the sash attached to his robe and pulled it tight around his midriff. He looked aghast that people he didn't know were in the house.

Randall looked to Moss. "I thought you said Mr Fung is in your car," he said.

"He is," Moss snapped.

"But this is Mr Fung. I recognise him," said Randall.

"No, believe me he's in my car…" Moss said.

"No. Believe me, this is Mr Fung," said Randall, leaving nothing to doubt.

"Are you sure?"

"Of course, I'm sure."

"How do you know him?" Moss asked.

"He's a committee member of the British Hong Kong association. I attended one of their meetings in Mayfair about a year ago. I was introduced to Mr Fung at the event. This is him," said Randall.

Moss looked stunned. "You're kidding, right?"

"No. I'm not kidding." Randall said in a curt tone.

It took a moment for the penny to drop through Moss's head. When it dawned on him his jaw fell open. "If this is Mr Fung. Then who the fuck is sitting in my car?" he asked.

Randall shrugged his shoulders. "No idea," he replied.

"Oh, shit" Moss immediately turned around, brushed past the uniformed cop and down the stairs as quickly as his legs could carry him. Randall was a few paces behind him. Once downstairs, Moss went through the door and into the basement, down the steps and along the corridor. Randall caught up to him outside, but stopped at the top of the stairs leading onto the pavement.

Moss scurried along the path at a brisk pace. Overhead there appeared to be the first crack of dawn light in the sky.

He was at his car within twenty seconds. He looked through the windscreen to see that the two people who, five minutes before, were sitting on the back seat were no longer there. They were nowhere to be seen. They had flown into the night. Literally disappeared into the dark. He couldn't do anything, but curse out loud. He was about to bang his fist on the bonnet when Randall caught up with him. He looked at Moss.

"You've got some explaining to do," he said.

Moss was too mortified to reply. He felt almost dumfounded and betrayed by his own sense of failure and lack of judgement. He put his hands to his head and just rested them on his forehead. DCI Randall asked him to accompany him back to number eighty-six.

By the time, they were back in the house, the two men who had been tied up were standing in the vestibule, alongside the two uniform cops, Crocker and the chap in the silk robe. The real Mr Fung. The smaller man had put on a pair of football shorts over his underwear. The stocky, heavy-built chap Moss had grabbed by and ankles and pulled down the stairs was seething with anger, as well he might. Randall could see it might be about to turn nasty, so he took Moss by the arm and pulled him to a side. "Let's go into this room," he said. He beckoned to Crocker to accompany them into the reception room. The one with the fine baroque furniture, tiled fireplace, the large desk and the comfortable sofa. "You too Mr Fung. If that's okay with you, sir?"

Mr Fung nodded his head.

Once inside the room, Moss went to the sofa and sat in the same seat he had occupied on his first visit to the house, to talk to the man who he now knew wasn't Ho Fung, but an imposter. The genuine Mr Fung sat in the black leather seat behind the mahogany desk. Randall and Crocker remained standing. The silver plate carriage clock atop of the mantel piece showed five minutes to three.

Randall looked to Moss. "You'd better tell us all about it," he instructed.

Moss sucked in a deep breath. "Where do I start?" he asked.

"How about at the beginning," suggested DI Crocker.

Moss felt he was in for a long stretch. "Twelve days ago, I received a telephone call from a man who said he was Ho Fung. He asked me if I would go to Hong Kong to find his daughter-in-law – Lily Fung – and persuade her to return home. I requested that I meet him face-to-face. I came here in the afternoon of the same Monday and I was shown into this room by the woman who was in the second-floor room. I sat in this very seat. The man who said he was Ho Fung sat behind the desk."

"What did he ask you to do?" Randall asked.

"To go to Hong Kong. To visit the home of a man by the name of Leo Sinnott – the racehorse trainer – to ask him where she was."

"How did this fellow, the racehorse trainer know where she would be?" Randall asked.

"Because he was paid to entice her to Hong Kong."

"Why?"

"I don't know for sure."

"What happened then?"

"When I arrived in Hong Kong, I looked up an ex-cop called Laurie Sullivan."

"Where do you know him from?" asked Randall.

"I met him when I went to Hong Kong on an extradition case ten years ago. Sullivan showed me the sights and helped to find the assailant. We found Leo…"

"Who's the we?" Randall asked, cutting him off in mid-sentence.

"Sullivan and me."

"What did this Leo say?"

"He didn't deny any of it. Said Ho Fung had paid him to meet her in London. Get a love thing going then take her to Hong Kong. We asked him where she was. He said she was with him for two weeks, but she had left his pad without leaving a forwarding address. He hadn't seen her since. Both

Sullivan and I asked him to take us to his apartment, so we could check it out. He obliged. She wasn't there."

"What next?" asked Randall.

"It was a Wednesday night. Race night at Happy Valley so I went there to try and get Sinnott on my own."

"Why would you want to do that?" asked Crocker.

"I wanted to get him on my own, so I could ask him a few questions."

"Did you succeed?" Randall asked.

"Yeah. Sure."

"And?"

"And he didn't tell me a lot more. He confirmed he was paid to catch her eye and use his good looks and charm to persuade her to return to Hong Kong with him."

"So, they could form an everlasting relationship?" asked Crocker.

"Something like that," said Moss.

Mr Fung was listening to the conversation in silence.

"Okay. So, you established that this guy was paid to entice this woman back to Hong Kong by someone who said he was Ho Fung."

Randall looked at the real Ho Fung. "Was that you Mr Fung?"

"No. Of course not," he retorted, as if such a thing was an absurd suggestion. "My son and daughter-in-law they live in Kensington."

"If it wasn't Mr Fung's daughter-in-law, then who is it?" Crocker asked.

"I've no idea," admitted Moss.

"Okay. So, you speak to this guy who convinces you that the woman's gone. What happened next?" Randall asked.

"After I'd been to the racetrack to speak to Sinnott I returned to my hotel only to discover that my room had been broken into, but nothing was taken."

"Who did it?" Crocker asked.

"Not a clue. But it was obviously someone connected to all this."

"And?"

"The following day I meet with Laurie Sullivan in a bar in Wanchai. My drink was spiked and I passed out."

"Really?" said Crocker.

"Yeah. Really. I came around in a dark cell in God knows where. There was a bright white light shining into my eyes. Like something out of a spy movie. I couldn't see who was there. I was interrogated for a while, then I was injected with some drug. When I woke up two days later, I found myself in a wooden shack, laid on a mattress next to a dead body."

Both Randall and Crocker looked at each other. Randall blew out a shallow breath. "A body of whom?" he asked.

"The woman I had gone to Hong Kong to find."

"How did you know it was her?"

"Because of this photograph." Moss reached into his jacket pocket and extracted the photograph the man who said he was Ho Fung had given him. He handed it to Randall.

Randall looked at it. He had a non-descript look on his face, but that changed after a few brief moments. His expression became one of puzzlement. "Oh, my word. Is it her?" he said to Crocker.

"Who?" Crocker asked.

Randall handed the photograph to his colleague. "Is it her?" Randall asked Crocker for a second time.

"Is it who?" Moss asked.

"A missing woman called Lia Chung," replied Randall. Crocker examined the photograph. Randall finished the sentence. "She's been missing from her home in north London for three weeks."

"Who is Lia Chung?" asked Moss. "And why haven't I heard about her?"

"She's a L.S.E academic and activist in the London branch of the Hong Kong pro-democracy movement. Her partner is a leading member of the movement. The reason why you haven't heard the name is because her family requested a news blackout in case they began receiving bogus ransom demands."

"Is her partner Lee Wang by any chance?" Moss asked.

"Might be," said Randall.

Moss sniffed. "He's the brother of Lily Fung. Is that right Mr Fung?"

"That is right," said Fung.

"How did this female die?" asked Crocker.

"There was drug paraphernalia all around the room," Moss replied.

"Such as?" Randall asked.

"A white powdery substance. A syringe. Tinfoil. A spoon and a lighter. There was even a Bong for smoking something. It looked to me as if she may have died from a heroin overdose."

"Why would anyone want to kill her?" Randall asked.

"To send a message to those who would challenge the Hong Kong government," said Fung.

"What message is that?" DI Crocker asked.

"That the Hong Kong government has a long reach and can kill anyone who causes a problem. Or maybe they were trying to implicate Lee Wang."

"Do you know this, Lee Wang?" asked Randall, looking at Ho Fung.

"Yes. He's been to my home on few occasion. I give him some money for the Free Hong Kong pro-independence movement."

Randall blew out another sigh as if to say this is heavy stuff for which he and his partner were not paid enough to get involved in. DI Crocker gave the photograph back to Randall. He took a couple of steps towards the desk.

"Do you recognise them?" he asked and passed the photograph to Fung. He ran his eyes over it.

"Yes. That is Lia Chung with Lee Wang," he confirmed.

Randall bit his lower lip and rubbed a hand across his chin. It was late. He was tired. The synapses in his brain were finding it difficult to make all the necessary connections. If the truth be told so was Moss.

Randall looked to Moss. "So, after you woke up next to the dead body. What did you do then?" he asked.

"I managed to get out of the place and walk to a nearby town, from where I took a bus into Wanchai. I decided to pay Leo Sinnott a visit. I managed to sneak into the tower block and get onto his floor."

"Was he there?" DI Crocker asked.

"Yes, he was there."

"And?" Randall asked.

"He convinced me that he knew nothing about the death of the woman in the shack."

"Is that all?" asked Randall.

"He didn't believe me. He said he wanted to see the body."

"And you took him?" Randall asked.

"I took him to the place. When we got there everything had been removed. The body and all the evidence except for one item…"

"What was that?" Crocker asked, interrupting him in mid-flow.

"They'd failed to remove a piece of curtain that was snagged on a nail."

"Is that all?"

"Yeah."

"What did this Sinnott do then?"

"Another man turned up. Between them they tried to silence me. He may have been one of the men who had interrogated me in the cell."

"When you say silence you. What do you mean?"

"Sinnott pulled a blade on me. A dagger of some type. He came at me."

"How did you get out of that?" Crocker asked as if he had serious doubts about the veracity of this whole story.

"I had to fight my way out. I stabbed Sinnott in the neck with a syringe…" Crocker put his hand to the base of his throat and rubbed his Adam's apple. "I managed to fight them off and escape. I got out and drove to Wanchai in Sinnott's car. Then I went to Kowloon and I was able to find Laurie Sullivan."

"What did he tell you?"

"Sullivan told me it was all about an attempt to discredit the pro-democracy movement."

"He told you *that*?" asked Randall.

"He couldn't very well attempt to wriggle out of it. I had him tied to a chair."

"Okay," said Randall.

Moss glanced to the window where the dark of the night was still very much intact.

"What exactly was his role?" DI Crocker asked.

"Whose?" Moss asked.

"Sullivan."

"To be brutally honest, I don't know for sure. I'm not sure of anything if the truth be told. I'm definitely not sure that anything he told me was true."

"What did he tell you?" Randall asked.

"Lots of things. Said it was an attempt to kill Lily Fung to discredit the British government at the same time. He said Lily Fung was involved in funding the pro-democracy movement. That the Hong Kong authorities were keen to stop her…."

"But it wasn't Lily Fung, was it? The person they wanted was Lia Chung," said Randall.

"So, it would seem. If that's her in the photograph," said Moss.

"Why was Sullivan talking about Lily Fung?"

"I've no idea. Maybe that's what he was led to believe. He also said that Ho Fung is a spy for the Beijing government here in London with the task of monitoring and keeping tabs on Chinese dissidents."

"That is rubbish," said Fung raising his rasping voice for the first time.

Randall looked at Fung. "Who were the people in the house?"

Fung expressed an air of not understanding the question. "Which people?" he asked.

"The pair who were tied up?" Randall clarified.

"He is my personal assistant. Wan Jok and his wife. We long suspect that he was spying on me and working for the Hong Kong government. We suspect he was impersonating me to create confusion and spread misinformation among the Chinese community here in London."

"How long have you suspected them?" Randall asked.

"A few month," Fung replied.

"Why didn't you do anything about it?" Crocker asked.

"We not know for sure. It was only when he come here today…" Fung said looking at Moss…" that we know for sure. We question him, and he admits to everything."

"Admits to what?" Randall asked.

"That he was pretending to be me. He admit that he hire him…" he looked at Moss again… "to go to Hong Kong to find Lia Chung, but they already know where she is."

"So, when Moss came to the house to speak to you, he was actually speaking to your personal assistant. Wan Jok, who said he was you?" Randall asked.

"That correct."

"Where were you at the time of the visit?" Crocker asked.

"I in America visiting my daughter. She live there."

"So, your assistant had the house to himself?"

"That correct."

"What about your daughter-in-law. Lily."

"She live in Kensington with my son Hue."

"Is she involved in the pro-democracy movement?" Randall asked.

"Yes. We give a small amount of finance support."

"Where do you think Jok and his wife may have gone?" Crocker asked.

"I not know. They have help here in London."

"From whom."

"People in the Chinese community."

Randall sucked on his back teeth. He was perhaps considering the ramifications of this in diplomatic circles. After all, a British citizen – or at least one with dual British-Hong Kong citizenship had been enticed to go to Hong Kong to be murdered by elements attached to the Hong Kong administration. This could get very messy. He didn't want to go there or contemplate where it may end. He elected to say nothing for the moment.

"What was the racehorse trainer's role in all this?" DI Crocker asked to no one in particular.

"He a racehorse trainer, but I no longer have any horses with him. I sell my stake in a consortium called 'Ho Fung Belgravia Racing' a long time ago," said Fung.

"Why?"

"Because I discover that he work for Hong Kong government."

"What about Laurie Sullivan?" Crocker asked.

"I know Laurie Sullivan. He work for me in Hong Kong."

"Doing what?"

"Security task for my organisation. But he also work for Hong Kong government."

"How do you know?"

"People tell me."

Randall glanced at his watch, then he cleared his throat. "What I can gather is that both this racehorse trainer and Laurie Sullivan were working for the Hong Kong authorities, along with the guy who worked for Mr Fung. Mr Jok. Someone wanted to entice Lia Chung to Hong Kong so they used this trainer fellow."

"Is he some kind of stud?" Crocker asked.

Moss answered the question. "Yeah. Something like that. In all seriousness he's a cool, good-looking guy with a reputation of a lady killer. He was rich, sophisticated and handsome. More than enough to turn any girl's head. I guess he was paid or told to contact her in London and persuade her to return to Hong Kong with him. She fell for him. She stayed with him for days, maybe a week or two. The man on the desk in the apartment building confirmed this."

"Confirmed what?" Crocker asked.

"That the woman in the photograph had stayed with Leo Sinnott in the apartment for some time, then she disappeared. If it was all a plot to kill her and implicate me then it very nearly came off."

"You talk of this guy in the past tense," said Crocker.

"Sinnott, might be dead," confessed Moss.

"How?" Randall asked.

"I stabbed him in the neck with a syringe," said Moss.

Neither Randall or Crocker chose to pursue this angle.

"Was it Sullivan who led you to the racehorse trainer?" Randall asked.

"Yeah. The man I spoke to who now turns out to be this Jok fellow gave me the last known address of Lily Fung, who from what I am hearing now turns out to be Lia Chung. I knew Laurie Sullivan so decided to ask for his help. They must have known I would do that all along. When they were concocting the plot, they banked on me contacting Sullivan to tell him I …"

"Then they were right," said Randall cutting him off in mid-sentence. He looked at his watch and expressed surprise that the time was three-twenty. "May I suggest we wrap this up for now," he said. "I'll contact you tomorrow," he said addressing Ho Fung. "It seems to me as if this is now an issue for my superiors to see where they want to go with it. At the end of the day, we may have discovered what happened to Lia Chung. If you're right..." he broke off to look at Moss... "she could be dead. Let's leave it for now and I'll resume my investigations in the coming days. Are we in agreement?" he looked to Mr Fung. Fung didn't say a word but confirmed his agreement with a simple and almost prosaic nod of his head.

"Do you have any idea where Mr Jok and his wife could be?" Crocker asked Fung.

Fung shook his head. "They be on their way to China in the morning," he said with an air of inevitability in his tone.

"Okay. There's probably not a lot we can do until much later. We'll leave you in peace," said Randall.

With that Randall and Crocker led Moss out of the room. The two uniformed cops were still standing by the front door. The thick set guy with the whiskers went into the reception room to consult with Ho Fung. The other guy in the t-shirt and shorts opened the front door and allowed the four cops and Moss to leave by the most direct route.

Outside in the dark of the morning, the temperature was chilly. There was an edge to a northerly breeze wafting down the street. The first chink of light in the sky suggested dawn was two hours away. The thick, black painted door to number 86 Seaton Place was closed.

Moss slipped his hands deep into the pockets of his jacket. He wondered if he would ever hear about this again. He surmised the British government would want to hush it up. No one wanted to create a rift in diplomatic circles or jeopardise the relationship between Britain and China. There was too much to lose. This entire episode might never see the light of day.

Moss was going home to rest. He was convinced that tomorrow, or today as it now was, he wouldn't get much sleep. He would spend most of the day wondering what the hell happened to him in Hong Kong and why. The truth was he didn't know and perhaps he would never know the truth.

# Chapter 20

Three days passed, Dave Moss hadn't received any communication or correspondence from DCI Randall or anyone else in authority. He was starting to think he never would, but all that changed on Wednesday morning when he received a telephone call in his office.

He picked up the telephone, and introduced himself in the usual manner. "Dave Moss Private Investigator. How can I help you today?" he said and waited for the caller's opening words. When they came, they were a little unusual to say the least.

The caller said: "My name is Roderick Smith from the Quaker Reform Fellowship Society." It was a middle-aged man's voice. He had a plummy Surrey accent.

"What can I do for you, Mr Smith?" Moss asked.

"I'd like to invite you to a meeting of the society on Friday in a hotel close to Euston station," the man said.

Moss assumed it was a crank call or a mistake. He was about to hang up on the caller, before something told him not to. He was intrigued if not a little confused. Perhaps he shouldn't have been. "I've never had any connection with the Quaker Society. Neither have I ever expressed any interest in joining such an institution," he said.

"Perhaps you should reconsider," said the caller.

"Why would I want to do that?"

"The society has postings all over the world."

"Like where?" Moss asked.

"Hong Kong," replied the caller.

"Is that right?" Moss said.

"It certainly is," replied Mr Smith. Moss doubted it was his real name.

"So how can I assist you, Mr Smith?" he asked.

Mr Smith didn't reply for a long moment. "By attending the meeting," he said after the pause. "We need to meet with you to discuss your recent visit to Hong Kong. We need to know how you found the locals and what you learned about the place." His tone of voice had become more assertive and laced with subtle cadence and innuendo.

Moss waited for a moment before replying. "I think in hindsight, I'd like to meet with you. Where and when do you want this to take place?"

"You'll receive some special delivery correspondence very shortly," said the caller. "The details of the location and the time of the meeting will be in the letter," he added.

"I look forward to receiving the letter," said Moss. Before he could utter another word, the caller terminated the conversation. Moss immediately pressed 1-4-7-1, but the message said the caller's number couldn't be traced.

He put the telephone down, sat back in his swivel chair and swung around one hundred and eight degrees to face the window with the view down to the street below. At ten-thirty, the activity on the street had reduced to little more than a thinly-spread number of people going about their business and few cars passing by. Sunlight was splintering through the edge of a cloud to splash a gold tipped wedge of light across the street and the rooftops of the building's opposite. The well-known coffee outlet on the corner was doing steady business. One and half hours before, during the morning rush hour, it was packed to the rafters.

He spun back to the desk, took the keyboard and typed 'Quaker Reform Fellowship Society' into the search engine and pressed the return button. A list of links popped up. The organisation or institution looked genuine enough. He assumed it was a front for another organisation, possibly one that was linked to a government agency. M.I something or other. Perhaps he was getting ahead of himself. Maybe it was an offshoot of the Serious Crime Unit based in New Scotland Yard.

As he replayed the conversation in his head there was a sound of someone pressing the button in the intercom at the front door downstairs. He got up from the desk, stepped out of the office and went down the stairs to the door at the bottom. At the door, he looked through a fish-eye spyhole to see a man dressed in the uniform of a Royal Mail postman, standing there with a manila envelope in his hand. He had a peaked cap on his head with the common livery on it.

Nonetheless, Moss was conscious of his own security and decided to stay on the alert. He made sure the thick metal safety chain was securely hooked into the locking device nailed into the door frame, then he opened the door to a narrow degree. When it was wide enough, he peered out through the gap and clapped his eyes on a skinny, short fellow with a pale face who was holding a A5 size envelope in his hand.

"Hello," he said to him.

"A special delivery letter for Mr David Moss of Moss Private Investigation," said the postman.

"That's me," Moss said. "Slip it through the letter box, will you," he requested.

The man narrowed his eyes as if to say why can't you just open the door like anyone else? "You've got to sign for it. It's special delivery," he said. He dipped a hand into a jacket pocket and withdrew a pad and a pen.

"Pass them through the door," said Moss.

"All right."

The postman slipped the envelope through the door. Moss took it, then the chap threaded the pad and a cheap biro pen through the gap. Moss took the pad. It looked authentic. He signed it against his name then handed it and the pen back to the postman, then promptly closed the door on him.

The envelope was marked with a 'Special Delivery' stamp. It was addressed to:

Mr David Moss
46A Borthwick Street
Soho

London
SW3

He climbed the stairs back to his office, sat in the swivel chair behind the desk and ripped open the envelope. He extracted a piece of letter quality paper. It was headed: 'The Quakers' Reform Fellowship Society'

He read the content. It said:

*Tuesday, 2nd May 2017*

*Dear Mr Moss*

*We are delighted to invite you to attend the monthly meeting of the society, which will take place on Friday 5$^{th}$ May in the Lawton Hotel on Grafton Way, Euston Road. NW1 3BT.*

*Please arrive for a prompt start at 12 noon. The meeting will last for one hour.*

*Tea and Coffee will be available at the meeting.*
*We very much look forward to meeting you on the day.*

*Yours sincerely*

*Roderick Smith*
*Society Chairperson.*

Mr Smith had signed it. At the bottom was a long number and a reference to a charity. How very cloak and dagger, thought Moss. A simple telephone call could have done that or an email, but both those forms of communication could be easily traced, whereas the Royal Mail can easily lose a signature.

He had never been to the Lawton Hotel, so he looked it up on-line. He discovered it was a small hotel, mainly catering for budget travellers and those wanting to be close to Euston, St Pancras or Kings Cross railway stations.

It would be interesting to discover what transpired at the meeting. He was in no doubt that it was either an information gleaning exercise or perhaps a diplomatic service, organised event.

## Chapter 21

Friday began overcast and cool. As the morning progressed towards noon the clouds cleared, and the temperature went up a couple of notches. The traffic on Euston Road was nose to tail. That was nothing unusual. As a major link road, serving routes into both north and east London, Euston Road was always busy. Moss knew the vicinity well having worked in nearby Bloomsbury when he was first drafted into the Met's detective core.

He was dressed in a dark lounge suit, blue shirt and blue tie. He was carrying the black leather document holder which contained the report he had written for Ho Fung. The one he had never been able to give to the client, as he had vanished into the night. He was still very much reflecting on his negligence and the haste which had caused him to be less than professional when he took the job. It was a lesson he had learned the hard way.

Since receiving the telephone call on Wednesday and the letter, he had been wondering who the Quaker society were. He would soon find the answer to the question. He slipped down the street off Euston Road in the area close to the entrance to Regents Park and made his way along Grafton Street. The Lawton Hotel was just ahead. The time by his watch said two minutes to twelve. He turned off the path, through the entrance and into the hotel reception area. It was nothing special. Not very inspiring at all. It was a small hotel. No more than twenty rooms at a guess, catering for transient business travellers and those on a moderate budget.

He stepped close to a tightly hemmed-in counter where there was an unmanned desk, that held a computer and telephone. A replica grandfather clock chimed twelve noon.

Then he saw the display board attached to the wall by the side of a corridor. A notice said: 'The Quakers Reform Fellowship Society' in the 'Tavistock meeting room'. A pointed finger sign signalled the way down the corridor.

As there was no one close by he stepped down the corridor, found a door marked: The 'Tavistock' and tapped on it.

Within a couple of seconds, the door opened and a man who looked remarkably like the postman who had handed him the envelope appeared. This time he wasn't wearing a postman uniform, but a worsted jacket, and matching trousers. The jacket had a pin badge in the lapel. He looked far more debonair in the jacket, shirt and tie, than he had in the postman's garb. He wasn't a big man by any stretch of the imagination. He eyed Moss for a moment. "Come in," he said and opened the door wide.

Moss stepped into a relatively cramped meeting room which was dominated by a large rectangular, walnut topped table at which two men were sitting in stout chairs, down the left side. A lady of about forty or thereabouts was at the top of the table. Everyone was dressed in smart-casual office attire. The lady was sitting with her back to a pair of French windows that opened onto a small garden. She was in a frumpy looking dress and matching cardigan. The natural light pouring into the room through the door was enough to brighten the setting, though the bulb in a round glass shade attached to the ceiling was on. A hostess type trolley along one side held a tea and coffee machine, plus cups and saucers, and individual packets of custard cream biscuits.

The man who had opened the door went to take a third seat next to his colleagues. "Please be seated," he said to Moss, gesturing to the right side of the table.

Moss sat down in the first chair. He made eye contact with the two men and they exchanged nods of the head. It was a few moments before the man opposite him began to talk. He introduced himself in rather a bumptious manner.

"Mr Moss. My name is Anthony Wordsworth and I'm the society president and chairman of this meeting." He was a tall, thin guy in his mid-forties. He spoke with a home counties accent. No doubt public school educated.

"This is my colleague Mr Raymond Smalley." He was an equally well turned out, balding chap, older than the chairman and had the look of a university professor or academic. He was unsmiling but not as serious looking as the chairman. A pair of wire-framed, thick lens spectacles covered his eyes. He looked as if he had been ordered to attend a meeting he didn't want to be at.

"And this is Miss Stannard. She is the society secretary and will be taking minutes of this meeting."

She cracked a half-smile at Moss. She was a dowdy looking woman with shoulder length auburn hair. She didn't go heavy on make-up. "You've met Mr Smith before."

"Anyone for tea or coffee?" Miss Stannard asked.

Mr Wordsworth requested a tea. Mr Smalley asked for a black coffee with no sugar. Mr Smith didn't want a drink. Moss also declined the offer of a hot beverage. He got the impression it was all stage managed and orchestrated. He had few doubts that they were Security Services aligned to MI5 or more likely they were Foreign Office personnel. Definitely not police. They were not coarse enough for bobbies.

Miss Stannard went to the tea and coffee machine and prepared the drinks for the men. Moss had to smile to himself. He now knew for certain that these were Foreign Office people. The lady in the party was expected to make the men their beverages. Equality and diversity hadn't quite reached organisations like this. They were still behind the modern times.

Once he had a cup of tea, Mr Wordsworth looked at Moss, but waited for Miss Stannard to be seated before getting underway. She sat down, took a pen out of her handbag and placed it down on a thick pad of paper in front of her.

Wordsworth began. "Mr Moss, I understand that you recently undertook an assignment in Hong Kong. Would you like to tell us about it? I understand you went there to try to locate a missing person." His accent was very similar to Mr Smith's. The aroma of the hot coffee made Moss wish he ought to have accepted the offer of a drink.

He pursed his lips. "Perhaps you wouldn't mind telling me just who you are?" he said.

"Why? We're the Society of Quakers," said Mr Smith. Miss Stannard wrote something onto the pad of paper.

"Yeah. And I'm…" he was going to say something witty but went off the idea. It would attract zero laughs. He decided in that moment to play ball.

"Perhaps you may like to start by telling us exactly how you were made aware of a missing person," said Smith.

"Fine. I received a telephone call from a man purporting to be Ho Fung. He asked me to go to Hong Kong to find his missing daughter-in-law. That was his brief. Plain and simple."

"When was this?" Wordsworth asked.

"The telephone call and subsequent meeting were three weeks this coming Monday."

"When did you leave?"

"The day after."

"Where did you stay?"

"At a hotel in Wanchai."

"What was the name of the hotel?"

"The Wanchai Mandarin Garden."

"When you set out to find the missing woman who did you contact first?"

"A guy by the name of Laurie Sullivan."

"What was your connection to him?"

"I knew him from the time I went out there to extradite a wanted criminal back to these shores." Miss Stannard wrote the name on her pad.

"What did Mr Sullivan advise?"

"That I contact someone called Leo Sinnott."

"Can you spell that?" asked Miss Stannard.

"L-E-O  S-I-N-N-O-T-T."

"Who is he?" Smith asked.

"He was the name of a person I was given by a chap who said he was Mr Fung."

"Why?" asked Mr Smith.

"He told me Sinnott had taken his daughter-in-law to Hong Kong and he knew of her whereabouts."

"What does this chap do?" asked Mr Smalley.

"Do? For a job?"

"Yes."

"He's a racehorse trainer at Happy Valley racetrack."

"And what is his connection to all this?"

"He's a kind of stud I'd guess you'd say," Moss said. He wasn't in any way embarrassed to use such a term in the presence of the woman. She didn't bat an eyelid. "I suppose you could say he put it about a bit. According to Mr Fung he had whisked Lily Fung to Hong Kong on a romantic quest, but in reality, it was a scheme to get her back to Hong Kong for other reasons.

"But she wasn't Lily Fung. She was Lia Chung. Is that right?" asked Smith.

"Yes. From what I now understand. When I was first shown a photograph by a man pretending to be Mr Fung, I was told it was Lily Fung, not Lia Chung."

"And he wasn't the real Ho Fung. Was he?"

"That would also appear to be the case," said Moss picking his words carefully.

"Thank you," said Smith. "Perhaps you would like to tell us in your own words the full story from the word go."

"Let me do that."

Miss Stannard turned over a fresh sheet of paper. Moss obliged them. He told them the full story from the very top. He effectively told them the full account in a statement spanning five segments. He told them of how he was first approached by the bogus Ho Fung to the moment he felt dizzy in the 'Old Country' pub. Then from the time he woke up in the cell to the moment he woke up on the bed next to the naked dead body of the person he believed to be Lily Fung. Then how he managed to get out of the shack and make it back into Leighton Hill to find Leo Sinnott. How he stabbed him in the neck with the syringe and so forth. The fourth segment began when he went into Kowloon to find Laurie Sullivan. Tied him to the chair with the beads of the door curtain and how he whacked him in the face with the base of the pan. The fifth and final instalment covered the events of last Sunday morning in Belgravia.

When he had completed telling them the account, those in the room could only reflect on what he had told them. They then asked him a series of questions which he answered to the best of his ability and truthfully. They seemed satisfied that he had furnished them with a true account of what had happened.
    The meeting lasted for five minutes short of one hour, then he was invited to leave. They never told him who they were. He suspected they were Foreign Office personnel who were assigned to investigate the Lia Chung case.
    He doubted that he would ever hear from them again, but he couldn't be sure.

It was just a few minutes before one when Moss left the hotel. As he stepped out onto the street, he looked at the brightening sky and felt a warm edge to the breeze, but he still shuddered his shoulders, sunk his hands into the deep recess of his jacket pockets and made a fist of his hands. It wasn't cold. It was just a trait of his.
    He would have loved to have been a fly on the wall in the meeting room, listening to what those people were discussing. If they were Foreign Office personnel, as he assumed, they would have a tricky balancing act to perform. A crime had taken place in the jurisdiction of a rising political and military power. He doubted if the British

government would want to make many waves when it came to dealing with the aftermath. The amount of trade Britain did with both the Hong Kong authorities and the Chinese - not to mention the inward investment – were far too important to be derailed by the death of a British citizen who also held Hong Kong citizenship. What they reported to their superiors and what they recommended would determine the course of action they would take. Moss doubted those at the top would want to take it much further.

That is exactly how it turned out. Eight days after the meeting in the Lawton Hotel, the story broke in the mainstream news media of how the body of the twenty-nine-year-old missing L.S.E lecturer – called Lia Chung – had been found washed up in a rocky cove close to a remote beach on the south side of Hong Kong Island. Apparently, the theory was that she had gone for a late-night swim in a bay close to a beach resort. She must have got into difficulties because of the strong currents that took her out of the shallow water. Her body was found trapped under rocks then washed up on the shore. Hence the delay in finding her. The official cause of death was drowning by misadventure.

Within a day of the announcement, Moss received a telephone call from Roderick Smith from the 'Quaker Reform Fellowship Society'. He made Moss an offer he couldn't refuse. Smith told him that he would receive a cheque from the society for the sum of £15,000 if he signed a confidentiality agreement. The agreement was that he would never tell anyone about his assignment in Hong Kong. Moss agreed.

It was all over. He would never receive another telephone call or another request from the 'Quaker Reform Fellowship Society'. He never did discover if Leo Sinnott and Laurie Sullivan had survived. Perhaps they were alive. Perhaps they were eliminated by their masters for their failure to kill Moss and failure to put him in the frame for the death of Lia Chung. He never did discover if the authorities had managed to apprehended Wan Jok and his wife. He thought there were two chances of finding them: slim and none.

He wanted to forget all about it. To be honest, he decided, missing person tasks were off his to-do list for some considerable time to come. He could do without them. They were far too dangerous.

**The End**

# Book II

## The Dark Web

Chapter One

David Moss took another swig of the coffee from the thermos flask in his hands. He had almost drained it dry. All that remained were the cold dregs swimming at the bottom. Those that were lukewarm and tasted very bitter and not very pleasant. At least the liquid was wet and still hit the mark.

The digital clock in the dashboard said the time was 06.45AM, on this, a day in early August. The AM letters on the LED screen stood out like a Belisha beacon and blinked, on and off, for a reason he had never been able to fathom out or turn off, despite looking in the handbook on a few occasions. Therefore, the flashing digits irked him a touch. That, and his back ached from having to sit in the same position for the past two hours and twenty minutes, in a seat that had lost most of its springs and comfort.

Out there, the early light of dawn was spreading over the city and Moss was witnessing the first hint of sunlight as the huge ball of hot air and gas rose in the east to cast a golden edge over the rooftops of London town. This was the third consecutive morning he had parked in the same spot at the same time, waiting for 'the POI' (the person of interest) to emerge. Little wonder he felt fatigued and a bit zonked-out due to a lack of sleep from all this surveillance. A neighbour, in one of the houses along the row facing the open plains of Ravenscroft Park, had told him the POI sometimes went for an early morning jog across criss-crossing paths that cut across the lawn, before it got too warm for running and doing such activities that could become a hazard to body and mind. Believe me, London in early August could get really hot and as energy sapping and humid as a Turkish bath. Therefore, the early morning was the best time of the day to get out for a run.

The guy Moss was trying to find, lived, according to what he had learned, in one of the plush, three storey Georgian style houses directly opposite the long line of wrought iron rails that separated the park from a road on the western edge of the verdant, tree lined vista. Ravenscroft Road was a cul-de-sac that slanted in a south-north direction to an enclosure – an acre in size – containing a set of clay court tennis surfaces, and several five-a-side football pitches or netball courts.

As Moss peered through the car windscreen and over to the right, he saw the door atop of the three steps at the end of the long path come open, and a man emerge out onto the top of the steps. He wasn't the first person to come out that morning, a lady in a trim business suit had emerged thirty minutes earlier as a black Hackney cab pulled out outside the garden gate. This individual was male and what's more he was wearing jogging gear. Moss thought there was a fair to good chance that he was the guy he was looking for. As if to confirm this believe the chap set off to the end of the path at a quick brisk pace, turned right onto the pavement, along the stretch and walked at a decent speed towards a pedestrian crossing. Moss marginally fatigued and absently daydreaming and not at all primed by his sudden appearance, fumbled to open the door, get out of his car and stretch his legs. Once the pins and needles had ceased to make his leg muscles feel less like jelly, he walked, at a brisk gait, in the same direction as the man in the jogging gear. The Pentax camera dangling at the end of the straps slung around his neck, bounced against his chest with a thud. The entrance to the park was a six feet wide gap in the railings, on the other side of the road, about another fifty yards along the path. Right opposite the pedestrian crossing.

The point of interest was a debtor who owed a Lincoln Inn's Field law firm approximately £200,000 in unpaid legal fees. David Moss's investigation skills, which he had horned and garnered in the service of the Metropolitan police, had served him well. With the help of a former DI, currently in the force, he had been able to locate the address where the debtor resided.

The POI was soon close to the crossing and near to the opening to the park. When he paused, at the broken white line to let a car pass, Moss, about one hundred yards behind him, raised the camera to his eye, found the viewfinder and clicked the exposure button half a dozen times with a rapid click-click-click. The motor made that audible, whirring sound that told him it was operating to its maximum charge. To the casual observer he was a man taking a photograph of the crisp morning sunlight splintering through the branches of the park side trees that splashed a light and shade pattern on the ground.

The target sauntered across the road, stepped through the gap in the fence and into the interior of the park. Moss quickened his pace, glanced left and right, then cut across the road to the opposite side, walked forward, through the opening in the railings and into the park. The guy in the black shorts and pink string running vest was ambling along a central walkway towards a path that dissected the glass-land in two. Several dog walkers were taking their pooches for an early morning walkies. A second jogger came into shot. An attractive looking lady in all the necessary gear that included a thick headband to keep her long hair in place and mitten like gloves on her hands.

Lifting the camera to his eye, Moss pressed the exposure button a further three times in rapid succession. It captured the man starting to jog, close to the lady, and they jogged, side by side, along the path not at Olympic standard pace, but at a steady speed. Whilst chatting and dodging around a couple of people exercising their canine friends on this a delightful early, August morning.

Armed with the required evidence, Moss turned full circle and headed out of the park. He was content with his morning's work. He would now contact the client and send the photographic evidence to him, informing him that the man they were chasing for £200k did, indeed – one hundred percent – reside at the address he had been given.

You see, this is what Moss did for a living. He found people, many of whom didn't want to be found. With the right methods and contacts no one was unfindable, not even in a city of ten million people, not even someone who was hiding from a £200k debt.

He sauntered back along the pavement to the front of the house from where the target had emerged, paused for a moment, engaged the zoom lens to get the front door in focus and took another snap. Then he returned to his car, got in and settled into the driver's seat. He took a few moments to fix his eyes on the camera screen and scrawled through the half dozen snaps he had taken. They were good enough for him to be able to recognise the person in the centre. There was little doubt it was him. His profile matched that of the images he had been given by the party chasing the debt. Finally, after three, fruitless early morning visits he had achieved his objective. He dropped the camera onto the passenger seat, started his Lexus saloon and pulled away from the kerbside. From here in west London, he headed the relatively short distance to his office in the Soho backstreets.

Chapter Two

Nearly two months after his return from the trip to Hong Kong, Moss had had plenty of time to reflect on that investigation and the less than satisfactory way in which it had concluded.

Despite thinking about the possibility of moving to a location on Haymarket, the address of his office hadn't changed. It was still on Broadwick Street, on the edge of Soho. In truth, that rather cramped two-room space on the first floor of a building above a pastry shop on the aforementioned street. The interior was just the same: the desk, a PC, two leather covered armchairs, and several metal cabinets full of files. Therefore, not a lot of character. Nor a lot of colour or charm come to that.

He opened a drawer in the desk, extracted a lead, plugged one end into the camera, the other he threaded into the USB port in the back of his PC. He turned the camera on and swiftly downloaded the photographs to the hard drive. He gave the file a name, added some lines of text to confirm the date and time, the address of the debtor then saved it all to the hard drive. Then, opening the email package, he typed in the client's address, added a main title and a few lines of text, then sent it and the attachment to the client.

When it had gone, and he received a message to that effect, he sat back in his swivel chair, turned one-eighty, crossed his legs and looked down onto the street below. A sheet of newspaper, left behind by one of the early morning fruit and veg traders, had become trapped under the back wheels of a parked van. A near non-existent breeze was blowing down the funnel of the street like a vacuum in a tunnel. The time, by the clock on the wall, was quarter to nine. People were going back and forth across the scene, either from or to their places of employment or to one of the eateries that lined the street. To think he had already been working since six. Three hours ago. Little wonder he was feeling beat and light headed. He swung back to face the desk and the PC screen, just in time to hear the landline telephone ring. Before he could reach out to grab the receiver it went straight to voice recorder and the following message kicked in.

*'Hello, this is David Moss Private Investigation'....* He snatched the receiver out of the cradle before it said, *sorry, but I'm not here right now.* He put the mouthpiece to his lips. "Hello, David Moss," he announced in a crisp business-like manner, then "how can I help you today?" It was the standard patter.

The caller seemed to be thrown off balance by the sudden change of tone and sound from a that of a recording to a real live human being at the other end of the line.

"Hello. Is that you?" came a distant female voice down the wire. It wasn't enough for him to make a determination of her age, class and ethnicity, but he could hear the feminine lilt in her voice.

"Hello, I'm here. How can I assist you today?" he enquired in an engaging, fully-awake, tone. The lady at the other end seemed hesitant, as if still off balance by a voice asking her a question. "You can talk openly; how can I assist you?" he repeated.

A couple of heartbeats of dead air were broken. "It's my friend," she uttered in a sotto- voce voice.

"Your friend? What about *him* or *her*?" he enquired.

"She's gone missing." She held the word *she's* for a couple of octaves higher than the 'gone missing' part.

"For how long has she being missing?"

"Close to two weeks... I reckon."

"What's her name?"

"Heather."

"Does she have a second name?"

"Hart."

Moss took the open pad of paper lying close to him, grabbed a pen and wrote down the name – *Heather Hart* – in thick, black biro ink. "Where does she live?" he asked.

"Some place in Canary Wharf."

"Does Heather have any family?"

"No. Not that I know of."

"How old is Heather?"

"About twenty-five. Twenty-six at the most."

By the caller's replies Moss figured that actually she didn't know Heather all that well. That the caller was an acquaintance of a kind rather than a fully blown friend. "Has anyone called the police to report her missing?" he asked.

"Not that I know of. I don't think so," she uttered.

He thought his perception wasn't far off from being correct. "What does Miss Hart do for a living?" he asked.

"That's just it…She's…." she didn't finish the sentence and there was another lapse of dead air that lasted several more beats.

"What's just it?" he enquired.

"She's an adult entertainment star."

*"Oh right,"* Moss's reaction was slightly over gasping. He sought to get his head and his mind back on an even keel. "Is Heather Hart her real name or just her professional name?" he asked quickly to regain a semblance of professionalism.

"She's an adult entertainer! That's a made-up name."

"What is her real name?"

"Heather Lockwood."

"How long has Miss Lockwood been in the adult film business?" he enquired.

"About three years, I guess. That's how long I've known her." Perhaps she assumed that David Moss was going to ask her if she was in the same business, so she volunteered the information to get it out there. "I work for a production company. I'm a sound recordist…That's how I know her," she added for the record.

"Does Heather work for one production company or for others as well?"

"Just one."

"Which one?"

"She's contracted to Justin Thomas Productions." Moss had no idea if that was a made-up name or if Justin Thomas was actually a real person.

"When and where did you last see her?"

"Three weeks ago. At the studio in Bethnal Green."

"You say you work as a sound recordist."

"That's right."

"Is her disappearance unusual? I mean has she done something like this before? Then returned to the studio?"

The caller spent a few moments to ponder over the question. "Not that I'm aware of," she offered.

"If I need to search for information on her, then where can I find an example of her work?" Work wasn't perhaps the most appropriate word to use, but he had said it all the same.

"You can look on the likes of Nudevista, and a host of other providers. You'll find most of her recent free to view videos on those sharing platforms."

"When did she *star* in her latest video?" Rather than *'star'* he maybe should have used the word 'feature'. Too late.

"Around three weeks ago. You could try to see her on the Justin Thomas site. It shows two-minute samples of longer videos. They're aimed to get people to become members, so they can buy and view the full run time version." She volunteered the last line of information as if she was doing a marketing plug to a possible purveyor of smut.

"I'll have a look at the free to view examples." She didn't reply. "By the way. What's your name? I don't think I've got it."

"Estelle."

"Estelle?"

"Yes." He wrote it down on the pad under the name Heather Hart, then underlined it with a double black line.

"Estelle. I think we should arrange to meet in order that I can put a face to a name and vice-versa. Is that okay with you?"

"You're in Soho, aren't you?"

"That's right."

"I can meet you in…Let's say in Golden Square at one o'clock. I'm coming into town this afternoon."

"That's an excellent idea," he agreed.

"Does anyone else know she's gone missing?"

"Justin does. Along with several of the production staff."

"Is anyone else concerned by her disappearance?"

"Not sure. We've all being asked to say nothing."

"Who?"

"The staff."

"By whom?"

"Justin Thomas."

"Why?"

"He said he doesn't want it to go public. It doesn't sound good in the industry if one of his major stars gets up and walks out on him. It's not good for his image."

It sounded to Moss like a plausible reason, but maybe there was something else in it or another reason, all together. "Is Justin Thomas his real name?" he enquired.

He was slightly surprised when she confirmed that as far as she was aware that was his real name. He paused for a brief moment to let any more questions drift into his mind. He looked at the clock on the wall. The time was nine-thirty. "I'll meet you in Golden Square by the water feature. The circular pool. Do you know it?

"Yes."

"How will I recognise you?" he enquired.

"I'll be wearing what I've got on now. A loose fitting, red tan leather jacket and a long flowery dress. I've got long ginger tinted hair with black extensions."

It was almost too precise a description to be made up. "Okay, I'll see you at one in the square."

She said see you later, then put the telephone down and she was gone, but for the telephone number that still remained lodged in the window. He wrote it onto the pad of paper, then gently placed the receiver into the cradle. This was the first time in his ten-year career as a private detective that he had been asked to search for a missing star in the adult entertainment industry. There was a first time for everything, he supposed.

Pulling his seat closer to the desk, he reached for the mouse, opened the internet icon at the bottom of the PC screen. It opened straight onto the Google page. Pulling the keyboard closer to him and the edge of the desk he typed: 'Heather Hart+adult entertainment' into the box and tapped the return key.

Several lines of information popped up before his eyes. He opened the videos option at the top of the page. Small captured images appeared adjacent to the entries.

Ms Hart had certainly been prolific in her short career. He counted at least twenty entries on the first page. He chose one of the options by random choice. It was a free-to-view video lasting for precisely eight minutes and six seconds. He hit the play button and the screen was filled with two fully clothed performers in close-up, to the accompaniment of a sassy jazz number. He turned the volume down to almost mute, reached back, took the blind cord behind him and closed the slats. It wasn't because he was fearful that anyone would see him watching a movie. It was to reduce the glare of the sunlight reflecting on the monitor screen.

Chapter Three

The storyline had a fake date-rape-punishment theme. The male star was called Devante Parker. He had taken her, Heather Hart into detention. He was now in the process of parting her from her clothing. Beyond the schoolgirl persona, Heather Hart looked like an attractive twenty something year old with a nice body. In this set-up, she had long straight dark hair, a whiter shade of skin and visible tan lines, compared to Parker's all-over milky coffee complexion. He had the body of an athletic light skinned black man, with plenty of muscles, a sculptured body and all the attributes.

The setting was a mock-up of a classroom with tables and curved brown plastic alloy type chairs, a blackboard and a desk. Heather played the part of a submissive semi-willing partner very convincingly.

It was all too sordid, crude and very close to the bone, but not that extreme in terms of content. Still, it wasn't pleasant viewing. The actual film quality, the sound and the production were pretty much par for the course. The dialogue was, at best, soap opera narrative quality and the acting was pastiche and wooden, but it did what it said on the tin. It got the viewer off. It wasn't by a long way the most disgusting thing he had ever seen in his life.

Moss clicked out of it after three minutes into the eight-minute-long taster. Less than halfway through. He pushed his chair back, leaned back, put his hands behind his neck and gazed up at the ceiling. He spent the next couple of minutes wondering how many voyeurs had watched that video, then secondly where did he go with this case. Perhaps the best thing to do would be to speak to a chap he knew. A fellow by the name of Murray Maxted. Maxted had worked in the industry as a distributor of films, but that was a few years ago. Moss debated in his mind whether to contact him to ask him if he was still active in the business and if he knew anything about Justin Thomas and his set-up. He decided to leave it for the time being. Maybe, he could contact him after he had met and spoken to Estelle. He returned to his PC, closed down the site, then spent ten minutes searching for any information about Heather Hart.

There was plenty of information, such as fan testimonials and movie reviews. A list of all her credits could be found on various sites. There were some industry insider opinions. Wikipedia revealed that she had worked in the industry for five years. In that time, she had made around fifty movies, which very nearly worked out at one for every month she had been active in the business. She had earned a reputation as a performer who would turn her hand to anything. She had won newcomer of the year in her first year, plus a few other awards since. Geez, thought Moss. What had the world come to? Awards for adult entertainment stars!

Moss left his office at close to ten to one. He was in nearby Golden Square precisely five minutes later. The square was right in the heart of bustling, busy Soho. There was the hum of sound from the surrounding streets and people, both tourists and local workers wandering around. Both in healthy numbers. Shop and office workers, tourists, the curious and the punter. On entering the square, he headed straight for the central water feature which had a jet spraying a funnel of sparking liquid a few feet before it fell back into the reflecting pool. As he looked around, he saw someone who could have been Estelle sitting on a wooden frame bench, close to the edge of the pool. It had a slatted backrest and armrests.

She was the second female of the six people sitting on the surrounding four benches. And the only one on her jack jones. She was wearing a ruby, oxblood shoe polish tinted, stressed leather jacket over a simple, three button blouse top. Her legs were hidden under a flowery dress, the hem of which was three inches above her black Doctor Martin booted feet. She looked to be long legged, and lithe and someone conscious of style. She had a mane of thick, dyed ginger hair with black extensions.

He stepped towards her. As his shadow poured over her, she raised her head, looked at him and gave him a stiff, manufactured smile. She was a pretty, attractive light skinned black lady with an appealing mouth, cherry red lips, lots of white teeth, lovely eyes, and smooth, blemish free skin. When the sunlight splashed across her face it reflected on the curve of her cheek bones and her eyes which had a deep melancholy appeal. Her fingers were long, and the nails were clean and manicured and finished by a sky-blue colour nail polish. She wore a chunky gold link chain around her neck.

"If you haven't already guessed it. I'm Dave Moss," he said as a way of an informal introduction.

"Hi. How's it going, Dave?" she asked in an easy-going tone.

"Good," he replied. He noticed that her fingers were ringless, though she did wear a thin silver bangle around her left wrist. She held her hand out and invited him to sit down next to her. He took her hand, exchanged a couple of *how are yous*, then he sat down, leaving a two feet wide gap between them.

## Chapter Four

For such an attractive early thirty-something, Moss wondered how Estelle had ever got into the business. She could have been a sought-after model. However, he didn't plan to ask her. It wasn't something he had to know as this stage of the investigation. He could ask her later. Perhaps the answer would be simple. That there was a dearth of opportunities at the time she was looking for a job and that working in the adult industry was the only decent job offer she received. He glanced around in a wide sweep to take in the surroundings and the front of the buildings looking over the square. The glare of the sun was reflecting in windows, many of which were open. She crossed her legs, turned marginally towards him, and leaned in ever so slightly closer to him. He could smell a fragrance that he liked but had no idea what it was.

He smiled at her. "Nice day," he commented and let his eyes wander to the overhanging sweeping tree that was dropping its pine needles over the soil at a rapid rate.

"Not too bad," she replied in a less than convincing tone.

"How far have you travelled?" he asked.

"From Bethnal Green."

"Not too far then."

"No. Just a few minutes away."

"Can I ask you some questions?"

"Fire away."

He relaxed and edged even closer to her. "When did you first realise that Miss Hart had gone missing?" he asked.

"As I said, about two-and a-bit weeks ago." She spoke with a slight lisp he hadn't picked-up over the phone. She didn't have a London accent. She may have originated from the south-west, though it was difficult to know precisely where.

"Where's the production studio? Where they make the movies."

"In Bethnal Green. It's an old school building that was converted into a film and recording studio. Justin Thomas purchased part of it and turned it into a facility to make adult."

"How many people work there?"

"What? Production staff?"

"Yeah, and the others. Office. Ancillary. Admin. That type of thing."

"A few. Let me see there's a couple of admin people. Three for camera and lighting. Two sound recordists, of which I'm one. A couple of dialogue writers and an editor stroke director. How many is that?"

He wasn't counting. "A few then," he replied.

"And one chap who deals with all the fan mail and promotional stuff."

"And this Justin Thomas owns the whole kit and caboodle?"

"I think I'm right in saying he's the outright owner of the production company."

"What's he like to work for?"

"Okay, I guess you'd say."

"Only guess?" She didn't reply. "Is it just films for the adult market?"

"No. There's some commercial stuff as well. But not much."

"Such as?"

"Say, a business wants a promotional video making. One that they can give to their clients. That kind of thing."

"How many videos do they make in a year?"

"Adult entertainment?" He nodded his head. "About sixty to seventy."

"Not a massive number then?"

"That's one a week. Compared to some nickel and dime units that's a high number. But it isn't Los Angeles valley or anything like that."

"Tell me about Heather. I watched part of a video before I came out here, in…" he paused to recall the storyline, "…in which she was supposedly a victim of a teacher rapist."

"Very popular," she admitted.

He didn't reply specifically to her remark. "What kind of person is she? Temperament wise?"

"Bubbly. Everyone on the set liked her." He noticed the past tense and it hit like a soft breeze wafting over him.

"No reason for anyone to dislike her then?"

"No."

"What about fellas? Boyfriends?"

"None that I know of."

"Okay."

"If you think one of the male stars was in a relationship with her, then think again. That's miles off the truth." He noticed the past tense again.

"What about any rumours? Any office gossip?"

"The rumour mill is that she fell out with Justin."

"Why?"

"He refused to give her a new contract based on the number of sales of the videos in which she starred in."

He pondered on the answer, then changed the subject. "How are the videos distributed?" he asked.

"Through the internet. Customers gain access through the web site. Pay for the videos of their choice, then once payment is received, they are downloaded by the client using a code. That's the way it's done in the electronic age," she said in a slightly 'know-all' and barbed tone, for a reason he couldn't figure.

"Do you have many customers?"

"Could be as many as one hundred thousand, each paying twenty to fifty pounds a time."

He did the maths, then filled his cheeks as he blew out a tuneless whistle. "Wow. Big money, then?" She gently closed her eyes and bobbed her head from side to side, but said nothing. "Let's get back to Justin Thomas. You say there was an argument?"

"A disagreement more like."

He glanced around to see a young couple arm-in-arm saunter by, then stop to admire the spray of water falling into the pool. The benches were beginning to fill up with office workers from the nearby businesses. Some carrying their packed lunch in plastic containers or paper bags.

"What about family and friends?" he asked. "Could any of them know where she might be?"

"I don't know. I don't think Heather has many friends." Estelle was being very precise and straightforward. He pondered for a few brief moments while he considered his options. "Can you supply me with a photograph of her. A publicity, promotion type of picture would be fine. Something I can print off from my PC should be adequate."

"That shouldn't be a problem. I can get one to you later this afternoon."

"Thanks."

"What about the police?" she asked.

"The police?"

"Will you contact them?"

He considered the question. "Maybe not for the time being. Let me give it a couple of days. See what I can come up with. Remind me, why doesn't Justin Thomas want to contact them."

"Because, he doesn't want the bad publicity."

"Which might suggest to me he knows what has happened to her. What about her going abroad or to some other producer?"

"No. She would have told me if she was planning to do something like that."

He judged from that answer the pair of them were closer than he initially assumed. Maybe lovers? Or just good pals? He didn't know the answer, and neither could he guess. "If she was able to, would she tell you where she is?" he asked.

"Yeah. I think that's a pretty fair assessment of our friendship."

"Which means she could be being held against her will. Or alternatively she is no longer alive. Or thirdly she isn't talking to anyone for a reason we have no knowledge of. What about a relationship with someone else in secret? Always possible," he said as if to put something into her head to think about. She didn't reply verbally but her body language and the single shake of the head suggested that was unlikely. "Tell me how many people know that you've contacted a Private Investigation to find her?"

"Just me."

"Good. That's the way we need to keep it. Just a couple of more things. Can you let me have a list of names of everyone in the production company who knows her? That's performers. Lighting staff. Everyone behind the scenes."

"Male and female?"

"Yes."

"I can write a list and let you have it with the photograph."

"Fine. That's good. One further question. Do you know how much she made last year from Justin Thomas productions? Care to hazard a guess?" he asked.

"Not for certain. But all the performers take a percentage from the video sales. When all considered it's probably going to be in the £100,000 a year bracket."

Moss pursed his lips. "That much?" he enquired.

"Yes."

"Who is the biggest earner?"

"Two of the male stars. Devante Parker and Troy Steel."

Troy Steel! He thought. As if that wasn't an adult star's name. For crying out loud. "Who is the big favourite of the two? Who sells more?" he asked.

"Devante Parker."

"Why?"

"He's in big demand. He's an Adonis." Moss recalled the scene from the video he had watched. Sure, he was a big man. "He's very muscly, and can go on forever without popping."

"Oh, right yeah," he replied slightly embarrassed by her candour. He looked around again to take in the scene. The number of people loitering around the square had doubled in the past few minutes. People were sitting on the raised surface around the edge of the reflecting pool. Soaking up the rays, smoking cigarettes, eating lunch or chatting in groups of two and three. Others listening to ear pods.

He looked at Estelle. "I think we'd better call it a day for now. Just in case someone sees us talking together. We can't be too careful. If you email me a photograph and the list of names as soon as possible. I can begin to work through them."

"What are you going to do next?" she asked.

He didn't have an immediate reply on his lips. He adjusted his posture. The hard wood slats of the seat were digging into his backside and making him feel uncomfortable. He pondered for a moment.

"Just a couple of questions before we part. What is her height?"

"About five-eight."

"Weight."

"Slim to medium. Size nine." It didn't mean much to him.

"Any distinguishing marks or tattoos? Any piercings?"

"She's got the petals and stalk of a twisting winding vine plant arching around her waist and up her back."

Classy, as you do, he thought. But, maybe not so much a tramp stamp, more like body art. "Any piercings?" he asked.

"One in her tongue. One in her tummy button. Where will you start?" she asked him directly.

"By ringing around a few contacts. See if anyone has heard anything. Put the feelers out." He pulled back a touch as if he was about to get off the bench and stretch his legs. "Oh, just one more thing," he asked.

"What's that."

"Your name."

"Estelle Gifford," she replied.

They chatted very briefly about his fees which she agreed to meet at the end of the first week. Then she would review the cost to see if she wanted him to continue. Maybe the most sensible thing would be to contact the police, but she clearly didn't want to do this in case the name of the squealer got back to Justin Thomas.

After clarifying a couple of minor things, they parted and went their separate ways. She went towards Shaftsbury Avenue. He went towards Oxford Street. He was back in his office in less than six minutes.

## Chapter Five

The first thing Moss did, when he was back in the sanctuary of his office was to fill the kettle, put it on and make himself a cup of very black, strong coffee. The early morning was starting to catch up on him. He checked his email inbox to see if he had received a message from his client on the missing debtor case he was working. There was. It was a reply, acknowledging receipt of the photographs and the other details, like the address.

He let the PC go into sleep mode, then took a copy of the morning newspaper he had purchased from a local newsagent, and swiftly scanned through the pages. After some thinking time he decided to put in a call to a former colleague in the Metropolitan police. DI Luke Terry had, at one time, worked the Soho square mile, helping to close down unregistered vice dens and illegal gambling parlours. He would still know some people in the business who might know something about a missing actress.

Moss called him on the private contact number he had for him. After the usual pleasantries he explained what he was working on and why he was contacting him. He was looking for a missing adult entertainment star, Heather Hart. Real name Heather Lockwood. DI Terry said he would ask some of his snouts to make some enquiries on his behalf. Moss thanked him. When he had completed chatting to his former colleague, he half contemplated calling someone in the Met's Missing Persons Bureau to ask if a Heather Lockwood had been placed onto that list, but went off the idea because he couldn't trust everyone in there.

It was getting on for close to four o'clock when Luke Terry called him back. He had made some, what he described as, 'initial' enquiries. From what he told Moss no one had heard a thing about Heather Hart's disappearance. She was a well-known actress, a starlet turned star, but nobody he talked to knew her personally, or that she was missing.

With nothing much in the way of concrete feedback coming from DI Terry, Moss had to think of a new angle. By five p.m. he had received the promised email from Estelle Gifford which contained an attachment in the form of a photograph of Ms Hart. He was able to save the jpeg to the hard drive and print it off on the attached colour printer. Ms Gifford also supplied him with a typed-up list of twenty names of those people who worked in and around the production company and those who worked closely with Justin Thomas. With nothing much coming from other sources, he had to think of a new strategy, though it was still very early in the investigation.

That evening, at around seven-thirty, Moss contacted Estelle Gifford on the landline phone number she had given him. He introduced himself. She sounded hoarse and a little fatigued from the day's activities. She told him she had been working on the sound of a new Justin Thomas production, starring Troy Steele and a newcomer to the business, Patsy Reynard.
 "I've been thinking," he said. "Is there any chance you'll be able to get me into the studio?"
 "Why?"
 "So, I can have a nosey around. Maybe speak to a few people."
 "That's a strict no-no," she warned. "The premises are off limits to snoopers and fans, and *voyeuristas* wanting to watch the action." He didn't know if the word *voyeuristas* was in the Oxford-English dictionary or if it was a made-up word. He blanked over it.
 "So, no chance? How about as an extra?"
 "What. In one of the adults?"
 "Yes. Are there any opportunities of me getting a part?"
 She said nothing for a few beats. "Not easy. There are strict entry requirements. The performers have to produce a

doctor's certificate on a regular basis to evidence that he or she is free of STDs. It's many a man's fantasy to appear as a performer in an adult video. Very few ever make the grade. Very few can perform in front of the camera." She was not only being earnest, but truthful. She continued. "For a start there's a strict audition process. Only those recommended by industry insiders are invited to take part in auditions. The male performer has to be well endowed in the meat and two veg department." Moss almost laughed out loud, but managed to stifle a reaction. He would say that he was average at best in that department. Estelle explained that the studio, did from time to time, invite potential studs and babes to audition, but that was a rare occurrence. She was being candid with him. She told him he didn't have the appearance or the camera profile to be able to pull it off. He knew what she meant. He was hardly star material. Though the manner in which she put it to him and put him down at the same time did leave him feeling a little disheartened. He ended the call not long after she had given him a frank assessment of his chances of gaining legitimate access to the studio.

The following day was Friday. Now armed with the list of names from Estelle, Moss set about trying to discover anything pertinent about them. The only way he could do this was to summon the assistance of DI Luke Terry. Before he could call him to ask him if he could do some work for him, the telephone rang.

He looked at the thin clear Perspex cover over the console. He didn't recognise the telephone number. He pressed the loudspeaker option before the recorded message kicked in.

"Moss Investigation Services," he said as the standard introduction. "How can I help you, today?" There was no reply. "Moss Investigation Services. How can I help you?" he repeated. Still no reply, though he could swear he could hear what sounded like the laboured breathing of the caller at the other end of the line. "Anyone there?" he enquired. He clocked the number in the display and swiftly wrote it down onto the pad of paper.

The caller hung up without saying a word. How bizarre, he thought. Something like that had happened a few times previously. Then it was a caller who had decided not to go through with it and backed out at the last moment. Silent callers always left him feeling rather edgy and vulnerable. He turned off the loudspeaker. Now acting with haste, he brought up the Google search engine on the screen and entered the eleven-digit telephone number. It came back as an unknown number. Did the caller know him and did he know the caller? Therefore, he or she chose to remain silent? Because Moss would have recognised his or her voice.

This was something of an unsettling development. No talkers always were. In truth there was no guarantee it had anything to do with the Ms Hart case. After a delay of around ten minutes, Moss decided to put in that call to DI Terry in his Charing Cross base. He had the list of names he wanted him to run through the system to see if any set off any alarms and whistles ringing. Moss gave him the list of names. He also gave him the telephone number of the mysterious caller and asked him to run it through the system. They agreed a sum of five hundred pounds for the information. Moss couldn't expect him to do it for free. His former colleague was sticking his neck out to do this for him, so it was only right that he was appropriately rewarded.

Terry told him he would have a look at the names, but couldn't promise he would get back to him any time soon, plus he hadn't supplied him with dates of birth, addressees or any other information to make the search easier. All Moss could do for now was to wait for his call back.

At noon there was a development that may have told them what had happened to Heather Hart. On the BBC News web page, a report appeared to say that the body of a twenty-five-year-old woman had been found on Clapham Common early that morning by someone out walking a dog. The discovery had been made before eight o'clock that morning. It sounded as if the case could have been solved, but of course there was no indication that it was Heather Hart.

If it did prove to be her the task for which he had done very little work would be over before it had begun. He braced himself, thinking in a strange way that if it was her, she would be at peace. Rather than being held prisoner in some dark and dank dungeon by a crazed fan who wanted to get up close and personal to a star. He believed such a scenario was a possibility.

A further update came from a communique from the Met police at two p.m. It wasn't Heather Hart. The victim was named as a twenty-five-year-old woman called Dina Morales. It looked as if she had been murdered in another location, then dumped on the common sometime during the previous evening. A possible suspect was being sought, but no one had been arrested. Knowing that it wasn't Heather Hart meant he was back on the case.

He considered the next set of options to pursue. Outside, the cool of the day had come as a much-needed fillip to the hot and sultry weather of the past week. In the meantime, Moss was looking forward to hooking up with a lady he had met a couple of weeks before. He had met her at a party given by a former colleague. A fellow copper. Her name was Claudette Munro. She was a thirty-five-year-old divorcee on the lookout for some fun. He was pretty much in the same category so there was nothing to stop them from seeing each other, and possibly taking it to the next level.

Moss wasn't married. Well, not any longer. He had been married to Jenny for eight years. It had ended a decade ago. He still referred to her as his wife, but she wasn't. He concluded he wasn't the marrying kind. He loved his independence too much. That perhaps was his excuse for leaving the marriage.

He pulled himself up from his desk, edged around it, then went into the tiny area set aside as a kitchenette, grabbed the kettle, ran the tap in the sink, filled the kettle a quarter full, then plugged it into the juice. He made himself a cup of powdered coffee, but placed far too much of it into the cup, so he had to pour half of it down the plughole, then fill the cup again with the remaining water.

Taking the cup to his desk, he sat down in the comfy swivel leather seat. The eleven-digit telephone number of the mystery caller intrigued him. He proceeded to tap it into the number pad, then put the device onto loudspeaker. It went straight to voice mail. He had anticipated this so read out a brief message he had already written in his head. He said:

*This is Dave Moss of Moss Investigations. Perhaps you'd like to talk to me. Give me a call back. I look forward to the possibility of chatting to you at some time in the next day or so. Thanks.*

He put the telephone down. He knew there was absolutely no guarantee that anyone would call him back. For the next couple of minutes, he drank the coffee and ran his eyes over some papers relating to a case, his most important client, an insurance company had sent him to look at.

## Chapter Six

It was now just over twenty-four hours since Moss had met with Estelle Gifford in Golden Square in the heart of Soho. He had been giving the case plenty of consideration, but was in a place where he couldn't progress it as he was waiting for other people to do work for him. He wanted to put a couple of questions to Estelle, specifically around fan mail. He had a theory that the solution to this could lie within the Fan base. Specifically, an obsessed fan. He considered a scenario that a fan had kidnapped her and was now holding her captive. It wasn't beyond the realms of possibility. A kind of 'Misery' scenario in which a fan kidnaps a movie star then keeps her prisoner in a makeshift cell of some description. It would be common knowledge amongst the aficionados of adult production and the fans of Justin Thomas that the production facility was in a former school building in Bethnal Green. Therefore, anyone loitering around would know where to find Heather Hart when she was shooting a movie.

He elected to call Estelle to put some questions to her. He got through to her on her mobile phone after listening to the ringing tone for twenty seconds or so.

He introduced himself. "Estelle. Its David Moss. I want to ask you a couple of questions about fan worship?"

"Okay. It's not something I'm familiar with, but fire away."

"Do you know, or can you find out, how many letters the company receives from crackpot fans?" He kind of regretted using the word 'crackpot', but couldn't think of an alternative. "What I mean is, fans who want to fulfil their fantasies by meeting the performers or actually wanting to take part in a scene."

She hesitated. Perhaps she didn't have an answer to the question or an opinion. "Quite a few I'd think. I'd have to ask the person who runs the fan club side of things."

"What's his or her name?" he asked.

"Lyndon," she replied.

"Is that a male or female Lyndon?"

"Male."

"Perhaps you could ask him if he receives more fan mail from any particular person or persons. You know eighty percent of the letters for Heather Hart are received from twenty percent of those who care to write in. Can you ask him if anyone stands out more than the rest? Anyone who exhibits the trait that would suggest an attempt to fulfil a fantasy to be near to Heather Hart."

"I can ask him," she replied after a long moment's hesitation.

"This Lyndon. How long has he been there?"

"Longer than me. Probably five years. He also helps to run the admin office."

"What's his full name?"

"Lyndon Cole," she replied. It was a name Moss recognised from the list she had supplied to him.

"Can you ask him out of curiosity only, of course."

"I can ask him when I see him, but in truth he isn't here all that often."

"Okay. It will be a start." He recalled the Clapham Common death. "Did you hear about the discovery of a body on Clapham Common?"

"No."

"A body of a twenty-five-year-old called Dina Morales was found by someone out walking a dog. Therefore, it wasn't Heather Hart."

"Just a minute, I'm sure Lyndon Cole lives in that area," she said as if it was too much of a coincidence. That is all it was a coincidence because the police were already looking for someone whose name wasn't Lyndon.

He dismissed it as having no relevance or connection to the case. He informed Estelle that a former colleague of his was looking through the list of names she had supplied. Once DI Terry had chance to run them through the system, he would get back to him, but it might not be a quick and easy task. In truth, Moss didn't think the answer lay with anyone working for Justin Thomas productions. He still thought it could be fan related, though he recognised that he could be wrong on that score. If DI Terry came back with some hits of anyone of interest, he might have to have a rethink.

He ended the conversation with Estelle, wished her a good day, then rang off. The coffee in his cup had gone cold. It was still half full. He thought about holding his nose and gulping it down, but then he recalled the bitter sting of the coffee he had drank in his car and thought better of it. He put the cup out of his reach, then stepped to the window to look down onto the street below. Pedestrians were waltzing back and forth. The overhead clouds were dark and mournful, angry and perhaps full of moisture. Within less than a minute, the cloud burst, and the first drops began to pitter-patter against the window frame. He watched the people starting to scurry for cover like an army of ants seeking shelter. It was a dim day. A mere date on a calendar. One to cross off and forget. It was as dark as it had been bright the day before. The thought depressed him a little. He got out of the chair, took the half full cup full of cold coffee, stepped into the kitchen, to the sink and poured it down the plughole, then ran cold water into the mug before drying it with a paper towel.

As he was stepping back to the desk the landline rang. He peered at the console to see it was the same number as the silent call he had received yesterday. Rather than lift the receiver out of the cradle, he selected the handsfree option and set the volume level to a halfway around the dial.

"David Moss Investigation Services," he announced in an upbeat welcoming tone of voice. There was another stone-cold silence at the end of the line, but he was certain someone was there. "Private Investigations," he said, just like Mark Knopfler sang in the Dire Straits hit of the same name.

"The girl," came a deep guttural male voice on the other end of the line. It was impossible to rake up an image of the caller, but if he had to guess he would say a male in his mid-fifties. Possibly an authority figure in a suit, shirt and tie.

"Which girl?"

"Heather."

"Heather. What about her?" he asked.

"Why are you looking for her?" The caller asked him directly.

"It's what I do. I look for missing people."

"If I was you, I'd stay out of it." there was a clear nuance of warning in the tone. "There might be more to it than meets the eye," said the voice in a careful, controlled, calculated and brusque tone. The tone was sand paper gritty.

"Sorry, who is this?" Moss asked. He didn't expect to receive an answer to the question. "Can we meet?" he added. Again, he didn't expect to receive a positive response. "I've got no idea why you want me to stay out of it." The voice was silent. There was a dead air silence lasting fifteen seconds. The only sounds were from the street below, and the beat of rain against the window. Drifting into the room to create a soft melodic backdrop. "Do you have any information on her whereabouts?" he asked.

"I have classified information," said the caller.

"About Heather?"

"Yes."

"How classified?"

"Very."

"Can you give me a hint?" There was no immediate reply. It seemed as if the caller was summing up his options, or playing a game with him.

"I can give you ten minutes of my time to talk, but not over the telephone."

"A face-to-face meeting. Where? Name the place," Moss said.

"Meet me on the corner of Portcullis's House and the embankment at Westminster Bridge in one hour from now."

Moss looked at the clock. It was close to one-thirty. "Two-thirty is fine. How will I know you?"

"I'll know you," said the voice in a terse, dominant and ominous tone. The voice of the person wasn't anyone Moss recognised. Before he could ask another question, the caller said: "By the corner of Westminster bridge in one hour from now," then promptly hung up and he was gone.

Moss blew out a deep, long sigh. This was becoming intriguing, perhaps too intriguing. He turned in the swivel chair to see his face reflected in the glass in the window against the dim backdrop. The sun was now trying to peer round the edge of a grey cloud, so the light on the street was speckled in a sombre glow of light and dark.

It was only a ten to fifteen-minute walk to the north end of the bridge by the Houses of Parliament. He wondered how the caller with the curt, abrasive way of speaking had known to call him. The only people who knew he was looking into the case of a missing star were Estelle Gifford and DI Luke Terry. But of course, the mystery caller had first rung him before he had spoken to DI Terry, so it couldn't be his former police colleague. That suggested it was Estelle Gifford. Why would she inform anyone else? It didn't sound plausible. Unless she was somehow involved in her disappearance. Or unless someone had tapped his phone or had his internet connection under surveillance, which was always a possibility.

## Chapter Seven

Moss left his office around forty minutes after talking to the anonymous caller. He wanted to walk the half a mile or thereabouts to the beginning of Westminster bridge. He could do with the exercise. Too much sitting at his desk had left him feeling lethargic. Getting out would, at least, give him some fresh air.

He ambled down Regents Street, onto Haymarket then up to the Pall Mall end. For some peculiar reason he found himself walking against a tide of people coming in the other direction, few, if any of the other pedestrians, were walking in the same direction as him. The traffic on the road was busy, but nothing out of the ordinary, after all this was London with its congestion and abundance of traffic control obstacles and crossings. Overhead, the sky had seen the last of the dark rain-soaked clouds drift away with the assistance of a stiff southerly breeze. The skies were now dominated by fluffy candy floss cumulous clouds that were merging together to form a dimpled cover of pale blue and white. The stench of fumes and the activity from the various grab-a-bite eateries along the street provided a busy backdrop.

He was soon sauntering through Trafalgar Square, and stepping onto Whitehall. The looming presence of the Houses of Parliament in the distance told him he wasn't that far from the river's edge. He passed the entrance to Downing Street, on the opposite side of the road. A protest of some description was taking place outside the tall, black wrought iron gates that blocked access to the street. He walked past the end of the street, then one hundred yards ahead, he turned left onto the walkway up to the bridge with the looming presence of Big Ben tower just across the street at the other side.

The edge of Portcullis's House was at his side. He turned around the corner, crossed the road and stepped onto the embankment. Just over the block-granite barricade the

Thames lay dank, dark and choppy. The surface whipped up by the stiff breeze.

He had just moved along the path in an easterly direction when he heard a call of 'Moss' come from behind him. He turned a one-eighty to see an individual in a long Crombie style coat striding manfully towards him.

It took him a few moments to put a name to the face of the man who had his eyes on him. DCI Rod Wilkie. Moss hadn't seen him for some time, probably just shy of three years, or so. Wilkie was a high achiever. He had ascended the greasy pole on the back of some alleged favours, he did for some of the top Scotland Yard brass. He had been promoted from a lowly DS to a more senior position in double quick time. When Moss knew Wilkie, he was an amiable type of chap, though Moss would admit he didn't know him that well and hadn't had much connection with him during his time in the service.

Wilkie was in his late forties to early fifties. He had a solid frame, a thick chest, brown wedge shape hair and a blunt, granite face. He was wearing a navy-blue, calf length coat over a shirt and tie. It could be that he had just emerged from the old Scotland Yard building, though there was no obvious indication this was the case. He had the appearance of a tv news political correspondent from maybe a decade before. Not young, or cocky, or aspiring to get one over on the opposition, but experienced, well balanced and bland with it.

"Rod Wilkie?" said Moss in a questioning tone of voice.

"That's right." When Wilkie was in reach, he offered his hand to Moss who took it and they shared a brief, but firm handshake.

"Long time. No see." They both said in almost perfect unison.

"You weren't the person I spoke to on the phone."

"I never said I was," said Wilkie in a grinning so-what kind of a way. "Let's walk along here for a while," he suggested as he looked across the width of the river to the far bank and the circular, white stone front of the County Hall building on the south embankment.

Moss was open to that. They set off to idle along the wide path to the beginning of the red brick ornate building that was the old New Scotland Yard. A line of people were queuing at one of the kiosks from where tourists could purchase tickets for one of the many sightseeing boat trips that went up and down the river. The walls of the buildings on the opposite side of the Thames, looked distant. They provided the quintessential London background. The edge of the London Eye, in the distance, was just visible from this angle.

"Who do you work for now?" Moss enquired.

"The Diplomatic Protection Service."

"You don't say."

They sauntered at a gentle easy going pace along the pavement towards the beginning of the Ministry of Defence building, on the other side of the road, with its stout grey walls and the various sculptures in the garden in front of the cold, granite stone façade.

The river looked dark and miserable and without much warmth. Several glass-topped tour boats were stationary at a pier, as they bobbed like corks in the water and waited for passengers to board. The giant arch of the London Eye turned partially in a slow clockwise direction. The glass in the observation pods reflected the emerging sun. It was just possible to see the shapes of those inside the fifty or so, cubicles, pressed against the glass.

"So," said Wilkie, as he reduced his pace and turned to face Moss side on. "You're looking for an adult starlet. Is that right?"

"Aren't we all?" Wilkie chuckled. "Why, may I enquire, has the disappearance of an adult entertainer grasped the attention of the Diplomatic Protection Service?" Moss enquired.

"We think there's a good chance a number of men may have abducted her. Diplomats from a foreign power," said Wilkie.

"What? You're kidding me!"

Wilkie smiled in a knowing expression. "It has come to our attention that she was seeing a high-ranking member of a foreign embassy. She perhaps didn't know who he was, or maybe she did. We suspect that he knew she was in the business. He splashed the cash. Lavished gifts on her. Thing is his countrymen didn't approve. When he dropped her on the orders of his bosses she might have clucked in anger and threatened to reveal the affair to one of the Sunday newspapers. To stop her talking she was kidnapped and is currently being held against her will. Of course, news of this breaking-story getting into the media could cause a diplomatic incident and cause both our countries a great deal of embarrassment."

Wilkie looked ahead. "Come on, let's walk as far as Northumberland Avenue, then we'll go our separate ways."

"How did you know that I've been asked to look at the case?" Moss asked.

"We've been speaking to the owner of the concern. That Justin Thomas chap. He advised us to keep our eyes on Estelle Gifford. We know that she called you and that the pair of you met in Soho to discuss Miss Hart. The thing is our brief is to keep a lid on it to prevent it mushrooming into a fully blown diplomatic incident. That's why we want you to drop it."

Moss took in a deep sigh. "Is that it?" he asked. He did wonder why if it was classified information Wilkie would be telling him. Though it did sound plausible.

They were now close to the underside of Hungerford bridge. An emerging train coming out of Charing Cross station was crossing the river at a gentle speed. At this point the river bent at an angle and curled towards Blackfriars and London Bridge which were just visible in the distance.

"So, what do you want me to do?" Moss enquired.

Wilkie looked at him. "Drop it. Don't pry. It's too sensitive."

"Which country is it?"

"That's classified. Let's just say a major partner of the UK in a number of ways."

"What do I tell my client?" Moss asked.

"Anything you want. Give her, her money back."

"She hasn't paid me anything, yet."

"Well, in that case, tell her its *finito*, or whatever they say nowadays." Wilkie took the knot of his tie and loosened it from his throat, then ran a hand through his stiff wedge of hair.

"So, no one has any idea where she might be now?"

"No. The smart money is that she's either in the embassy or in a second secret location. Or maybe even the ambassadors own private residence."

"What about the official?"

"Back home in wherever. Probably getting fifty lashes as we speak." Wilkie chuckled at his own acid wit. Moss didn't have time for people who laughed at their own jokes, though he sometimes did the exact same thing.

"What for knocking off some young vixen."

Wilkie tittered. He paused at the end of the path, close to where it turned into Northumberland Avenue. He threw his eyes in that direction. "I've got to be on my way, so we'll go our separate ways. Do as I ask. Drop it. Will you? There's a good chap."

Moss ran the tip of his tongue over his lips to get the tiny salt particles off, then gave him an open face. "I'll consider it," he replied.

Wilkie didn't look pleased by his reluctance to agree to drop it here and now. Perhaps the next time he spoke to him it would come with a much sterner warning of serious consequences if he didn't do as he was told. Wilkie didn't say a word, moved from him and stepped away at a quicker pace than he had walked along the embankment.

Moss watched him turn onto the avenue and go out of view, then he, himself, turned and headed back along the embankment in the same direction he had come. He didn't know what to make of it for sure. If Wilkie was being on the level with him. If he was, the job was as good as over.

Moss made it back to his office for two-fifty after first stopping off in a coffee shop on a side street off Haymarket for a takeout latte. He ruminated on his next move. If there was credence in the story Wilkie had told him then he shouldn't get too hung up about it. Though it kind of did sound like a storyline dreamed up by a skilled writer of crime fiction. All in order to throw the investigation off the scent? He added the question mark of his own.

After thinking about it for ten minutes he opted to call Estelle Gifford on the telephone. Rather than tell her about his meeting with Rod Wilkie, he informed her of a theory he had developed that might explain what had happened to Heather Hart. It may have something to do with her past. Could something that happened in her recent history have caused this? Even before she became a star? Something which had led to this episode? He asked her if she knew of anything from Heather's past. Like a failed relationship. A crime she had committed. A crime she knew something about. About a villain she had befriended in the past and something she had learned of interest. He didn't want to know if she had ever been voted 'Miss Most Likely' to become an adult entertainment star. He asked Estelle, but she said she couldn't help him out. He ended the conversation without knowing if she accepted his theory. She never said.

Next, he logged onto the internet and looked at the local BBC London news. There was an update about the murder of Dina Morales. She was a twenty-five-year-old sex worker, who had been found dead on Clapham Common. It would appear that the chief suspect had been released on police bail. The police believed she had been killed in another location then dumped on the common. She had been strangled, not before being tortured with a brandling iron that had left several scorch marks on her body. The fact that she was a sex worker just added to the depravity of the murder.

That evening, Moss left his office at six. He was in his flat at the Harrods end of Knightsbridge for seven. This evening, he was taking his latest squeeze, Claudette Munro, out to dinner at a restaurant in Brompton.

That evening Claudette and he enjoyed a lovely meal in the restaurant. He had known her for these past four weeks. He liked her a great deal. She had a warm, bubbly personality with a friendly nature and a great sense of humour. When he met her, he told her what he did for a living. She had made a funny quip about wanting to get to the bottom of his secrets. He liked that she saw everything with an element of fun. She was the best thing to happen to him for some time. It was now a decade since his marriage had come to an end. In that time, he had dated a couple of women. Claudette was by far the one he wanted to develop a long-time relationship with. He might get lucky tonight. But he was the kind of guy for whom things in love never ran smoothly. There was always some imperfection that would ensure it would crash around his feet.

He was at the restaurant table tucking into the meal when his mobile rang. He had to leave the table in order to take the call. It was his former colleague, DI Luke Terry. Terry told him he had been able to run the list of names through the system. He had only got one hit. It was someone by the name of Lyndon Cole. Eight years ago, Cole had been charged with aggravated assault, GBH, against a female. He had managed to wiggle out of the charge on a technicality.

However, he also had one other pinch on his record for deception.

Moss knew from Estelle that Lyndon Cole was the name of the man who was responsible for dealing with fan mail and sending out signed photographs of the performers and other such menial PR tasks. He couldn't have earned a lot doing that. It sounded more like a part-time role.

Moss thanked DI Terry for getting back to him. Before returning to the dining table to re-join Claudette he asked his former colleague if he knew DCI Wilkie.

What Terry told Moss next was like a lightbulb moment. A bright white light sparkling in his head. Rod Wilkie had at one time being head of the vice unit based in Soho. Therefore, he must have known the likes of Justin Thomas when he was a kid cutting his teeth by peddling his tapes around the dirty mag stores and the 'under the counter' proprietors in the area. Maybe the pair of them had linkage. Some kind of connection. Such a notion was highly speculative. Maybe it had legs.

However, perhaps there was some truth in what Wilkie had said. That Heather Hart had been involved with a senior diplomatic from a foreign embassy and their liaison had caused an embarrassment and a problem that had to be nipped in the bud for the sake of bilateral relationships. Moss returned to the table in the darkened secluded part of the restaurant to continue his meal with Claudette. The other diners around them were in conversation. He tried to relax and engage in conversation with her, but was finding it difficult to take his mind off what he had just learned from DI Terry.

He attempted to recall the one and only time he had worked with DCI Wilkie. It was a serious crime squad case concerning a white-collar crime committed by a City of London worker, who had turned investment fraudster. He recalled that Wilkie had been okay with him. He wasn't cavalier in the way he had approached the investigation, nor did he flout the rules or run risks. He was a straight down the middle kind of a guy and played it with a straight bat. Moss had, soon after, lost contact with him when he moved across into vice, then his swift elevation up the greasy pole to bigger and better things.

After leaving the restaurant Moss took Claudette home to her place in Bow. He stayed there the night.

## Chapter Eight

The following day was Friday. Moss was in his office for nine-thirty. He had left Claudette's home at eight-fifteen, that morning. He had not been home, so he was still wearing the clothes he had gone out in last night. Still, he felt refreshed and reinvigorated after a decent night's sleep and was ready to progress the Heather Hart investigation with renewed vigour and zeal. The morning was fine. Sunny spells interspersed with slow moving cloud; therefore, the temperature hovered and either went up or down like a fiddler's elbow. Soho was a hive of activity, like a constant moving part of a larger machine that fed and watered the entire west end of the city.

At a time just after ten a.m. he put in a call to Estelle Gifford from the comfort of his office. She wasn't in the production room or the studio today, therefore she could talk freely. He asked her if the name of Rod Wilkie meant anything to her. It didn't. She didn't recognise anyone of that name or the description he provided. He asked her for details about Lyndon Cole.

According to what she knew, Cole was close to fifty years of age. She said she hardly knew him, but described him as a ballsy, extrovert, slightly madcap individual. He came into the office on an irregular basis to collect the post, reply to fan mail and do several other low-level administration tasks like keeping the petty cash stocked. What was interesting from the conversation was Moss learned that Cole tended not to talk about his background, as if he was guarding some dark secret or secrets from his past. When Moss informed Estelle that he had a record and a conviction for violence against a woman she was neither stunned or surprised.

"Have you been able to speak to him about obsessive fans?" he asked.

"No. Not yet. I haven't seen him," she replied.

"Do you know his address?" he asked.

"No."

"Is there a way of being able to find out?"

"I can ask."

"If you can find out it might be a big help, but if it means the possibility of getting into any danger then don't attempt to," he advised.

She maybe wanted to know why he was asking questions about Lyndon Cole but held back. The warning to be careful was perhaps playing on her mind.

Moss continued. "I believe that Rod Wilkie knows Justin Thomas far better than he's willing to admit." He informed her that Wilkie had been speaking to Justin Thomas, but not what Thomas had told him about her. He didn't know if this was a good or bad thing.

"Thomas didn't appear to be concerned about her disappearance, telling us that he doesn't want the publicity," she commented.

Moss took in her words and ruminated on them in silence for a few short moments. "Was he just saying that to cover up the fact that he knows what has happened to her?"

She seemed not to take in the gravity of his words or chose to skirt around them. "Of course, performers do come and go, some retire and some move on to pastures new."

"Such as?" he enquired.

"The growth area is on the internet for perv cams and the like. To such an extent that most internet traffic is adult industry related."

"What does it consist of?" he asked.

"The performer sets herself up with a camera and streams live on the internet. Viewers can buy her time. The more extreme the more they pay to see it."

"Okay. Going back to his time in vice Wilkie must have known Thomas. I gather that Thomas cut his teeth making cheap movies and peddling them around the old dirty magazine parlours. About the same time Wilkie was in vice."

"What about Lyndon Cole?" she asked.

"Who knows."

"What do you think might have happened here?" she asked.

"I'll level with you. I've got a hunch, but its only that," he admitted.

"A hunch," she asked as if she had no real idea what the word meant.

"A hunch," he replied. He had said that word on more than one occasion, but hadn't fully elaborated because, if the truth be told, he didn't know where he was going with it. "I'll be in touch," he said, then ended the call without offering an explanation. As soon as he put the telephone down, he elected to put in a call to DI Terry.

Terry picked up after a few rings. Moss introduced himself. "Luke. Do you have a current address for Lyndon Cole?" he asked.

"Why?"

"He could have something to do with Heather Hart's disappearance. I've got a feeling she's been kidnapped, or worse, by one of several people or by a trio of men including Cole."

"What are the names?"

"Lyndon Cole, Justin Thomas and finally DCI Rod Wilkie of the Met's Diplomatic Protection Service."

"You're kidding me. Right?"

"No. I'm deadly serious."

"Wilkie. Why him?"

"I met with him yesterday. He advised me to drop the case from a great height. He told me some cock-and-bull story about she'd been kidnapped by a bunch of diplomats from a foreign embassy. Its frankly a bit over-the-top. Too crazy to be true. He told me about national security and the like. I think it's got a large element of bullshit attached to it."

Terry made a loud 'mmmm' as if it was a line that intrigued him, but assumed it did come with a large health warning attached. Perhaps Wilkie did have influence and shouldn't be messed with.

Moss continued. "Wilkie told me it's all hush-hush. No publicity in case it creates a diplomatic incident, but I've got a feeling that's crap. I think it's possible that all three of them, Justin Thomas, Cole and Wilkie, have teamed together for some reason and she, Heather Hart, has been abducted."

"Why?"

"I'm not sure why. I need the address to check their places to see if she's being held there against her will."

"To do what. Exactly?"

"Go around there. Check-up."

"You'll require some back-up."

"Are you offering your services?" Moss enquired, with his tongue firmly in his cheek.

There was a period of dead air, DI Terry seemed to be considering his options or where this could be heading. "Who is Cole?" he enquired.

"He's the guy at Justin Thomas Productions who deals with the fan mail and the publicity stuff. Then there's Thomas himself and lastly, but not least former vice-squad chief Rod Wilkie."

"What do you think could have happened?"

"Not sure. But I don't buy Wilkie's explanation that it's a hush-hush operation to prevent a diplomatic incident. He's only saying that as an excuse because he's actually involved and implicated somehow in her going walkabout."

"Look, I'd better inform my chief super about this. We could do some investigating of our own. You said that Heather Hart has been reported as missing for a couple of weeks."

"Correct."

"You'd better leave it with me. I'll speak to my superiors and let you know the outcome."

Moss considered the offer. "Okay," he said after a few brief moment's reflection. Saying 'okay' was agreeing to approach the missing perp case from a different angle and with a fresh course of action.

Within two hours of the end of the conversation with DI Luke Terry, a cop called Detective Chief Superintendent Carla Sheriff contacted Moss at his office. She wanted to know what the case was about. He told her the tale from the very top. How Estelle Gifford had contacted him. If he was in the right ballpark Heather Hart had come to harm at the hands of some fans who had met her courtesy of Messes Thomas, Cole and Wilkie. That was former, Metropolitan police, vice-squad chief Rod Wilkie who would be acquainted with the likes of Justin Thomas and even possibly Lyndon Cole.

    At the end of the day, Moss decided that honesty was the best policy. It was a cliché and he knew it. He wanted to see if the police came up with any theories. In truth, he really didn't want to ride in there recklessly, like a gunslinger hero, a one-man band on a horse heading into an ambush at the corral. He wasn't the police. He was a private citizen with a licence to be a private detective. He wasn't a knight in shining armour about to save a damsel in distress.

Twelve hours passed. Moss hadn't heard a thing from CSI Carla Sheriff or DI Terry nor anyone else. He did receive a visitor to his office. It was a guy called Ray Bentley. He was an investigator from one of the insurance companies who used Dave Moss to look into possible bogus insurance claims and the like. These cases were his bread and butter. They paid the rent and provided him with a reasonable living. He charged, on average, two thousand pounds for each and every case, if the value of the claim was over fifteen thousand pounds his rate went up.
    On other matters, he had learned by listening to the early evening news that the alleged murderer of Dina Morales had been arrested. Of course, the suspect would

remain innocent until such a time he was proved guilty of her murder in a court of law. That's how the justice system worked.

That evening he invited Claudette to his flat and cooked her a spaghetti meal. They had a fruity bottle of wine with it. They were a well-matched couple. He had high hopes for the future, but wouldn't be drawn at this time on its long-term success.

# Chapter Nine

On Saturday, Moss was in the office for nine-fifteen. There was still no call-back from DI Terry or CSI Sheriff. He spent an hour browsing through the set of six case files Ray Bentley had left with him. They were the usual suspects. Fraudulent claims. Claims for things which the claimant maintained were true. He would investigate them to try to determine if they were being cavalier with the concept of truth. Bogus injuries sustained in a car accident. Falls, trips and slips. The usual mishmash of human folly. He didn't mind these cases because they didn't contain extreme violence. Just good old greed. One of human kind's deadliest sins.

He had just completed making some notes on the fourth case when his telephone rang. He hit the loudspeaker button, said hello and listened to DI Luke Terry at the other end of the line. Terry told him he had something to discuss with him.

"Fire away," said Moss, using the same expression Estelle had used on several occasions. DI Terry refused to discuss it over the telephone. "Has it got something germane to do with Heather Hart?" he asked him.

"Yes," Terry replied, sniggering that he had used such a lofty word. He informed Moss that a colleague, a DI Pamela Bent, and he would come to his office in about one hour from now to speak to him. Moss said he would put the kettle on. Terry told him not to bother. What they had to say shouldn't take that long.

It was almost one hour and thirty minutes after the call ended when Moss heard the sound of the doorbell at the bottom of the staircase being pressed. He got up from the desk, went out onto the landing, then descended the steep stairwell to the door at the bottom, opened it on the safety chain, and put his eyes on DI Luke Terry and a lady, none other than Detective Inspector Pamela Bent. He invited them to come in, led them up the stairs and showed them into the cramped space of his small office.

DI Bent was a very nice-looking young, light skin black lady. She had plenty of detective experience and nous. She was at least five, nine tall and slim. She had a slightly flattened nose and the welt of a scar above her top lip which suggested she had been born with a cleft pallet. Still, she was very cute and had these large brown eyes you could swim in. She was dressed in a trim light-coloured trouser suit. The jacket had a thin silver thread along the lapels. DI Terry was a reasonably presentable chap. Around six-foot-tall and with an athletic frame, but not that he stood out as an athlete or anything. He was a young Detective Constable, new to the role when Moss was just finishing his time in the detective core. Now in his late-thirties, DI Terry was maybe one of the more senior guys. The first sign of grey was beginning to invade the temples of his light brown hair which was starting to show the first signs of thinning on his crown. Still, he retained a modicum of freshness and a face that was yet to be invaded by a preponderance of wrinkles and lines. Not that men ever got wrinkles.

Moss asked them both to take a seat in the armchairs he had placed before his desk. He couldn't help but notice the shape of her figure under the sheen of her blouse or the smell of the tangy cologne she wore. Behind the desk, at the window, the midday sunlight was arrowing in between the gaps in the strips of the slash blinds over the window. He sat in the armchair behind his desk and put his eyes on his two guests. There was a scent of the microwave pasta meal he had recently consumed.

"I guess you being here has got something to do with Heather Hart? I assume you've been able to follow up on the leads."

DI Terry took in a sharp breath. "We've found her alive, though barely," he revealed in a tone that suggested this had been a surprising and positive outcome.

"When?" Moss asked.

DI Bent cleared her voice with a light cough. The whites of her eyes were like puddles of stone against the dusky backdrop of her skin. "This morning. Colleagues in Essex raided a house in Brentwood and found her in the home."

"Whose drum was it?" Moss asked.

"Justin Thomas," said Terry. "She was barely alive," he added.

"Okay. What happened?"

DI Bent adjusted her posture. "We got the full SP from Lyndon Cole."

"The whole nine yards," DI Terry added.

"The dark web at play," she said.

Moss pricked his ears up at the mention of the *dark web*, but wasn't any the wiser. "How?" he enquired.

"We're still trying to piece it all together. It would appear that Heather Hart had reached her sell-by-date according to Justin Thomas. She was to become a kind of plaything." Maybe, 'plaything' was used as a substitute for something else.

Moss thrust his head back and narrowed his eyes into a squint. He recalled the scene from the fake-rape teacher-schoolgirl video just as Devante Parker was about to perform.

"Where did it all start?" he asked, though he knew they didn't have to tell him anything.

DI Terry sniffed then wiped a finger across the base of his nostrils. "It would appear that Cole received correspondence from a fan who promised he would pay Thomas a great deal of money if him and five of his friends come spend some time alone with Heather Hart."

"How much are we talking?" Moss enquired.

Terry glanced at DI Bent and she at him. "Around a quarter of a million," she said.

Moss was stunned and widened his eyes. "Wow. Oh, my word. Yes, that's serious money. That's incredible."

"Six businessmen formed an allegiance. Each agreed to pay forty thousand for the privilege of spending some time with her."

"Geez. Some party attraction."

"Cole told Thomas who agreed to facilitate the request. He got his old pal Rod Wilkie to contact the people in order to get the money and to set it up. Wilkie contacted the interested party and the arrangements were made."

"Heather Hart was told of a party taking place in Thomas's home, but of course it was a ruse to get her there."

"On arrival she was bound and gagged, then the party of men were giving free rein to abuse her as they saw fit."

Moss clenched his teeth. "Oh, my God. This sounds really gross."

"For the next sixty or so hours she was raped on numerous occasions, as they took it in turns to abuse her."

Terry didn't have to go on. Moss got the sordid picture. "When did all this take place?" he asked.

"Over the recent bank holiday weekend," Terry replied.

It was his female colleagues turn to reveal more of the information. "According to her, Heather, she was threatening to leave Justin Thomas productions. So, he wasn't that concerned. He and Wilkie saw that they could make one hundred thousand each, with what remained going to Cole."

"After sixty hours of full-frontal attack, she did well to come out of it in one piece."

"Where is she right now?" Moss asked.

"In hospital recovering from the ordeal."

"Who are the men?"

"We're still looking into that. We hope to confirm their names and background pretty soon and we'll be giving them an early morning call. Once we get all their identities, we'll be dropping on them from a great height."

"Needless to say, the whole thing was filmed. Edited highlights of the party might be already going viral on the dark web. With members paying as much as one thousand pounds to bag a download."

Moss wasn't a choir boy – by any stretch of the imagination – but even he was astonished by the sheer depravity and lust of some people. He knew of the dark web and that it was a repository to which users and abusers could access such material. The dark web's structure was very much like a web with its tentacles spreading far and wide. Stopping it and restricting the content was a constant battle. Many battles had been lost, but the war was far from being over.

Content was mostly encrypted. Like scenes of torture, bestiality, hardcore pornography, flogging and perhaps even more disturbing material, which turned the stomachs of even the most hardened cops.

Moss, in his time as a serving detective had heard stories that the horror that some cops working on paedophilia witnessed, meant they could only stick it for a year or two before they asked to be taken off the job. He also guessed that the edited highlights of the video of Heather Hart being attacked might be available to view on some of the free-to-view platforms in one form or another, at some time in the near future.

Moss wasn't so astounded by the revelations, but saddened. What did surprise him was the involvement of DCI Rod Wilkie. What had driven him to get into bed with a load of scumbags like Justin Thomas? And agree to such an enterprise? After all, it wasn't as if he stood to make a million. His career as a top-ranking Met officer was now has good as over. Still, it could have been a lot worse. Heather Hart could have been murdered. The question was what did Thomas, Wilkie and Cole have planned for her? Moss didn't know, and nor did he ask the question of DI Terry and DI Bent. They asked him to keep silent on the details of this revelation for the time being. That was until they had been able to locate the six businessman who had been involved. He couldn't even give Estelle Gifford a call to tell her that Heather Hart had been found alive.

At the end of the conversation, he took both the DIs down the staircase, out through the door and back into the surroundings of the early evening. He bade them farewell and watched them saunter into the distance before they turned onto Regents Street and went out of view. He did wonder if Luke Terry was involved with DI Bent romantically? If he was. Good for him.

He returned to his office, sat in the comfy seat behind his desk, took the first of the insurance case files and refamiliarised himself with the notes he had written on the pad. He would have to prioritise all his notes to determine which of the six cases to tackle first. He rose from the desk, slipped into the kitchen, filled the kettle, turned it on and put coffee into a mug. He needed to stop drinking too much caffeine. It was making him jumpy and on edge, but he did appreciate the wide-awake feel.

**The End**

# Going Dutch

Chapter One

The stand-out case in the pile of six new insurance investigations was the one in which the claimant maintained he had a Rolex watch worth £6,000 stolen from a hotel room in Brighton. There was little doubt that he had been robbed, but the inclusion of such an expensive timepiece didn't look right. After all, the value of the other items didn't come anywhere close to £6,000.

Sadly, for him, the claimant, he never provided a bill of sale for the watch. He did eventually submit an invoice, but it was the kind of thing a school kid could have produced in five minutes on his or her computer. Therefore, it cut little ice with the insurance company. Nevertheless, the claimant still maintained it was a genuine claim.

When David Moss questioned the fellow over the telephone the claimant was never able to explain how he could tell a genuine Rolex from a fake. Neither was he able to provide the serial number. Okay, that didn't mean to say he was lying, but it certainly put more doubt on his story.

The following day, after talking to Moss, the claimant contacted the insurance company and dropped the claim for a stolen watch. Due to his deceit the whole of the claim was kicked into the long grass. He was given a warning that if he ever submitted a mendacious claim in the future, it would land him in a courtroom. His name was now on the list, circulated to all the companies, of customers to keep a close eye on.

It was now getting on for two months and some loose change since the end of the culmination of the Heather Hart investigation. Those in the frame for her kidnap, Justin Thomas, former Met police DCI Rod Wilkie, and Lyndon Cole were in the process of being hauled before a magistrate to answer the charge of kidnap, false imprisonment and malicious wounding. The identity of four of the six businessmen, who had each paid £40,000 to abuse her, were known. That just left two others to find. In between that, and the new batch of insurance claims, Moss had had a fairly simple case of a missing person to solve. Now with the year at the back-end, Christmas was only eight weeks away.

Today was a Thursday, the last but one day in the month of October. Four days before the clocks had fallen back one hour to signal the start of the autumn-winter period. It was close to four p.m. The sun was already going down on the horizon and the temperature was dropping.

Moss received a telephone call into his office. Despite the gathering gloom outside, he took the call in his usual upbeat tone of voice. The caller sounded educated, sure of herself, confident, studious and shrewd. She said she wanted to hire him to do some work, but steadfastly refused to discuss what she actually wanted him to do over the telephone. Possibly fearing that her phone was bugged or whatever.

She said her name was Annabel, but didn't provide Moss with a surname. Rather than chat to him over the airwaves she wanted to meet him, face-to-face, to tell him precisely what it was that she required him to do. He said fine. Not a problem. When he pressed her, she told him it was something to do with her father, but that was all she was prepared to say at this juncture.

Moss agreed to meet her tomorrow afternoon. Rather than a neutral venue she said she was coming into *town* tomorrow and would be happy to meet him in his office. It wasn't usual for him to meet clients here, but, on this occasion, it suited them both. A three o'clock appointment was agreed.

The following afternoon – Friday – Moss spent an hour, from 2pm up to 3pm, tidying the office though it wasn't too bad. He sprayed a can of furniture polish over the desk top and over the top of the three stack metal drawer cabinets to rid them of the build-up of dust and to give the air a nice lavender aroma. He even borrowed a cordless Dyson vacuum cleaner from the pastry shop owner below. He ran it over the rug on the floor and the varnished planks to force out the bits of dropped food lodged in the grooves. He also gave the surface of each of the picture frames hanging on the wall a wipe with a dry duster. He soon had the room gleaming, but not exactly sparkling.

The client arrived right on the stroke of 3p.m. She was just as he had imagined her. Tidy and stylish. Svelte and blonde with long curly hair that reached her shoulder blades. She had an expensive dress sense and a bit of a 'lady about town' appearance. She wore a white Dior jacket and skirt combo over a bow-tied silk blouse. The Chanel handbag she was carrying looked genuine. Her makeup was maybe a little over done, but she was able to carry it off. She had nice eyes and blemish-free skin. She had the look of an actress, whose name escaped him. She had played opposite George Clooney in an agreeable Rom-Com about failed relationships and having to look after their kids whilst both combining stressful, but successful careers. That was when he, Clooney, had dark hair, was ten pounds lighter, and long before he was able to produce his own movies.

 Moss showed her into his office and asked her to take a seat in the armchair he had placed by the side of his desk. The scent of her perfume easily trumped the smell of the furniture polish that still lingered like a cloud of chlorine gas. She sat uncomfortable on the edge of the seat, then eased back and crossed her smooth, stocking covered legs. Her knees under the stockings were round and perfectly formed. The light cutting in through the strips of the vertical blinds at the window settled on her face in an alternative two-tone shade of light and dark. He placed her in an age range of thirty-two to thirty-four, somewhere in that ballpark, though he could be mistaken. He noticed the diamond-encrusted ring lodged against the wedding band on her ring finger.

"How can I help you?" he asked as he sat forward in his swivel chair, placed his elbows down on the table and turned fifteen degrees to face her. He left out the word 'today' at the end of the question. As it was obvious that today was D Day. Or decision day. Though she may have made the decision to seek the assistance of a private detective some days before.

She observed him through her soft brown eyes that were as dark as teak. "It's my father. He needs you to do something for him."

"Okay. Such as?"

"I'd like you to visit him."

"What's his name?"

"Max Kirton. I'm his daughter. Annabel Litten."

The name Max Kirton struck a chord with him, but he couldn't place it for the moment.

"Where is your father?" he asked.

"In Belmarsh prison. He's doing eighteen years." She replied without hinder or hesitation.

Then it came to Moss. Max Kirton was the name of a criminal who had been involved in a daring heist on a Hatton Garden safety deposit centre about three years before. It was a celebrated heist because of the ingenuity of the caper, but also because it was carried out by a rag-bob set of old geezers who had showed that senior years were no hindrance when it came to pulling off a daring caper. The Hatton Garden job had really captured the British public's collective imagination. It had resulted in the spin off mini-series on tv, starring a load of senior, mostly retired actors. A large percentage of the thirty million haul taken was still unaccounted for. Those responsible had refused to tell the police where the loot was hidden. The reticence to tell the authorities had resulted in most of them receiving longer sentences than the statute set. Rumours were rife that the gang had managed to hide some of the stolen gear out of the country, or into secret hiding places dotted here and there around the Home Counties.

Max 'Dutch' Kirton, as he was known by his friends and associates, had been a property developer and builder throughout a criminal career that had lasted perhaps thirty years. He was known as 'Dutch' because of the urban myth that as a child his mother had made him wear wooden clogs to school. The nickname had stuck to him like a limpet mine for the rest of his days. He must have been in his mid to late sixties by now.

"What does your father want to speak to me about?" he asked.

"I don't know for sure. A task," she replied candidly.

"What kind of task?"

"I don't know," she repeated, shrugging her shoulders. Her face was set in stone. He could see that she held her hands tight and that her body language was strained. She came across as hard-edged, but in reality, she may have been more petite than the image she tried to project.

Moss was intrigued by her. He knew that following the heist Max Kirton would be two-years and some months into an eighteen-year stretch. It would be halved, to nine, if he kept his nose clean, while serving his sentence.

He chose not to question Ms Litten too tersely at this point, because even if she knew why he wanted to see a private detective she might not be willing to tell him.

She fidgeted in the round back armchair. She was never comfortable and repeatedly crossed then uncrossed her legs that looked muscled and perhaps indicated a keen squash or tennis player. Her body language was stiff, and her face was drawn and taut. He told her of his daily rate which she agreed to meet. With that settled there wasn't a great deal to discuss, other than the preparations for him to visit Max 'Dutch' Kirton in Belmarsh prison. She told him she would contact her father forthwith and inform him that Moss was willing to visit him in prison to discuss the ins and outs, therefore, he, her father, would have to make the necessary request for a visitor to come and see him.

Moss was going to ask her why she had chosen him, but didn't. He asked her if she wanted him to keep her up-to date on progress. She thought about it for a few long moments then said 'okay', but never seemed that happy or convinced it was a good idea.

With little else to discuss, he took a few contact details from her in the form of a mobile telephone number, then she said she had an appointment in town. He escorted her out of the office, down the staircase, then out of the door next to the pastry shop window, watched her turn and elegantly saunter towards Regents Street. She had left him to wait for the formal official letter from the prison asking him to visit Max 'Dutch' Kirton in Belmarsh nick.

Chapter Two

Several days passed. It was now November. On the Wednesday morning, the day before Bonfire Night, five days after the visit from Annabel Litten, a letter arrived on the mat at the bottom of the staircase. It was from the Home Office. The content informed Moss that an application from an inmate of Belmarsh prison had been made for him to pay a visit.

The time of the visit would be Monday of next week, the 9$^{th}$ of November at 2pm. Moss had to call a telephone number written in the letter to confirm he accepted the appointment. He would have to bring some photo identification with him. A current British passport would suffice.

On receipt of the letter, he called the number to confirm he would attend the appointment.

Monday, the 9$^{th}$ of November soon came around. It was now ten days since he had met Annabel Litten in his office. Moss arrived outside the prison gates at 1.30pm and parked his car in the visitor car park on the outer side of the tall, sandy textured wall. Belmarsh prison in south-east London was a Category A correctional facility for societies bad boys. It was perhaps the largest Cat A prison in the whole of the country. It housed the most serious of offenders from terrorists to hardened criminals. Though at sixty-five years of age, classing Max Kirton as a hardened offender was perhaps a little over the top. He was hardly a menace to society. Odd that Lords of the Realm and establishment figures who do wrong spend their time housed in open prison camps by the seaside, whilst public heroes like Max Kirton are housed here, Moss pondered to himself.

He entered into the administration block, through the public entrance, after first passing through one of those airport-style metal detectors. He showed the letter, he received from the Home Office, to a uniformed official, then his passport. His details were checked and recorded in the log. He was handed a lanyard to place around his neck which had the word 'VISITOR' emblazoned across the glossy plastic surface. He was then taken by a second official and shown into a room where perhaps two dozen other people were congregated.

A further couple of minutes elapsed before the visitors were taken through a double door and into a wide, very bland and sterile looking area that was lined with tables and chairs. This was the meeting room. Four columns of tables were set out across the floor with about ten rows, making forty tables in all. Each table was separated, from the other, by a gap of around six feet or so. A three feet high partition in the form of a Perspex sheet split the table into two halves. It was pretty much a stark place, unwelcoming and devoid of any colour or attraction. It had plain blanch walls and a polished white tile floor. The ceiling was high. Light was blazing in through windows at the angle of the wall and ceiling. Brightly lit bulbs, inside circular green industrial lightshades, were hanging down from the ceiling on the end of long grey-black cables. The echo of opening and closing doors seemed to vibrate and ping around the high ceiling. This was Moss's first visit to Belmarsh as a visitor to see an inmate.

As each visitor entered the room a uniformed officer stopped them to ask for their name and to check their lanyard. He ticked off the names on a list attached to a clipboard. He told Moss to go to table eighteen. It was in the second column, the eighth table along the line.

He strode across the floor, along the second aisle and came to the table which was marked with the number eighteen on a piece of card attached to the Perspex screen. He sat down on the visitor's side. The clear glass sheet had small round holes punctured into it, so the visitor and inmate could communicate without having to resort to raising their voices.

Due to there only being two dozen visitors the tables were well spread out amongst the visitors. A prison officer in uniform came clip-clopping along the aisle and cast his beady eye over those seated.

Once all the visitors were seated, a door at the other end of the room opened and the inmates began to file in in single file. They were all wearing the same grey sweatshirts with a thin single yellow stripe across the front. Several were wearing knee-length black shorts. Others were in jogging pants of various colours and style. Nearly all the inmates looked glum, melancholy, and distracted as if a visit from a member of their family was the last thing they needed.

Moss had never met Kirton in his life; therefore, he didn't know what he looked like. He had only seen photographs of him taken a few years before, so his appearance might have changed. He could have aged significantly. After all, prison time was hardly conducive to fine living and health.

One of the inmates wended his way to table eighteen, put his eyes on Moss, then paused to give him a *once-over* look before he sat down at the other side of the table-tennis size table. This was Max 'Dutch' Kirton. He looked younger than his sixty-five years. With his grey, thinning hair pulled back tightly in a ponytail he had the look of an ageing rock star who hadn't strummed a guitar in ages. Or maybe a retired snooker player, who once upon a time had a successful career and was known to be flamboyant. As soon as he faded from the limelight, he hit the buffers and was now down on his luck. Hence, a period in prison. In the grey top he had a hard-bitten grizzled appearance. He had loose deep lines under both eyes and his jawline sagged into jowls. Other than this he looked okay. He peered around the room with a wide sweep of his green eyes. A big clock high on the wall said 2pm. There was a large notice telling victors they had one hour. Moss didn't think it would take that long. One of the uniformed guards made his way down the aisle, the clip-clop of his booted footwear on the tiles told you he was close by.

Kirton took the metal tube chair, pulled it back, sat down and put his eyes on the chap at other side of the clear, transparent partition. He placed his forearms down and edged forward. His face was serious and glum. He didn't crack a smile. He had the faintest resemblance of his daughter across his eyes.

"Who are you?" he asked.

"I'm David Moss. The private eye you've hired." Kirton shifted his posture and adjusted his legs to sit side on, so he was the model of a chilled out easy-going character. "What can I do for you?" Moss asked.

"It's my wife."

Moss reached into a jacket pocket and extracted a slim notepad. A short, thin pencil was attached to it by an elasticated ring. He put them both on the table before him. "What about her?" he asked.

"According to my daughter she's seeing a bloke. I want to know his name."

"All right. How long has she suspected this?"

"A while. I want you to investigate it and get me his name."

"Okay. What's your wife's name?"

"Eleanor. She ain't my first wife or my kids' mother. She's my second wife. Twenty-five years my junior. I wouldn't mind if she had asked for my permission, but she ain't."

"She's not your daughter's mother."

"That's what I said, didn't I?" he snapped.

"Who's your first wife?"

"Bernie."

Moss shifted his position ever so slightly. "Tell me a few things about Eleanor. What's her age?"

"Thirty-five."

"Where does she reside?"

"South Kensington."
"Is it your home?"
"Yes."
"What was her name before she married you?"
"Eleanor King."
"What did she do before she met you?"
"Airline stewardess."
"What does she do now? If anything."
"She owns and runs her own travel shop."
"Where?"
"In Pimlico."
"Does she have any children?"
"No."
"Do you or your daughter have a recent photograph I can have."
"My daughter might have one."
"What's your wife's current address?" Kirton provided him with the address which he wrote onto the pad.

Moss continued the fact-finding exercise. "Did she have many male friends before?"
"Before what?"
"Before she met you."
"Probably, but not while I was out on *civvie* street."

The clip-clop of the prison guard's boots came by the table. Moss waited until he was out of earshot before speaking.

"How does your daughter come to think your wife is seeing another man?" he asked.

"She's seen her on the arm of some suave young buck."

"And you'd like to know who he is."

"That's right." Kirton titled his head back and looked up at the ceiling. His old rocker's ponytail fell down over the back of his head and his leathery neck stretched. His teeth were whiter than white for someone his age. By the size of his arms and the roundness of his chest, it looked as if he was well acquainted with the prison gym equipment.

Moss wrote the details of what Kirton had said in his notebook. It sounded a simple task. He had to find out who Eleanor Kirton's man friend was, then channel it back into the prison for him to consider what to do next. If anything. Not that he would get involved in scaring off the 'young buck' or anything like that. That would be for someone else to do.

Moss was right. The meeting didn't last too long. Kirton seemed keen to be on his way back to his cell, as if he had a chess match or card game to complete, and he had the other guy in check or by the balls.

The visitor was heading out of the door and back into the prison entrance, not fifteen minutes after stepping through it. He had met 'Dutch' Kirton and felt privileged in a way. Kirton was the archetypal kind of anti-hero villain revered by many people and adored by his peers. A long stretch in prison was an occupational hazard for people like him. If he kept his nose clean, he could be out in six or seven years. He'd still only be in his early seventies. Therefore, still young enough to enjoy his wealth and ill-gotten gain.

## Chapter Three

One day after meeting Max Kirton, Moss was on the street checking out the address he had been given. Cornwall Gardens in south Kensington was prime London real estate. Eleanor Kirton's home was in a property in a row of white walled stucco fronted, four-story homes on the edge of swanky, elegant and posh London.

Moss believed that good surveillance was mostly about patience and good timing. It was seventy percent perspiration, fifteen percent patience, and the rest luck. It was also about being in the right place at the right time. In truth, if Eleanor Kirton was seeing another man or men, who could blame her? Her husband had said much the same. It wasn't her fault that her old man was banged up inside doing prison time. Though if she lived off his money, then perhaps, he had a point and a right to know who she was seeing. He doubted she would know where Kirton had hidden his part of the loot stolen from the heist, but maybe she did, and that is why he wanted to know who she was seeing. In case she told her beau where the money was stashed. Then it was likely to soon disappear, and him with it.

It wasn't too long before the POI (point of interest) emerged from the front door of her elegant home and Moss put his eyes on Eleanor Kirton. She was a cracking looking woman with a nice dress sense and the poise of an actress. Her dark hair, and the way it was styled, with the straight cut fringe, gave her the appearance of a modern-day Cleopatra. Old boy Kirton was certainly punching way above his weight to marry such a beauty. She was taller than her husband. Around five feet ten or thereabouts. She was well proportioned and made-up. She must have had a stable of male admirers.

She stepped towards a Mercedes soft-top convertible, parked in the kerb outside her home, opened the door, got in, started the engine and proceeded to drive away. Moss followed her in his own car, the relatively short distance, to her travel shop business on a street in Pimlico, not too far from Victoria railway station and just off the busy Belgrave Road. It was an independent travel agent, in that it wasn't part of a franchise nor one of the big chains. It was a nice-looking place with several promotions inside the window displays and plastered onto one of those old-fashioned sandwich boards on the pavement just by the entrance. He parked fifty yards along the road, from the shop front and settled down to watch the front.

Over the course of the next couple of hours a thin line of customers and clients came and went. She didn't leave, well not from the front. He did see her a couple of times in the doorway at front of the store, looking out onto the road. It would appear that she stayed indoors for the majority of the time.
    It was just after three-thirty when she emerged, closed the store for the day and left. She got into her car, took off into the mid-afternoon traffic and drove to a nearby supermarket where she parked in the car-park, went inside and took the opportunity to stock up on groceries and whatnot. She came across to him as a classy lady in her mid-thirties, going about her business. From the food store he followed her to her residence in Cornwall Gardens and watched as she parked on the street, got out, took her shopping from the boot, then went inside the front door.
    He was prepared for the long haul to discover if anyone turned up or if she went out. He couldn't hang about in front of her home all evening. Nor did he want to. Someone was bound to notice him and wonder who he was and what the hell he was doing. He had to perhaps create a couple of roles for himself. For now, he sat in his car watching the front of the house from around one hundred yards away.

The previous night, after the visit to Belmarsh, he had done some desk research on 'Dutch' Kirton. Kirton had been a relatively low-level criminal in his early career before he became far more professional and choosier about who he hung around with. He became pally with a few 'movers and shakers' to become a more well-known face around town. He had served a couple of short prison terms for various crimes, but nothing major. His big break came when he met a guy called Harry Darnell. Darnell took him under his wing and the pair of them became bone-fide businessmen dealing in both legal and illegal activities, such as stolen cars, jewellery and gold bullion. His last and final big job was the raid on the safe deposit centre in Hatton Garden.

The gang of ten thought they had perfected the perfect crime and had got away with it. A year went by with the police obtaining few leads. If it wasn't for the witless behaviour of one of the gang members, who couldn't keep his mouth shut, they might have got off with it. He blabbed to an undercover cop, who had followed him to Ibiza, sought the chap's company and created a fictitious backstory which the villain took to be gospel. The copper had told him he was interested in purchasing some of the stolen loot. The chap couldn't help but blab about his role in the caper. The police collared this individual and set up a sting to draw him into a trap. Once he had admitted to being involved in the job the cards quickly fell into place. The other nine members of the outfit were quickly identified and arrested. Once the questioning began it all came crashing down around their ears. When one of them went under, the rest soon followed. Fourteen months after the robbery the other nine members of the team were banged up on remand. Six months later a jury at the Old Bailey found them all guilty in less than two weeks of hearing the evidence. Max Kirton, one of the ring leaders, got eighteen years. That was two and a half years ago. He still had seven years to serve before any chance of being considered for parole.

Moss was conscious that he had to keep a low profile. He knew he didn't have the manpower to keep a full twenty-four-hour surveillance, so he decided to call a friend, a former Met police colleague Bob Ambrose and ask him for his help. Ambrose agreed to help out starting at noon tomorrow.

That evening Moss was back on the street for seven p.m. With the start of the second week of November the evenings were turning cooler. The nights were drawing in at a rapid rate. It was dusk and dim by half past five. Houselights were burning inside the long line of residences, and the streetlamps were bright.

Moss was in his car peering through the windscreen. He had a flask of coffee with him and a few snacks, like a family-pack of chunky KitKats and a packet of mints to keep him nourished. A few residents were coming and going, but it wasn't busy. The street was a cul-de-sac so there wasn't a throughway for vehicles seeking to beat the traffic. However, there was a pedestrian walkway at the end of the block cutting through to the next adjoining street.

Moss's mobile phone rang. It was Bob Ambrose asking him how things were going. 'Slowly,' he replied. He was digging in for a long haul. If she didn't emerge by ten p.m., he was going to call it a night and go home.

Bob Ambrose soon rang off. Moss took his coffee flask. Screwed off the cap and took in a quantity straight from the rim. Most of the liquid ended up in his mouth, but some down the front of his jacket. He swore as he brushed it away, as best as he could.

It was getting on for eight-thirty when a car, an opal blue coloured BMW 4 series – new model – slowly trundled down the street. It slid into the kerb and came to a halt directly behind her car and outside of the Kirton home. A slim well-dressed dark-haired man, maybe in his early thirties got out. He was carrying a bunch of flowers in one hand and a bottle of something in the other. He stepped across the path and up to the front door, where he went out of view under the storm porch overhanging parapet, above. Moss noted the time and the arrival of the car. He couldn't make out the number plate because of the angle and the distance.

The front door must have been opened because the fellow never came back into view.

Moss waited for a few minutes, then got out of his car and walked up the path towards the house. The cold of the night wrapped around him and coated his skin with goosepimples. He increased his pace and soon came level to the step leading up onto the storm porch in front of the door. Indeed, the man must have gone inside because he was nowhere to be seen.

He noted the licence plate number, repeating it over and over until it was wedged in his head, then walked to the top of the street and the path that cut through to the adjoining street, then he did a *one-eighty* and walked back the same way he had come. He repeated the licence plate number over and over again. When he was back in his car, he wrote the number on a pad.

Thirty minutes past with no movement at the front of the house. It was now close to nine o'clock. It was dark as hell. The lights beaming out of the houses and the streetlights were bright. It was a further five minutes before two figures stepped out from under the porch and appeared on the path. They turned and came in this direction, towards his car. It was her, Eleanor Kirton, and the dark-haired chap. They sauntered by, arm-in-arm, walking close together in a way an old married couple might do. She was in a calf length dark coat. Dark glasses over his eyes. He had the swarthy good looks of a film star. All teeth and eyes and perfect smile. He was in casual slacks and a brown leather button up jacket with a wide lapels and collar. It would appear that they were either going for a walk or heading to a local eatery or a public house.

Moss had seen enough. As the pair of them were about to come level with the parked car behind him, he waited a few moments, then put the key in the ignition, got the engine running and gently pulled away from the kerb. He wasn't prepared to follow them. He knew by what he had seen they were a couple. Rather than hang about any longer he left the street before the police descended on him and asked him who the hell he was.

That evening he was home for ten-fifteen. He had the number plate of the car the chap had arrived in. That was as good as a name. He only needed to ask Bob Ambrose or DI Luke Terry to run it through the DVLA database to get a name and address of the registered owner. He would have the identity of her admirer. Assuming it wasn't a hire vehicle, of course. The man Max Kirton's daughter said she was seeing. From what he had observed the chap looked at be five years younger than her, though he'd admit it was difficult to be precise on the numbers.

## Chapter Four

The following day – at 10 a.m. – Moss contacted DI Luke Terry and asked him to do a favour for him for which he would pay him two hundred pounds. He asked him to run the licence plate of the BMW through the database – provided by the DVLA, of all known vehicles in the UK. Luke Terry said he was sticking his neck out for him doing this. If he was caught, he would be disciplined or worse still, suspended. It wasn't such a simple request anymore. Moss offered him another one hundred pounds. DI Terry said he would get onto it straight away.

One hour passed before DI Terry got back in touch with him. He informed Moss, he didn't want to give him the name of the registered owner of the vehicle over the telephone from the office. Passing information down the line wasn't the wisest thing to do, in case his phone was being monitored. He would use his own personal mobile phone.

Moss said all right, he would ensure he had his phone on. Meanwhile, before the call from DI Terry, Bob Ambrose had been in touch to let him know he was on the street watching the front of the house on Cornwall Gardens. He would stay for one more hour. There had been no comings and goings from the address. Eleanor's car was still parked there. The BMW was no longer on the street. If anyone turned up at the house, within the next hour, or if she left Ambrose would let him know.

It was just after eleven when Ambrose called him back. He had seen the person of interest leave the house and walk onto nearby Gloucester Road where she had met a chap outside of the tube station with the same name. They had gone, from there, into a public house directly across the road.

Ambrose described the chap as a man in his early to mid-sixties. They had left the pub together after about forty minutes inside then ambled back to the house on Cornwall Gardens. Luckily, Ambrose had a camera with him. He had taken a couple of snaps of them. He described it as being a non-romantic liaison. In other words, there was nothing which suggested any intimacy was involved. He said he would send him the snaps as soon as he was able to download them and put them in an attachment to an email. Moss thanked him. The conversation ended at that point.

It obviously didn't sound like the chap Moss had seen her with the day before. This chap was much older. Could it be her father? An old friend? Her former boss? The possibilities were endless. There was no evidence to say there was any love interest. The relationship could have been purely platonic.

Thirty minutes passed before Moss's phone pinged. It told him he had an incoming email. He logged onto his PC, went to his email account and saw that the file Bob Ambrose had promised had flown into his inbox, with an attachment. He eagerly opened it and feasted his eyes over two snaps of Eleanor Kirton together with an older chap. The guy looked well-groomed and moneyed. He had a bouffant of carefully styled hair turning from grey to white. Mid-sixties. Like an old-style matinee idol from way back when. Rich and sophisticated like a swashbuckling Lionel Barrymore type. Nicely dressed in an easy-going, sober style. Moss didn't recognise him. He could have been anyone. Her father. Uncle. Confident. Who knew?

He sent the photographs to the case file, then to an external hard-drive for back-up. He might have to contact Annabel Litten to ask her if she recognised the chap. But maybe not yet.

DI Terry called Moss back after a wait of about ninety minutes.

"Who is he?" Moss asked him eagerly.

"I got a colleague to search the database. The owner of the BMW with that registration is a Darius Litten," he revealed with little fanfare in his voice.

"Who? Just repeat that name again, please," asked Moss.

"The registered owner of the vehicle is Darius Litten."

"Okay. Thanks. What about an address?"

DI Terry read it out slowly. Moss wrote it onto his notepad. He thanked DI Terry after first telling him that he would get the three hundred pounds to him shortly, then rang off.

What were the chances that Darius Litten was the husband of Annabel Litten? Was the husband of the lady who had been into his office Eleanor Kirton's love interest? Was Max 'Dutch' Kirton's son-in-law involved romantically with his father-in-law's wife? It would look that way. And stranger things had happened.

As soon as he had concluded the conversation with his former colleague Moss left the office and drove to the house on Cornwall Gardens to relieve Bob Ambrose. Mrs Kirton's Mercedes was still parked on the street. The activity in the vicinity wasn't as busy as it had been the previous day. Now, well into the second week in November, the afternoon sun was as weak as watered-down lager. There was zero warmth in the air. A developing thin frosty mist was just visible against the failing light.

It wasn't too long after he arrived when the four series BMW appeared at the end of the street and parked close to the rear of Eleanor Kirton's Merc. The driver went inside the house. It wasn't long before the pair of them, Eleanor and the good-looking younger chap, emerged and walked arm-in-arm along the street and out through the walkway at the end and into the adjoining street. She was wearing a blue buffer type sports coat. Darius Litten was in a thick wool jacket. Moss watched them saunter down the passageway and go out of view.

Moss concluded that he had seen enough to be able to inform Kirton that his wife was involved with his daughter's husband. He wasn't sure how much further he could go with this investigation. He had what he needed to end it now.

He returned to his office and logged onto his computer. He ran a check on the electoral register for the address DI Terry had given him. It listed two people as living at that address. Darius and Annabel Litten. That confirmed to him that it was her husband who was having the affair, well definitely seeing Mrs Maxwell Kirton.

The second chap, Bob Ambrose had snapped with her, was a mystery. He elected to try and discover his identity by running the photos past several of his compatriots in the private investigation game. First, he pixelated the two photographs to hide Eleanor Kirton's face, then he emailed the images to several contacts and asked them if they could identify the man.

The answer of who it was came back within the hour from a guy called Steve Howson. The man in the photograph was Roderick 'Rod' Kirton. No less a figure than Max Kirton's younger brother. Rod Kirton was a former theatrical agent. He had made loads of money negotiating deals for some top of the list actors and actresses, then he got out of that business and retired after he was accused by a Sunday newspaper of some financial improprieties.

Moss congratulated himself. After only a few days of investigating he had managed to obtain two names that Kirton would be interested in. How he would react to the information was a different matter. Maybe well. Possibly badly. Who knew?

## Chapter Five

After debating about it in his own mind for a couple of hours, Moss decided to put in a call to Annabel Litten to inform her he had a couple of names for her father, though only one of them was the candidate for her lover. Over the course of a call lasting a couple of minutes he explained to her that he had seen two men, but he hadn't witnessed either of them in bed or in a passionate embrace with Eleanor or anything like that, therefore the evidence was in some ways still a little bit circumstantial.

Annabel ended the conversation by telling him she would get back to him once she had been able to chat to her father. She would let him know what he said. He said okay, he would wait for her return call.

During the course of the conversation, he hadn't provided her with any names, though, in truth, she never asked for them. During their chat it had crossed his mind that it was all very open, as if actually it was all a set-up of some kind, that he was supposed to see them together. All done for a reason that wasn't, as yet, obvious. They had never sought to hide the fact. Maybe it was all manufactured and scripted like the plot of a tv drama. He parked the thought to the back of his mind for the time being and got on with his day.

It was now close to four-thirty. The signs of the rapidly developing cold snap were drifting across the sky in the form of menacing grey clouds. The daylight was fading faster than an England cricket team batting collapse. Down on the street, below his office window, people were starting to make their way home from the businesses in and around Soho. The nearby Oxford Circus tube station would be starting to become clogged with commuters trying to get home.

He turned to his PC, pulled up the pages of the main BBC news site, and began to browse through the content. Then he heard the bell at the door downstairs sounding. He twisted around to turn and look down onto the street, through the gaps in the blinds, to the space in front of the entrance. He was not expecting anyone to call this afternoon or this late, so the sound of the doorbell came as a total surprise. He could make out two figures standing there. Despite the gloom and in the light drifting out from the front of the pastry shop he could make them out. One was Met police detective, DCI Steve Rice, the other was DI Pamela Bent. They were both suited and booted and wrapped up well against the cold nip in the air.

He pressed a button in the intercom unit connected to the front door. "Hello, how can I help you guys?" he asked.

"David?" asked DI Bent.

"Yes."

"Can we pop up for five minutes?" she asked.

He held off from saying 'about what?' "Just a minute, I'll come down and let you in," he replied. He got out of his comfy seat, headed out of the office, onto the landing, then down the rickety staircase to the door at the bottom. The streetlight was pressing against the glass panel above the door. Before opening the door, he peered through the fish-eye lens to see them still standing there. Two obscured figures like goldfish in a glass bowl. He flicked up the latch and pulled the door inward, then stepped aside.

Moss knew DCI Steve Rice from his days in the Met. He was an okay kind of guy. Non-aggressive and not too pushy. Now in his mid-to-late forties. Average appearance and looks. Fair hair that was starting to thin at the crown to reveal a balding patch. He had a sort of harassed football manager look. He was a *teckies-tecky*. Straight down the line. If such a moral, highly principled person existed in the ranks, anymore. A detective in the old CID, now better known, in some circles, as the Serious Crime Unit. Moss hadn't cast his eyes on him for a while. At least a couple of years.

DI Bent was just as attractive as the last time he had seen her during the Heather Hart case, which was now a fading memory. Both of them were dressed for the job in warm jackets and trousers.

"How can I assist you, today?" Moss asked them both as he closed the front door behind them.

"Just a couple of questions about Max Kirton," said DCI Rice, straight out. No messing about with banalities.

"Okay. Come up."

Moss led them up the staircase, onto the landing, through the door, past the door to the kitchen area, then into the tight surroundings of his office. He asked them to grab a chair from down the side, close to the metal cabinets. He had, sort of, been expecting a visit from the police to ask him about his visit to Kirton, so their appearance wasn't totally unexpected.

"I'd offer you something warm to drink, something medicinal, but I've only got coffee, and it's from a jar."

"No thanks," said DCI Rice. "We don't expect to keep you that long," he added.

Moss raised his eyebrows, but didn't say good. The pair of them sat down in the two round back armchairs and glanced around the room. Maybe finding it hard to understand why a former Met detective worked out of a couple of cramped rooms above a pastry shop in Soho.

Moss edged around his desk and sat in the swivel chair and rested his forearms on the padded armrest. "So how can I help you?" he asked again, looking at DCI Rice.

"We understand you've been talking to Max Kirton."

"News quickly gets around the bush telegraph," he replied.

"We'd just like to know what it concerns." DCI Rice asked. His voice hadn't changed. He still had an accent that told of his north of England roots.

"Oh, you know, this and that. Client-attorney privilege and confidentiality and all that."

"Leave it out," she said. "This is not America." It reminded him of a lyric in a David Bowie song, but he couldn't place the title right now.

"It's nothing earth shattering," he admitted. "He's asked me, through his daughter, to check on his wife who he thinks is having an extra marital affair while he's banged up in Belmarsh."

"Nothing to do with where he's stashed away what we failed to recover from the Hatton caper?" Rice asked.

"No. Far from it." replied Moss, keeping a straight face.

"Just *good'ole* infidelity then?" she asked, partly grinning as she said it.

"Not sure if it's that. She's having a bit of fun while he's away. Who can blame her? I mean she's an attractive lady who's bound to have many male admirers."

"Like flies buzzing around a lightbulb?" Rice put it crudely.

"You could put it that way. I suppose."

DI Bent sat forward in her seat. "So, nothing about where the missing loot is stashed?" she asked.

"No, I'm afraid not."

"Why are you afraid?"

"Figure of speech."

"So, is she?" Rice asked.

"Is she what?"

"Having an affair."

"She might be, but who can deny her a bit of male company in these darkening days. I dare say he knew she'd be seeing other men while he's away on secondment. Not even he would deny her that. He just wants to know who it is. I don't think he's going to put out a contract once he gets a name. I don't think that's Kirton's style."

"Might it have something to do with the location of where he hid the stolen cash and jewels, he stole from out of the deposit centre?"

"I don't think so. He never said that much to me."

"The rumours are that he's told some people where he's hid the stuff."

"He never told me."

"He did it in a clever way."

"How?" Moss asked DCI Rice.

"He told five people, but only gave each of them part of the location."

"So, like a puzzle to solve."

"Yeah, something like that. He told one person one detail, then another the next and so on. If the people all come together, they'll be able to work out where he hid the merchandise. There must still be about a couple of million pounds worth of stolen jewels out there somewhere."

Moss made a face by chewing on his bottom lip and creasing his brow. "Wow. Oh, I see, but I'm not sure it has anything to do with that. He wants to know who his wife is having a fling with…By the way. Do the five people he told know who the others are?"

"That we're not sure."

"We think the five are his first wife. His daughter. His brother Rodney. His son-in-law Darius. And lastly his second wife."

"But there could be a sixth person who holds the vital, key piece of information," DI Bent added.

"Like a puzzle or a riddle then? The key piece of information will solve it. Just join the dots to solve the riddle. Sadly, when I visited him in Belmarsh he didn't confide in me."

DCI Rice grinned. "Why does he want to know what his wife is up to?"

"No idea. I suppose he just wants to know what is happening outside the walls."

"Who is it?"

"I'm really not at liberty to divulge a name. It doesn't appear to be anything that heavy. I mean it's hardly a state secret. From what I've witnessed she seems content. She's not guarding the crown jewels."

"Okay, let's leave it there," said Rice. "But we'd really like to find the sixth person to solve the riddle."

"How intriguing," said Moss in a rhetorical, heavy-laced theatrical tone.

"Yes, indeed. Intriguing isn't the word I'd use." Rice commented. He stretched his long legs, then got up onto his feet. His pretty female colleague followed his lead. They stepped to the door, then took the long, steep wooden staircase to the door at the bottom, then out. Moss turned in his chair to watch them step away along the pavement. His landline telephone rang. He could see it was Annabel Litten, returning his call from earlier.

He put the phone on loudspeaker, then sat back and rocked on the springy legs. She introduced herself. He could gauge from her sharp delivery that she was tense and on edge. He asked her if she had spoken to her father. She said, 'no not yet' in a terse, dismissive tone of voice.

"I'll need to visit your father in order to pass on the two names I've got."

"I don't want you to do that," she said in stiff tone that contained a hard edge.

"Why not?"

She paused for a brief moment as if to collect her thoughts. "I know that my husband's name is one of them. He's been seeing Eleanor for these past few months," she revealed. "I'm going to visit my father to tell him."

Moss was thrown-off balance for a few long moments. He leaned forward in his seat and placed his arms down on the desk. He didn't know what to say in the face of the revelation she had openly volunteered. She was admitting that she knew her husband was the name of the person he had seen. "How long have you known?" he asked.

"For a while. Six months. I guessed it was his name when you didn't tell me earlier. It's no secret. They've been seeing each other. Darius hitches his wagon to one woman then moves onto the next. It's nothing I can't handle."

"All right."

"What's the second name?" she asked.

He debated in his own mind whether to tell her, but now that she knew about her husband he thought why not. "His brother Roderick Kirton," he revealed. "With him I guess it's more of a case of infatuation or simple friendship."

"I'd prefer it if you didn't arrange to go to see my father. I'll go to see him. I'll tell him the score."

Moss thought that it was an odd thing to say, but brushed over it. "If that's what you want then I can hold off making an application to go and see him."

"Thanks," she said softly.

"Look there's something you'll need to tell him."

"Such as?"

"Two detectives came to see me today."

"What about?" she asked.

"They came to question me about why I'd been to visit your father. I claimed client confidentially, but they wanted to know. I told them it was an investigation into his wife."

"Is that all?"

"Like what?"

"Is that all they wanted to know?"

"No. They started to ask questions about the missing loot from the Hatton Garden heist. They think your father has hidden a lot of items and that he's given the details of where it is to five different people. Maybe six."

"My father was in the property development business for a long time," she said as if it was a significant piece of information to part with. He couldn't grasp why. He remained silent so there was some dead air between them. She coughed at the other end of the line to tell him she was still there. "He gave me part of a postcode. His former wife, my mother, has the second part. His brother has a two-digit number. Darius was given the word, water tank. Eleanor was given the word loft. The sixth and final part is the name of the house, but nobody knows who has the sixth part. It is only when my father is released from prison will we know who has the sixth part, or failing that he will tell us who has it, so we can find the missing gear."

"That's quite amazing."

"No, not really. There's something you must know about my father. Even while he was married to Eleanor, he had a number of affairs with various women. He was, at one time, seeing both Eleanor's sister Emily, and Darius's sister Donatella. Either one of them or someone else could have the sixth part."

Moss smiled to himself. In truth he didn't much fancy going back to the jail to visit Kirton, so on that score she had saved him a job. The place depressed him to high heaven. He was pleased he won't have to go back if she didn't want him to.

"Tell me. When I observed your husband and her together, I got the impression that the affair wasn't that serious. That they openly didn't care who saw them because there wasn't anything to hide."

"We are all adults," she said. "I'm in another relationship. We agreed to stay married because we choose to. This is the way we live our lives. Now in regard to a prison visit, I'll see my father in a few days. Tell him. He'll probably forgive them. Hell, no I'm positive he will."

"Okay, I'll go along with that," said Moss. "Oh. Just one more thing."

"Which is?"

"Who shall I send my invoice to?"

"How much do I owe you?"

"Make it a round one thousand pounds."

"I'll write you a cheque and get it into the post today."

"Will you please make it payable to David Moss Investigation Services?"

"Of course, I will."

"Thank you."

He heard Mrs Litten sigh, then softly say goodbye before placing the telephone flat.

He couldn't do much, but make a face. He turned off the loudspeaker, sat back in his seat and looked at a crack in the ceiling. In the yellow-orange light from the table lamp it looked like a line cutting through a sandy desert or a river winding its way through the Nile delta. He turned to look through the slits in the blind over the window. The last embers of light in the sky were visible. It gave the sky a delightful silvery shade. He reflected for a moment. He did feel a little short changed in a way and a little blown away by the ending, but he'd get over it.

He climbed out of his seat, grabbed his jacket from off a coat hook and swung it over his shoulders. He elected to leave the office to take a five-minute walk to a confectionary shop on Regent Street to purchase a bar of chocolate. Then perhaps he'd wander into the tube station to listen to a busker and people watch for ten minutes. He contemplated life for a few moments. He wondered why a man like Max Kirton would give up a beautiful young wife in order to take part in a heist. There you go. Such was the pull of carrying out a daring caper. Anyway, it was back to the reality of the insurance investigations for him.

He raked in his pocket to find a few loose coins, then got up and stepped onto the landing. He counted the value of the coins. He had just about enough money in twenty - and ten-piece coins to purchase a candy bar. Happy days. He thought. He reminded himself that he was going round to see Claudette Munro this evening at her place. Happy days indeed!

**The End**

# Little Sister

Chapter One

The two sisters, Jacqui Farlow-Brodie and Amanda Farlow-Defoe said they were concerned. They hadn't seen their younger kid sister, Samantha, or spoken to her for some time now. All of eight months or thereabouts. To Moss, that seemed like a long time for siblings to go without any contact. The older sisters told him they believed their brother-in-law, Sam's husband, had forbidden her from contacting them. When they first met Calvin Martin, he came across as a bit of a controlling, coercive type of man. Not a nice person, but eh that was their opinion. Maybe it was tainted in some way by an event that had caused a fall-out. Moss didn't say that. He diplomatically kept his powder dry and his thoughts to himself.

Samantha hadn't been in contact with them for such a long time. According to them, sisters shouldn't go eight months without talking to each other. They were worried. They had talked of their concern to the police, but the officers of the law said there wasn't anything they could do about it, because they had never been asked by Mrs Martin to assist her or anything remotely like that. There was no indication to the police that Samantha Martin was in any danger from her husband. Perhaps, she had fallen out with her sisters for a reason they were not sharing with them. The two sisters, Jacqui, aged thirty-six, and Amanda two years Jacqui's junior, sought the services of a private detective to investigate if their sister was in danger at the hands of a control freak husband. David Moss was the chosen one.

Calvin Martin was six years his wife's senior. He was a professional footballer who had a reputation as a hardman on the pitch. He took no crap from anyone. Martin had never fully reached the potential he had shown as a youth to become a footballer who got to the very top of the pile. His entire career had been spent playing for several London clubs in the third and fourth tier of the English football league. Never in the top league. He was now what fans might term as a 'journeyman'. A player in the twilight of his career. He had started out at Chelsea, but soon moved on. He had represented Queens Park Rangers, Fulham and Brentford in his time. Calvin Martin was a light skinned black man with seriously good looks and a twinkle in his eye, along with plenty of charm when it came to a pretty lady. Today, he played for a league one club in south London. He was a father to two children by his first marriage to an actress called Rosetta Coning. He was on his second marriage to Samantha Farlow. She was the daughter of the former tv actor Barry Farlow and mother Mary Livermore, the celebrated tv cook.

Jacqui Farlow was married to the film director James Brodie. Amanda was the wife of a rock musician, Terrence Defoe. When the sisters sought out a private detective, they visited Moss in his Soho base. He was most impressed by their persuasive argument that something wasn't right. Both of the sisters were tall, and pretty and possessed plenty of their parents' class and good breeding.

The sisters told Moss that Calvin Martin was an intimidating so-and-so who had once threatened them. Therefore, he was a source of fear. Their younger sister, twenty-eight-year-old Samantha had married him a couple of years before. Jacqui and Amanda told Moss that they had discovered that he, Martin, was the manipulative kind, who had bullied his first wife into submission, to such an extent that she had had a nervous breakdown. Therefore, there was little reason to doubt that he wasn't up to his old tricks with their sister. They wanted David Moss to get to the bottom of it. To discover if Calvin was mistreating her.

They informed him they were shocked when their sister fell for a lower league footballer and even more shocked when she agreed to marry him. Telling her it wouldn't last long. The Martins lived in some style. In an apartment building on Park Road, close to the north-west corner of Regents Park, directly across from its open fields and tree lined vista.

Moss began his investigation by researching the career of Calvin Martin. In truth there wasn't a real lot to discover except for the number of first team appearances he had made for the five clubs he had represented in a professional career spanning sixteen seasons. He was in the last year of his contract with his current club. It was rumoured that the club wouldn't offer him a new deal for next season, but had to stick with him as they couldn't afford to off load him now that the transfer window had closed. Therefore, the curtain was being drawn on his career. Still, he had done well to make the number of first-time appearances he had, in the cut and thrust of lower league English football. No small achievement.

His Wiki page said he had married Rosetta Coning at the age of eighteen. They had two children. The marriage lasted for eight years. Eight years later he married Samantha Farlow in Marylebone registry office. There was absolutely nothing to suggest that Martin was a nasty person, portrayed by the sisters. On the contrary, he had a good reputation as a hardworking footballer who was an ambassador for his current club and a local children's hospital in South London. On the football field, he was someone who wouldn't shirk a tackle or a confrontation. There was nothing to suggest he was like what Jacqui and Amanda Farlow painted him to be – a controlling coercive bully with a nasty streak. It was beginning to look as if they were, at best exaggerating, or at worse, making it up. Still, Moss was compelled to investigate why their sister had gone quiet on them.

## Chapter Two

One explanation for the silence could be was that there was something from the past that had tainted the relationship, like a family dispute leading to a falling out.

Moss sought to commence the detective work by contacting his old Met police pal, DI Luke Terry, to ask him if he would pull up Calvin Martin's sheet to see if there were any offences or cautions against him. If so, it might back up the sisters' claims. He called DI Terry, spoke to him for a couple of minutes about the old times, then asked him to do him the favour and see if he came up with anything.

Terry said fine. He'd get back to him as soon as possible. Following on from that call Moss pulled up the Wiki page on the well-known tv actor Barry Farlow, Jacqui, Amanda, and Sam's father. There was nothing much to interest him, other than his bibliography of work in the form of his acting credits, which were mostly on the small screen and in modern or gothic type of dramas.

Sam's parents were now divorced. Barry Farlow was now married to someone who was a former prominent figure in the tv industry. He was the kind of actor who frequently appeared on screen, but few people would know his name. He wasn't that high profile. He wasn't in any of the soaps. He had had quite a few appearances on pocket-size dramas like Midsomer Murders, Spooks, Poirot, Casualty and such like. It would appear that he had a good agent and plenty of friends to give him small parts. Being the former husband of the former tv cook and style guru Mary Livermore hadn't done his profile any harm.

Following the divorce, he had appeared in one or two of those tv schedule type of magazines that came with the Saturday newspapers. Mainly to lament the passing of his marriage, though he had swiftly remarried again. In one article he had referred to his 'brilliant' relationship with his three daughters who had provided him with much comfort and joy. He had two grandchildren. He said he was enjoying his twilight years on tv more than ever, but writing for a tv magazine he would say that, wouldn't he? His personal wealth was put around the £5 million mark, which reflected the fact that the Farlow family were an old money family.

A day elapsed before DI Terry got back in touch with Moss to inform him that Calvin Martin's sheet was as barren as a seedless Jaffa. He had never been arrested or even cautioned. He had zero offences against his name. His only cautions had occurred on the football field where his discipline record was patchy. He had mellowed towards the twilight of his career. He was a hot-head in his earlier days, then turned down the gas a little. He hadn't been sent off in two seasons. Which was a record for him.

Moss had the Martin's home address. He checked it out on Google Earth. They lived in a block of apartments on Park Road right opposite Regents Park on its western side. Samantha didn't have any obvious income, but when he investigated a little deeper into her background, he discovered she was the owner-manager of a flower shop on Grove End Road in St. Johns Wood, called 'Six Red Roses'.

When he pulled up the shop website, he stumbled onto a photograph of a lady who was Samantha Farlow-Martin, standing in the store entrance holding a bouquet of six red roses and beaming lovingly at the photographer. She was a strikingly attractive woman. Blonde and bright eyed. Tall and slender and with an easy going none eclectic dress sense. Cal Martin had done well for himself. She was a good looker. He was a handsome guy too, with dark features, an athlete's physique and a sportsman's granite features. He wore his hair short. His smile was wide and contained plenty of ivory. She had done well herself to bag such a handsome beefcake. If anything, they looked like a perfectly-matched couple.

That afternoon Moss took a trip to the southern fringe of St. Johns Wood to visit the area around Park Road. The apartment building, they lived in, fronted onto Regents Park and looked over the boating lake. Therefore, it was expensive, prime central London property. The façade contained a lot of reflective, gleaming glass beaming out of a jagged face in a representation of modern architecture. It was six floors high with penthouse terraces along at the top floor. The greenery of a rooftop garden was visible from the ground. Each of the forty or so apartments had a balcony with a view out across the wide-open plains of the park, looking north over central London. A private car park snaked underneath the building and there was a garden at the rear in which residents could relax on long loungers. It also came with a gymnasium, a ten-metre length swimming pool, a communal laundry and even a child's play area. It was exclusive to a degree. Two bed flats would probably change hands for between £2,750,000 to £3,000,000, minimum.

From Park Road, Moss drove the short distance to North End Road to find the 'Six Red Roses' flower store. It was in a row of shops running along the ground floor of a four-storey block of private residence flats. There was a café at one end. A store selling up-market kitchen apparel, and an Indie bookstore, then the 'Six Red Roses' flower shop. It was very much smart central-north London suburbia. Plenty of daytime traffic edged along on the road so there must have been a healthy amount of passing trade. Road signs erected on the lampposts pointed the way to Lords Cricket Ground, which was just around the next corner from here.

Moss parked his car in a vacant bay in an off-road parking space, got out, strode over the path, then a forecourt, through the central entrance and into the flower store. There was a notice attached to the window advertising the *Interflora* delivery service. Vases of flowers were displayed on the floor and on shelving on both sides of a central walk up to a main counter. It was a narrow store in a compact T-shape configuration. The fragrance of the flowers and the colours were almost overpowering to the extent that it knocked his head back a touch. The air was cool and filtered.

As he approached the main counter a lady who resembled Samantha Martin appeared from out of a side doorway. The website photograph had done her justice. She was as pretty as the picture. Her eyes were deep blue. Her face exquisite. High cheek bones and thin lips. She greeted him with a warm smile. She was wearing a light, baggy wool jumper that reached down to the thighs of faded blue jeans. Her boobs under the jumper, were firm. She was, at a guess, a thirty-two in a C cup. The jeans were tight and showed off her thighs and hugged her hips. He noticed the thin silver, tennis-bracelet, around both her wrists and the rings on her fingers. Cal Martin was a lucky man to have such a fine-looking lady on his arm.

She mouthed the word 'hello' at him then asked him how she could help him.

He had rehearsed his lines. "I'd like to send my partner a bunch of six red roses. It's her birthday tomorrow. Can you arrange for their delivery?"

"Certainly."

She took a pad from off the top of the glass counter and he watched her long fingers take hold of a cheap biro. There must have been every flower under the sun in here. The scent was gorgeous, but not good for someone who suffered with a pollen allergy. She asked him for the address to where the roses where to be sent, then asked him if he wanted to fill out a card to go with them.

As he chatted to her, he gauged her mood. She certainly didn't appear to be stressed or under any kind of anxiety caused by a possessive, coercive partner. On the contrary. She was garrulous and vivacious. He was keen to engage her in conversation, so quickly dreamed up a line of enquiry.

"The name 'Six Red' Roses' were did it come from?" he probed.

"It was my idea to give it a name that was a little quirky. It hit the mark," she replied in a modest manner.

"It definitely does," he agreed.

She grinned more than smiled at him, reached to a side, took a card from a cardboard dispenser and handed it to him along with the pen. He took them, thought about what to write for a several short moments, then wrote:

*Happy Birthday Claudette. All my love Dave*

followed by a line of x's and a smiley face.

She asked him for fifteen pounds. He gave her his credit card, which she fed into a chip and pin reader, then gave him it to complete the transaction.

"How long have you been here?" he asked to keep the conversation going.

She touched her face gently and brushed a loose strand of hair from her forehead. "About three years," she replied.

"What was here before?"

"Err. I think it was a shop selling oriental rugs and carpets."

He nodded his head as if in agreement. She asked him, once again, for an address to send the flowers. He gave her his own address. It wasn't Claudette's birthday tomorrow and she definitely didn't live with him. Not yet. He would admit that he had failed on two occasions to persuade her to move in with him. He might ask a third time, but that would be the last time. They were still romantically linked, but not to the extent that they lived together as a married couple.

She wrote the address on the pad, handed him back his credit card and a receipt and the transaction was complete. She, Claudette, could expect the roses tomorrow afternoon at a time between one and three. He smiled at her and she forced a similar expression across her cherry lips. She didn't appear to be in any way subdued or harassed or deflated. On the contrary. She was lively, vibrant and more than responsive to his words. Her personality and characteristics were akin to anyone else of her age. If she was being coerced by a 'control freak' husband she might not even be here, serving and dealing with customer enquiries in a natural thoughtful and rational manner. It wasn't the usual scenario. He concluded that the sisters claim was wrong, or at best, farfetched. He did wonder if someone had put the sisters up to it or they were just misguided? There had to be another reason why she had not spoken to them in over eight months.

He felt as if he should go back to the sisters to tell them that, in his opinion, their younger sister was not under any duress or anxiety caused by her husband's controlling and coercive behaviour.

Rather than contact Jacqui Farlow-Brodie immediately Moss called his friend and associate Bob Ambrose and asked him to do some snooping for him. He wanted him to do some trawling to find the mobile phone telephone number for Calvin Martin – the lower league footballer – if he could. Bob Ambrose had the ways and the means of finding this kind of information and digging further in order to produce a record of all the calls he had made from that number in the past two months.

Ambrose informed him it would take him at least three days to trace the number and the list all the calls he had made. That was assuming Martin had a contract with one of the major service providers. Moss said okay, he would await his reply.

## Chapter Three

On leaving St John's Wood, Moss returned, the short distance, to the apartment block in which the Martins resided. He parked along a nearby road, walked up to the front entrance and discovered by looking at the names of those listed at the front door, that the Martins where in flat number twelve.

Flat or apartment number twelve was on the second of the six floors. It was at the front of the building. The first on the left-hand side looking at the building from the front elevation. An orange and white stripe awning that matched all the others was down and stretched out over the balcony terrace to provide some privacy and protection from the sun's rays. The view over the wall along Park Road towards the boating lake would be unrestricted.

Once he had the number of their flat, he returned to his car, climbed into the driver's seat, but didn't drive off just yet. He elected to wait around for a while to watch the comings and goings. In the end he only hung around for another fifteen minutes, then drove away and returned to his office in Soho.

The evening would be the best time to return to see if either of the Martins would emerge. The unseasonably warm September evening might be a good time to go walkabout in the park or elsewhere. Maybe taking a dog for a walk, though he suspected that was unlikely as the landlord-tenant agreement would exclude any pets. He had no idea what their habits were. He knew that, the day after tomorrow, Saturday, Calvin Martin had a football game up north in Doncaster, for his club. Assuming he was in the matchday squad, he would probably travel up there with the team tomorrow, Friday. It would be unlikely that Mrs Martin would accompany her husband up north, but he didn't know for sure if she wouldn't travel to the game.

It turned out to be another forty hours before Bob Ambrose got back in touch with Moss. He had the information he required. Ambrose provided him with a full list of all the calls Calvin Martin had made in the past two months from his iPhone device. The list came in an email attachment. Alas, it didn't list any calls he had received.

Moss spent a couple of hours compiling a summary of all the dialled numbers. Martin had made a total of two hundred and sixty-eight calls from that one phone. Of the fifty-three numbers he had rang, six appeared more frequently than the rest. Martin tended to make most of his calls out in a period between 7pm and 11pm. There were very few in the afternoon, and even fewer in the morning hours.

Moss assumed that most of them would be to his wife, however, the times possibly didn't suggest this would be the case. There would be some to his team mates and other people connected to the club he played for and others perhaps connected to football in one way or another. Like former team mates. These people tended to stay in touch with each other, or so he assumed. The current team he was playing for had played nine games already this season. They were lying tenth in the fledgling league table.

Today, Martin had featured in the game at Doncaster which had ended in a nil-nil draw. Martin had received a mixed bunch of on-line reviews from fans on a fans' forum message board, from a high of: *he's a quality worker who drives the team forward and always gives 100pc*, to a low of: *he's a useless knackered journeyman who gives the team nothing and is a waste of a shirt*. The manager-coach had *shepherds hooked* him after seventy-two minutes in a game that sounded like a bore draw. This season, he hadn't finished any of the games he had featured in. He had scored one goal.

Moss made a list of the telephone numbers, in ascending order, from top to bottom, in terms of the number of times Martin had made a call to that number. As there was no record of the name of the person Martin had spoken to, he would have to ring the number to determine who he was calling so frequently. This was the nitty-gritty detective work. The work he had to do to determine if Calvin Martin really was the manipulative prick he had been made out to be. He seriously doubted he was anything of the sort.

On Saturday evening Moss left his office at seven for an hour to visit a close-by eatery in Soho. Tonight, Soho was just beginning to get busy and the revellers and the sounds escaping out of the pubs and bars were beginning to increase. On return to his office, he sat in the seat by the window and powered up his PC.

He had only just finished reading a summary on today's sporting headlines when he received a surprise buzz at the door downstairs. He went down the staircase to peer through the fish-lens peep hole. His visitor was none other than his ex-Met police detective colleague DI Luke Terry. His arrival at his office was totally unexpected. Moss showed him in and led him up the stairs, into his office and invited him to take a seat. Terry was in his Saturday casuals as if he was really out on the town with a few chums he had left in a nearby pub.

Terry wouldn't have called around to say hello. Unless he was just passing the time of day with a face-to-face call to his favourite private detective. Moss wondered why he had come to see him on a Saturday evening? It wasn't his style. Terry didn't waste any time with idle chatter. He told Moss that he wanted to know why he was looking at Calvin Martin.

"An accusation from his wife's two sisters that he's a controlling arsehole," was his response to the question.

"Is he?" Terry asked.

"Is he what?"

"A controlling prick."

"Not that I can tell. His wife seems pleasantly relaxed and cool."

"When did you see her?" Terry enquired. His face was serious and studied in thought.

Moss shifted his posture. "When I visited her in her flower store in SJW. She sold me a bunch of red roses. Which I received yesterday."

"Calvin Martin and his wife have been mentioned in dispatches recently," Terry revealed, right out of left field.

"Why? How?"

Terry ran the tip of his tongue over his lips and rubbed the side of his neck. He displayed a cautious pause before continuing to speak. "Something about laundering money through the flower store."

"You're kidding me?"

"Would I kid you?"

"No, you wouldn't. What's the angle?"

"Calvin Martin receives dirty money from some south London villains and they rinse it through the flower shop. We're not talking massive figures, but it soon adds up. Five grand here and there. It's recorded as profit from the business. It comes out at the other end cleaned and smelling of carnations."

"Grief," was Moss's somewhat underwhelming response.

"Not big numbers," DI Terry repeated, as if that was okay, then he volunteered some more classified, information without being prompted to do so. "A snout in south London told Croydon serious crime that Cal Martin knows some people who deal in people trafficking. These illegal migrants do black market jobs. The thing is the bosses take a cut of their wages as a finder's fee for a job finding service. It's all highly illegal of course."

"Of course."

"To clean the money, it goes through the books of the flower store. The money is banked as takings, then comes out at the other end rinsed, then distributed back to the villains. Some bogus paperwork completes the paper trail."

"Phhrrfff,' Moss let out a scoff. "Come on. A flower shop is hardly likely to be a cash-cow of a business. Martin must be on ten grand a week playing football. Even if he's in the third tier," said Moss. "That's half a million a year."

DI Terry came back to him. "But he's coming to the end of his career. He'll need something to fall back on. He's also got a divorce to fund. Child allowance and all those expenses."

That was a fair point, thought Moss. "Still, she'll be fairly wealthy on her own. The Farlow family aren't short of a few bob."

"Still the cut and thrust of doing something illegal. It must give them something to get excited about. The thought of doing something against the grain."

"Yeah, but as you say it's only a grand here and there. It's hardly a massive amount."

"Less chance of being caught then."

Moss conceded that DI Terry had a point. "But why would he do it?"

"Who, Cal Martin?"

"Yeah."

"The opportunity. The buzz."

"Have you got anything else on him?" Moss asked.

"No, just that."

"Not a Mister Big then?"

"No, a nickel and dime merchant."

"He seems to have landed on his feet. Gorgeous wife. I bet he looks forward to bedtime every night."

DI Terry chuckled out loud at him like a mischievous schoolboy who had just heard a lewd joke for the first time. "Just thought I'd let you know," he said.

Moss thanked him for the heads-up. After a visit lasting a minute short of twenty minutes, DI Terry said so-long, excused himself, got up and left him in peace. He never told Moss why he was in the neighbourhood.

Chapter Four

The revelation that the Martins might have been involved in laundering money for a criminal enterprise through the shop was a serious eye-opener and a game changer. Moss didn't want to speculate if it was true. He asked himself if the sisters were aware of it and were using it as a way of trying to get to their sister. He thought that unlikely. There was no reason to believe the sisters knew anything about a money laundering operation. Assuming it was true, of course. If the police knew about it, why hadn't they become involved and arrested those running the operation? Perhaps it was nothing short of garbage.

Moss wondered if any of the phone numbers provided by Bob Ambrose were related to the operation. Perhaps, Martin used a special phone, a burner, to contact the key movers and shakers. Moss considered ringing some of the numbers to see if he got a response.

After thinking about it for five minutes he decided to call each one of top ten most frequently dialled numbers. The first number went straight to a message saying: the other party wasn't available to talk to at this time.

He ended the call, then rang the second eleven-digit number on his pad. A male voice said. "Yeah, who's that?"

"It's Dave. Who's this?" Moss asked.

"You must have the wrong number," said the receiver before he hung up.

The third number was answered by a female who sounded as if she was twelve years of age. When he asked, 'who's that?' She replied by saying she was Abigail Martin. Cal Martin's daughter. Moss said, 'sorry wrong number' and promptly terminated the call.

The fourth number went straight to voice mail. He hung up.

The fifth number was answered by a female with a sassy sounding voice. "Hello. Who is this?" she asked in a breathless manner as if she'd just been involved in some vigorous physical activity.

"It's Dave," he replied.

"Well, hello Dave," she said submissive tone of voice.

"Hello."

"Which Dave is that?"

"Dave Jarvis."

"Dave who?"

"Dave Jarvis."

"I don't know a Dave Jarvis."

"Calvin Martin gave him your number," he said.

"Cal?" she asked, instantly recognising the name.

"Yeah, that's right."

She hung up before he could utter another word.

He put his phone down onto the desk top then swivelled around to peer down onto the street, which on a pleasant evening in September, was remarkably quiet for a Saturday in Soho. His telephone sounded. The number, displayed in the glass, was the fifth number he had called. It was the female with the sassy voice ringing back.

"What do you need?" she asked.

"What have you got?"

"Everything, you've ever dreamed of baby love."

"Can we meet?" he asked.

"Which hotel are you staying in?"

"The Dorchester."

"Which room?

"Four-one-two."

"You certain?"

"That's what it says on the door. What's your name?"

"Jennifer."

"How much?"

"What do you want?"

"What do you provide?"

She told him what she provided. Reeling off a list of services.

"Sorry. I think I've got the wrong number," he said, then hung up and breathed out a long sigh. He didn't expect to hear anything like that, but he wasn't stunned into thinking what the hell was going on. It didn't take a rocket scientist to work it out. Calvin Martin was a pimp, or a contact person for an 'executive' escort agency. It didn't seem plausible, but that is exactly what it sounded like. There might have been a lot more to Calvin Martin, the footballer, than met the eye.

Surely, his wife didn't know about this. Surely, she wasn't one of his stable. Highly unlikely, but he couldn't dismiss the notion out of hand. He wondered if Jenny was actually Samantha, but he couldn't match the voices. The escort had a manufactured edge, like a phone sex talk operative, talking to a telephone client. Samantha's voice was much more natural.

Jenny would be likely to charge top dollar and be expensive. Maybe as much as a thousand pounds for an hour. Three thousand to spend the full night with a client.

That got him thinking. He debated about whether to go to the apartment block on Park Road this evening to see if Samantha left the building at any time. Then he debated whether to call Cal Martin's number to see if he got a reply. He thought about the common-sense aspect of calling him, but decided to go for it. He took his iPhone and prodded the number into the keypad. It rang for a while before the call was answered by a male voice.

"Hi. Is that Calvin?" Moss enquired.

"Yeah."

"I'm looking for an escort tonight. I got your number."

"Who from?"

"Called herself Jenny."

"Jennifer?"

"That's right. She said to give you a call to fix me up with a date."

"Who are you?"

"Dave. I'm in London on my own for a couple of days. I'm on a business trip. I could do with some female company tonight."

"Dave?"

"That's right."

"I can give you a number to call. She'll be free this evening and tomorrow. Jenny gave you, my number. Right?"

"Yeah. That's right. Do you have many girls available?

"I'm only the contact. I don't run the girls. It's a genuine escort service."

"Sounds good to me."

"I'll give you her number. She's called Isobel."

"Isobel?"

"Right."

"Okay. Give me her number and I'll speak to her."

"Got a pen?"

"Yeah."

Martin went silent for a few brief moments while he must have been consulting a pocket book or a second telephone to find the list of contact numbers. He came back on and read out a long phone number very slowly. Moss wrote it down. "Get it?" Martin asked.

"Yeah. What about Sam? I was told she might be free."

"I don't have anyone called Sam."

"No, Sam? Okay, I must have misheard. I'll call Isobel in a minute."

Martin didn't respond. He terminated the call at his end. Perhaps mention of the name 'Sam' had spooked him and thrown him off balance. Moss was tempted to call Isobel, but decided he had heard enough to know what was going on. He guessed that Cal Martin was either a pimp or a middleman running a stable of escorts for the people he was connected to and for whom he did the money laundering favours.

Chapter Five

There was absolutely no evidence to suggest that Samantha Martin was an escort or in any way involved in the management of a harem of girls for lonely business types and clients. She may have known what was going on, but wasn't involved in the day-to-day running of the operation.

Moss decided to leave the office for the day. At eight in the evening, with the sky now dominated by dark clouds it was chilly. He grabbed his fleecy jacket from the back of the door, swung it over his shoulders, then took off. He went out to his car, pointed it towards the north-west and drove the relatively short distance along Marylebone Road towards the Regents Park area.

The time was getting on for eight-twenty when he drove past the Regents Park Mosque, turned onto Lodge Street, parked his car in a free space, then walked back the three hundred yards to the front of the apartment block facing the parkland, with its jagged face, brown brick façade and wide windows and open terraces. Some of the green bushes along the ledge at the rooftop garden were billowing in the stiffening breeze.

Lights were blazing in the windows behind the curtains and blinds. The foliage of the rooftop garden was in silhouette against the fading light in the sky. There was a low light presence in the Martin residence. There was little traffic on the road, except for the occasional passing taxi or bus or car, but nothing happening in the entrance area. He closed the zip of his jacket all the way to his throat and held himself tight for a moment. The temperature had dropped a few degrees in a short space of time. The chill had him wishing he had put on a warm pullover under the fleece jacket.

This was perhaps the time of evening when some of the residents might take a walk in the park, but there was no suggestion that the Martins would emerge, assuming they were at home. That wasn't looking favourite at the moment.

The trees stretching over the wall by the park side were still full of leaves. With the days of October not too far away it wouldn't be too long before they began to turn from green to amber, then the shade of burnt orange.

He turned on his iPhone and saw that he had missed two calls, one from Jenny and one from Cal Martin. He elected not to return their calls right now.

The half-light coming from their apartment looked to be from a lampstand in the lounge-sitting room. Maybe neither of them were at home. He didn't know what he was likely to see. Samantha Martin in a low cut, short dress on her way to meet a client? He doubted that very much. She didn't look the type to flaunt herself like a common everyday escort on her way to meet a client in a West-End hotel, but he didn't know the type. Escorts came in all shapes and sizes. Every creed and colour, though most of the high earners would be in the twenty-two to twenty-eight age range. He guessed.

The glass front entrance door came open and a couple emerged walking a boxer type dog on the end of a long leash. They were dressed appropriately for the chill in the air. The door closed before Moss was able to get there, but he didn't want to get inside, not yet. Anyway, what would be the point? He didn't want to invade their flat or anything like that. What would he say to him or her? He couldn't say something on the lines of: *Hi, Sam. Do you know your husband manages the appointments of a group of girls who act as escorts to lonely gentlemen who are looking to cop off with a bird?*

He hung around the front of the block for twenty minutes. When he thought he had outstayed his welcome and was beginning to feel too conspicuous and on edge he walked the two hundred yards onto the road he had parked his car.

As he plunked into the driver's seat, his phone pinged at him. It was another incoming call from Cal Martin. He hit the accept button and lodged the mouthpiece close to his lips.

"Hi," he said as a way of introduction.

"Who are you?" Cal enquired. Moss felt like saying 'your worst nightmare', but didn't. He said nothing. "Isabel never received your call," said Cal Martin.

"That's true."

"What do you want?"

"I would have liked to have met her, but I had cold feet right at the death. I guess I'm not cut out for these things."

"What things?"

"Meeting escorts in hotel lobbies."

Cal didn't reply, but neither did he ring off. He kept the line open as if he was expecting him to reveal who he was. He took a short-controlled intake of breath. "You mentioned the name Samantha," he said.

"Your wife, Samantha. Does she know you launder money through the flower shop? Six Red Roses. Not big amounts though, granted."

"Who are you?" he asked again.

"A private detective." Cal said nothing. "What makes a professional footballer turn to helping out a few small-time criminals to launder their scam cash through a small business?" He didn't reply. "A gambling debt? A skeleton in your cupboard? Does Sam know?"

"Leave her out of it."

"Out of what? Does she know? Or alternatively she doesn't care because she loves you too much?" Cal stayed mute. "I'm quite prepared to give you a heads-up."

"Like what?"

"The cops are aware of the scam with the illegal migrants working for peanuts then having money taken from them. Is Sam happy for you to do this? Does she know you're in debt to some south London crims? If I was you, I'd stop doing this! It's only that the figures are so small that the cops don't think it's worth doing anything, but if the figures change that might change. It might be a few months, a few weeks or a few days before they pull you in for questioning. The escort business might be a different kettle of fish. It's nothing illegal. Consenting adults. Do you also launder the kickbacks through the flower shop? Be careful Cal. I'd be gutted if I lost a wife like Samantha Farlow." Cal didn't reply. "So long," said Moss then he terminated the call.

He immediately thought about calling Jacqui Brodie to request that she call in to see him. With the time fast approaching 10 p.m. he decided to hold fire and wait until tomorrow morning. He started his car, slipped away from the kerb and drove home to Knightsbridge.

# Chapter Six

Sunday was one of those damp, late September days that smell of wet earth and the approaching autumn to come. Everyone had to get used to it. The short-lived Indian summer which had seen record warmth in the first two weeks of the month was well and truly over. Colder chilly nights were ahead.

Moss decided to leave it until 1pm to contact Jacqui Farlow-Brodie. He got through to her within ten seconds of hearing the dialling tone at her end. He didn't waste any time with idle, banal chit-chat. He informed her that he had reached the end of his investigation and that he was now going to write a report of his findings. He would present it to her and her sister as soon as they were able to meet with him at a place of their own choice. He didn't want to discuss what he had discovered over the telephone and neither did she ask him to.

She immediately told him she and her sister would be with him in three hours from now in his office. He said fine. He looked forward to seeing them later. It would be exactly four days to the minute when they had visited him to tell him of their concerns.

As soon as he put the telephone into the cradle he began to work on a two-thousand-word report that detailed what he had discovered. He rewrote it a few times, settled on a final version, then wrote a shorter version in an executive summary with bullet points. It was complete by two o'clock. He left his office to take a walk onto, close by, Dean Street to visit an eatery. He had a coffee and a slice of apple pie with cream, then returned to his office. He put in a call to Claudette to ask her if she wanted to meet with him this evening. She said okay. He wanted to take her to the restaurant in Brompton they liked. If he got lucky, he would stay the night at her place.

Jacqui and Amanda Farlow arrived promptly at four o'clock that afternoon. He heard the doorbell downstairs. He went down the staircase, opened the door, greeted them with a pleasant good-afternoon, then led them up the wooden hill. They were dressed as if they were going to one of the auction houses in Mayfair to attend a sale of artwork and etchings by some famous 18th century English artist. They were in smart Christian Dior jackets and matching skirts. Both of them had their hair up and held in place by silver coated grips.

It was nearly exactly four days, to the minute, since they had last graced his office with their presence. There was the smell of a cafeteria of fresh ground coffee bubbling on a hot plate in the kitchen area. They came into the small space and sat in the two round back armchairs he had placed in front of his desk. He sat down in the swivel seat with his back to the open slats of the blinds over the window. He smiled as he took the six-page report he had prepared and placed one each, for them, on the edge of the desk.

He opened it to the first page. Over the course of the next six or seven minutes he read the findings detailed in the executive summary. He told them that, in his opinion, Calvin Martin didn't exhibit any coercive influence over their sister. What he did tell them was that Martin was likely to be involved with a gang of relatively low-level, south London criminals who had something over him, and used him and the flower shop to launder money. If that didn't come as a shock. He informed them that Martin was also involved in the running of an escort agency that supplied ladies of easy virtue to clients, rich or otherwise, who were willing to pay their dates the going amount for such services.

He suggested this could be the reason why Samantha chose not to converse with her sisters. She was simply too embarrassed to admit that her husband was on the edge of something dodgy. Whilst she may not have been frightened to inform on him, she was fearful of the reaction she could receive from her sisters. Therefore, she chose to bottle it up.

There was no reason to suggest that she was in anyway connected to either the money laundering or the sexploitation angle.

What the sisters now chose to do with the information was up to them. It was their call. There was nothing to say that Martin was breaking any law with regard to the escort service. It wasn't something he would want people to know about. If the escorts were not being coerced or forced to do something they didn't want to do, then there was nothing to suggest any exploitation or the breaking of any anti-slave laws was taking place.

He handed the sisters each a copy of the report. They left thirty minutes after arriving. Jacqui gave him a cheque for £2,250. His fee.

In truth, he hoped that Calvin Martin would heed his advice and end his association with the group of criminals. It might only be a matter of time before he was pulled in for questioning.

Moss had no idea what Martin would do, or if his marriage to Samantha would survive a crisis. He couldn't talk for anyone nor would he offer an opinion on Calvin's character or make a judgement call.

As soon as the Farlow sisters departed, he took a walk onto the street then to a local watering hole, called the Lord Nelson public house, to meet with Bob Ambrose. Moss handed him two hundred pounds in cash for the information he had provided. After all, the list of telephone numbers had given him the breakthrough he required to crack the case.

It was done. It was over. He had a couple of beers with his former colleague and they spent a couple of hours chewing the cud and going down memory lane. He got the impression the sisters were disappointed with the outcome. He couldn't make up false stories to satisfy their need to have the outcome they desired. At the end of the day, it was what it was. Whatever that meant.

The End

# In a New York Minute

Chapter One.

Sometimes in life, things come at you with an element of a massive surprise. Take this on board as the perfect example. After a dearth of jobs over the past couple of months Moss had two in a short period of time. One week after the conclusion of the Samantha Farlow-Martin investigation he received a call from a chap calling himself Hector Monserrat. The client wanted Moss to travel across the pond to New York City to collect two items from a literary agency. They were a manuscript and a hard drive device. Both had to be in London in one week from now.

    To emphasise that he was deadly serious about the timeframe, he, Monserrat, agreed to pay him two thousand pounds for the task, but also to pay his travel and hotel expenses to a maximum of two and a half thousand pounds. He was most insistent that Moss had to be in Manhattan next Tuesday morning to collect both a packet containing the hard-physical manuscript and an external hard drive device. The items could be collected from an address in an office tower block at 845 x 5$^{th}$ Avenue in Manhattan. They had to be here in London two days later on the Thursday at 12 noon. Precisely one week from today. The literary office in Manhattan was the New York office of 'Hector Monserrat Literary Agency'. The agency also had an office in London on Bond Street. One in Los Angeles, and a fourth in Berne, Switzerland.

    Monserrat was most adamant that he didn't want anyone else to collect the items other than a fully qualified and hard-bitten private detective who had the wherewithal to look after himself. He didn't trust one of his staff not to get robbed on the streets of the Big Apple.

    Moss had been to New York City on three previous occasions. Once when he attended an Interpol conference for his then employer, the London Metropolitan Police Service. Twice as an everyday tourist visiting the must-see sights. Though he had never been there in October, he guessed New York at this time of the year was the same as London. Changeable and potentially warm, but also cool.

New York City was one of those places he liked, but wouldn't say it was his favourite choice for a city break. That was reserved for Berlin for which he had a great fondness. Though he would admit that he hadn't visited every tourist place on the planet. Far from it. He wasn't that well-travelled. If the truth be told he tended to favour visiting European countries because he would never have much of a problem with the language barrier. In all seriousness, he wasn't that adventurous when it came to travel.

The client for this job, the seventy-two-year-old Hector Monserrat, was the owner of a literary agency that had a few well-known authors for clients. He described the device Moss had to collect as a hard drive in a zip-up container about the size of a rolled fist. The device was currently in safe keeping in the Manhattan office. The packet contained three hundred pages of a manuscript. Moss had to collect both items at precisely ten o'clock on Tuesday morning and bring it back to London, safe and sound.

An all-expenses paid trip to the US east coast was all the doctor ordered, though he wouldn't be in the city for long. From landing to leaving it would be all of forty-eight hours. Hardly enough time to visit Central Park never mind the other attractions. He had to be back in London on Thursday at noon, therefore no time for sightseeing.

Hector Monserrat never did explain why the manuscript couldn't be attached to an email and downloaded in seconds. Obviously, he had his reasons why someone had to go and collect it. Perhaps he feared the communication would be infiltrated or hijacked and the content of the file stolen by a competitor. He preferred to have the hard-drive physically device and manuscript in his hands.

Moss wasn't complaining. He met with the client in his Bond Street office, heard the details of the assignment, and received a banker's cheque for four and a half thousand pounds up front. Therefore, it must have been important to the client. Monserrat had also handed him a letter of introduction on company headed paper to give to the manager of the New York office, a chap by the name of Morton Frankel, as a way of ensuring he gave the items to the right person.

After hearing what Monserrat had to say, Moss accepted the assignment. As soon as he left Monserrat's office, he visited a travel bucket shop on the nearby Piccadilly to book a flight from Heathrow to Newark, New Jersey, in five days from now, Monday and a two-night stay in a four-star Manhattan hotel on East 26$^{th}$ street.

From Newark Liberty airport he would take the New Jersey Transit train to Penn Station, then a short taxi ride to the hotel. He had it all worked out in no time. He just about knew Manhattan well enough to know he wouldn't get lost or drift into the wrong area. Just follow the street and avenue numbers and you always had a good idea if you were either downtown, midtown, or uptown and in which direction to go. It was that simple.

Chapter Two.

The time of his arrival in the Big Apple was at 3pm Monday, east coast time. He soon made it to the hotel on East 24$^{th}$ street, close to the junction with 3$^{rd}$ avenue, checked in, went to his room, put his clothes away, then crashed onto the bed and caught up on some sleep. New York City in the first week in October was pleasant. It didn't have the stinging humidity of the summer heat, nor the debilitating cold of the winter months when the temperature could plummet to freezing. On a previous visit to the city, in the middle of March, when he had been here on police business it had snowed solidly for most of the two days.

The first day was pleasant. The sun was shining, and it was warm out of the shade. That was until the sun began to sink at around 6pm, when it became chilly. The 'Regency Hotel' on East 24$^{th}$ was typical New York chic. The front was Renaissance style with many windows and a solid decorative block. The interior decoration was fancy and kitsch. The majority of the clientele were tourists who were paying over inflated prices for what was a pretty standard hotel.

Tomorrow, he would go uptown in a taxi to 845 x 5$^{th}$ Avenue, visit the office of Hector Monserrat Associates in suite 1258, which he assumed was suite 58 on the 12$^{th}$ floor. Or maybe it was the other way around.

Later that Monday evening he stayed close to the hotel and visited an English theme pub bar at the junction of 24$^{th}$ and 3$^{rd}$ avenue for a few beers and a plate of wings. He spent much of the time watching Monday Night football on the large tv screens hugging the walls.

The following morning, Tuesday, Moss went down for breakfast at 6.30am, spent an hour in the dining room, then returned to his room. His body clock was still on UK time, so he had been wide awake since around 3am.

It was close to 9am, local, when he stepped out of the hotel, turned right onto 24th street and ambled down the street to the junction with 4th Avenue. He crossed the road to the other side, in the same direction as the traffic, and began walking uptown. He was still a little unaware that he was in Manhattan. It might take a few hours to sink in. The jetlag was still in his body, so his senses were nullified to a degree. As he set off, he looked forward to the towers in Midtown, he could make out the old, wide 'Pam Am' building, now renamed the 'MetLife' looming high across the backdrop.

By the time he had reached the junction with 32nd street the time had raced around to nine-twenty. He stepped to the kerb and raised his hand to flag down a cruising yellow cab. A taxi with its light on soon appeared and pulled into the kerbside. He climbed into the back and asked the driver to take him to 845 x 5th Avenue, which he knew was in a block sandwiched between 44th and 45th streets, right in the heart of busy Midtown.

The taxi driver veered off down 33rd street, then took a right onto 5th avenue and drove north through the canyons with the huge steel and glass skyscrapers soaring for seemingly miles into the white cloud filled sky. Delivery vans were parked into the kerbsides and operatives were emptying the backs of the vehicles. Buses, taxis, cars, vans, trucks and limos jostled for space. Horns blared and provided the quintessential Manhattan soundtrack, but at least the traffic was moving fairly freely. Sitting on the rear seat of the cab, Moss began to reminisce about all the iconic movies that were set in this setting. Particularly those in the 1980s, 1990s and later such as 'Goodfellas', and 'Carlito's Way', to name just two. Ironically, many of those films were actually filmed in other cities, such as Toronto. Moss had been to Toronto on a few occasions. He couldn't, for the life of him, see the resemblance between the streets of downtown Toronto and Manhattan. Clearly someone with authority in the production department could, and that's all there was to it.

The office block at 845 x 5$^{th}$ avenue was a typical glass and steel midtown high-rise tower. Probably fifty plus floors high, but by no means the tallest on the avenue. It was a combination of both office space and some residential apartments. The entrance was a double glass enclosed doorway, sandwiched in between a row of small to medium stores, underneath a wide canopy that stretched across the path to the lip of the kerbside. There was a baseball concession store on one side, partially hidden under the overhead canopy, and a Disney store on the other. A line of Stars and Stripes flags were fluttering from the top of the parapet over the sidewalk. As the taxi pulled in, a FDNY fire truck came rushing by. Its heavy bull horn working overtime. There were plenty of people walking on the sidewalk. With the time now close to five to ten the morning rush hour was starting to reduce, but there were still people heading to their place of work.

Moss had had a topsy-turvy night's sleep. His neck had a rick caused by an overstuffed pillow, or the constant blast of cold air coming out of the overhead AC unit. He was wearing a simple blue shirt under a button-up jacket and dark easy-fit trousers. The letter of introduction given to him by the client, Hector Monserrat, was lodged in the inside jacket pocket.

He entered the building through the revolving glass door and into the interior of the lobby. It had a kind of blush-orange colour scheme, a white tile floor and a simulation marble slate covered walls. Nothing too over-the-top in the way of embellishment, but for some abstract, colour splashed artwork attached to the walled surface. There was a long counter at which several people dressed in a pale blue security guard uniform were standing checking the credentials of those making their way towards the bank of three elevators. Everyone who worked in the building had to use a credit card size 'Swipe & Enter' pass which allowed them to gain entry through the barriers. A notice on the wall advised visitors they had to report to the security desk before they were allowed through the barrier that led to the elevators.

Moss placed himself in a short queue of four people who were lined up at the counter. As he reached the top of the line, he withdrew the letter of introduction, given to him by Hector Monserrat, opened it and passed it to a tall, nice looking young dark-skinned chap.

"I've got an appointment to see a chap called Morton Frankel at ten in the suite of Hector Monserrat Associates. Perhaps you can tell me which floor is suite one, two, five, eight on? I'm not sure," he asked.

"That's the twelfth," he replied in a blunt downbeat tone. He examined the letter, fleetingly, handed it back to him without smiling and waved him through the barrier.

Moss went through the barrier and aimed for the middle of the three elevators. The lift was on the $6^{th}$ floor and heading down to the $1^{st}$ floor, which happened to be the ground floor. There was no ground floor in Manhattan office tower blocks.

As the elevator door opened, he stepped into the car along with five other people. The button for that floor was already illuminated. Someone else was also heading to the $12^{th}$ floor. The door soon closed, and the car began its ascent up the lift shaft.

The first stop was the $7^{th}$ floor, then it stopped again on the $9^{th}$, then the $10^{th}$. Three people got out. Nobody got in. That just left him, another younger male and an elderly lady. He glanced at his watch. The time was now two minutes after ten. He was two minutes behind schedule.

When the car stopped on the $12^{th}$ floor, he stepped to a side to let the lady out first, then stepped out onto the landing. On a grey-blanch wall directly opposite was a laminated notice pointing in the direction to take. Left for suites 1201 to 1232, inclusive, right for suites 1233 to 1260.

He turned right. The lady who had also alighted on the twelfth went in the opposite direction.

The corridor wasn't that wide, but wide enough for four people to pass each other with just a narrow section of space down the centre. The surface was carpeted with thin carpet tiles in a brown shade. The walls were plain white-grey. Picture frames were attached at intervals of every ten yards or so displaying a variety of colourful splashes of colour. Much like the artwork in the foyer. He passed a chap, wearing a shirt and tie and business suit, walking hurriedly in the other direction – a briefcase in his grip. They passed within a couple of feet of each other.

There wasn't a standout fragrance, and neither was there much in the way of sound, but for the whine of an AC unit embedded in the ceiling. It blew a waft of cold air along the corridor. He passed the single door entrances to suites numbered 1233 to 1252. Odd numbers on the left, even on the right side.

At the end of the corridor was a second direction finder, pointing left or right. Suites 1253 to 1255 to the left. Numbers 1256 to 1260 to the right. He turned to the right and soon came at a solid plain teak wood door to suite 1258. The words: 'Hector Monserrat Associates' was ingrained into the surface and white letters against the brown veneer background.

He had made it. The time was four minutes after ten. He raised his hand and gave the door a solid tap. He could feel the sharp points of the letter of introduction lodged in his inside jacket pocket. He took it out and held it tight.

It was around twenty seconds before the door was opened by a cherub-faced girl who appeared to be in her mid-twenties. She seemed to be slightly animated and took a step back at the sight of a visitor. Almost as if she was on the end of a taut elastic band. She was wearing a burgundy-coloured jumper over pink leggings. Behind her was the interior of an open room which had book shelves along both sides and a variety of hardback books on display on a central, circular mahogany topped table that also held a curvy shape vase containing imitation daffodils. Beyond the table was a sliding frosted glass door which was open six inches to reveal a space into a larger room. A splash of natural light was beaming in from the left. The young lady looked at Moss expectedly. Her eyes were a study in concentration. She must have been wondering who the hell he was.

"Can I help you?" she asked in a local accent. Almost as if she believed he had knocked on the door seeking directions to the nearest bathroom.

He unfolded the letter of introduction in his hand and gestured for her to take it out of his hand. The one given to him by no less a person then the owner of the agency. She seemed reluctant to take it. He thrust it in her direction. "I've come to collect the storage device and a packet containing a manuscript for Mr Monserrat in your London office. I'm David Moss," he said. "That is my letter of introduction." She didn't appear to react in any way or in any shape to his British accent.

Her face went from one of concentration to one of eyes screwed confusion. Just then there was movement in the space behind her and an average build, plump, balding chap appeared in the opening at the sliding door. He was wearing a plain open neck white shirt and dark shiny stay-press trousers. His stomach hung over the rim of the belt holding up his trousers. He looked on to observe the unknown visitor and saw his colleague take the letter, open it and read the content.

"But," she said hesitantly.

"But what?"

"There must be some mistake," she said.

"Mistake? Such as?" Moss asked in an appropriate tone.

"Someone with this same letter has already been to collect the items. Not two minutes ago."

Moss expressed puzzlement. "What? Who?" he asked.

The man came forward to join them. He took the letter from his colleague and read the content. "He said he was David Moss," she said.

"I'm Moss. That's me."

"What?" the chap asked while still running his eyes over the content of the letter.

"I'm David Moss," he repeated.

The man folded the letter closed. His face was serious and drawn. "Someone has already been to collect them," he said in a tone of utter confusion. His stiff face was still bathed in quandary. "Said he'd been sent by Mister Monserrat in the London office."

"Who was he?"

"I don't know. Said he was you."

"I'm Moss."

"He said the same."

"I'm the one who was told to come here."

"There must be some mistake," the chap uttered.

"No mistake. There's my letter," said Moss gesturing to it with a point of a finger. "What did he take?"

"The packet containing the manuscript and external hard drive about…" he made a shape with his hands… "six by four inches in size. In a proactive hard back container."

"I was supposed to collect them on behalf of Mr. Monserrat."

"He said the same thing." He explained. The chap spoke with a Brooklyn edge and in a tone that was marginally wheezy and weary.

The girl turned to him and looked on as he poured his eyes over the letter for a second time. He looked at Moss. "The guy who got here first had the exact same letter. He took the case packet containing the hard drive and the manuscript. I gave it to him not three minutes ago."

"So, you keep saying. You were supposed to give it to me. Have you got another copy?"

"No."

"Did this person speak with a British accent?"

"Sure did. Just like you."

"What did he look like?"

"Not a lot different from you. Maybe a bit younger. A bit taller."

"Was he wearing a dark suit, white shirt and tie? Maybe late twenties or early thirties?" Moss asked.

"Yes."

It seemed as if it could have been the hurrying chap he had passed on the corridor. Moss was in two minds about running out to try and find the guy, but he could be well gone by now. He was in a quandary over what had happened. He was still finding it difficult to grasp that someone who said he was him had been here and taken the packet he was supposed to collect.

He glanced at his watch. The time was now twelve minutes past ten. It would be ten past three in the afternoon in London. "Can I use your telephone to make a call," he requested.

"To whom?"

"To your boss in London. To tell him what's going on."

The plump chap glanced at the girl, who looked at him and they shared a grim stony face. "Err, yes. Be my guest," he said. "Good idea. Follow me. This way."

Moss stepped away from door, into the room, around the central table, through the partition and deeper into the next room. He followed the chap along a corridor and into another smaller office which had a window looking down eleven floors onto a side street. The room had a desk, a couple of chairs and a sofa. Two close-up photographs of someone who might have been Ernest Hemingway were side by side on one of the walls. It was quiet but for a hum of the AC unit blowing warm air into the space.

The chap went behind the desk to the telephone unit. He lifted the receiver and pressed several digits. "That will get you straight through to our London office."

Moss took the receiver and put it to his mouth. He could hear it ringing at the other end. It rang for thirty seconds or thereabouts before it was answered.

A London accent said, 'The Hector Monserrat Agency.'

"Mr. Monserrat, please. Quickly."

"He's not at his desk at the moment. He's gone out on business."

"Can I leave him a message?"

"Sure."

"It's David Moss. Tell him that someone pretending to be me, got here first and took the packet I was supposed to collect from your Manhattan office."

"Tell him what?" asked the voice down the line. "I didn't catch some of that."

"What did you catch."

"Not a lot."

"Tell him it's David Moss calling from your New York office. Someone got here before me and has taken the packet Mr Monserrat hired me to collect. I'll be in my hotel room at the Regency Hotel on east 24$^{th}$ street in about forty minutes from now, should he want to contact me there. He's got my contact details."

"Who are you?" asked an upper crust Surrey accent.

"Dave Moss. I'm the chap Mister Monserrat paid to collect the packet from your New York office."

"Okay," the person said as if he had no idea what he was talking about.

"I'm staying at the Regency hotel. I'll be in my room in about thirty minutes time. Room eighty-three. I suggest you ask him to give me a call as soon as he can. I'm also on my mobile. He's got my number."

The chap asked for the number, just in case. Moss obliged, then he thumped the phone down with an impatience thud then reached out and took the letter of introduction out of the plump man's hand. The girl in the pink leggings looked on.

Before he walked out, he told Morton Frankel and the young lady where he was staying. With little cooperation and even less concern they didn't appear to be all that concerned. As if they suspected Moss, was the one who was pretending to be the real deal. Or in other words a fake.

# Chapter Three

**M**oss turned away and walked out of the office, threading the introduction letter back into the jacket pocket as he stepped through the door, onto the corridor and headed back along the landing. He couldn't begin to explain what had happened, but there wasn't a lot to explain. Someone had got here before him. Clearly something wasn't right. It dripped in intrigue and deceit. He felt as if he had his tail firmly rammed between his legs. He had been done, for the want of a better word.

He retraced his steps to the elevator. The fact that the client hadn't been in the office to receive his call also didn't fit well with his mood. Something didn't smell right. But what?

He rode the elevator down to the first floor alone, stepped out, went through the barrier, and across the foyer floor towards the double door then out into the hustle and bustle of 5$^{th}$ Avenue. He stepped out from underneath the overhead parapet, close to the edge of the sidewalk and looked up to see the sunlight reflecting in the face of the huge skyscrapers in this part of Midtown.

The sound of the traffic, the bleep of car horns and the smell of vehicle exhaust fumes filled the senses. He lost his orientation for a second and turned right along the sidewalk instead of left, quickly realised his mistake, stopped and turned back in a downtown direction.

When he was about fifty yards along the sidewalk, his mobile phone sounded. To get off the street and out of the noise he had to dodge into a store entrance to take the call. It was Hector Monserrat calling from London. He sounded virtually mute, listless and speaking in a kind of monotone voice.

"What the hell happened?" he asked. Just those four simple words.

"I didn't get the packet. Someone pretending to be me got here first. Someone knew I was going to be there at this time. Someone was ready and waiting to impersonate me."

Monserrat didn't reply. Moss didn't know if he had dropped out. "You still there?" he asked.

No reply. Moss waited for another twenty seconds with the phone still lodged to his ear, but there was no sound from the other end. He gave up on Monserrat and snapped the phone closed. He walked out of the store entrance and carried on in a southerly direction. He moved out of the dark shadows to the edge of the road, but opted to walk further rather than hail a passing taxi, just yet.

He swiftly made it to the junction of $5^{th}$ avenue and $42^{nd}$ street, turned right and sauntered by the side of the New York library building, then along the edge of Bryant Park. Behind him in the gap between the tall buildings he could make out the top of the Chrysler Building with its flamboyant rococo design summit. The light was reflecting in the overlapping tear drop pattern. He felt fatigued and his mind numb. The jet lag was still in his system. It would probably be with him until the time he was due to board the return flight to London at seven-thirty tomorrow evening.

At the junction with $6^{th}$ avenue he crossed over to the other side of the road and walked down to the start of $41^{st}$ street. Stepping to the edge of the kerb he paused and raised his hand in an effort to attract a cruising yellow cab.

The time was ten-thirty. The morning was sunny with horizon-to-horizon blue sky, but chilly in the shade and the shadow of the skyscrapers. It was about a minute or so before a cab appeared and pulled to a halt to let out a passenger, Moss swiftly edged forward, slid onto the rear seat and took her place. He asked the driver to take him to the junction of $4^{th}$ Avenue and East $24^{th}$ street. He was heading back to his hotel to wait for a call from Hector Monserrat should he choose to call him. There was no guarantee he would do that, for a reason that as yet wasn't obvious to him.

It took the cabbie less than ten minutes to drop him off on the corner of 24th street and 4th avenue, right outside a Starbucks coffee outlet on the corner. He walked the final one hundred yards to the Regency Hotel and entered into the darkened lobby, then through the vestibule, past the front desk and around a corner to the bank of two elevators that served the eighty or so rooms on twenty floors. The inside of the hotel was cool. A blast of cold air from an overhead fan, caught flush him in the face. The smell of cooking food coming from the adjoining restaurant wafted up his nostrils to make his mouth water.

As he reached forward to the side of the elevator to press the call button he was aware of two guys casually sliding up to him with the guile and presence of silent assassins. One stood to one side of him, the second at the other side. It looked as if they were together. Both were wearing henchman type dark suits, shirts and ties and stout shoes. They didn't resemble hotel guests or staff. This wasn't a business travellers' type of hotel. This was a tourist hotel. The spread of languages he had heard earlier in the dining room, told him it was the place in which airlines pilots and crew, and tourists from Europe would use. He had heard French, Italian and German voices during breakfast, plus a few other languages he didn't recognise.

These two were silent. Moss glanced to one side, made eye contact with one of them and gave him a three-quarter strong smile and a nod of the head. Both of them were in the thirty to thirty-five age range. Both were over five-ten in stature and both were slim and athletic looking.

The car was on the eighth of the twenty floors. It wasn't a new building therefore the car wasn't the quickest in the world. Before it reached the ground floor three other people emerged from around the corner and joined the three waiting. Moss let out a shallow breath. Two of the newcomers were babbling in a language that sounded French. They were carrying brown paper Macy's bags. Moss felt marginally relieved. The two men could have been genuine hotel guests. Maybe he was getting ahead of himself. The third person was on her own.

The car came down from the eight floor and was at the ground in less than ninety seconds. As it arrived a bell sounded, and the door slid open with a hydraulic 'siss' to reveal the inside of the car with its light coffee shade and semi-transparent roof.

Moss was in first, followed by the two suited men, then the French couple who were still chatting, then the single lady. Moss reached over to a side and hit the 12$^{th}$ floor button in the panel of buttons. The French chap did likewise with the 7$^{th}$ button, the other three didn't do anything. Moss was put on edge by this omission. He considered getting out with the French couple on the 7$^{th}$ floor, then using the emergency staircase to walk up to the 12$^{th}$ floor.

The lift door closed, and the car began its ascent. The Macy's 'Little Brown bag' the French lady was carrying brushed against Moss's jacket. He smiled at her and she smiled back. The two men in suits were standing to the rear, almost resting against the solid brass handrail along the back panel. The third person, a lady in her sixties was to Moss's side. The bulbs in the overhead panel flickered momentarily. The sound of the motor filled the silence.

The car was soon at the 5$^{th}$, then the 6$^{th}$ floor. The two French people were preparing to exit on the 7$^{th}$ floor. The car reduced speed, came to a stop on that floor and the doors slid open. Moss thought what the hell, he elected to stay put. If the two men wanted to confront him then so-be-it. He might learn something from them. The two French people and the single lady stepped out onto a tangerine-amber and black coloured pattern carpet. A laminated notice on the wall opposite said: 7$^{th}$ Floor.

The door closed with a solid clump and the car set off with a slight shudder. Moss felt the urge to say something crass like 'which floor are you guys on,' but chose to say nothing.

The car sailed by the 8th, 9th and 10th floors. The two guys behind him were silent and hardly moved a muscle. He could see their shapes reflected in the sheen of the metal door in front of him.

The car was soon on the 11th floor. It sailed by that floor and was now slowing down as it prepared to stop on the 12th.. There was no movement from behind. They weren't here to harm him. He had been getting ahead of himself, as usual. As the car slowed, then stopped, a bell sounded, and the doors began to slide open from left to right. Moss, his head down, stepped forward onto the orange and black pattern carpet, then turned to his left only to see a blur of a fist swinging towards him. He took a sucker punch straight to the jaw that came at him at a swift pace. The blow knocked him off balance. Before he knew it, his legs collapsed from under him and he was on the deck. The attack was as vicious as it was sudden. Stars danced in front of his eyes and a weird scent rushed up his nostrils. The two men in the car, accomplices of the person who had attacked him, rushed out and pinned him by the shoulders to the carpet. The one who had hit him swiftly bent over him, reached down and began to pat him down in a professional manner, as if he had done it many-many times before.

"You Moss?" he asked. Moss could feel that his jaw had been dealt a blow that had caused his back teeth to bite a chunk out of his tongue. The chap, leaning over him, was a big white man with a large head and thick arms, though it was hard to be precise because Moss was laid on his back looking up at him from an unnatural position.

"What?" he asked.

"You're Moss," said one of the two who had been in the car. "Aren't you?"

"Yeah. Who are you? The tooth fairy?" He replied without knowing why.

"Less of the funnies. Where's the packet?"

Moss sought to pull himself up, but was prevented from doing so when one of the guys placed his foot on his chest and forced his shoulders down.

"What package?"

"The one you were paid to collect."

"I didn't get it. Someone got there before me and took it." He could feel blood in his mouth, leaking from the cut to his tongue, along with an ache in his jaw.

One of the trio snorted then cursed a word Moss didn't hear clearly. The man reached down and ran his hands over his torso to feel for a concealed packet. He didn't find one. Moss, though stunned by the attack, was beginning to come around. The chap towering over him completed the search. "He ain't got it," he snarled at the other two.

Just then there was a sound of voices from further down the corridor, coming from around a corner. As if spooked by the sound the trio of attackers straightened themselves, then without any further delay they scurried away, to a door by the side of the elevator shaft and opened it. Moss knew that it led onto a stairwell that ran around the back of the lift shaft. They disappeared into the opening and were gone. Meanwhile, the close-by voices grew louder. Moss managed to turn and pull himself onto his side, then spin round, get onto his butt then sit up and rest his back against the side.

He put his eyes on the door to the stairway, which said: STAIRS – ONLY TO BE USED IN AN EMERGENCY. As he turned to look at the source of the voices two men appeared from around the corner. They instantly put their eyes on the chap sitting on the floor and came to a shuddering stop.

"God man. What happened to you?" Are you okay?" one of them asked. He was an American as was the chap with him. They were both in their late twenties and dressed as tourists in casual clothing. Jeans, warm jackets, baseball caps and stout footwear.

"You okay, man?" the second guy asked in an incongruous tone. Moss rubbed his jaw which was still throbbing from the punch that had floored him.

"I slipped and lost my balance," he said. "Nothing to worry about."

"Okay," one of them said as if he was relieved to hear that. Perhaps he thought he was under the influence of alcohol or some other substance.

The one who had asked him if he was okay held his hands out. Moss took them, and the chap helped to pull him up onto his feet. Moss propped himself up against the wall. "I think I had a funny turn," he said.

"You, okay?" the other one asked again.

"Yeah, think so," he replied, then nodded his head and shrugged his shoulders. "I'm fine. Thanks for your help. Thanks for asking."

"You Australian?" one of them asked.

"No. British."

"What room are you in?"

"Eighty-four."

"You want help to get there?"

"No thanks, I'll be okay."

"Okay, sure."

"I'm sure," Moss said, almost forcing a beaming smile at them. He ran a hand over his chin. "I just need a second to get my bearings." The two Americans watched him step away and head down the corridor to find his room. He dipped a hand into a back trouser pocket, found the slippery coated room key-card, took it out, felt its sharp edges and shiny surface in his fingers. He felt a buzz in his head and an ache in his back teeth. The chap had certainly hit him with a solid sucker punch. But why? The debate could begin as soon as he got into his room. The corridor was dim and in permanently shadow, but for the dull light in the overhead panels, along with a small trace of natural light coming from the end of the corridor to the right. He ambled down the corridor to the end and came to the door to his room.

He slid the pass card into the opening device, waited for the green light, took the handle, pushed it down and entered into his room.

He closed the door behind him, then made sure it was both bolted and chained, then he went by the door leading into the bathroom, then into the bigger wider bedroom, aimed for the Queen mattress and fell onto it. A combination of the shock of the attack and the fatigue in his body soon had him in a light, drowsy sleep.

## Chapter Four

**M**oss must have slept, on and off, for the next forty-five minutes. He woke up, disturbed by the sound of a horn on a fire engine on the street running parallel to the back of the hotel. The sound of a distant pneumatic drill on a construction site was the like that of a demented woodpecker repeatedly banging its beak into a tree trunk. He pulled himself off the mattress, headed into the bathroom, ran hot water into the basin, stripped off the top half of his clothing, then had a wash in hot soapy water. The shock of the attack was slowly working its way out of his system. Once he had dried himself with a fluffy white towel, he headed back into the room and sat in a seat by a desk and peered at his reflection in a mirror. The time by the digital clock on a bedside table said fifteen minutes after noon. The workmen with the drill had stopped for lunch.

    He sat back in the seat, raised his legs and rested them on the edge of the mattress. A couple of minutes went by before his thoughts were disturbed by the sound of the bedside telephone ringing. Maybe it was the desk clerk asking him if he was okay. Perhaps the two guys who had found him had reported seeing the guest in room eighty-four sitting on the floor having suffered some kind of a seizure.

    He got up, went around the bed, reached out and lifted the receiver out of the cradle. "Hello," he said. There was no reply. "Hello," he repeated.

    "Is that David Moss," asked an unfamiliar British voice from down the line.

    He stalled for a moment. "Who is it?" he asked.

    "Is that Dave Moss?"

    "Yes."

    "The packet."

    "Who is this?" he enquired.

    "A friend," replied the stranger in what Moss thought was an oddly termed reply.

"What about the packet."

"I collected it."

The voice sounded like a man in his thirties. He sounded streetwise, solid, educated and adroit.

"You collected it, so why are you calling me? What do you want from me?"

"You've got to know what happened there."

Moss took his words in. "There? Where?" he asked.

"In the New York office of Henri Monserrat."

"Have I?" he asked. "For your information, I've just had three men have a go at me. One of them whacked me with a sucker punch."

"Were they British?"

Moss had failed to register that the men had spoken with English accents until the caller asked him the direct question. "Yeah. You know, come to think of it, they were."

"I thought so."

"What's going on?"

"If you want the truth, you were the decoy in all of this." The stranger said in his polished London accent.

"A decoy for what? For whom?"

"For me."

"Why?"

"For the contents in the packet."

"I've got no idea what you're talking about. And no idea what the hard drive contained."

"Sensitive information."

"Why, if you've got it, are you telling me?"

"Good question. Just that it's because I didn't collect it either."

"I'm not with you."

"I collected the packet, but I've since discovered it's empty of anything."

"What is that supposed to mean?"

"It means I have also been short changed."

"What was on it? I guess you know the answer."

"The memories of a person who worked for a Wall Street financier who had connections to Jeffery Ellis and some senior establishment type figures in the UK."

"I'm still not with you. You're not making much sense."

"I'll explain it to you. Can you meet with me in two hours from now?"

"Why?"

"So, I can tell you what should have been in the manuscript and on the hard-drive device."

"Tell me now."

"I'd prefer speaking to a face, not down a phone line."

Moss waited for a moment to assess his words. He had no idea where this was heading. He thought about it for a long ten seconds. "Okay. Fair enough. Where?"

"Do you know pier thirty-eight on the Upper East side."

"Yeah. I think I'll find it. Pier thirty-eight on the east side."

"It's from where the ferries going across the East River set off for the journey over to Queens. Meet me there by the rail looking onto the East River. 38th Street. Can you find it?"

"Yeah, I'll be there. At the pier at the end of 38th street?"

"Correct. At the eastern end of 38th street. In two hours from now. I make that two-thirty or thereabouts. Do you know it?"

"I'll find it."

"Good."

"All right. I'll see you there, but how will I know you?" Moss asked.

"I'll know you. See you then."

"Okay."

Before Moss could ask him how he knew to call this hotel in order to speak to him, the anonymous caller was gone. Maybe Hector Monserrat or the chap in the office, Morton Frankel, had told him. Maybe there was some truth in the fact that he had been employed as a decoy.

## Chapter Five

Moss arrived at pier thirty-eight at close to twenty-five past two. Despite the sunshine the air was cold, and a strong sharp tipped breeze was whipping up the surface of the East River. The swell bounced against the quayside with a fierce slapping motion that was strong enough to send a small amount of spray onto the path. The water had a dark green tint to it. The pier at 38th street stretched out about fifty yards into the river. Several ferries with their traditional yellow and black livery of the East River Ferry taxi service were moored to the pontoon. A ferry was about to set off on the quarter of a mile, or so, crossing to the spots on the Queens side of the river. Several seagulls swooped and hovered on the breeze. Two were standing on the top of a silver galvanised handrail of the metal pole fence that prevented people from toppling into the river.

Moss took in the scenery. He held himself tight, wishing he had put on a thicker jacket to the one he had selected when he set out from the hotel thirty minutes before. The ache in his jaw had long since gone. His back teeth did feel a little tender to the touch of his tongue and he had taken a bite out of his gum which felt swelled and twice the size it should have been. The attack had left him feeling a little vulnerable and tense, but it wasn't anything he couldn't handle. He parked himself on a bench overlooking the river with the pier just twenty feet away. He sat back in the hardback seat, stretched his legs and could just about rest the soles of his feet on the middle of the galvanised metal rails that formed a barrier between the path and the river. At his back was the sound of the traffic on the elevated section of FDR Drive which cut along the side of the river for several miles.

To his left was the structure of the Queensboro bridge and the southern tip of Roosevelt Island. On the right he could just make out the east side towers of both the Brooklyn and Manhattan bridges, but, from this angle, little of the actual spans. The tall but incredibly narrow building that was the United Nations headquarters wasn't that far along the riverside from this point. The number of high-rise apartment buildings on the Queens side of the river seemed to converge into one and emerge to create a barrier to the rest of the Queens skyline. The sunlight, though strained by gathering white cloud, was reflecting on the surface of the river like slashing silver blades.

Ten minutes drifted by. He was still on the bench with his legs resting on the rail. A group of tourists were taking photographs of the Queensboro bridge or the Manhattan skyline from advantage points along the pedestrian walkway which ran along the edge of the river. A gleaming leisure craft was gliding up the river, travelling in a south to north direction. Two people were visible, high up on the upper deck and shielded by a high windscreen in front of the area that must have contained the controls.

Moss glanced to a side as a single white male figure appeared in his eyeline. He was a tall, slender chap in his thirties. He was wearing a dark, motif sports type of coat over a suit. He sat down, at the other end of the bench. A couple of feet from him. Moss had seen him before. It was the same guy he had passed on the corridor on the 12th floor of the building at 845 x 5th Avenue.

"You must be Moss?" he enquired in a surreptitious tone.
"You must be the man on the telephone."
"That's right."
"You've got an advantage over me."
"How?"
"You know my name."
"Call me Steve if you want."
"Does Steve have a second name?"
"Steve…Kean."
"How are you doing, Steve Kean?"

"Not too bad."

"How did you know to contact me at the hotel?" Moss asked him.

"Hector Monserrat told me you were staying there."

"You've spoken to him."

"In the past couple of hours."

"How do you know I was a decoy?"

"Because it was me who set up the operation. I was even on the same flight as you coming over."

"What the hell is going on?"

"The plan was that I would impersonate you to collect the package containing both the manuscript and the storage device. You were the decoy."

"What is on the hard drive?"

"A manuscript that contains the memories of someone who worked for a Wall Street financer called, Jeffery Ellis."

"That Jeffery Ellis?"

"As far as I know there was only one. That person worked for him. She was his assistant for a while. She is the author of the manuscript."

"So, what's so important about what she wrote?"

"It's about her time with the financier. She has records detailing a lot of dodgy deals that he did with leading members of the British Royal family, plus various other establishment figures on both sides of the pond."

"Oh, my word. A kind of kiss and tell." He didn't reply. "So, what happened?"

"When I got the hard drive and plugged it into my laptop there was nothing on it. The manuscript was also empty."

"Who do you work for?" Moss asked.

"I'm employed by Hector to do things for him."

"What kind of things?"

"Like collecting packets."

"What kind of dodgy, high finance deals are we talking about here?"

"Ellis ran schemes. He said he could make rich people even richer than they already are. He invested the money in the stock markets and could guarantee a ten percent return on investment. The thing is it was nothing much more than a Ponzi scheme. It was never going to be successful unless he got an infinite number of investors. Which he didn't. He creamed money from the top in fees and made several millions of dollars."

"It's a pyramid scheme then?"

"Exactly. Those who got in early got their money back, plus a return. Those who came in too late lost their shirt. It was basically a scam. The US authorities were investigating him. The penalty could have been twenty years in a federal jail cell."

"So why the hiatus."

"Some prominent members of the British royals invested in it. They got their fingers burnt. If this became public knowledge it wouldn't look good for them. Who needs bad publicity in difficult economic times like these?"

"Not them. I guess."

"The assistant had access to all the records. She knew who had invested what. Thing is she wrote it all down in a manuscript."

"What's her name?"

"Rebecca DeMornie."

"Why would she write a book?"

"To make a great deal of money. I guess. She had access to all of his dealings and wrote the manuscript revealing all of his client's names and activities."

"Where does she live?" Moss asked.

"Here in Manhattan."

"I guess it wouldn't look good for the royals to be mixed up with a character like Jeffery Ellis"

"Exactly. But let's not get into the rights and wrongs of those caught up in the scam."

"Okay. Fair enough," Moss said. He had no wish to criticise the actions of those who had fallen victim to a clever confidence trickster. No matter who they were. "Tell me about Rebecca what's-her-name."

"DeMornie. She wrote a manuscript of around one hundred thousand words from the records she kept. She had first-hand knowledge of everyone who had passed through his hands. Hector Monserrat offered to buy the manuscript from her, then offer it to a number of British publishers and sell it to the highest bidder. That's why I came here to collect the hard drive and manuscript and to take them back to London with me."

Just then, a group of several people dressed in tourist garb came ambling by. They were heading onto the pier. One of the yellow and black vessels was cutting across the river. A horn on a barge blew out a loud repost. Someone in the group dropped an item of fast food onto the floor which was immediately bounced on by an alert seagull.

"I came to collect the packet. I showed them the same letter as you. I was ten minutes in front of you." Kean admitted.

"That's why Hector was so insistent that I got there at ten."

"Precisely."

"How come the drive was empty?"

"I guess the manager of the office, Frankel, either wiped it or gave me a dud."

"Why don't you got back and confront him?"

"Something tells me he's either sold it on for personal gain or the FBI or British intelligence have persuaded him to part with it."

"Why would three heavies, think I've got it?"

"Perhaps he told them he gave it to you as Monserrat had planned."

"All this talk of the FBI and British Intelligence is beginning to worry me. I didn't sign up for this." Kean didn't reply. "Tell me this," Moss continued. "Why are you telling me all this?"

"To keep you up to speed."

Moss doubted his sincerity. "Okay. But, why?"

"So, you'll help me"

"Help you do what exactly?"

"Visit the home of Rebecca DeMornie."

"Why?"

"To obtain a copy of the manuscript."

"What makes you think she'll have one."

"She must have kept a copy on her computer or some other storage device."

"But why should I help you when you've told me my role was as a decoy?" A seagull landed on top of the galvanised rail in front of them and just stood there gawping at them. It was a little spooky. It was almost as if it was here to listen in on their conversation, record it, then fly back to its handler. It hung about for ten seconds then flew away, squealing like crazy. "Why do you need me to accompany you to the home of the whistle blower?" Moss asked.

"For back up."

"From what?"

"Anyone hanging about. When I tell Monserrat, you helped me to get the document he'll be so pleased he'll agree to pay you extra."

"Where does she reside?" Moss asked.

"In an apartment in a house over on West 12$^{th}$ street. Just a stone's throw from Washington Square."

Moss had never been to Washington Square. Well couldn't recall ever been there. He tended to get it mixed up with Union Square, which, in truth, wasn't that far from Washington Square. He knew of a bar on Union Square, which he had frequented on a previous visit to New York.

"Do you agree to come with me?" Kean asked him directly.

"Why should I? I took a sucker punch to the jaw for you people. If it wasn't for two hotel guests coming along, I might have taken a few more."

"Occupational hazard," Kean said dryly.

"True," he begrudgingly admitted.

"We'll get to the bottom of it."

"Is that the royal we?"

"Might be."

"When did Rebecca DeMornie contact Hector Monserrat?"

"I guess, about six months ago."

"Who has seen the manuscript?"

"That I don't know. I would think the New York office worked on it for a while to get a few bugs out and to polish it into the finished gem."

"Who did the work? The manager chap. That Frankel fellow?"

"Probably him and his assistant."

"So, you want me to go with you to the home of this DeMornie lady to see if she's got a copy?"

"That's about the size of it. Go there first. If she doesn't have a copy, I'd have to go back to confront Frankel. I'd have no other option."

"In that case, I'll come with you."

"Thanks," he said. "I really appreciate it." Kean seemed eager to be going as soon as possible. He got up from the bench, stretched his legs and raised his hands above his head, then put his hands deep into the coat pockets. Moss had his doubts about this. Whether it was all genuine, but he had no way of knowing for sure. Big financial shenanigans involving seriously wealthy people was slightly out of his ballpark and his usual caseload. He could only assume that the chap who called himself Steve Kean was telling him the truth.

## Chapter Six

The pair of them stepped away from the pedestrian walkway close to the pier. They walked under the elevated section of FDR Drive, along 34$^{th}$ street then left onto 1$^{st}$ avenue for one hundred yards and into a district that was fringe Midtown. On 1$^{st}$ avenue Kean flagged down a cruising yellow cab. He asked the driver to take them downtown to the junction of west 12$^{th}$ street and 8$^{th}$ Avenue. It was in an area roughly designated as the beginning of Greenwich Village, and close to Washington Square.

It took around twenty-five minutes, after setting out and struggling through the mid-afternoon traffic, to get to the start of 12$^{th}$ street on 8$^{th}$ Avenue side, just south of Chelsea and the Meatpacking district. The cab driver turned onto 12$^{th}$ Street.

The thoroughfare leading up to Washington Square was a narrow tree-lined street with nice looking tightly packed homes converted into apartments on each side. Cars were parked along the right-hand side under trees that were shedding their leaves and dropping them into the rain-soaked gutter.

They hadn't travelled far along 12th street before they were stopped by a line of stationery vehicles ahead. They were told by the cab driver that the street was blocked by a number of police cars with their lights flashing. Indeed, up ahead there was evidence of an ambulance. Its alterative red and white lights were flashing out of the rear end. Clearly, there had been or was an ongoing live incident in one of the homes along the street. A few people, in groups of two and three were loitering on the sidewalk. The cab driver said something on the lines that he wasn't going to be able to get much further any time soon.

Moss had a distinct feeling that he wasn't ever going to meet Rebecca DeMornie. Kean suggested to him that they bail out here. He thrust a twenty-dollar bill through the gap in the glass partition between the driver and the rear. He told the driver they were getting out here. The driver had little option but to let them out.

Moss climbed out of the cab, stepped through a gap between two parked cars and onto the sidewalk right outside of number 64 west 12$^{th}$ Street. Kean soon joined him. They walked onward along the narrow tree-lined sidewalk. Passing numbers 62, then 60. The number of the building in which Rebecca DeMornie resided was 54.

Up ahead a group of people were standing, congregated on the path in a tight knit foursome. It looked as if they were in front of the steps that led up to the entrance of number 54. Moss counted three NYPD vehicles in a line on the street. He could hear the crackle of amplified sound coming from one of the police car radios, echoing against the wall of the three-storey buildings. The sun at three-fifteen was dipping over the rooftops so it left a wide shadow across the width of the street.

Moss turned his head to look at the person he knew as Steve Kean. "I think we've got here too late," he commented. Kean didn't reply. He was mute and looked apprehensive about what he would discover had happened to Rebecca DeMornie.

The horn from one of the cars in the line sounded and bounced down the street. Moss edged forward a few paces and came level with the steps leading to number 56. Outside, a young, light-skinned black man in a crisp shirt and tie and dark trousers was sitting on the second step from the bottom, observing what was going on.

"What's happened?" Moss asked him.

The chap glanced up at him. "Pardon me?"

"What's going on?" he repeated.

"Eh," the chap looked at Moss with a blank stare in his eyes. His brow was glistening with perspiration though it was hardly a warm day.

"What's going on?" Moss asked once again.

"Oh yeah. One of the residents in fifty-four's just been found dead," he said in a clear and strong voice.

"When?"

"I don't know. About fifteen minutes ago? I guess."

"Did she have a name?"

"What?"

"Does she have a name?"

"Not sure."

"Could it have been Rebecca DeMornie?"

"Yeah, that's it? Did you know her?"

"No, I didn't."

That chap looked at him with a questioning face as if flummoxed by the exchange, but he didn't utter a word. Kean came to stand level with Moss.

"Got here too late," said Moss softly. Kean didn't say a thing.

In the next moment a uniformed cop emerged from out of the doorway to number 54, remained standing at the top of the stairs and asked the small crowd of onlookers to step back. He was followed twenty seconds later by the sight of two uniformed Emergency Medical Service personnel carrying a gurney on which lay a dead body inside a black body bag. The outcome was unmistakable.

As the gurney was manoeuvred down the steps the crowd of five people stepped back. Moss watched as the gurney was carried across the sidewalk, onto the street, then up into the back of the ambulance where it was manoeuvred inside. The doors were slammed closed.

One person in the group of five onlookers, inadvertently backed into Moss and gently bumped into him. They both apologised instantaneously.

"Who was she?" Moss asked. "Could it be Rebecca?"

"Yeah."

"How did she die?"

The fella squinted at him through narrow eyes. "How the hell do I know?" he said, as though he thought Moss was a police detective. "She's just dead."

It was another minute or two before the ambulance moved off, followed by one of the police cars. There was no siren. The person inside the ambulance was in no need of a siren.

The cars in the line were now able to move forward. The taxi, they had arrived in, went by.

Moss reflected for a few moments. He knew that 'Hector Monserrat Agency' would never be getting the manuscript. That was gone. He knew that the content of her PC would have been taken out of her home by the same people who had killed her. As he stood watching the action two cops dressed in detectives garb emerged from the entrance, both were carrying large clear plastic bags that contained a lot of papers and other material. Two uniformed cops who had followed them were chatting amongst themselves. The group of five onlookers split up and went their separate ways.

Moss glanced to a side to see where Steve Kean was, but he wasn't anywhere to be seen. He turned and did a full three-sixty. The man who called himself Steve Kean had literally melted away and vanished into thin air, just like one of *Willow the Wisp's farts*.

Moss stood there on his own. What the hell he thought. Occupational hazard. He walked by the steps leading up to the entrance of number 54. Ahead in the near distance he could just make the beginning of Washington Square. It wasn't that far. A couple of hundred yards at the most. Union Square was close by. Perhaps he could go to the bar he knew. There would be some people playing chess in the courtyard by the entrance to the subway station. Whatever had happened to the author was like a game of chess. Check mate had been delivered in one way or another. Moss looked at his watch. It was fast approaching four p.m.

He wondered if he went to the airport now, he might be able to get onto a London bound flight. Then he thought what the hell. He still had another night in the hotel. He may as well stay the second night and stick to his original plan. Visit a bar and have a few beers. Watch some football in a Hell's Kitchen pub. Chill out. Head back this time tomorrow as planned. Alas, without the packet in his possession. Move on. Put it all into storage for when he wrote his memories. He chuckled to himself at the thought of doing that. It had all happened in a New York minute. Or perhaps, in this case, a New York five and three-quarter hours, was more apt.

**The End**

# The Wayward Genius.

Chapter One

The office of 'DeVere Management' was located in a building on New Oxford Street. It was sandwiched in between Tottenham Court Road on one side and Bloomsbury Street on the other. Moss sauntered in through the glass entrance and stepped up to a counter which doubled as a security desk. The names of the two dozen or so small and niche businesses who had an office in this facility were displayed on a board attached to the back wall.

Moss had an appointment in five minutes time with the gentleman from 'DeVere Management' who had requested that he come here to chat to him. It was no less a figure than Mr DeVere himself. The owner of an agency that had stars of stage and screen on its books.

The chap at the desk, wearing a dark uniform with all the trimmings, was officious to the point of boredom. He took Moss's name, wrote it into a visitor log, recorded the time, then he called someone in DeVere Management to announce the arrival of their eleven o'clock appointment.

He then directed the visitor to the third floor of six and told him how to negotiate the maze of corridors to find the DeVere Management suite. Moss stepped through a gate and into a space by one of the two elevators that fed the six upper floors. He was wearing a smart jacket, matching trousers, a freshly pressed shirt and tie. His shoes had a smooth polished finish, that, while not mirror like were reflecting the overhead spotlights. The grip in his hand was attached to the black leather document holder into which he had inserted a thick pad of paper and a pen with plenty of ink in it. Plus, a copy of his private detective licence, issued by the High Court, should the potential client ask to see it. It allowed him to practice as a private investigator in the city.

Crazy as it may seem even private investigators had to be regulated, just like everyone else in this day and age.

Moss had spoken to James DeVere at three o'clock the previous afternoon. It had been their first ever communication. DeVere informed him that he wanted him to find one of his clients, though in truth he didn't say a lot on the phone, not even the name of the POI. He, no doubt, much preferred to disclose this key piece of information in a face-to-face – tete-a-tete –rather than announce it over the telephone, should anyone be listening in.

Moss made it to the third floor, walked down a long, bare wall internal corridor, around a corner and eventually came to the single glass panel door leading into the suite of 'DeVere Entertainment Agency'. Agent to the stars of tv, film, stage and just about anywhere else where people performed to make a living. He paused to read the words stencilled onto the door, they read, 'please knock and enter'. He did just that. He opened the door and stepped into a tight room which was nicely appointed with a light carpet, and a three-seater sofa-settee running down the side of a partition. A single display unit with several shelves, held several picture frames on them, containing portraits of some of the star clients. It was plush, posh and provided an insight into the way they did things. Though, if truth be told, he didn't recognise any of the artists, mainly because this agency tended to deal with people from the let's say, the more, 'arty-farty', hi-brow side of the arts, from famous opera singers, to divas, classic musicians and cool, young dude jazz stars. A bunch of daffodils in a silver metal vase added a touch of nature and colour to the surrounding.

Moss closed the door behind him. As he turned back inside, a door came open and a young lady in her twenties, who was wearing a simple purple, shiny blouse tucked into a plain knee-length dark blue Gingham skirt appeared. She gave him a warm welcoming smile.

"Mister DeVere, will see you now," she said, as if there had been some debate about it. "Please follow me."

Moss followed her through the door and straight into a wide room that doubled as both an office and a lounge. A chap who must have been James DeVere was sitting back in a high wrap around black leather chair behind a large ornately carved teak desk. Light was streaming in through a blind-less wide window that must have looked down onto the side of Tottenham Court Road.

The walls were covered with rectangular shape picture frames containing the faces of people Moss didn't know from Adam. James DeVere was wearing a white shirt with a plain blue bowtie at his throat. He looked to be only in his early forties, therefore he had the looks of a man in transition from his thirty-somethings to his middle years. Though his mop of hair was nicely arranged but suspiciously abundant for someone of his age. He got halfway to his feet, stretched out a hand and beckoned Moss to take the chair set in front of his desk.

"Make yourself comfortable. Is coffee, okay?"

"Yes. Thanks."

"Two coffees, please," he requested to his personal assistant. DeVere had a pleasant non-bully-boy manner about him. He didn't have the look of senior maturity, but the presence of someone who was both studious and shrewd.

Moss had done his homework. He knew that DeVere management, managed the careers of a host of internationally recognised musicians and singers, but not the type who would figure on 'Top of the Pops' any time soon. He sat in the seat in front of the desk and jousted eyes with DeVere for a few brief seconds. The girl closed the door behind her to leave them alone.

Moss glanced around. "Nice interior," he commented. DeVere showed him the lower row of his white teeth with a half-smile that pinched the cover of his waxy skin. Moss reached down to a side to place the document holder by the stout legs of the chair, then back up to him.

"How can I be of assistance to you?" he asked.

"You may or may not have heard the name of a concert pianist by the name of Marcus Parris."

Moss took in the name, didn't recognise it and shook his head. "No sorry. I don't believe I have."

"Marcus Parris is what the music press might term as a phenomenon. A classically trained pianist who has played for some of the best conductors and the best orchestras the world has to offer. He's also trained on the flute, oboe, clarinet and saxophone."

"An all-rounder then?" said Moss, though he didn't know if he would appreciate the term. DeVere wasn't describing a cricketer, for crying out loud. He was describing a musical boy genius.

"Yes. You could, I dare say, say that." DeVere said with an air of a playful, snobby attitude. He had a clipped, upper-class accent with a sort of public schoolboy educated lisp. "He's a piano virtuoso. One of the best Europe has to offer."

"Marcus Parris?"

"Yes. I manage his career. And he's my client, but we currently have a problem with him."

Moss nodded his head once. "He's gone missing?" He knew that because DeVere had revealed it during the telephone conversation.

"That's correct. He's a virtuoso, but he's also flawed."

"In what way?"

"He suffers from mild autism."

Moss didn't know if you could suffer from mild autism as opposed to any other level of autism. He had no recollection of ever meeting anyone with the condition. "And he's gone missing."

"That's right. He's due to perform with the LSO in three weeks from now, but he has not turned up to rehearsals in these past ten days. No one knows where he is."

"Does he have any family? Or someone who may know where he is?" Moss asked.

"He doesn't have any family. I understand that his mother had to give him up for adoption when he was only one year old. He's had a long line of foster parents, due to his temperamental behaviour brought on by frustration caused by his autism."

"His condition sounds severe."

"No not really. But he's got little idea when it comes to the concept of responsibility."

"Has Marcus gone missing before?" Moss asked.

"Yes, but not for this long."

"How long previously?"

"A few days."

"Not ten?"

"Never this long."

"When did you last speak to him?"

"Just over two weeks ago."

"How was he then?"

"He sounded well and said he was looking forward to the Chopin recitals."

"Chopin?" Moss asked.

"He's a famous piano composer."

"Of course." Moss regretted displaying his ignorance on such hi-brow musical matters.

Just then the door to the office opened and DeVere's assistant returned, holding a white plastic tea tray carrying two cups of coffee on saucers, along with a couple of chocolate biscuits on a plate. She placed the tray on the corner of the desk and asked them to help themselves.

DeVere and Moss both said 'thanks' in unison.

"What was his last known address?" Moss asked, then stood up, reached out to take one of the saucers. He took it, then carefully sat down again and held the saucer tight.

DeVere opened a khaki-coloured file on the desk in front of him. He extracted a single white sheet. "It's all on here. His address and other contact details." He lifted the sheet.

"Tell me about his autism. What are the key symptoms?" Moss asked.

"His communications skills are not the best and he is socially awkward…"

"But it's not stopped him from becoming a concert pianist."

"That's true. He's not got much understanding of the value of money either. But he's a virtuoso. He was an accomplished soloist by the age of fifteen. He was performing Bartok, Rachmaninov, and Debussy piano concertos faultlessly by the age of eighteen."

"Have you ever had a disagreement with him?" Moss enquired.

"Nothing too serious."

Moss took a sip of the coffee in the cup. It was bitter and strong. Just how he liked it. DeVere delved deeper into the file. He pulled out an A4 size glossy backed photograph of Marcus Parris and held it aloft. It was one of those promotional type of images. From what Moss could see Marcus Parris was a light-skinned black fellow with mixed race features and appearance. He was standing close to a piano gazing at the photographer. In his black bow-tie, 'bib and tucker' he looked like a top-class musician. His hair was a kind of afro frizzy mullet combination. He looked to be in his mid-twenties, though it was difficult to be precise. The black-rimmed spectacles over his eyes contributed to a geeky like appearance.

"When was that taken? And how old was he at the time?" Moss asked.

"Six months ago, during a London Philly outing at the Royal Albert Hall. He'd be twenty-five."

Moss was suitably impressed. "Does his condition stop him from performing?" he asked. He wished he could find a replacement word for 'condition', but couldn't think of one.

"On the contrary. He's in his element when he's at the piano. It's like his release mechanism from the pressures around him."

DeVere pushed his cushioned chair back, got to his feet, stood up, stepped around his desk and passed the information sheet and photograph to him. The sheet had his Date of Birth, address and contact details on it. His full name was Marcus Adam Parris. He had an address in Wood Green, north London. He was six months north of his twenty-fifth birthday.

Moss ran his eye over the information. "You say he doesn't have any family. No brothers or sisters."

"Not that I'm aware of. He never knew his parents. He lived in foster homes from the age of one right up to eighteen. His autism was a problem in that he could be disruptive."

"How bad?"

"To the point where he went from home to home."

"Where did he learn to play the piano so well?"

"At one of his foster parents' homes. They encouraged him to learn to play as a stress release mechanism and they soon discovered he was a gifted child."

"Amazing. The address in Wood Green. Is it his only address?"

"It's the only address I have."

"How many years have you managed his career?"

"Since he became an adult at seventeen. Eight years ago."

"How high is he in the list of gifted piano players?"

"In the UK?"

"Yeah, and Europe."

"He's in the top three in this country. Perhaps the top, say, eight in Europe. The top twenty in the world."

"Wow. That high?"

"That high."

"That's some achievement for someone with a condition." There he was again using that word. "Does that make him rich?"

DeVere's face became slightly pinched and palsied. He waited a few beats before responding. "He's comfortable for a young man of twenty-five," he offered, ruefully.

"How much is comfortable?"

"I'd say he's earned in excess of one and a half million pounds from concert appearances."

"That much. But you say he's got little conception of the value of money."

"Money doesn't seem to interest him, but that could be his illness."

"If he's got no family or guardian. Who manages his fortune?"

"I do."

"And you'd like me to try and find him?"

"Yes."

No wonder thought Moss. How much did DeVere take from his earnings? He asked himself. "Then what?" he asked.

"Just let me know where I can locate him."

"I can make enquiries, but of course I can't guarantee I can find him, especially if he doesn't want to be found."

"What do you mean?"

"How do you know he wants to be found?"

"He's contracted to this agency for another two years."

"Does he realise the significance of this and the ramifications?"

"That, I can't be sure about. Which is why I want you to find him quickly, so I can speak to him and manage this situation."

"How quickly do you need to find him?"

"Within one week of today."

"What are the ramifications if I fail?"

"He'll lose his contract to appear with the London Philly at the Royal Albert."

"Is that serious for his career?"

"Absolutely. It might signal the end. That's why we need to find him. Will you be able to do that?"

"I can try by asking around. I've got his mobile phone number which is a good start."

"Good," said DeVere. "I'd appreciate it if you got straight onto it."

"I will, immediately." Moss changed the subject and asked him if he was happy to meet his fees, which were £100 per hour, plus expenses."

DeVere said fine. No problem. With that Moss slipped the glossy photograph of Parris and the information sheet into his document holder. He didn't waste any more time with idle chatter. He placed his barely touched cup of coffee onto the tray. He left the office of DeVere Management Agency in the next minute and returned to his office in nearby Soho. The chocolate biscuits had stayed on the plate.

## Chapter Two

On returning back to his office, the first thing Moss did was to turn on his PC and type the words: 'Marcus Parris + concert pianist' into the Google search engine. He pulled up the Wiki page and read the content. Everything James DeVere had said was true. Marcus Parris was a world-renowned pianist. He had won the prestigious Leeds Young pianist competition title when he was nineteen years of age. He was in big demand in his early years. There was also a fleeting reference to his autism which had, in some ways, stifled his career. He had developed a reputation as someone who could be difficult to work with.

Next, Moss hit the YouTube app, opened the welcome page and typed 'Marcus Parris' into the top bar. It opened onto a number of videos of Parris playing the piano in a classical concert setting. He was playing the likes of Debussy, Rachmaninov, and Bartok like a seasoned pro. He was very impressive, indeed.

Moss knew what to do to start the task of trying to find him. He called his good friend and ex Met police pal Bob Ambrose to ask him if he could trace his telephone records.

"Okay," said Ambrose, without asking why he wanted to trace the chap. Moss gave him the eleven-digit mobile phone number from the sheet DeVere had supplied. Ambrose said he'd get back to him in a couple of days.

Moss thanked him then rang off. He then spoke to someone, a contact, in the Metropolitan Police's Missing Person Bureau. He persuaded her to run the name of Marcus Parris through their records. She ran the name for him, but it didn't receive a hit. Nobody had reported him as missing. Not even James DeVere. Moss thanked her. He then brought up Google Maps, entered the address on the sheet, and looked at the place where Parris was supposed to be residing.

It turned out to be a local council authority owned flat in a fifteen-storey block in an area of Wood Green, north London, not that far from Alexandra Palace. It was hardly the place where you'd expect a world-renowned pianist to be living, but it just goes to show you. It was maybe close enough to the centre of the city to be deemed cosmopolitan chic, but not near enough to be called inner London squalor. Wood Green was on the Liverpool Street over ground line going north into Barnet and Enfield and the fourth to last station at the northern end of the Piccadilly tube line.

He thought for a few moments about James DeVere's words that Parris didn't have much idea when it came to the money he had earned. Someone outside of the agency must have had an idea that Parris had accumulated quite a fortune and therefore perhaps had an interest in him. He considered the possibility that Parris was being held against his will. In other words, he had been kidnapped and DeVere had received a ransom demand, but he wasn't keen to report this or tell him.

It was close to one o'clock when Moss grabbed his jacket and swung it around his shoulders. He headed out of the office, down the steep bank of stairs, out of the door, turned right and walked the short distance onto Regents Street. He flagged down the first available black cab and asked the driver to take him north into Wood Green. The day was fine, though a little overcast and cool for a mid-April day.

Wood Green was very much a distant north London suburbia. A mixture of private dwellings and local authority owned properties in large housing estates that hadn't changed much over the past forty years. Bounds Green Road snaked through a maze of side streets and provided the best shopping and entertainment amenities. It was a racially mixed area and quite diverse.

The block of high-rise flats in which Parris lived was in the same location as three other blocks that were all of the same construction. He counted fifteen floors, from top to bottom. All brick with colourful cladding across the width, balconies and wide windows arranged in straight lines. Moss arrived outside of the entrance to the block which matched the address on the sheet. It had, of course, a security-controlled access system. Entrance could only be achieved by the use of a 'door to flat' intercom system.

Parris was in flat number, thirty-eight. Moss pressed the number three button, then the eight, then hit the bell icon and waited for a response. He assumed Parris lived on the third floor. There was no reply to his call. He pressed the three, then the seven, which he assumed would be next door. Still no answer.

As he hovered by the front door, a figure appeared inside the inner glassed-in vestibule, came to the outer door and opened it. The person, a male in his late twenties, briefly looked at Moss as if to enquire who the hell are you? Moss smiled at him. As the chap came out, Moss stepped inside. The chap muttered something incoherent, but didn't challenge him and carried on his way. Moss watched him for a few moments, then stepped the five paces to the lift door and pressed the call button.

The lift door glided open to reveal the dark of the car. He stepped inside and directed it to the third floor. On arrival, the door opened, and he found himself in a glass-enclosed communal landing. One long corridor to the left and one to the right. Both leading to a window from where daylight was streaming in to reflect across the tile floor.

There were eight homes on each floor, making a total of one hundred and twenty, in all. Some had two bedrooms, others three. Four flats to the left, numbered one to four, and four on the other side, numbered five to eight. He stepped to the right, opened a glass door and walked onto the corridor leading to the window at the end. There were Perspex panels in the ceiling with those movement sensitive devices inside, so they lit up as he walked. The air was cool. The colour scheme was neutral in the extreme, blanch-grey walls with a dash of sorbet and pink in a pretty winding pattern.

He made it down the corridor to the last door on the right. Flat number 'thirty-eight'. There was a thick woven mat in front of the door with the word 'Welcome' ingrained into the bristle. A peep hole was inserted into the surface. He pressed the door bell and took a backward step. There was no pane of opaque glass in the door, just the numerals 'three' and 'eight' in black on a white background, just like the others.

He knocked on the door. No one came. A few seconds past then he heard a sound from behind him and turned to see the door to the flat directly opposite, number thirty-seven, come open. A middle-aged, plump, black skinned lady, holding a tv remote control in her hand, appeared. She was wearing a lemon fluffy type of wool jumper and blue jeans. She eyed Moss with suspicion from behind spectacle-covered eyes.

"Did you press my bell?" she asked.

Moss felt like saying something witty, but refrained. "I'm looking for Marcus Parris. Have you seen him lately?" he enquired.

"Who are you?" she enquired, straight out and with little nicety in the tone. She took a step back inside the entrance to her home from where the escaping aroma of a spicy sauce was evident. She took hold of the edge of the door as if she was prepared to slam it closed in a heartbeat.

"I'm from his management company. Mr DeVere is trying to locate him at this time."

It didn't mean much to her. "I haven't seen him around for a while," she replied, relaxing her tone.

"Neither have we. That's why we're looking for him."

She was a nice-looking lady with bright eyes, thick lips and an appealing grin that almost give her an elfin-like appearance. She gave him a quarter smile that made her look a great deal friendlier than she had ten seconds before.

"I think a girl's moved in with him," she revealed.

"In here?"

"Yeah."

"Oh right. Do you know her name?"

"All I know is that she calls herself Simone or Sienna. Something like that."

"Simone or Sienna?" he asked for confirmation.

"Sienna. I think. I've seen her a couple of times with him."

"With Marcus?"

"Yeah, that's right."

"Where? Here?"

"Yeah. And in the pub down the road."

"Which pub?"

"The Prince Regent."

"Do you go in there?" he asked.

"Sometimes. They play in a band every Tuesday and Friday night."

"Who do."

"Them two."

"Which two?"

She frowned at him briefly. "Marcus and his girlfriend."

"Where? In the pub?"

"Yeah. That's right."

"Do they have a name?"

"Who?"

"The band. The group."

"The Wandering Minstrels, or summat."

"Okay. Thanks for that." He told her he'd maybe come back later to see if he could catch them at home. He thanked her, wished her good afternoon, turned away and headed back along the corridor to the communal area by the lift doors. Excellent, he thought. Finding Marcus Parris might be easier than he had anticipated.

## Chapter Three

The 'Prince Regent' public house was a decent size establishment at the junction of Trinity Road and Bounds Green Road, not that far from the location of the tower blocks. About a quarter of a mile, at a guess. It had a kind of dullish aquamarine paint job on the front, large windows and the look of an olde-worldly east-end pub made famous by a tv soap. A set of three tables and benches were outside for those who enjoyed a cigarette with a pint. A picture of some real-life or mythical prince was in a panel attached to the front elevation. There was some graffiti on a nearby brick wall which read *'Potch's Yid Army'* along with a Star of David symbol. It must have been a reference to the former manager of Tottenham Hotspur Football club, Mauricio Pochettino, and the club's Jewish owned heritage. Moss saw a notice plastered on a window close to the doorway which advertised live music every Tuesday and Friday night. The Wandering Minstrels. It seemed absurd that a classically trained pianist would play in an out of the way pub for beer money. Then he remembered he did have a condition.

Moss stepped through the door, into a vestibule, then into the large room. It was a one room pub, set across the corner of the two roads. It was a typical London boozer. High ceiling. Large windows, plenty of character. Plain laminate boards lined the floor. A dark painted ceiling. A stout central pillar had loads of notices attached to it, along with a Spurs flag and an Enfield Town football club fixture list. The lights on a bandit machine were flashing as were the illumination on a Wurlitzer Juke box. There were zero customers inside at this time of the day. Ten minutes to three.

He stepped up close to the bar and eyed the options in the liquor bottles attached to a metal frame. He caught his reflection in the mirror and noticed that his eyes were displaying deep dark lines due to a lack of sleep and vitamin

C. His flesh looked a milky white-pink shade and in need of some UV.

A moment past, before a busty, blonde barmaid in her fifties appeared in a doorframe She put her eyes on him and came to serve him.

"What is it you'd be after?" she asked in an Irish brogue laced accent.

"I'll have a shot of Bacardi and a bottle of coke." he requested. "And get one for yourself."

"That's very kind of you," she said grinning at him.

"She took two short glasses, placed one under the Bacardi optic and pushed it. She placed the second glass under the Teachers whisky bottle and poured herself a free one.

She placed his glass on the counter, then turned to the cold unit, opened the door, reached down and extracted a 250ml bottle of coke.

"That's six fifty," she requested.

"He handed her a ten-pound note and suggested she place the change into a 'Help for Heroes' charity collection box behind the bar.

"You're not from around these parts, are you?" she enquired.

"No. I'm out west."

"So, what attracts you to green plains of Wood Green?" she asked inquisitively.

"The Wandering Minstrels."

"How?"

"I hear they're good."

"They're all right. If you like that kind of stuff," she said without a great deal of enthusiasm or care in her voice."

"What kind of music do they play?"

"Covers mostly. Fleetwood Mac. Some Beatles. Stones and Bowie classics."

"Do they have Marcus Parris on piano?"

"And sax."

"They're on tomorrow night?" he asked.

"Well, it is a Friday tomorrow," she confirmed.

"How many are in the band?"

"Five of them. Is it?"

"I don't know."

"Yeah, it's five."

"Is it five guys?"

"No," she said stiffly. "It's three girls and two guys."

"Of course, it is. What time do they appear?"

"Nine to eleven usually. You some kind of a talent scout, then?"

"How did you guess." He took the bottle of coke and emptied half of the content into the Bacardi.

She took her whisky neat. He saw her drop the change from the ten-pound note into the plastic charity container. He put the rum and coke to his lips and took in a good mouthful. It hit the spot at the back of his tongue.

One of those, old style, big railway station waiting room type clocks with a white face and black numbers, behind the bar, hit the hour of three. According to him it was six minutes fast. A couple of customers came into the room, carrying plastic bags containing grocery shopping. The landlady, barmaid, whoever she was, went to serve them and engaged them in lively chit-chat. Moss quickly polished off his drink, called out 'goodbye and thanks' to the barmaid, then he left the public house. He decided to walk the few hundred yards to Wood Green underground station to take a south bound Piccadilly line train back into the centre of the city.

On the train he thought about calling James DeVere to inform him of progress in the search for Marcus Parris, but stopped himself before he made the call. The thought of a ransom demand was still lying heavy in his thinking.

By the time he got into Soho the time was edging close to four-thirty. He decided he would contact DeVere tomorrow morning to tell him that he had traced Parris to a pub in Wood Green, from where he would be performing covers to a score of well-known middle of the road contemporary classics from the past two decades, or so. Though after a night to sleep on it he could change his mind.

## Chapter Four

The following morning – Friday – Moss left his Knightsbridge flat early and drove the short distance into Soho. He parked his car in one of those 24 hours car parks that cost a reasonable twenty-pounds for all-day parking. He arrived into his office at seven-twenty and concerned himself with doing some homework on a couple of the insurance cases he was working on.

It was eleven o'clock when he received a call from Bob Ambrose to tell him of his findings on the trawl of Marcus Parris's mobile phone. The update he gave Moss was interesting. It would appear that the volume of calls he had made from that number had dried up, significantly, over the past two to three weeks. He had been fairly active over the past few months, making on average one hundred calls a month, from the same number. This further supported the theory that he had been kidnapped and was being held against his will. But this was wild speculation, at best. A simpler explanation could be that he had changed his phone number, which was always a possibility. Moss didn't think a lot about it. He asked Ambrose to email him a summary showing the numbers called and the volume of calls made.

Ambrose sent the information before lunch. In the period over the last three months. Parris had made about three hundred and seventy calls from that number. Moss spent the next hour analysing the numbers and making a simple list to discover the mode. He learned that fifty percent of the calls were made to just six numbers. The other fifty percent were to a variety of forty-eight different recipients.

At two o'clock he received a surprise telephone call from James DeVere asking him if he had made any progress. Plenty, he replied. He told him what he had learned, that his client was in a pub band called the 'Wandering Minstrels' who played twice weekly in a north-east London watering hole. DeVere was stunned into silence.

Moss asked him if he wanted to accompany him this evening to see the band. Somewhat surprisingly, perhaps, DeVere turned him down, stating that he already had an appointment at that time to meet with another one of his charges in a central London eatery. Plus, it would look as if he was checking up on Marcus. He didn't want to come across like that. He asked Moss to try and chat to Parris, to ask him to call his manager as matter of great urgency. Moss thought it odd that De Vere didn't want to chat to Parris face-to-face, but he couldn't be in two places at once. He let it go. Maybe he had a justifiable excuse. He agreed to help him by giving Parris the message. After all, he was on the clock.

During the afternoon Moss received a visit from Ray Bentley, his contact in the insurance company he did investigation work for. Bentley handed him three new case files he wanted him to investigation in order to determine if the claims were bogus. As soon as Bentley departed, Moss spent the next couple of hours reading through the files and making notes. One of the cases related to a car accident in which the claimant claimed he had sustained whiplash. One was for the theft of some jewellery during a burglary. The other was a claim relating to a supposed attack by a neighbour's dog. He got them all. The cranks and the bizarre.

It was five o'clock when he left the office to visit a pub on a nearby street. He stayed in there for one hour, then returned to the office to do some more preparation work on the insurance cases. The early evening was okay. The afternoon had been fine, but now the sky was darkening so the warmth of the day was being reduced by a cooler temperature.

It was getting on for ten past eight when he left his office and walked the short distance to the car park to reclaim his car. This being a Friday night, in the centre of the city, the west end was becoming busy as the pubs and the restaurants were welcoming patrons. The theatres along Shaftsbury Avenue would be opening their doors shortly and putting up the 'house-full' or 'seats still available' notices.

From Soho, he drove east along Euston Road, then north and into the northern denizens of the greater metropolitan area. It took him around forty minutes from exiting the car park to reach the fringe of Wood Green. He was on Bounds Green Road by ten to nine. He parked his car on a street around two hundred yards from the 'Prince Regent' public house.

The night was now dark so the streetlights and those in the premises and homes in the vicinity were on and glowing. The light from inside the pub was splashed onto the pavement and across a section of grassland that stretched to the lip of the roadside. He stepped into the same entrance he'd used the day before and into the public house for a second time.

In the evening, the pub had a different feel and ambience than that in the afternoon. It was far starker and not as subdued or shaded as in the day time. With the sound of chat and the sight of a Friday night crowd it had a far grittier feel to it. He entered the big room and cast his eyes around the crowd of say two dozen people who were congregated inside. An area in the corner where the two outer walls met had been cleared of tables to create a space for a band to set up. Two guys were arranging the mikes at the front. A set of drums and cymbals had already been erected, along with a pair of Marshall amplifiers. There was also a Fenway type of electrical pop-up organ, and guitars on stands. All ready for musicians to play. A few people were standing at the bar, others milling around the edges. There was still some free seating at the tables in the centre of the room. A rig had been erected from where a few beams of light were aimed at the makeshift stage. It looked like a fairly professional set-up. Moss was impressed. As he glanced around the faces of those gathered, he couldn't spot anyone who looked anything like Marcus Parris. He negotiated his way to the bar. The busty barmaid he had spoken to yesterday was behind the counter, pulling pints and chatting to the patrons. Another younger version of her was also serving. There was that general pub banter in the air. People were waiting for the band to appear and get down to delivering some Friday night entertainment. The weekend was here and most of the customers were determined to have a good evening. The noise from the bandit was low. The juke box had been disconnected.

Claudette would have enjoyed the vibe. Alas, he had not seen or spoken to her in several weeks. He had blown it, to a degree. He had pushed at the door a little too hard, when he had misread the signals. He didn't want to think about it.

## Chapter Five

After a wait of a minute at the bar the young barmaid came to serve him. He asked for a pint of lager. Then as the clock hit nine, several of the young people who had been sitting at a table close to the gear, got to their feet and moved into the area set aside for a stage. Not one of them resembled Marcus Parris. There were three females and two males. All racially diverse. One white guy and a light-skinned black chap. Neither of them was Marcus Parris.

The Asian looking guy slipped behind the organ and got himself comfortable. The female drummer feathered the cymbals. The house lights were lowered to dim, and the beams were cranked up to three-quarter power to catch the majesty of a live performance. The light splintered off the guitars which were in the grasp of the other two females. One white girl. One black girl. One had an acoustic guitar plugged into an amplifier. The other had a long neck black and white bass. The white guy picked up a saxophone and slipped the harness around his neck.

"Good evening," one of the girls said into a mike. "We're the *Wandering Minstrels*. And we're here to entertain you for a couple of hours." A couple of the on-lookers clapped and whooped, as you do. "We want to start with Stevie Wonder's Superstition."

Moss held his pint glass close to his lips and took a sip of the lager. He didn't know what to think, other than feeling a little deflated and confused. What was clear was that nobody on the stage looked like Marcus Parris.

"Various superstition," the lead singer sang. "The writings on the wall." Moss, still resting against the bar, tapped his foot to the beat of the music and the vibe, bouncing out of the amps. The sound, the music and the strength of the beer took him back down memory lane for a few wishful wistful moments.

He sipped his drink. The Minstrels completed the Stevie Wonder cover, then revved up and got down to a cracking version of Gerry Rafferty's 'Baker Street'.

On completion of the second track the lead singer took a few moments to introduce the band. Dave was on Saxophone. Louise was on drums. Marcus was on the Fenway organ. He wasn't Marcus Parris, perhaps this was another Marcus Parris. She introduced her co-female, front of band singer as Molly, then introduced herself has Sienna. The same name as the lady in the flat had given him. Were they Marcus and Sienna? Moss had no idea. He did wonder if James DeVere had given him the wrong address. Mixing him up with some other Marcus? That could have been the case.

He purchased a second pint which he consumed far less quickly than the first. By ten-thirty most of the audience were starting to drift towards the exit. At ten-thirty-five Sienna announced this would be their final track. Appropriately, a cover of the Moody Blues song, 'Go Now'.

As the gig reached its zenith, Moss decided it was time to slip away. He went outside, went to his car, got in, but didn't drive off. From here he could see the pavement in front of the pub. He sat in the comfort of the seat, looking ahead, waiting for the chap who called himself Marcus to appear. He wanted to see where he went and who with.

It was around ten-fifty, when the members of the band came out of the doorway, carrying their instruments and gear. Meanwhile, a blue, battered looking, Bedford type of van, several years old, had pulled up outside the pub. The driver opened the back doors. The gear, the instruments, amps and mike stands were put into the rear storage.

The six of them, the five members of the band and the chap who arrived in the van stood around the back door of the vehicle chatting for ten minutes, smoking cigarettes and generally passing the time.

Then the band members split up. Two of them. The girl called Molly and the sax player called Dave, went to a parked car and climbed in. Then a second car, a Mini, appeared on the scene. Two of them, Marcus and Sienna, squeezed onto the rear seat. The car was soon on the move. Moss turned on the ignition, moved off and followed the Mini onto Bounds Green Road. The time was close to eleven o'clock.

It wasn't too long, a matter of minutes, before the Mini was close to the high-rise blocks of flats. It came to a stop outside the entrance and exit of the block he had visited. Marcus and Sienna and the unknown male driver got out, went to the glass enclosed entrance, opened the security door and headed inside.

Moss parked in a free bay opposite the entrance. He swiftly got out of his car, locked it, then made his way across the forecourt to the doors. Lights were blazing in the windows spread across the fifteen floors. After all, it was only just after eleven on a Friday night. That said there were no people outside the entrance. He would either have to wait for a resident to arrive or try to get in by stealth. Or maybe there was another option.

It would take the residents of flat thirty-eight a couple of minutes to reach their place. He decided to give them a few extra minutes. The lager he had drank repeated on him. His ears were only just losing the buzz caused by the decibels of music. He had an idea what was going on here, but couldn't be sure. Nothing was certain.

Then his mobile phone rang. He saw it was James DeVere calling him. He took the call. DeVere wanted to know if he had spoken to Marcus Parris.

"No not yet," he replied. He told him that it looked as if someone was impersonating Marcus Parris. Why he wasn't sure. Maybe it was to get at his fortune.

"Where is the real Marcus?" DeVere enquired.

"That I don't know, but I'm determined to find out."

He advised DeVere he would update him shortly, definitely before midnight, then he terminated the conversation. He stepped up to the entrance, concentrated on the digits in the intercom number pad and pressed the figure three, followed by the figure eight, then hit the bell symbol.

He could hear the sound of a buzzing intercom phone ringing in the flat. It rang for about thirty seconds before it was answered by a female voice asking, 'Who is it?'

"Where's Marcus Parris?" he asked straight out in a curt enquiry. There was no reply. "Where is he?" he asked again.

There was silence then a male voice took over and asked. "Who's that?"

"My name is David Moss. I'm a private detective employed to find Marcus. And that is what I'm going to do. If you don't start to answer my questions, I'll have little alternative but to call the police. Who are you? And what are you doing in his flat? Your call. You've got exactly one minute to decide."

"Err… Okay," said the voice cautiously and in genuine hesitance.

"I'll call you back in sixty seconds from now," said Moss.

There was no reply and the other party hung up on him. Moss looked at his watch. He concentrated his eyes on the second hand and watched it go around. Twenty seconds…Thirty… Forty… Fifty… Sixty. One minute was soon up. He reached out and pressed the figure three and the figure eight and hit the bell icon.

There was 'zzzz' sound out of the intercom, followed by the sight of the automatic door sliding open. Moss stepped inside the entrance and headed to the shiny lift door. He pressed the call button. The car was on the third floor. It was down on the ground in around fifteen seconds. He didn't know what he would find in the flat or where this was going to end, but didn't think he was in any kind of danger. His mobile phone sounded. He turned it off. He had to keep his wits about him.

When the lift arrived on the third floor, the doors opened, Moss cautiously stepped out onto the landing and thrust his eyes along the corridors on both sides which were in semi dark. A light in the overhead panel was reflecting in the shiny finish of the floor tiles. He noticed the lack of graffiti and the lack of anyone to meet him. He stepped out through the door to the right and headed along the dark corridor. As he progressed a light came on in reaction to his movements to illuminate the spread of the floor before him. A radiator was cold to the touch. At the window at the end of the landing the thick dark of the night was pressing against the glass. The lights of urban north London towards the city of the centre were spread out far into the distance. His heart was beating a little faster, but not that it caused him any discomfort or consternation. When he came level to the door leading into flat number eight, he paused for the briefest of moments, then knocked on the plain wood board.

He took a step back. The time was now five past eleven. He could hear a sound. In the next moment the door came open. Standing there in the opening was the chap he had last seen sitting behind the pop-up Fenway organ in the 'Prince Regent' pub. He was still wearing the same *'Fresh Ooutta Compton'* t-shirt and blue jeans. The girl known as Sienna was standing behind him. He was a good-looking light skinned east Asian man. She was in a sweatshirt and shorts combo with a rock band logo plastered across the front of the shirt. She had a kind of post Punk appearance with the thick eyeliner and an anaemic whiter-than-white complexion. There was the tangy smell of dope and the sound of a Muse track playing in the lounge.

Moss put his eyes on them. "Where is he?" he asked.

"Who?" she asked.

"Marcus Parris. Because that isn't him." He nodded his head to the guy, who took a step back.

"Come in and we'll explain," he said.

"Why can't you explain out here?"

"You ain't got anything to fear from us. We ain't the violent type," he said in a *I'm okay* way.

"Pleased to hear it," replied Moss.

He eyed him and wondered what were the chances of this guy attacking him. Perhaps eighty-twenty in favour of the unlikely category, so he elected to take a chance. He edged forward, stepped over the threshold and into the flat. The fruity aromatic smell of the dope was stronger, and the music had a kind of an occult, menacing vibe to it. The chap closed the front door behind him.

"Where is Marcus Parris?" he asked for a second time. "And why are you pretending to be him?"

"Believe it or not we've swapped identities," said the man, straight out.

"Why?"

"To give him some peace of mind and freedom away from the pressure."

Moss wasn't stunned, and neither was he surprised. "Is that right?" he asked.

Sienna cleared her throat with a light cough. "The truth is its all getting too much for him to handle. He's suffering from stress and anxiety. He needs to get away from the pressure. He needs to get away from…."

"From who?"

"The pressure his management company is putting on him," he said.

"He hasn't got anyone to care for him, except for us," she added defiantly.

"Okay," said Moss in a reflective tone. He felt like saying something on the lines of how Christian are you, but swerved the opportunity. "Where is he?" he asked.

"In my flat."

"Where's that?"

"On the twelfth floor," replied the Marcus Parris doppelganger.

"How come the lady in the flat across the landing has seen him in here?"

"What. She's only lived here for two weeks."

"She doesn't know who he is. She thinks I'm Marcus," he said.

"Okay. Got it. Is he in this block?"

"Yeah, on the twelfth floor."

"Can I see him?"

"Why?"

"To make sure he's alive and well and who's with him."

"With someone we've asked to be his minder and buddy."

"Can I see him with my own eyes?"

"Why?"

"To know you're telling me the truth."

"Who are you anyway?" she asked.

"David Moss. A private detective. I was hired by his management company to find him. His management want to know where he is so they hired me to locate him. To be honest that wasn't very difficult."

"He's too stressed out to see anyone," she said.

"How do I know that you're being honest with me? And that you haven't kidnapped him and stolen his identity? Helped yourselves to the contents of his bank account?"

"We wouldn't do that," he said.

"Then take me to see him."

"Take him," she instructed her bloke, then put her eyes on Moss. "What are you going to tell his manager?" she asked him.

"That I've seen him and he's alive. And that he's not in any kind of danger. But he's in no fit state to carry on performing, due to a breakdown of some kind."

"Would you do that for us?" she asked.

"One hundred percent. If it's true."

"He doesn't require medical help. He just needs to be left alone," she added.

"If that's the case, that's okay. But I need to see him."

"I'll take you," he volunteered.

## Chapter Six

The pretend Marcus Parris reached out and took a jacket off a coat peg. Moss took a step back down the corridor towards the front door. He didn't expect anyone to come at him, therefore he wasn't on edge, but he had to keep his wits about him. It would appear that the pair of them – the pretend Marcus and Sienna – were on the level with him. The guy slipped his arms into the sleeves of his jacket, brushed past Moss, opened the front door and stepped out onto the landing.

Moss followed him out of the flat. They walked down the corridor side by side. Moss noticed they were the same height, but the younger man wasn't half as solid as him. He might have been younger, but he wasn't as streetwise as the former Met Police detective.

The pair of them were soon at the lift doors. They each had nothing to say. The ride up to the twelfth floor was without any drama. The guy was cool. His body language told of a realisation that he was about to be found out as an impersonator of a well-renowned pianist. Perhaps he liked playing the part. Or maybe he didn't.

When the car reached the twelfth floor, the doors slid open. The younger fellow was the first out. He stepped into the communal landing, then through the glass door on the left and onto the corridor containing the four flats numbered one to four. At the large window the lights of Enfield or Barnet or wherever were spread out on a carpet of urbanisation, until they petered out to the Essex countryside. They were soon at the first flat on the left-hand side. Flat number 1204. The chap extracted a key from a jacket pocket, threaded it into the lock, opened the door and stepped inside. Moss was close behind him. They went along the internal corridor, and straight into a sitting room in which two people were sitting on a centrally placed sofa watching a movie or something on a large wide, flat-screen television.

One of them was the real Marcus Parris. The person by his side was a male of the same age. It could have been the chap who had collected both Sienna and the guy from outside of the pub less than thirty minutes ago.

"This is the guy," said the pretend Marcus Parris to the real one. "He's been sent by James DeVere to find you."

Moss breathed in the smell of stale tobacco. He let his eyes wander around. The interior was bland, nothing of great interest. The colours were either grey or had a grey tint of beige. Long mauve and orange stripy curtains covered the French doors that led onto an enclosed balcony. On a coffee table were a packet of cigarettes and a lighter. No alcohol of any kind and evidence of drugs were on display. The blinds over a window were open. The lights of north east London looking towards the centre of the city were lit up like a magic carpet.

Marcus Parris lifted his head and turned to face Moss. He didn't appear to be drunk or zonked out on any substance or otherwise. He was lucid. The light from a wide screen reflected on his face to make his features appear blunt. His afro hair had been tied back and was less bushy than it appeared in the promotion picture. He was sitting slumped in the sofa, with his legs stretched out. He was very much alive. He was breathing. He wasn't dead. And neither did he look in any distress or held against his will.

The unknown chap sitting with him, looked up at Moss. "I've told DeVere he's not up to performing. He's burnt out and fatigued." Parris looked at Moss, but said nothing. "His manager rips him off. Takes most of his money. Uses him as a kind of cash-cow."

"I don't know anything about that," Moss said in his own defence.

"Take it from us, man. He charges the orchestras top dollar for him to perform. He's fed up at being a rich man's slave. We're looking out for him," said the pretend Marcus.

The scene reminded Moss of the scene in 'Once Upon a Time in Hollywood', when the character Cliff Booth, played by Brad Pitt, went to check on a former work colleague, called George Spahn, to ensure he was not being manipulated and taken advantage of by a bunch of hippies.

Parris was gazing at the tv screen, almost as if he was in a trance. In truth, he was absorbed by the action movie. Moss had no reason to doubt his friends' motives. That they were looking out for him, and that was their only concern.

"Okay. I'm sort of convinced by your words, but I've got to tell DeVere something."

"He's only concerned that Marcus isn't making money for him. Tell him this. Tell him he's done with performing for the organ grinder. He's not his friggin monkey," said the chap on the sofa. Moss thought that wasn't fair or called for, but brushed over it.

"What about the contract he has?"

"Sod the contract," said the real Marcus Parris, opening his mouth and expressing himself for the first time. He forced himself up to sit on the edge of the sofa and pulled his legs up. He reached out to the coffee table, took the packet of cigarettes, took one out and lit it with the lighter.

"I've seen enough," said Moss, looking to the guy who had brought him up here.

"What will you tell DeVere?" he asked.

"What you've said. That he's out of action for the foreseeable."

"Yeah, do that. Will you?" said the real Marcus Parris. He put the cigarette in his lips and took in a deep pull that released a plume of fumes.

"He's done his time as a concert pianist. He's going to learn how to play boogie-woogie and go on tour playing that kind of old-style rock and roll. It's what he wants to do."

"Boogie-woogie," Parris repeated. He chuckled out loud as if the word tickled his whimsical elbow.

"Fine, let me leave you guys in peace," said Moss. The music on the tv reached a crescendo as the car chase ended abruptly as a vehicle smashed into a low wall, throwing the driver out of the windscreen and over the barrier. Moss sort of knew how he felt. He turned to leave the flat. The chap who had brought him led him to the front door, out of the flat and onto the landing.

The time was eleven-thirty. He didn't know what he was going to tell James DeVere when he spoke to him. What words to use or how to phrase them or the tone of his voice he was going to use. He would cross that bridge when the time came. He had better say it as he meant it. Tell him up front. A classical pianist was no longer willing to perform like a circus animal. It might come as a blow to his prestige and his pocket. But that's the way it was. He had no need to sugar-coat it. Such things did happen from time to time.

It was precisely two minutes to midnight when Moss put the call in to James DeVere. He had promised he would call him before midnight, so he was true to his word. He had pulled down a side street off Euston Road, just on from the front of St Pancras railway station. Parked in a bay and killed the engine to make the call, hands free. It was almost exactly thirty-six hours and fifty-eight minutes since he had first met with him in his office on New Oxford Street.

"I found him," he announced as soon as DeVere answered the call.

"Did you manage to speak to him?" DeVere asked eagerly.

"Yes, I did."

"And?"

"It doesn't sound to me as if he's inclined to return to the fold any time soon."

"What does that mean?"

"I got the impression that his days as a leading concert pianist may be over. In truth he wants to become a boogie-woogie player, playing rock and roll in pubs."

"Can you explain what you mean?"

Moss took in a long deep breath. He informed DeVere that he had found Parris in the flat on the twelfth floor of the block of flats. He had surrounded himself with what appeared to be genuine friends and buddies who were seemingly looking out for his wellbeing. There wasn't maybe a lot that DeVere could do but to let him go. Perhaps he already knew this.

They chatted, back and forth, for a couple of minutes. Moss couldn't tell him a great deal other than inform him of the number of the flat. He told him he would complete a full report detailing everything he had seen. He would drop it off in his office at ten tomorrow morning, along with an invoice for his fee.

DeVere rang off after saying he would speak with him tomorrow. He hadn't displayed any great sadness or surprise at the outcome, perhaps he had expected it all along. Then Moss recalled the chap telling him that he had already spoken to DeVere and told him he wasn't returning. Therefore, he must have already had an inkling what the end-game would be from the outset.

Moss got his car moving and drove through the quiet central London streets to his place in Knightsbridge. Now it was back to the bread-and-butter stuff. Investigating possible bogus insurance claims. The staid and the mundane. The everyday stuff that was his stable diet.

Strange things human beings, he mused to himself. Highly unpredictable and difficult to fathom out on any given day. It was the final summing up to the evening's proceedings.

**The End**

# Old Soap

Chapter One

Roseanne Massey, had, at one time, been a fashion model who had featured in the glossy pages of the likes of Vogue, and Cosmopolitan magazine. From the on-line images of her when she was in her prime, she was an attractive and classy lady who resembled the models who had paved the way in the 1960s. Such as the likes of Jean Shrimpton and Twiggy, who had been around in the beginning. Roseanne's signature look was the 90s, but with an early twenty-first century twist. Now, perhaps twenty years later she still had the looks and the style to turn heads. She had graced the glossy pages of the trade mags for a decade, before turning her hand to doing a spread in one of the – let's say – top shelf publications. Moss was sort of reminded of the time he would occasionally browse through the pages of a girlie magazine left lying around in the detectives' office. Those were the days when the job of a detective was, by and large, a male preserve. Not anymore. How the times had changed! Now some of the Met's most experienced and best detectives and senior investigation officers were female. He knew that in changing times, the days when men ruled the roost in the corridors of power were diminishing, but not long gone.

It was now around twelve years since he had last walked along the corridors of a police station as a bona-fide Metropolitan police detective. Did he miss it? No, not that much, if the truth be told. He liked being his own boss, without anyone, male or female, telling him what to do. Though he would admit that he did miss the salary to a degree.

Roseanne Massey had contacted Moss to ask him to help her to find someone, who, she said, had stolen the best part of £250,000 from her mother, the former television newsreader, Melinda Falkland. According to what Ms

Massey told Moss, in the telephone conversation they had had. Her mother, who was now in her mid-sixties, was as vulnerable as a stray puppy, and easily duped and taken in by a sob story. Melinda Falkland had been a widow for these past seven years. Her daughter told Moss she had fallen for the charms of a good looking, much younger man who had the sleaze and the patter of a snake-oil salesman, a sweetness of voice, and an expertise for taking money off mature ladies who fell for his smooth dark looks.

When she, Roseanne Massey visited Moss in his Soho office, above the pastry shop on Broadwick Street, she told him the tale. Roseanne was an attractive lady of around forty years of age. She had a healthy tan. She told him that she spent six months of the year living in Spain, and the other six months at her home in the Surrey countryside.

In the two hours, following the phone call, he had received from her, to actually meeting her in the flesh for the first time, Moss had conducted some desk research into her family background. The Massey-Falklands were a well-to-do family who lived in a fine home close to Wentworth golf course.

Basically, Ms Massey wanted him to find the man who had left her mother feeling down, on edge and in a state of depression. What she told him was like one of those 'oh my word,' type of stories you hear about on tv or read in the fifty pence sleazy tabloids from time to time. In which some vulnerable person had been rinsed by a smooth-talking lounge lizard who used romantic liaison as a tool to get his victim to part with her money. Especially a victim who had lost her partner to a sudden illness after being married for thirty or more years to the same man.

That had happened to Melinda Falkland. A chancer and a scammer had taken advantage of her delicate mental state to ask her for money. In truth, this wasn't one of those internet dating type of scams. Melinda Falkland had met the man at a party given by a former work colleague. They had wined and dined on a few occasions and even been on holiday to Miami Beach, together. Apparently, it was six months after this that the love interest began to pull at her purse strings with requests for money.

She, Melinda Falkland, had, according to her daughter, given the chap around £265,000 in a series of cash gifts over a period of six months. Now the chap had disappeared from her life leaving Melissa Falkland full of remorse for being taken for a fool. Now she lacked the confidence to even leave the family home for more than a few hours on each occasion. Roseanne wanted Moss to trace the whereabouts of the man, so she could commence the task of trying to get back some of the money.

'That could be difficult,' Moss had told her during their face-to-face chat, because the chap could turn around and say her mother had agreed to give him the money as a gift and not a loan. There was nothing to tell him the guy had broken any law or done anything fundamentally wrong.

Roseanne Massey did understand this, but she was still determined to find the chap to give him a piece of her mind. Or maybe to hire a few heavies to pay him a late-night visit in order to knock his porcelain white teeth down the back of his throat, or to give him such a beating his face wouldn't be attractive to anyone anymore. Not even to his mother. He didn't know, but could only speculate. She didn't tell him, and he didn't ask her. What she did tell him was the name of the chap and a last known address for him, which was in Putney, west London. But she then informed Moss the POI was no longer living there. He had flown that nest in a midnight flit.

The chap's name was Henri Barrington. In a photograph of her mother and Barrington together he looked to be twenty years her junior. He was a handsome, hirsute and well-dressed chap with devilishly good looks. Privately educated, stylish, debonair and all those words that describe someone with a love cheats and scammers pedigree.

Roseanne told him the photograph had been taken on Miami Beach, around one year before, six years after her husband, Roseanne's father, Sir Raymond Falkland had passed away following a stroke. Roseanne said she didn't want her mother to know that she was hiring a private detective to find Barrington.

    She agreed to pay him the going rate of one hundred pounds an hour, plus any expenses to find Henri Barrington. He sounded like a character from 'Dirty Rotten Scoundrels' or some other heinous individual from a long running television drama. Roseanne asked Moss to keep contact down to a minimum and only to contact her when he had located Barrington.

Chapter Two

Moss began the search for Henri Barrington by browsing the internet. Barrington had at one time been a part-time actor on a daytime tv soap, five years before. He was written out after two years. He hadn't appeared on tv again and by the information Moss found on an actors' website, hadn't done any stage or repertory work. It looked as if the acting days had dried up or he had chosen to do something else to make a living. The information provided gave his date of birth, place of birth and the names of his parents, but that was the sum totality of the information. He was close to twenty-five years the junior of Melinda Falkland.

The Barrington family were wealthy. Members of an old London based banking family. It would appear that Henri wasn't short of money and perhaps didn't have to work that often to feed himself and live in a style he had become accustomed to. He did have a younger sister called Tabitha Young. She was a well-known socialite and a former style guru and influencer on a daytime tv programme. A one-time hit girl who hung around with other like-minded hit girls.

Barrington had a Facebook page that said he lived in Putney. He had been a frequent visitor to the 'Bona-Vista' club in the west-end where he had worked as a 'meeter and greeter' for a while. The club had once been the kind of place were film and tv stars and those who wanted to be seen, hung out. That was before the club lost its edge and the patrons moved on to some other place to be photographed by the *paps*. Perhaps he still hung around in there and he lived off his name as a former soap star.

The Bona-Vista club was in Mayfair. It wasn't that far from Moss's office. Perhaps it would make sense for him to pay a visit to the club to see if anyone knew Barrington and if so where he could be found. First, he called Bob Ambrose and asked him to do some digging around for him. Ambrose asked what kind of digging. Moss told him.

Ambrose said fine, he was up for it. Next Moss contacted DI Luke Terry to ask him if he could shed any light on Henri Barrington's whereabouts. Other than a Facebook page which hadn't been used in a long time, the fountain of knowledge on his whereabouts, had dried up.

Moss decided to take the short walk into Mayfair to see if there was anyone at the club who knew of his whereabouts.

The Bona-Vista club was on Mount Street, right in the heart of plush Mayfair. Blink and you'd miss the entrance. It had once, been the place to be seen in. All the hit boys and girls gravitated to it in the new romantic period. That was the best part of twenty years ago. How times had changed. Now it was just another night-club that had lost its pulling power and much of its attraction.

The entrance was just a single door. Nothing fancy. It had a black glass frontage. No flashing signs or swanky notice spelling its name. No notices, other than a request from the management for patrons to leave as quietly as possible as this was a residential area. That notice must have been there for some time because the ink had started to run and blend into one. As it was this area appeared to be mostly business. A spruce topiary tree sat in a glazed glass pot by the doorway. A flower basket hooked onto a frame was empty of plants. The club didn't appear to be open at three in the afternoon. There was a 'RING HERE' notice advising visitors to ring the doorbell. The path running along the side of the street was narrow at this spot, so the edge of the road was only a few steps away. A thin line of people were just ambling by, but it wasn't busy. No one was stopping to take a photograph of the once go-to place in the heart of Mayfair. The black glass, unpretentious, front gave it the impression of a place to be avoided. As if it was slightly seedy and out of limits. Like a dungeon for S&M lovers to partake in their wildest fantasies. It had three upper floors, covered in the same black glass cladding.

Moss thought he would be lucky to find anyone inside. Still, he pressed the bell and waited. There was no response, just as he assumed. He was just about to walk away when there was the sound of a bolt opening, then the sight of the single door coming open. A grey-haired, middle-aged man appeared in the doorway and gazed out onto the street. He was wearing a blue two-tone Ben Sherman shirt, and light trousers.

He looked at Moss. "Did you ring the bell?" he asked him.

"Yeah."

"What do you want? You're not the delivery man."

"That's true."

"We're not open today. Not until ten!"

Moss glanced at his watch. "I'm looking for Henri Barrington." He pronounced his forename with a French pronunciation.

"Aren't we all!" the man replied.

"Aren't we all, what?

"Looking for him."

"Did he work here?"

"He did once upon a time."

"I don't suppose you know where he is nowadays?"

"You'll be right. I don't. The last time I saw him was months ago. He was with some old bird. I ain't seen him since." He poured his eyes over Moss to give him the once over. "Why are you asking," he nosily enquired.

"I'm working for a client who's looking for him."

"Owes her money, does he?"

"How did you know?"

"Let's call it a lucky guess. He's a bit of a rake is our Hennie."

"Hennie?"

"That's what everyone called him."

"How?"

"How what?"

"How is he a rake?"

"How do you think? He's left loads of women in his slipstream. Loves'em and leaves'em. Mainly older than him. You're not the first bloke to come here looking for him."

Moss gave a chuckle. "So, you don't know of his current whereabouts."

"No. He could be anywhere. I know he used to frequent the Lord Nelson pub in Soho. There could be someone in there who knows where he is."

Just then a white box type van came along the street at a slow speed and pulled up in front of the black windows. On the high side it said: *'Ravens Supplies'*, then underneath that: *'serving the London pub and club scene'*.

"Here's my supplies," said the chap. He took his eyes off Moss as the wagon partly reared up onto the pavement and came to a halt.

Moss knew of the Lord Nelson public house. It had been a Soho fixture for the past fifty years. It was one of the many drinking spots in the locality. It was famed for its bohemian set who had, at one time, frequented the bar. Musicians and old rockers flocked there in its heyday as it was the pub to be discovered in. David Bowie was supposed to have written 'Fashion', and 'Fame' in the back room. It was probably nothing more than an urban myth. The Beatles, or at least George Harrison in particular, was supposed to have been a frequent visitor.

Moss made his way through the slowly developing late afternoon rush hour the several hundred yards from Mount Street onto Dean Street and the location of the public house. It was one of the closest watering holes to his office. Just a couple of streets away. Ironic in some respects that Henri Barrington may have been a patron. He entered the pub through the only doorway and headed into the darkened interior. With a name like Lord Nelson the pub had a nautical theme. Several paintings of Britain's greatest naval hero were placed on the walls in homage to another period in history.

At four in the afternoon the interior was less than busy. A juke box or the sound system was playing some music he didn't recognise. Over the bar was a glassed-in upper storage space lined with empty pint pots. The painted murals in the glass depicted scenes from some historic naval battles. It was frequented now by a few tourist types and maybe some local Soho residents. It was all dark rose leather upholstery seating along the walls. A few imitation copper-topped tables were dotted here and there.

Moss stepped up to the bar. He had to wait for a minute before someone behind the bar spotted him and waltzed over to serve him. He asked for a double 'Lambs Navy' rum and a bottle of coke. He parted with a twenty-pound note, and told the barman to get one for himself.

The chap returned with a five-pound note for his change. "Can I ask you a question?" Moss asked him.

"Sure, you can. But don't expect the right answer," he replied in a comedic joust.

Moss smiled at him. "Do you know a fellow called Henri Barrington. He might come in here now and again."

"Who?"

"Henri Barrington. He used to be on tv a few years ago on one of the soaps."

"Henri?" piped up a voice from behind. Moss turned his head to see a tall, portly, middle-aged man in a crumpled, dark suit standing by a mirrored pillar. He had a copy of the Evening Standard resting on a narrow shelf in front of him. It was open at the horse racing page. The chap was thick set and looked as if he liked his food. He had a grey moustache and hair in nostrils and ears. The hair on his head was thinning and swept back over an oily pate. He had the appearance of a tv personality who he hadn't seen for some time. It wasn't who he was looking for and he didn't know the man.

"Henri Barrington. Do you know him?" Moss asked, turning to him.

"I used to."

"Have you seen him recently?"

"Not in here for a while."

"How long?"

"About six months."

"Do you know where he's living?"

"Who wants to know?" the stranger asked.

Moss noticed that he had a near empty glass in front of him. "Can I buy you a drink?" he offered.

"Okay, thanks. A pint of Guinness."

Moss turned back to the bar and asked the barman for a pint of Guinness. He took his glass containing the rum and the bottle of coke off the bar, turned to face the chap and rested his drink on the shelf, close to the where the chap had placed is near empty glass.

"Why do you want to know?" the stranger asked.

"Believe it or not I work for a tv magazine. We're putting a feature together on old soap stars. A kind of 'what are they doing now' expose. I recall him from a few years ago and someone else put his name forward as a possible interviewee. We're seeking to locate him to ask if he wants to get involved. Last I heard he was a meeter and greeter in the Bona-Vista club in Mayfair."

"That was a few years ago. Barrow-boy. That's what we called him."

"Yeah. Barrow-boy"

"Character."

"That's what I hear."

A raised voice came from behind. Moss looked back to see the barman place a pint of thick, black stout on the top of the bar. He wanted a fiver in return. Moss paid him. He took the pint and placed it on the shelf before the chap.

"I can give you his mobile number," said the chap.

"Brilliant."

"Just a minute." The stranger dug his hand deep into his inside jacket pocket and pulled out a battered iPhone. He soon found the contacts page and waltzed through his speed dials. He found the number and read it out loud. Moss took his phone and after asking the chap to repeat the eleven digits, entered it into his contacts page, then saved it to the memory.

"How do you know Barrington?" he asked.

"Oh, through this and that," he repaid cagily. "We used to chat every now and again. About racing, mostly. I liked Hennie."

"Do you know where he's living now?"

"Last I heard. Out west with some posh bird."

"From what I hear he's a jack the lad."

"Yeah, always had a cracker on his arm."

"Do you know his current address?"

"It might be Earls Court. Or Barons Court. With some old boiler."

"Thanks for your help."

"Thanks for the pint," said the chap as he picked it up and placed the rim to his lips. "I hope you find him soon."

"So, do I."

Moss swiftly drained off the rum and coke. He left the public house shortly after and walked the short distance back to his office. He wanted to be back there before the chap in the pub had the opportunity to call Barrington to tell him that somebody was looking for him.

He got back to his office in five minutes flat. He got comfortable in the swivel chair behind his desk, took his phone, brought up the contacts page and hit the new entry. He didn't get through to him immediately. He didn't expect to. It went straight to the voice mail option.

Moss had, in the time it had taken him to walk back from the pub, composed a message in his head. He said:

*'Is that Henri Barrington? My name is Dave. I'm a freelance journalist doing a piece for a tv magazine about soap stars from the past. A kind of 'where are they now' feature. I wonder if you might give me a call when you have a minute? Perhaps we can meet to discuss the assignment?*

He ended the call. He thought he had sounded genuine enough. He had given his voice a little pushy edge, something a journalist might do in order to get a story. If Barrington was interested, he would have his number on his phone. He might fall for it. He might not.

## Chapter Three

A couple of hours passed. It was now just after six in the evening. Henri Barrington nor anyone else had called him. Had he hit an impasse? With nothing much to do Moss left the office, hailed a taxi and went home to relax. He had not seen his lady friend, Claudette Munro, for a week. They were back as an item after falling out for a month or two. They had developed an understanding that the relationship wouldn't develop into anything too deep.

At eight that evening just as he was thinking about her, she called him. Sadly, it wasn't the best piece of news he had received. She told him that just two hours before she had been mugged on a street in east London by a lad on a scooter. She had been to visit her mother who lived in Bethnal Green. She was a little shaken by the experience, but other than that she was okay. The culprit had driven up behind her on the path, then with brute force, ripped her bag off her shoulder. It contained a little bit of cash, not much, a ring that was worth next to nothing and a credit card, which she had cancelled almost immediately.

Moss was fuming with rage. What he wouldn't have given to have been coming around the corner at the time of the theft. A local chap had reacted to her shout for help, and chased after the villain but he was on a fast scooter. He had easily got away. Who the hell in their right mind would attack a defenceless lady in broad daylight? It was almost beyond comprehension. Claudette said she was okay. But she would say that. She had contacted the police who had opened a file, but it wouldn't develop into a full investigation. It wasn't violent enough.

Her attacker was wearing a helmet therefore she had no description of him. The number plate had black tape over it. Obscuring the letters and numbers. Moss wanted to find him more than anything in the world. To deliver him instant justice that the court wouldn't. To give him a beating he wouldn't forget in a hurry. But he couldn't do that. He would be just as bad as the scrote. He would leave it to the police to find the culprit, though he knew the chances of that were slim. Still, she wasn't hurt, only shook up by the incident. He told her he would put tomorrow to one side to visit her and take her out into the countryside for the full day. She told him she would see him tomorrow night and not to fret too much.

That night Moss retired to bed at midnight. He found it difficult to get to sleep. He got up at around two in the morning and made himself a stiff drink. He sat at the kitchen table and contemplated his life. He didn't know how he had got to this point in his life. He felt himself tumbling down a long dark tunnel that threw him out onto the street. The turns he had taken that led him here? He didn't feel happy. He couldn't put his finger on why. Maybe it was the case. His relationship with Claudette? He didn't know for sure. His relationship with her seemed to go from high to low over a short period of time. One minute it was good. The next it was so-and-so. The snatch of her handbag had left him feeling angry and useless. That the world was a dangerous place. Full of horrible people who gave the human race a bad name.

He returned to bed at three o'clock and managed to get three hours sleep. He got up at six, showered, then made himself some breakfast, watched morning tv for five minutes, then left his home for seven and walked to his office in Soho. He decided to drop into a café at the junction of Regent Street and Broadwick Street and sat in there for thirty minutes drinking their coffee and flicking through the pages of a morning red-top newspaper.

He made it into his office for eight. The telephone rang at half past the hour. It was Roseanne Massey wanting to know if he had made any progress finding Henri Barrington. He told her his investigation was ongoing. He had a few people making enquiries for him. He was still waiting for a former colleague in the Met police to get back to him. Other than that, he was on the case and continuing to make enquiries. She seemed happy with his explanation, then rang off moments later.

For the next thirty minutes Moss concentrated on one of the insurance cases he had been asked to look at by Ray Bentley.

The next telephone call he received was close to eleven o'clock when his phone rang again. He looked into the window to see it was Henri Barrington returning his call. He took a deep breath then hit the accept button.

"Hello, its David," he said, but intentionally left his surname out.

"You called me yesterday. Something about an article?" the caller asked.

"Is that Henri Barrington?"

"Yes."

"Oh. Many thanks for calling back so swiftly."

"You said something about a feature."

"That's right."

"Who are you?"

"I'm a freelance writer. I'm doing an article for a tv magazine about previous soap stars. A kind of where are they now exclusive."

"For whom?" Barrington's accent had an upper class, Harrow educated la-di-da edge to it. He used words sparingly. Perhaps it was an indication that he was suspicious.

"It's aimed at the tv listings magazines. The Saturday supplements."

"Who else have you contacted?"

"A few people from the soaps."

"Who like?"

"I'd rather not say at the moment, until they've signed up." he thought he had made an error saying that so sought to gloss over it. "To be honest you're the first I've asked. I'm going to contact a few others from EastEnders and Corrie and the other soaps."

"How come I've never heard of you?"

"I'm just starting out on a new career. This is my first big assignment." Barrington was wary. Moss thought he had covered his back well. Or as well as possible in the circumstances.

"How much are we talking?" Barrington asked.

"Money wise?"

"Yeah."

"The budget's a bit tight, but I can go to two thousand up front."

"What's the format?"

Moss had to think on his feet. "It's a Q&A type of interview. I'll ask you a few questions in a light-hearted way. Record your answers."

"What type of questions?"

"What are you doing now? Do you miss the tv? Other actors, etcetera. Any funny stories. I'll have a photographer with me. We'll take a few snaps. Pick the best one. See how you are now. A kind of before and after comparison."

"I hear that you spoke to Ernie, in the Lord Nelson the other day."

"Ernie?"

"The guy who used to be a tv producer."

"Oh right. The chap in the pub. He didn't tell me his name or his job."

"So how did you get my number?"

"Ernie gave it to me." Barrington didn't respond and there was a period of silence. "You still there?" Moss asked.

"Yeah. I'm still here."

"Can we do a deal? I'd really appreciate it."

"Maybe."

"What if the photographer and I come to your home one day soon? Do it in private. Get a few snaps. You sitting in your garden with your partner or whoever. Is tomorrow, okay?"

"Who do you work for?"

"I'm freelance. I don't work for anyone, but myself. What do you say?"

"Let me have a think about it." It sounded as if his suspicion antenna was bouncing from side to side. He was more streetwise than Moss had anticipated. Did he know this was a ruse to discover his whereabouts?

"Alternatively, we could do it in another venue."

"I'll consider doing it for three thousand," he said. "We'll meet in a hotel lobby. Or someplace like that. I'll also need to check out your credentials."

"Fine," said Moss trying to sound upbeat and to brazen it out. "Where shall I send my credentials?" he asked.

"Email them to me."

"All right. Let me have your email address."

Barrington supplied him with an email address. He was effectively pushing Moss into a corner and he knew it. Moss knew he could easily knock up some fake testimonials overnight. It wasn't difficult to produce something that would look authentic. He wrote the email address onto a pad and told him he would send them sometime tomorrow. The conversation ended at that point. What Moss did have was his email address. He wondered if Bob Ambrose would be able to trace his home address by the ISP. He didn't know.

Barrington said he would wait for his email, then ended the call without uttering another word.

In the seconds after the conversation with Barrington ended abruptly, Moss put in a call to Ambrose. He asked him if he could trace an address by the ISP or by his mobile telephone number. 'It wouldn't be easy', said Ambrose. It might take a while. The easiest way was through the ISP address, but only if Barrington responded to his fake email.

Moss gave Ambrose the email address Barrington had given him. He believed he was finally getting somewhere. He suddenly felt upbeat when he thought he could be on the verge of finding him.

After chatting to Ambrose for five minutes, Moss rang off, then he contacted DI Luke Terry. Henri Barrington did have a sheet going back a few years when he had committed a minor drug bust. His address at the time was in Brompton, west London. He had been twenty-two years of age at the time. That was three years before he landed the role in 'Tony's Place' the television daytime soap for lonely housewives, the retired and those who avoided working for a living.

After chatting to Luke Terry, Moss set about creating a fake ID for the fledging tv journalist. It took him the best part of two hours to create something that looked genuine. He sent it off to the email address Barrington had given him.

That evening, Moss left his office at quarter to six and set off to Bow to visit Claudette in her home. He got there within an hour. She was jittery and on edge. She hadn't suffered any psychical harm as a result of the theft. The harm was psychological. Such an incident could have a really devastating effect on the victim. Claudette, whilst not dismissive, remained positive and strong and more inclined to laugh it off in a gallows humour type of way, which was very admirable but maybe an indication that she was trying too hard to present a 'I'm okay' front. She cooked him a nice meal, then they settled down with a nice bottle of red in front of the tv.

He wanted to stay the night. She wasn't in the mood for him to stay over. He stayed nonetheless, and they watched tv until midnight, then he left and headed home. On his way home, he read a text message from Bob Ambrose. Barrington was proving to be more careful and cannier than he had imagined. His computer IP address was logged to a library in Putney. It was one of those public friendly facilities. People could use a PC for an hour; therefore, it wasn't his home address.

Moss had been further thwarted in his effort to find Henri Barrington. He texted Ambrose, thanking him for the message. He didn't know where he was going with this investigation. Perhaps nowhere fast was the answer.

Chapter Four

The following morning dawned bright but cool. The April days were lengthening and becoming brighter, though the temperature still hovered around a cool twelve degrees centigrade. That morning Moss left home at eight and took the tube for the short ride to Oxford Circus. From there he walked the short distance to his office in Soho. On arriving, he made himself a cup of strong, black coffee, opened the post, which included a cheque for five grand from one of the insurance companies he did work for. Then he looked on-line and checked his email to see if Henri Barrington had responded to his email.

He hadn't yet, and perhaps never would. He was proving to be very elusive. Perhaps more clued-up than he gave him credit for. During the morning he received a call from a client he had worked for previously, asking him to carry out a check on an executive who had recently left his employment. He wanted Moss to investigate if the ex-employee had taken some of the files with him in the form of customer profiles and account details.

He had just finished reading the brief when there was a sudden and surprise beep on the button at the door downstairs. He said 'hello' into the communication device and instantly recognised DCI Steve Rice's voice. Rice said he was here with DI Pamela Bent.

Moss went onto the landing, and down the staircase to let them in, then led them up into his office.

"What do I owe this pleasurable surprise?" he asked.

The plain clothed cops made themselves comfortable in the two armchairs along the wall from the three metal storage units. The morning light slicing through the gaps in the blinds at the window, gave the room a kind of shadowy atmospheric ambience. He offered to make them a coffee or perhaps something stronger from the bottle of whisky in the top-drawer of one of the three storey cabinets. It was way too early to start drinking hard liquor.

"Henri Barrington," said DCI Rice in response to his question.

"What about him?"

"We understand that you were talking to him yesterday."

"That's right."

"Why?" DI Bent asked.

"Why do you want to know? Is there something I should know?"

"He's in a hospital in west London, fighting for his life," was Rice's candid response to the question.

Moss was more astonished than mortified to receive this news. "Who? Henri Barrington?" he enquired. "How?"

"Someone mowed him down on the road last night," DI Bent revealed.

"Geez. Where? What? In a car?"

"Where were you at about two a.m. this morning?" Rice asked him.

"I'd been in my home for about one hour. I'd been to see a friend who was robbed the other day. I left her place at just after half past midnight."

"Can anyone vouch for you?" she asked.

"Come on. What do you take me for? I'm hardly likely to go around running people over."

Rice cleared his throat. "We checked his mobile phone. We saw your telephone number in the log."

"The log also contains details of the time you made a call to him yesterday," DI Bent added.

"For crying out loud. You don't suspect me. Do you?"

Rice made a face by rolling his bottom lip into his mouth. "Odd, that you're contacting him. Then this happens," he commented.

"If you must know a client put me onto a job to locate his home address. But he's as slippery as a snake, I've not been able to pin him down. How bad are his injuries?"

"Life threatening."

"Someone matching your description was seen hanging out near to the place he was living," she revealed.

"I'm beginning to smell a rat here. A set-up."

"By whom? Who hired you?"

"A lady by the name of Roseanne Massey. But I'm beginning to wonder if it's really her."

"What's the angle. Why the need to locate him?" Rice asked.

"According to her, Barrington conned her mother out of a quarter of a million pounds."

"And?"

"And I told her I'd try to find out where he is, but so far, he's proved to be as elusive as ..." he sought to think of a decent example... "as a pork sandwich at a bar-mitzvah. Trying to find someone in a city of ten million people who'd rather not be found, isn't easy."

"Will you pop into a police station to make a full statement?" DCI Rice asked.

"Of course, I will."

"What have you done to try and find him?" she asked.

"A couple of things."

"Like?"

"I've visited the old Bona-Vista club in Mayfair yesterday and spoke to some guy who I'm assuming is the manager. I went into the Lord Nelson pub just around the corner from here. I got lucky in there. I got chatting to this stranger, a customer in there, who said he had his telephone number. That's how I happened to be on his phone."

"Who was it?"

"Who was what?"

"The person who gave you the number."

"I didn't ask for a name."

"What did he look like?"

"Mid-forties. Maybe older. Average height. Portly. Grey salt and pepper moustache. Stylishly scruffy dresser. He was reading the racing section in a copy of the Standard. He had a polished look. Might be called Ernie."

DI Pamela Bent crossed her legs. He hadn't noticed the chain link bracelet around her ankle before. Her legs were really slim and delicate as if they'd snap under the least pressure. "If we contact Roseanne Massey, will she confirm that she has been talking to you?"

"If it's really her, then yes she will."

"What's the story she told you?"

"That Henri Barrington had met her mother and rinsed her out of a large amount of money."

"How much?"

"A cool quarter of a million."

"How?"

"Requests for money here and there, I gather it soon added up into a decent amount."

"But then he dropped her." DI Bent commented in a barbed tone.

"Are you asking me or telling me?"

"Neither."

"A statement of fact then?"

"So, her daughter comes to you asking you to find him. Is that right?" Rice asked.

"That's right."

"Why?"

"So, she can do something about getting the money back or at least some of it."

"Did you give her his address?"

"No. As I've said I haven't been able to trace his whereabouts."

"You sure?"

"Positive."

"But someone found him."

"So, it would appear to be the case. That's why I think I might have been set up by someone to take the rap."

"Looks that way."

"You guys know me. Am I the kind to go around knocking people over in my car? Surely the car will be damaged. Check mine there's not a scratch on it. It's not in my DNA. If I had his whereabouts, I'd have told her and that was it. The job would be over. I'd have no need to run him over. You know that."

"What did your visitor look like?"

"Who?"

"Roseanne Massey."

"Like a former highly paid fashion model. Stylish. Classy, I suppose you'd say."

"She fitted the bill?" Rice asked.

"Yeah, I'd say so. She came across as the caring daughter. Troubled by the thought that someone had conned her dear old mum out of a large amount of dough."

"What do you think has happened?" DI Bent asked.

"Someone obviously knew where to find him. Wanted to harm him for some reason."

"That would appear to be the case," Rice uttered.

"Who?" asked DI Bent.

"I don't know. Maybe he has pissed off someone else. Or maybe they were trying to put me in the frame for it."

"And you don't know who?"

"No."

"Maybe it's the person who said she was Roseanne Massey."

"Could be. But that's if she is really her. Someone could be pretending to be her."

DI Terry and Bent looked at each other. Moss was waiting to hear a code word they had created.

"So, you were at your girlfriend's. Until what time?" she asked.

"Just gone half twelve. Then I drove home. Getting there at around five to one, after stopping to take a text from an associate."

"Who?"

"If you must know, Bob Ambrose."

The conversation had the feel of one of those that would go around in circles. It started off okay, went around and around until it came back on itself like a returning boomerang.

"If we contact Roseanne Massey, she'll be able to confirm that she came here to talk to you." Rice said.

"If it's really her. Yes."

"How are you going to contact her?"

"She gave me a phone number."

"When?" Rice asked.

"When what?"

"When are you going to contact her."

"When I'm in a position to give her the information she wants. His address."

"If we contact Melinda Falkland, will she confirm she knows Henri Barrington?"

"The client showed me a photograph of them together on a beach somewhere. Miami. They know each other. Unless it was a photo-shop made up image, but I doubt it."

"Who showed you the photograph?" DI Bent asked.

"Roseanne Massey showed me the photograph as confirmation of a liaison. It would appear from it they did know each other."

Moss took in a deep breath. The penny dropping through his head told him that the lady who had come to see him wasn't Roseanne Massey and neither was the lady in the photograph Melinda Falkland.

"Will you pop into the police station in Charing Cross sometime today to provide a written statement of your whereabouts this morning? Just for the record," asked Rice.

"Of course, I will. Not a problem."

Clearly, they, Rice and Bent, didn't think Moss had been the driver of the car that had hit Barrington and put him in an ICU unit. If Roseanne Massey denied she had been into his office, it might make the situation a little tricky, but not lethal. If the police spoke to Melinda Falkland, and she denied knowing Barrington, then someone really was seeking to set him up.

## Chapter Five

As soon as the two detectives left his office, Moss compiled a six-hundred-word statement, first in long hand, then he edited it to take out any inconsistencies. In doing so, losing a quarter of the words for the useable version. He typed the final version into his computer and printed off a copy.

When he had read the content, several times, and was happy with the finished text, he signed and dated the statement. Once complete, he took a few minutes out to call Claudette at her home. She had slept right through to ten o'clock this morning. She was having the rest of the week off work courtesy of her employee, Camden Education Authority. He asked her what time he had left her home this morning. She said it was a shade after twelve-thirty. He ended the call with a 'goodbye', then immediately turned to his computer and brought up the local London news. He found a snippet of news about an incident in Chiswick, west London, in the early hours of this morning, in which a man had been badly injured in what looked like a 'hit and run' incident.

It revealed that the police were looking for the driver of a 4x4, possibly a silver body Range Rover. There was no description of the driver. The name of the injured man was not released to the public.

He took the statement he had written, put it into an envelope, sealed it closed, then he left his office and took a walk to the nearest police station. It was in Charing Cross. It was only a ten-minute walk from his office.

At the desk he asked for DCI Rice. He was informed that he wasn't here, and neither was DI Pamela Bent. He asked the officer behind the counter to ensure the envelope got to one of them. With no charges pending he was free to leave the station and get on with his day. Perhaps, DCI Rice believed he had given the address to the person who had tried to kill Hennie Barrington. Come what may, he couldn't second guess that someone would try to kill him.

When he left the police station Moss returned to his office, first stopping on the way back to purchase a tuna and mayo sandwich from a Greek owned deli. The time was close to midday.

It was just after one o'clock when he took a call from DI Luke Terry. Moss had been expecting a call from him. DI Terry, speaking in a surreptitious tone, gave him an update on what he knew about the incident involving Barrington. He, Barrington, had apparently, been returning home at close to 2am this morning. As he entered the street in Chiswick in which he rented a flat in a block of maisonettes, a 4x4 came hurtling around the corner and collided with him. He was thrown to the ground where he hit his head against a cobble stone surface and sustained a nasty injury. His condition now was thought to be non-life threatening, but he was badly concussed. He had been stabilised, taken out of the ICU and transferred onto a normal ward in an Ealing hospital. What DI Terry did provide him with was the address where Henri Barrington was currently living.

DI Terry also informed him that the Met police would be releasing a statement later in the afternoon, at 5pm, about the incident in order to engage the public with a request for help to find the hit-and-run driver. They would name Henri Barrington at that time as the victim.

Moss glanced up at the clock on the wall. The time was ten past one. He had four hours to get in touch with the lady who said she was Roseanne Massey before the news broke.

He called her mobile number. It went straight to voice mail. He asked her to call him back as soon as possible. There was little he could do now, therefore he turned away from the case for half an hour to do some prep work on one of the insurance assignments.

The hour passed by very slowly. It got to two p.m. and still no call from the client. Two o'clock soon became half past. He was beginning to doubt he would ever hear from the client. It was getting on for thirty-thirty when, much to his surprise he received a return call from someone who sounded like Roseanne Massey. She apologised for not getting in touch with him earlier. She sounded mildly stressed and out of breath as if she had been rushing.

"No problem," he said. "I've got the address you've been waiting for."

"For Henri?"

"Yes. Perhaps you'd like to come into my office or meet me in a place of your choice. I'll hand it over to you along with my bill."

"How much do I owe you," she asked.

"Make it a round one thousand pounds. Ten hours at one hundred pounds."

"I'll come into your office. Is a banker's cheque, okay?"

"A banker's cheque is fine."

Roseanne said she would be in his office in one hour from now. She told him she was at her home in Bermondsey. He said he looked forward to meeting her, then ended the conversation at that point.

As soon as he put the telephone down he turned in his chair to peer down onto the street below to observe the people ambling by. A small group of Chinese or Japanese tourists were being led by someone holding an umbrella aloft and taking them down the street to the junction with Regents Street. The twang of a busker's guitar vibrated and echoed against the high wall of buildings along the narrow thoroughfare. Then the sound of a voice singing the opening line of 'Halleluiah' cut through the quiet. That song written by that guy whose name Moss could never remember. It sounded like an angel singing a psalm.

Chapter Six

It was close to four p.m., one hour before the news of the incident concerning Henri Barrington was going to be released to the public, when the lady he knew as Roseanne Massey arrived on the path outside the door adjacent to the pastry shop. She was on her own.

He went down the staircase to let her in. She was wearing a Gingham-style summer dress with a wide, frilly hem. It was buttoned up like a bodice to her chest. Her mint white and green shade Versace jacket looked expensive. Her long hair was trimmed and bouncy. She had a splash of rouge on her cheeks and a blue edge mascara on her eyes. Her eyebrows were long and thin. The rings on her fingers contained turquoise stones and onyx jet. She smelt of Chanel number five. Her nail varnish was the shade of burnt orange.

He escorted her up the staircase, into his office and asked her to take the chair which he had placed in front of his desk. The incoming strips of light and shade splashed across her with a two-tone effect.

He sat down in the seat behind his desk, then reached to one side, opened a drawer and extracted a plain buff colour envelope and placed it down, in front of him on the desk top. He opened it to reveal a single white A4 envelope inside. He could see that her eyes were following his movements. She rested the handbag she was carrying on the edge of the desk, opened it and extracted a white envelope of her own.

"I have a cheque here for one thousand pounds," she said as she placed the envelope flat on the desk top.

"Thanks," he said. He took it, ripped it open, extracted a cheque and ran his eyes over the details. It was, as agreed, made payable to 'David Moss Investigation Services.' As it was a bank cheque it didn't reveal who she was or her bank details.

He slipped it inside the folder.

"What is Barrington's address?" she asked in a calm non-flustered manner.

He sat back in his seat and opened his chest wide. "Before I tell you that, I'd be very grateful if you would tell me who you are?"

She thrust her head back as if mortally wounded by the implication in his words. She screwed her pretty face into an instant manufactured frown. "Why, I'm Roseanne Massey," she protested.

"No." He shook his head from side to side several times. "I don't think so."

"What?"

"You're not Roseanne Massey. The real Roseanne spends six months of the year in Spain. Your colouring doesn't reflect that. Anyone in the sun for that long would have fairer hair and a deeper ingrained tan than yours. You have neither. That's why I think your someone else."

"Who?"

"One of Barrington's jilted girlfriends. A former lover. There's also a couple of other tell-tale factors."

"Such as?"

"You don't speak with a genuine la-di-da accent. Yours is made up. The Massey-Falkland's are a very well to do family from the stockbroker belt. The way you talk doesn't reflect that."

"Anything else?" she asked coolly.

"Yes. They are Home Counties people. When I talked to you earlier you told me that you were at home in east London."

"Why would I pretend to be someone I'm not?"

"Because you're impersonating someone you might know very well."

"Why?"

"You're someone who is seeking to get back at him. That's why you came to see me, but I think you already knew where he was all along."

"That's rubbish."

"Is it"? You wanted to create a smokescreen, so you came here, claiming to be the daughter of one of his old flames, but you dreamed that up in order to take suspicion away from yourself. I think you drove to his home address at 2am this morning, waited a while until you saw him then drove your car at him. You or someone you know."

"That's crazy."

"Is it?"

"What about the photograph I showed you."

"Henri Barrington gave it to you. You've fallen out with him. I don't know if you ever intended to harm him by running him over. That or you had something else in mind."

"Very interesting," she said.

"So, who are you really? His sister Tabitha? No, I don't think so. I'd guess his sister and he haven't spoken for a while. A former lover who he promised to give some of the money he rinsed out of Melinda Falkland to. I think that part is true. Perhaps you helped him, but he failed to honour his promise to pay you." She didn't stare at him and neither did she stir. "So, who are you?" he asked.

"Does it really matter?"

"Maybe not. But yeah, I'd like to know."

"Is it really any of your business?"

"That's true. You're the client."

"Client confidentiality."

"But not in a case in which you or someone you know would deliberately aim a lethal vehicle, a weapon, at someone. With the intention of killing him or if not killing him badly hurting him. That's called attempted murder. But you didn't succeed. He's still alive."

"Is he? I don't believe you."

"He survived. It's one hundred percent true. What isn't true is that your Roseanne Massey. I think you know her. Maybe she's your best friend. You're an accomplice. Maybe you know a lot about her and her mother. Perhaps you were the architect of getting them together, so you could ask him for money. Thing is he didn't give anything to you."

"That's rubbish."

"Who are you?" he asked for the third time.

"One of his old girlfriends," she admitted.

"When did you last see him?" he enquired.

"About three months ago."

"In the Bona-Vista?"

"No one goes in there anymore."

"How long have you known him?"

"For many years."

"When did you first meet him?"

"When we used to frequent the clubs and the scene around here. With the likes of the new romantic set."

"Who put you up to this?"

"No one."

"The real Roseanne Massey? She used to be a hit girl. Was it her?"

The look in her eye told him he had hit a nerve. He waited. "Yes." She admitted.

"Why?"

"Roseanne and Barrington were once lovers."

"Did she set up the whole thing with her mother?"

"Yes. That's true."

"Where did you meet Roseanne."

"In the Bona-Vista. That's where she got spotted and got her big break into the world of high fashion." She took a brief moment to reflect on what she had said. She looked at him with a stiff, pained face. "Are you going to tell the police?"

"Me?"

"Yes."

"No. Why should I? He probably got what he deserved." She didn't reply. "Who attempted to run over him. You or Roseanne or someone else?" She said nothing. The way she had responded to the news that Barrington had survived was interesting. Perhaps, whoever had ran him over, assumed he was dead. Maybe she hadn't been behind the wheel, after all. Maybe it had been the real Roseanne Massey behind the wheel.

He turned in his seat and looked down onto the street below. For a few brief moments he watched people going back and forth. All with different places to go. All leading different lives. Some happy. Some sad. Some rich. Some poor. No two the same. He thought of Claudette for a moment. Ironically, the motor scooter robber may have brought them closer together, though he wouldn't wish such an experience on anybody. He hated the thought that some pond life cretin had driven up behind her then brazenly snatched her handbag from her shoulder. Maybe he should try to find the robber and kick his arse from here to hell. Of course, he wouldn't do that. He would let the proper authorities search for the villain. He wouldn't risk losing his licence to practice as a Private Investigator. He put it to the back of his mind.

After a few brief moments he turned back to look at her. He still didn't know her real name. Did he care? Not that much, if the truth be told.

"I think we're done here," he said. With that he got to his feet. She did likewise. He escorted her out of the office and onto the landing. He thanked her for coming to see him and for the cheque, but also for fronting up. He said goodbye, then watched her step carefully down the staircase, open the door at the bottom and step out onto the street. There was something poignant about someone stepping through a door and going out of sight. It signalled the end game.

He headed back into his office, made for the top drawer of one of the metal cabinets, opened it and extracted a bottle of malt whisky and a single glass. In the best tradition of a hardened private eye he polished off a healthy tot of something strong, straight off, right down the hatch.

He took the file on his desk, opened the second cabinet drawer and placed it inside a suspended hanging holder. Then he went back to his desk and sat down. He picked up one of the insurance tasks he had been working on to re-familiarise himself with the facts. Happy days, he thought. Back to the bread and butter. The meat and the gravy stuff.

**The End**

# Five Angry Men

Chapter One

The thunder and pearl-necklace lightning, flashing across the sky, sent the pedestrians on the street below scurrying for cover into shop doorways and under pulled-out awnings. David Moss turned in his swivel chair to look down onto the scene as the first drops of rain began to splatter against the glass in the nine-pane window frame. Drops the size of marbles were soon ricocheting like bullets on the street. He took in the scene for half a minute before being distracted by the telephone on the desk. He nonchalantly turned his eyes away from the rain and pressed the loudspeaker button on the console.

"Hello, David Moss, private investigation service. How may I help you today?" he asked. He never knew why he said today. He couldn't say 'yesterday' or 'tomorrow' so the word 'today' was a bit of a misnomer.

"Hello…Are you a private detective?" asked a firm, but hesitant female voice from the other end of the line.

"Yes." He was going to say something caustic like 'that's what I said' but baulked at the opportunity. "Can I be of assistance to you?" he asked in a welcoming and pleasant tone of voice.

She sighed. "I need someone to do an investigation for me," she said. Then added, "before it's too late."

"Okay."

"I've been given your name by someone."

He didn't ask who. She already sounded hesitant as if she was unsure that this was the best route to take. He could hear it in her voice. A kind of stunted delivery, borne of uncertainty.

"What is it?" he asked.

"My son was beaten up by five men. I want to know who they are."

"Have you spoken to the police about it?"

"Yes, for some time."

"What did they say?"

"The police told us they couldn't do anything about it."

He picked up on the word 'us' but refrained from asking who the 'us' were. "Why not?" he enquired.

"They said they didn't have enough evidence to carry out an investigation."

"When did the attack occur?" he asked.

"Around six months ago."

"What's the name of the victim in this?" he asked. "The person who was attacked."

"My son. Bakayo Ostemabo"

Moss instantly recalled hearing that name and about the case. Bakayo Ostemabo was a sixteen-year-old boy who had been attacked on a street in Tottenham, north London, by five adult, white men, allegedly. The victim had been beaten to within an inch of his life. The case had attracted a lot of unwanted attention because it was implied, first by the family, then later by the community that two of those doing the beating were serving officers in the Metropolitan police service. An allegation the Met had robustly denied. The case had become one of those *cause celebs'* when the liberal left had taken it on board and turned it into a crusade for justice and transparency. The police had investigated the incident. Despite all the resources at their disposal they hadn't been able to identify any of the culprits. Which only created a great deal of mistrust and doubt that led a lot of people to the assumption there had been an institutional cover-up. The local police had been put through the wringer because they hadn't been able to bring the culprits to justice. There was a suggestion in some quarters that the police had made a cock-up of the investigation from the outset, on purpose, to protect two of their own serving officers. This was a suggestion vehemently denied by the chief of the Met police, herself.

Moss waited for a few moments to take in what he knew before he spoke. "Has there been plenty of publicity about the case?" he asked, knowing the answer from the outset. "Did it occur around last November?" he added.

"Yes. It did."

"Six months ago, in north London. Does it include a belief that two serving police officers were involved?"

"Yes."

Moss recalled some of the background to the incident involving a youth called Bakayo Ostemabo. He was accused of sexually assaulting a white girl, whose name he couldn't recall, at a teenagers' only party in a house in Noel Park, north London. Or maybe it had occurred somewhere close by. The lad had denied that he had done such a thing. Because the police had failed to charge him it was rumoured that a group of vigilantes took the law into the own hands, hunted him down and gave him a severe beating. Because the police failed to find the men and it was murmured that two serving police officers were in the group of five, then the charge of a 'cover-up' was muted. A left-leaning newspaper had investigated the case and the local MP had also raised the question of a police cover-up in the House of Commons, but the police steadfastly refused to reopen the case, telling the public that they had insufficient evidence to pursue it. In the six months following the incident a committee called 'Justice for Bakayo' had been set up and subscriptions had been collected to build a fund to help the family achieve the justice they thought they rightly deserved.

Moss found himself in a bit of a dilemma. He didn't know if he wanted to get involved in this. He could be in danger of alienating himself. After all, he did on many occasions ask his former colleagues for help in solving other cases. If he took on this case, it may cause problems for him in the long term. He opted to hedge his bets for the time being.

"Perhaps the best thing would be for me to meet with you in order to chat to you about your requirements and the case," he suggested.

"I want to find the names of the five men who put my son in hospital for four weeks." Her words were terse, impassioned and her tone was brusque. She clearly had a desire to find those responsible and bring them to justice. Perhaps she had detected the hesitation in his voice.

"I understand," he said. "I think the best thing to do is for us to meet and talk it through."

"I'll agree to that," she offered.

"I can come to you. Is that okay with you?"

She said she'd appreciate him visiting her, rather than the other way around. She gave him an address in Upper Edmonton in north London. He arranged to visit at three o'clock that very afternoon. Moss said goodbye and ended the call.

The next thing he did was to turn the hands-free volume down to zero, then spin in his chair to face the window frame, see his reflection in the glass, then look down to the street below. The thunder and lightning hadn't lasted long. In the two minutes he had been on the telephone the dark clouds had moved away. All that was left of the sudden storm was the rainbow arching above the roofs of the buildings across the area and a damp sodden street.

## Chapter Two

The Ostemabo family, all six of them, one guardian – the mother – plus five children, resided in a three-bedroom tenement flat in a mid-level block that was close to Edmonton Green railway station. There was Mrs Ostemabo and her five children. The man of the house was nowhere to be seen. It would appear that he had left her to bring up five children who ranged from six years of age, the youngest, to the oldest who was eighteen. Mrs Ostemabo told Moss she did two cleaning jobs to keep the family together.

Both her oldest son, Moses, eighteen, and Bakayo, sixteen, were good footballers who had at one time interested the likes of Tottenham Hotspur and Arsenal. North London's two biggest football clubs.

The flat was both cramped for space and crammed with gear. It had a homely feel and reminders of Lagos in Nigeria where Mr and Mrs Ostemabo had originated before coming to England, twenty-five years before. It was festooned with African artwork and face masks and colourful wall covers and ornaments. Moss would admit that he didn't know what they were called or if they were his idea of decoration. Still, they did provide some colour to an already drab interior of poor-quality furniture and fittings in this a local authority supplied home.

Mrs Ostemabo showed him into the lounge and asked him to sit on a straight back wooden seat at a dining table. The curtains over the windows were thick and blocked out a lot of the incoming light. The carpet was a dense pile and patterned like a fruit salad. Behind the wide but not high windows was a view down to a communal garden that had swings and a child's roundabout in it. The tv was off. In the middle of April there might have been a need to have the heating on. If it was on it didn't register much as the room was a tad chilly. There was a three-piece suite in a flowery design, light coloured yellowy-green shade. A chest and a small everyday kind of table for various use.

The flat was clean. It was quiet. At three in the afternoon her five children must have been out at school or a college or wherever they went during the day.

Moss made himself comfortable in the sturdy, straight back chair and crossed his legs. He placed his document holder he used to carry a pad of paper and a good supply of pens and pencils, on the dining table. He opened the zip and extracted a pad and took a pencil. The lady of the house was sitting across the table from him. She was perhaps in her mid-forties. A largish lady with very dark skin and curly dark hair that may have been a wig. Wide-framed spectacles over her eyes. He made eye contact with her and smiled, but she remained downbeat.

"Your son Bakayo. How is he now?" he enquired. "Six months after he was badly beaten up," he added.

"He's getting by," she said in a glum tone. "But since he was attacked, he's lost a lot of confidence." Her English was good, though delivered in a strong Nigerian accent.

"How about his football training? I understand he's a good player."

"He's not played much since he was hurt."

"That's a shame. What were his injuries?" he asked.

"He had five broken ribs. A punctured lung and a fracture to the skull. A lot of cuts and bruises to his face."

"I understand he was in hospital for nearly a month."

"That's right."

Just then there was a sound of the front door coming open and the evidence of someone entering the home. The door to the lounge came open and a youth entered. He paused in the doorframe and put his eyes on his mother and the unknown white man sitting at the dining table.

He was a tall, skinny black youth wearing a matching dark zip up top and sports pants, both plastered with the same trademark. He had Nike trainers on his feet. His hair was loose, braided ringlets that fell low around the arch of his eyebrows. He was at least six two, tall and lithe. He looked, for all the world, like a professional basketball player. All long arms and legs.

"This is Bakayo," she said.

Moss nodded his head and smiled at him, but didn't get a lot back in the way of an acknowledgement.

"Who's he?" Bakayo snapped, half glaring at the stranger in his home. He had an attitude. That didn't appear to be good for an investigation of the facts.

"He's the investigator I said I'd hire to find those who…"

"Forget it," he snapped this time in a louder tone than before. "I've told you a thousand times." He bellowed at his mother, made a 'huff', then promptly marched out of the room.

Moss chose not to say anything. He didn't know Bakayo was going to be here, not that it mattered that much.

"Bakayo, come back," she ordered. Much to Moss's surprise the lad came back into the room, edged inside and sat on the end of the settee. "Sit down and tell Mr Moss everything about that night."

"Which night?"

"The night you got attacked," she said in a high pitch.

"Oh, that?"

"Yes, that! Tell him."

Moss looked at him and gave him a neutral look that was open and not swaying in any direction. He didn't want to lead him or say anything that could be construed as leading, so didn't say a word.

"Come and sit at the table," said his mother.

Bakayo tutted. He got up from off the settee with a huff and a grunt, came to the table and sat down by his mum so Moss was at a ninety-degree angle to him. Bakayo placed his elbows down on the table top and rested his chin on both raised fists. There were no obvious scars or marks on his face, other than a deep line above one eye, that may have been the track of a healed gash. He put his eyes on Moss.

"Tell him about the party," his mother encouraged.

He took a deep breath. "I'd been invited to this party see, with two other friends. Across in Noel Park. At the home of this girl called Asthana."

"Who by?" Moss asked.

"By her bloke."

"Who went with you?"

"Two mates. Carlos and Jake."

"What night was it?"

"A Friday."

"What happened?"

"We went to the party. Got there for about ten. There was a load of beer and booze."

"Whose home was it?"

"This girl. Asthana."

"Did you know her?"

"No."

"Who invited you?"

"Her bloke." He'd already told Moss this.

"What's the name of her fella?"

"Tazza."

"How many people where there?"

"Loads. About thirty or forty."

"Raine Sizer. Is that the name of the girl who was allegedly assaulted?"

"Yeah. But it wasn't by me. I got blamed, but I swear it had nothing to do with me, see."

"Why would she blame you?"

"I don't know. I think she got me mixed up with someone else."

"Who was it. Who assaulted her? Do you know?"

"No. I don't."

"How long did you stay at the party?"

"I left the party about one. It was getting a bit crazy, man."

"Crazy? What do you mean?"

"The house was sort of getting *trashed* and some of the neighbours were saying they were going to call the cops because of the noise. I didn't want to stay and get into trouble."

"Did you talk to this Raine at all."

"Yeah, maybe a couple of times. But then she sorts of disappeared, and I never saw her again."

"Did you leave with your friends?"

"No. It was getting too crazy. A couple of guys were fighting. I decided to go before the cops turned up."

"Did you leave with anyone?"

"No. On my own, man."

"Where did you go?"

"I walked back here. It was only a mile or two."

"So, you have no idea what happened to Raine Sizer?"

"No."

"Why did she say that you were the one who assaulted her?"

"I don't know."

His mother sat up. "I reckon she thought it was my son, because she confused the lad with my son," she said. "I believe him when he said it wasn't him. I know my son. And I know he wouldn't lie to me."

Moss nodded his head. "What happened then?"

"Three days after the cops came here to say they wanted to question me."

"About an alleged assault on Raine Sizer. Is that right?" Moss asked.

"I told them it wasn't anything to do with me, see."

"They took him to Tottenham police station for questioning. I had to go down there to see what was going on."

"How long did the police keep you?"

"For about four hours."

"Were you charged with assault?"

"No."

"When did they drop the investigation against you."

"A couple of weeks after. The police said there was no evidence that it was Bakayo and told us there was no more investigating to do and that he wouldn't be questioned again."

"How long after was it before you were attacked on Tottenham High Road?"

"About another two weeks."

"What happened?"

"I'd just come out of the gym on the street. I was waiting for the two-four-six bus to come home. This car pulled in to the bus stop."

"Did you see it? See the model type?"

"It was too dark. It was getting on for ten-thirty."

"Then what?"

"These two guys got out and came into the shelter."

"Did they say anything to you?"

"No. Not at first. Then they grabbed me and pulled me out of the shelter and down an ally and into a car park at the back of them shops. The car came around and three more blokes got out."

"Did you say anything to them?"

"Something like what the fuck are you doing? They got me into the car park then started to punch and kick me."

"Did you see their faces."

"It was too dark."

"What about any words?"

"They said they were going to teach me a lesson."

"What for?"

"For Raine Sizer. I think."

"But did they mention that?"

"Sort of."

"So how do you know it was about the alleged assault on Raine Sizer?"

"It's got to be"

"What time was this?"

"Say twenty past ten. I left the gym at quarter past; the bus should have been there at twenty past."

"How long did the attack last?"

"About ten minutes."

"They knocked him unconscious."

"Were they all white men?" Moss asked.

"Yeah. I think."

"How did you raise the alarm?"

"I guess I must have woke up. I managed to get to my feet and stagger down the ally and back into the bus shelter. Someone there, called the cops and an ambulance."

"Why do you think you were jumped on?" Moss asked him directly.

"Because of what Raine Sizer said."

"Why did she say it was you?"

He shrugged his shoulders, opened his mouth a gave him an expression of someone struggling to see the light.

"She either got the wrong name or she was blaming my son on purpose."

"What to cover up for someone else?" Moss asked.

"Maybe," she said as if she had just considered this angle for the first time.

"How bad were your injuries?" Moss asked him.

"I lost loads of blood. They knocked out two front teeth. Broke three ribs kicking me. And gave me a fractured skull and a broken wrist."

"From which he is still suffering from headaches and pain," his mother volunteered.

"The police said they weren't able to trace the guys because the car they arrived in had false plates."

"That's rubbish," she said. "They did nothing because two of his attackers were police officers."

"But there's no evidence that that's the case." Moss said. He swiftly changed tack. "What did they say to you?"

"Who?"

"Your attackers."

"Loads of racial slurs."

Moss elected to say nothing.

"What can you do to find the men?" Bakayo's mum asked Moss directly.

"I'll make some enquiries. I'll see if anyone knows who they are. Five angry men."

"Five bullies. More like," she said as if disappointed that he had referred to them as angry men.

"Bullies are bullies," said Bakayo. "And these guys were mentally deranged."

There was the sound of the front door opening and a fourth person coming into the home. Moments later, the door opened and a girl of fourteen or so appeared in the frame. She was wearing a school uniform. Her tie was short and bent. She took one look at Moss. Didn't say a word then immediately backed out of the room and went away. Moss thought he had exhausted his time there. He told them it was time to be going.

Before leaving the flat he told Mrs Ostemabo he would take on the case to see if he could drag up the information to identify the five men who had allegedly attacked Bakayo in the car park behind the shops on Tottenham High Road. He wasn't the police and that did give him an advantage. Those who may not have been happy to talk to the police might speak to him. Ironically, he wasn't exactly delighted to say he would look at it. He didn't want to lose what police friends he had. Though something told him the chances of two serving police officers being involved in the attack on Bakayo were slim to say the least. If it was true, he could be opening himself up to the slings and arrows of misfortune.

He left the flat in the block in Edmonton about fifteen minutes after entering. He walked onto Edmonton High Street to the office of a mini cab firm and took a ride all the way to Kings Cross station, then a Hackney to his office in Soho.

## Chapter Three

The following morning, Moss was in his office for eight o'clock. He wanted to have a good think about how he was going to action this case. Perhaps the most sensible thing to do would be to refamiliarise himself with the facts. When he was sitting comfortably in front of his pc, he carried out a full and detailed trawl of all the information he could glean from the internet. From the volume of written newspaper reports to the visual in the form of clippings and videos and so forth. There was nothing much to get excited about, until a reference, popped-up, to the possibility that two serving members in the Met police service were part of the gang who had beaten Bakayo.

The rumour of police involvement developed following an apparent tip-off to a local free newspaper. The names of two police officers were released and soon became common knowledge. PC Shane Carlow was one of them. He happened to be the nephew of Leonard Sizer, Raine Sizer's father. Therefore, the cop and the victim of an assault, allegedly at the party house, were cousins. The other cop was named as PC Paul Menzies. Both were young uniformed cops working out of the Tottenham High Road police station. Both vehemently denied any connection to the event. The subsequent police enquiry cleared them of any wrongdoing and involvement in the attack that put Bakayo in hospital. It was believed that those making the accusations were just seeking to stir up trouble between the local community and the police. Which was a pretty sad set of circumstances. The area was still fragile following the riots in 2011 that had occurred in the area around Tottenham High Road. Now several years after those events, there wasn't much social harmony to be had.

The most senior police officer in London – the chief – herself, dismissed the accusation of a cover up as a malicious attempt to stoke up more mistrust between the police and the local community, by outsiders. She said the accusations had no merit whatsoever. A leading national newspaper had also come to the same conclusion, which drew a cry of foul from the local provocateurs. Moss wasn't convinced there was anything in the rumours. The men who had attacked Bakayo could be anyone. Raine Sizer's father, a well-known local hardcase, denied it had anything to do with him. His daughter had apparently told him she had been assaulted by a black lad at the party. The police were called in to investigate. Despite clear and irrefutable evidence that an assault had taken place the police were no nearer to discovering the identity of her attacker. The party had been attended by upwards of forty people, most of them in the sixteen to nineteen age range. Because news of the party had been spread on Facebook, a lot of those who turned up were not known to the party organiser.

Raine Sizer told police she recalled talking to Bakayo Ostemabo and that he was the one who had attacked her in the back garden of the house, but she also admitted that she was a little drunk at the time. Bakayo was visited by police and taken to Tottenham police station to be questioned by officers. As the police doctor found no DNA trace on her then it was her word against his. The police were forced to drop him from their investigation because of a lack of evidence. Less than two weeks later Bakayo was beaten up on the street by five men and put in hospital for a month.

If the truth be told, Moss wasn't sure where he should commence this investigation. After thinking about it long and hard for a day he put a plan together and mapped a course of action. He first opted to visit the scene of the incident.

First, he spent a couple of hours working on another case that was taking up some time. It had just gone one in the afternoon when he closed the file, got up, and grabbed his jacket from the coat beg behind the door. He went out of his office, dropping the latch as he left, stepped down the staircase and out into the afternoon light. It wasn't a bad day for mid-April. Quite warm out of the shade. A breeze was chasing away any clouds.

From Broadwick Street he walked the hundred or so yards onto Regents Street, stood on the kerbside and waited for the first available Hackney cab to come by.

It took the cabbie thirty minutes to fight through the early afternoon traffic to reach Tottenham High Road. The road was a busy thoroughfare that contained the usual suspects in terms of food stores, fast-food outlets and the occasional dentist's surgery or health centre. The locality had gone through a bit of a makeover and clean-up following the 2011 riots when the area became a tinder box. The Met police had shot and killed a local man called Mark Duggan, an alleged small-time villain and wannabe gangster. Despite the coat of new paint and some tinkering around the edges, the area hadn't lost any of its edge.

The location where the attack on Bakayo Ostemabo had, allegedly, taken place was in a car park at the back of a quick-stop food market and a row of small stores. According to him, he had been waiting for the 246 bus to take him home to Upper Edmonton, when he was dragged out of the bus shelter by two men, down an alleyway between the store and a fast-food outlet at the other side, and into the car park at the rear.

Moss took a walk down the alleyway. The walls were covered with a lot of unsightly graffiti, put there by the local Banksy. The sprayers' tags were everywhere. He soon emerged into the open space that was the car park. The dominant structure was an outbuilding, that apparently, belonged to the food store owner. At the bottom end, the alleyway led onto a street that was full of terraced, residential houses dating to the 1930s. It was very much working-class urban north London. No doubt about it. An area that was racially mixed and very multi-cultural.

The car park was a facility for shoppers to park and for store owners to give access to delivery vans and the like. According to the victim, after dragging him from the bus stop and into the car park, a car containing three other men arrived. They joined the first two. That's when the assault began in earnest.

At ten o'clock on a November night the area had been quiet. Less than five cars were on the tarmac. Now at two-thirty in the afternoon, there were around a dozen vehicles parked there. Running down the side of a chain link fence were a number of those large galvanised cage-like containers used to store discarded cardboard, along with a couple of charity collection receptacles for second-hand clothes, books and whatnot. The white lines outlining the parking bays were bright and sharp on the recently re-laid tarmac. There was a delightful smell of baking coming out of one of the out buildings that had a sign saying 'Coopers' Bakery' fixed to it.

If the truth be told there wasn't a lot to see. The incident had taken place, getting on for six months before, therefore there wasn't anything of significance to observe.

After a couple of minutes, Moss turned back, headed into the alleyway and out onto the high road. Across the road was a glass and stone building housing the Haringey Council community library, Tottenham High Road branch. He made it across the road, entered through the glass doors and went inside. In the glassed-in vestibule there was one of those pull-up information stands with information about a current exhibition. Local artists were displaying their latest work in an exhibition space beyond a glass partition. A couple of people were browsing in amongst the pieces on display, from the glazed pots to more contemporary work in the form of paintings, pencil sketches, and felt, pot and glass work.

He entered the exhibition space and clapped his eyes on a large dark-skinned, middle-aged lady, sitting at a desk, gazing into a laptop screen. She took her eyes from the screen for a moment, looked up and clocked him. She was dressed in a garish African type outfit all the colours of a Dulux paint chart.

"I've got a programme here. Should you want one," she called out to him and held a glossy sheet aloft. He smiled, said thanks and strode the ten feet towards her. "Tell me are these all made by local people?" he asked glancing around, as if genuinely interested, though he already knew the answer. After all, the exhibition was titled: 'Tottenham Art and Soul', with the tag line: 'Together We are Stronger' then under that in smaller words, 'inspiring local people in the community.

"All the exhibition pieces were done by people who attended a local arts and craft school," she revealed with a sense of pride in her voice.

"Wow, they're great," he said laying on the charm a bit thick.

She quickly assessed that he was not local to these parts. "You're not from this area, are you?" she enquired.

"No. You're right. I'm here having a look around. I'm a journalist looking at the place where Bakayo Ostemabo was attacked six months ago." He lied, convincingly.

"Oh, I see," she said cautiously, but with a look of interest on her face as if she wanted to learn more.

"I'm doing a follow-up piece for my paper into the allegations that two serving police officers were involved in the beating." She listened to him attentively, but her eyes didn't flinch. Maybe his admission had caught her flat-footed. "Do you know anyone who may be worth chatting to about it?" he asked. Not believing for a moment that she would say anything positive.

She diverted her eyes from his for a couple of beats, while she considered the question or her options, or both.

"The caretaker of this library knows the family. He said something about it."

"Which family?"

"The Ostemabos."
"Said what like?"
"About mistaken identity."
"Of whom?"
"I don't know."
"Can I have the caretaker's name?"
"Eric," she replied."
"Eric?"
"That's right."
"Is he here today."
"Not until about five when this place closes."

He glanced at his watch. The time was now getting on for five to three. "Thanks for that. Maybe I can come back later to chat to him." She smiled wanly.

He went to step out of the room then realised he had failed to take the pamphlet from her hand. He went back for it.

"By the way, what's Eric full name?" he asked.

She didn't know his surname, but informed him that Eric was a frequent visitor to the William Hill's betting shop across the road. He said thanks, then goodbye and left the library with the pamphlet firmly in his grip. He planned to be back in one hour to visit the betting shop across the road to see if Eric might be inside. Once back outside on the street, he paused to reflect for a moment. The disclosure about the possibility of mistaken identity made his skin itch.

Mistaken identity was one of the three possibilities he had considered, along with a prank gone wrong. The third concerned Bakayo's involvement with a criminal enterprise of one kind or another.

He stepped away from the library, turned right, ambled along the pavement and headed along the high street in a northerly direction. There were a few people coming and going, and some going into or exiting the stores and the businesses that lined the thoroughfare. The Ostemabo family home in Upper Edmonton was perhaps two to three miles further along the road, assuming the crow flew in a straight line. The 'Tottenham Spartans Boxing Club and Gym', the place where Bakayo said he was in on the night of the attack was at the end of the next street. Moss walked the forty yards to the location.

The boxing club and gym were nothing much to write home about. Just a rundown looking facility in a ramshackle building adjacent to a vacant plot of land which must have held a building before it was burned down to the ground during the riots.

Moss went through a double wood and glass door, and into a tight reception area. The gymnasium was on the bottom floor. The club, formerly called 'Gloves and Co.' was on the upper floor.

There was an unmanned counter on one side. Plain wood panel doors on the other side led into the male and female changing facilities. Ahead, a pair of glass-topped hardboard doors led into the gym space. The letters spelling the word 'gymnasium' were arched over the door. Tucked into a corner was a straight steep staircase ascending to the club.

Moss stepped up to the door marked 'gymnasium' and peered through the window. There were a line of exercise machines along two sides of the room. On the back wall was a large mat in front of a floor to ceiling mirror in which bodybuilders and those looking to pose could observe themselves working out. A frame held a good supply of loose weights. There was an area for other equipment like medicine balls, Bulgarian bags and kettle weights.

He counted three people, two men and a woman, then a third man emerged from behind a punch bag suspended on a long metal chain attached into the ceiling.

There was a sound from behind him as the door to the male changing room opened and a stout looking man in his forties, wearing shorts, a training vest and carrying a towel emerged. He had the appearance of a Greek or Turkish colossus. Huge chest and arms, though it looked as if he neglected his legs. He looked beefy and well ripped and had a bodybuilder's rocking gait. The logo of 'Golds Gym' was plastered across the vest. He saw Moss peering into the window.

"You looking to join the gym?" he enquired curtly.

"Yeah. Thinking about it," said Moss turning to greet him.

"It's okay here. You don't get many hard-ons in here."

"Many what?"

"Hard-ons? Posers."

"All right. I see what you mean. Are you local to the area?" he asked.

"Yeah. I'm a Tottenham boy."

"Do you mind if I ask you a question?"

His face changed, and his expression became marginally tense. "Go on then. What?" he asked, cautiously.

"I don't suppose you know the lad who got duffed up in that car park over there," he half-heartedly nodded in the direction of the car park… "about six months ago? Behind those shops over there."

"Yeah, you're right. I don't know him, but I know his brother."

"His brother. Moses. Is it?"

"That's him. Like twins they are."

"Dead ringers. Are they?"

"What you mean?"

"Lookalikes?"

"Yeah. I'd say so," the chap still maintained a poker face. "Who're you?" he asked. Perhaps thinking Moss was a copper.

"I'm an undercover journalist looking into the rumour that two cops were involved in his beating."

"What the attack?"

"Yeah."

"That's a load of horse shit."
"What is?"
"That two cops from the police station were there."
"How do you know?"
"The brother Moses. He was up to no good."
"Like what?"
"Use your imagination?"
"What's that supposed to mean?"
"It means he was involved in something well dodgy."
"Who Moses Ostemabo?"
"Right."
"What like?"
"I don't know," he said, though the gaze in his eye said he did.
"Who knows what he was up to?"
"Try the police. See you soon." He was done with talking to an alleged undercover hack, edged past Moss, forced open one of the doors and entered the gym.

The words: *try the police,* rang through Moss's mind like a 'Bill stickers will be prosecuted' warning. Did he really want to do that? Perhaps there was some mileage in it. Maybe the only way to get to the bottom of it, was to give the local police station a visit.

He turned around and took the fifteen steps to the door, and back out onto the street, then the twenty steps or so onto the high road. The time was a shade after three-fifteen. A bus, the number 246 'Kings Cross via Seven Sisters Road and Pentonville HMP', came by and pulled into a bus stop. There was a cop car behind it with its flashing blue lights, but no warning squeal of the siren.

## Chapter Four

The traffic wasn't that busy. There was a road sign pointing the way into Central London, and one on the other side saying: 'Seven Sisters Road'. Bruce Grove Railway station was perhaps another two hundred yards ahead on the left-hand side. The next station would be White Hart Lane and the home of Tottenham Hotspur football club. Strange that he was in the area of the Wayward Genius case so soon after it had ended. He reflected on that for a brief moment. Wood Green was perhaps three of four miles off in the distance, after Upper Edmonton.

He walked past the front of a small independent eatery just as the door opened and he caught the smell of fresh coffee. The place was called. 'The N17 Acropolis'. He headed for the open door and stepped inside. It was nothing out of the ordinary. A greasy spoon. Two sets of round tables covered by red-chequered table clothes. It had a Greek theme. The side walls were covered in a mural of a Greek island vista. He went to the counter, looked at the cakes and asked the assistant, a pretty looking Cypriot girl, for a coffee and a small piece of what looked like coffee-flavoured carrot cake.

She advised him to take a seat and said she would bring his drink and food to him. He was the only customer at three-twenty in the afternoon. The table had a Greek language newspaper on it. The girl was soon at the table holding a tray, which she put down and deposited a mug on a saucer containing the coffee and a plate holding a piece of cake.

"Can I ask if you live in the area?" he asked.

She gave a blank, introspective face as if she was asking him why he was asking her.

He decided to stick to the same lie. He smiled. "I'm a freelance journalist. I'm doing a piece about the riots of a few years back from an angle of how the area as changed, and if it's changed for the better." She glanced towards the counter and an open door that led into a well-lit room. Perhaps there was another person in there and all she had to do was shout for help if he became too pushy. She looked at the pretend journalist through dark attractive eyes that sparkled like pearls in a pool of dirty water. She couldn't have been more than twenty years of age.

"I wasn't here at the time," she said in a defensive tone.

"What about what happened around six months ago up the road?"

"What was that?"

"The attack by five men on an Edmonton lad called Bakayo Ostemabo."

"Who?"

"Bakayo. He was sixteen years of age at the time."

"I don't know about it."

"I gather it created a bit of tension, reminiscent of the riots, because it was rumoured that two serving police men were involved."

"Oh that," she revealed. She had heard of it.

He continued. "It created a situation where extra police had to be drafted into the area for a few nights to prevent it kicking off and happening all over again. You don't by any chance know the victim, do you?"

She shook her head from side to side. "I'd have remembered him," she said.

"Did you hear any rumours about it?"

"No. All I heard was that one of the family was involved with a gang."

"Which family."

"The one you just said."

"A gang? What type."

"They steal cars."

"To order?"

"She shrugged her shoulders. "I dunno."

"Cars from where?" he asked.
"I dunno," she repeated.
"Who is the leader of the gang?"
"Petras."
"Who?"
"Petras Monogul," she said.
"Where is he based."
"Haringey. I think."
"Petras Monogul," he asked, hoping he had pronounced it correctly.

She didn't reply. Just then the door to the café came open and two men with a west Asian appearance entered, babbling in a language that could have been Farsi or Hindi.

Moss took his mug of coffee and put the rim to his lips. The girl went behind the counter to serve the newcomers. Moss didn't hang about much longer, he rapidly finished the coffee and polished off the cake in no time, then he got up and left the café.

In another two or three hundred yards he was in an area close to the start of the stadium that was the home of Tottenham Hotspur Football Club. It was a very impressive, tall structure of glass panels in a variety of grey, black and white shades.

He crossed a road, stepped onto the forecourt in front of the high wall of glass and headed into the club shop on the ground floor. At this time there were few customers inside, unlike on a match day when it would be crowded with fans eagerly purchasing the merchandise on offer. Several members of the sales team, all wearing the same dress, were standing around in groups of two and three and chatting or watching the tv displays of famous Spurs matches from the long gone or recent past. There was also a wide selection of NFL gear from shirts to pendants. The football club must have had a deal with an American organisation to sell its merchandise.

Moss headed across the floor to the section displaying racks of replica club shirts. The cost of a new shirt, for the season which only had a few weeks to run, was forty pounds, reduced down from sixty. Shirts for next season, due out in June would retail for upwards of sixty-five pounds. He took one of the current shirts and held it against his chest as if trying to picture himself wearing it.

One of the floor walkers, one of the salesmen, clocked him and came over to chat or to assist him. He was a tall, solidly built black guy in his mid-twenties who looked very handsome in his uniform of jacket, matching trousers, shirt and tie.

"You looking for anything special?" he asked. He had an energising smile and a nice engaging soft voice.

"Yeah, but forty quid for a shirt."

"That's the going rate."

"Do you sell many?"

"Thousands. You a Spurs fan?" he asked.

"All my life," he lied in order to appease him.

"You become a Spurs club member and you'll automatically get ten percent off the price."

"Oh right. In that case its only thirty-six quid."

"That's right."

"Do you live in these parts?" Moss asked suddenly changing the topic of the conversation.

"Yeah, up in Enfield."

"Tell me. Does the name Petras Monogul mean anything to you?"

The chap made a face by scrunching his eyes and squinting at him. "Not to me. Leon might know who he is." He called out the name 'Leon' to one of the chaps in the group of chatting sales assistants.

"What's that?" Leon called out.

"Over here a minute."

The chap came over to join them. Leon was shorter than his colleague but wide and well-constructed. His shaved head reflected the overhead light in the ceiling. His corporate jacket fitted him well. He waltzed over to join Moss and his colleague.

"What can I do for you?" he asked.

"Petras Monogul. Is it a name you know?" The chap asked.

"Yeah, he lived close to me at one time."

"How do you know him?" Moss asked. Leon looked slightly taken aback as if the question irked him a little.

"He was an aspiring criminal who's got involved with some bad arses."

"Doing what?" Moss asked.

"Intimidation mostly."

"How about stealing cars."

"Yeah, that as well."

"What's he doing now?"

"Prison time. Last I heard."

"For what?"

"A couple of years."

"No. I mean what did he do?"

"I don't know. I guess his operation got sorted out."

"For what?"

"Stealing cars to order."

"When was this?"

"When did he go down?"

"Yeah."

"About four months ago. Dunno for sure."

"Just him or a few others?"

"His gang. About five or six of them in total."

"Were they stealing cars to order? From where?"

"Not from around here. Mostly up west."

Moss thought he had exhausted this line of enquiry and he could see that the chap was becoming restless at the tone and direction of his questions. He thanked him and his colleague for coming to chat to him. He put the shirt hook back onto the rail, then drifted over to another display that was selling knick-knacks like key-rings, mugs and pens. He opted to purchase a key-ring to give to a child of one of Claudette's friends and a pen for himself. He parted with seven pounds and seventy pence.

The time was getting around to ten to four. He left the store with the items in a white plastic bag loaded with the Spurs motif, turned left and walked at a slow pace the quarter of a mile or so back to the area around the library and the William Hill betting shop on the opposite side of the road.

## Chapter Five

He was soon outside the library and going across the zebra-crossing to the other side of the road. The bus stop shelter, the one from where Bakayo was supposedly dragged into the alleyway was less than fifty feet away. The late afternoon was just starting to lose its warm front, though it was still pleasant out of the shade of the tight buildings on both sides. The traffic was starting to build with the school run and the first evidence of the evening rush hour to come. The proliferation of one-pound shops and the gaudy eastern European stores gave the area a rough, tough working-class, and multi-cultural edge.

He made it into the betting shop for ten past four. There were a few people inside. Ten if that. Horse racing from somewhere, both real and virtual, was on the screens on the back and side walls. A few youths were hanging about close to one of those roulette machines that was beeping like crazy as the player tapped the numbers on the screen. Monte Carlo it wasn't, though the machine said it was.

Nobody gave Moss a second look. The sound of the roulette machine and the commentary over the airwaves gave it a feeling of a busy shop. The SIS broadcaster told the punters of the opening betting for a hurdle race at Newton Abbott. Moss scanned his eyes around the interior and put them onto a tall, thin balding chap who was consulting the racing form inside one of the glass-encased boards around the edge of the room. As the chap turned away Moss saw his karahi overall under an open brown leather bomber jacket. The chap had a betting slip in his left hand and a pen in the other. Was this the library caretaker called Eric? If so he was having a flutter before he went to work for a few hours.

He certainly looked the part. He was south of sixty, but not by much. He put a pair of black-framed reading glasses over his eyes, then turned to have a look at one of the newspapers lodged inside the glass case. Moss slipped along the counter and got close to him, so close that the fellow looked at him with a questioning face for a brief moment.

Moss winked, then smiled at the chap. "Are you Eric? The caretaker from across in the library over the street?" he asked in a convoluted manner.

"Who might you be?" he replied.

"My name is Dave Moss. I'm doing some investigating on behalf of the Ostemabo family into the attack on Bakayo about six months ago."

"What about it?"

"I heard from a colleague of yours in the library that you might have heard something about it."

"Who told you that?"

"*She* did."

"Oh, what about it?"

"I wonder if I could ask you a couple of questions?"

"About that?"

"Yeah. Specifically, that you told her it might be a case of mistaken identity."

"That's what I heard…" he was about to say something else, but wobbled slightly. "Who are you?" he asked.

"David Moss," he slipped his hand into his trouser pocket and pulled out a wallet that contained his ID. He opened it discreetly, and let him see his licence and the photograph of him looking serious and business like.

"What's in it for me?" he asked.

"Revealing the truth," he replied, though it didn't appear to please him. "How about a twenty-pound free bet. Is that okay?"

"Yeah. Good as."

Moss dipped a hand into a front trouser pocket, and pulled out a ten-pound note, followed by a second one. "When you said mistaken identity, what did you mean?"

The chap reached out and took the two notes from his hand. "The beating should have been for Moses Ostemabo, not his brother. They got the wrong guy."

"Who?"

"The gang."

"Which gang?"

"The one doing the stealing."

"Why Moses?"

"He was involved in eyeballing the cars for the boss."

"Who? This Petras Monogul character?"

"How do *you* know him?"

"I heard the name."

"They were stealing cars from fancy people over in the west."

"One of whom was Moses?" Moss asked.

Eric leaned into him ever so slightly. "That's right." He rubbed the two notes together as if checking they were genuine.

"What happened?"

"They might have stolen a car without telling the others."

"Kept it for themselves then?"

"Maybe."

"Did the gang find out and decide to teach him a lesson."

"That's right." Moss was now so close him that he could see the remnants of food on his bristled chin and his bloodshot eyes.

"But they got the wrong boy? Or couldn't find him so they decided to get his brother instead?"

"Maybe. That's what could have happened."

"How do you know this?"

"Because the other lad with Moses was my grandson."

"Did he get roughed up by them."

"No. He moved up to Birmingham to be with his dad and to get away from them."

"Smart move. So, let me get this right. It was Petras and his gang who attacked Bakayo either because they couldn't find Moses, or they got them mixed up." Eric looked at him and gently nodded his head. "So, it had nothing to do with an alleged assault on someone called Raine Sizer?"

"Not that I know of."

"By the way what's the name of your grandson?"

"Noah," he replied.

"Thanks," said Moss I appreciate you fronting up." Eric slipped the two ten-pound notes into a breast pocket of his work overall.

Moss left him to fill out a betting slip, then he headed out of the betting shop and walked out onto the high road. He decided to walk the one hundred yards to the Bruce Grove overground railway station to catch the next train into Liverpool Street station.

It was precisely six thirty when he stepped into his Soho office.

## Chapter Six

After some time to consider his next option Moss opted to call his former colleague DI Luke Terry. He wanted to ask him if he knew anything about the case, though suspected he wouldn't as it was not that high profile. Not anymore.

As he thought, Luke Terry wasn't up to speed on the case. As a way of helping, he said he would make some enquiries with his friend in the north, as he put it, then get back to him as soon as possible. Which might be a couple of days. Moss said okay.

Moss didn't hear anything for the next twenty-four hours. He wondered if it was time to contact Bakayo's mother to put her in the picture. He would tell her what he had discovered about her son Moses, and his association with someone called Petras Monogul. He didn't know how she would react to him telling her it was down to her eldest son, that Bakayo got a beating. The truth that her son was the victim of mistaken identity or had taken a beating for his older brother might be hard for her to take. Along with a confirmation that the two police officers were not involved in the attack and neither was it linked to the incident involving Raine Sizer.

After thinking it through for a while, he opted not to make that call, just yet. He considered trying to chat to Moses Ostemabo but had no idea where he was. He would ask him to admit to his mother that he was involved with a gang, stealing cars to order, led by Petras Monogul. Who it would appear was inside jail, along with the rest of the gang for their part in the car stealing caper. He decided to let it pass for now.

Ten hours went by with no word from Luke Terry. Moss was on the verge of calling him when Terry returned his call. Terry told him that Monogul and his associates were a band of small-time wannabes who stole plush cars to order. The crew were full of bravado and brazenly dismissive of the police. They would roll up in the early morning hours in a low loader and take cars left on the street in the likes of Chelsea, Brompton, Knightsbridge and south Kensington. They were prolific but by no means always successful. They would either sell the cars to crooked dealers or blackmail the owner for the return of their vehicle. It was only in the past three months that the gang, including Monogul had been sent down for an average of six years each. What DI Terry told Moss next was that two of the gang had been working for the police. He didn't name names, but Moss assumed those two were Moses Ostemabo and the other was the grandson of Eric the caretaker, Noah Bailey.

It was now Friday evening and Moss was looking forward to spending some time with Claudette Munro over the weekend. Then within three hours of the conversation with Terry concluding, Moss received a call to his mobile phone from a number he didn't recognise. He took the call, none the less. The caller said he was Moses Ostemabo. As a way of confirming his identity he said he had received a message from Eric Bailey, that he, Moss, had been talking to him.

Moses readily admitted that he had been a member of the gang stealing cars.

"Were you one of the guys feeding information to the police?" Moss asked him outright.

Moses didn't reply immediately. He waited for a moment. "Yeah, that's right," he admitted, but then he dropped a bit of a bombshell when he said that two policemen in Tottenham station had informed Monogul that Noah Bailey and he were police informers.

"That's why the gang either got your brother mixed up with you or they sought to hurt your brother to get back at you," Moss said.

"That's the way it looks," he replied.

"They gave him a beating that nearly killed him," said Moss.

"If it wasn't for them being spooked at the time, they would have killed him," he revealed.

"Who were the police officers. Do you know?" Moss asked him.

"I don't know their identities," he replied.

"What did you do after your brother was attacked?"

"I went up north for a few months."

"What did you tell your mother?"

"What I had to. That I was working up there."

"I'd like you to do me a big favour."

"Such as?" he enquired.

"Tell your mother the truth. She's convinced that Bakayo was beaten up because of the alleged attack on Raine Sizer. Tell her that I'm prepared to waive my fee. But you must promise me that you'll tell her and your brother. What do you say?"

He thought about the offer for a few moments. "Okay, I'll do that."

"Promise?"

"Yes, I promise."

"By the way how did you get my number?"

"From my mother, she told me you were looking into the case. She gave me the card you left."

"You'll tell her. Won't you?"

"Absolutely," he replied.

Moss said thanks, then terminated the call as there was little else to discuss.

He swung around in his seat and looked down to the street. He couldn't ever recall giving Mrs Ostemabo his card, but maybe he had. Maybe he was losing his memory. He got up out of the chair, grabbed his jacket, and immediately left the office.

It was six-thirty on a Friday evening. He was planning to visit the Lord Nelson public house for a beer and a bite to eat, then he would make his way into Bow to visit Claudette. The weekend was young. According to the weather people, it promised to be a decent couple of days, though it seldom was. He pondered on that for a moment, then closed the door to his office, dropped the latch, then headed down the staircase to the door and out into the vibrant vibe of the city. There was a smell of food in the air and the sound of Soho ringing in his ears.

## The End

# The Gingerbread Man

Chapter One

The insurance company representative was a man who had a penchant for wearing tight jackets and chatting endlessly about his favourite movies. Raymond Bentley said he was forty-five years of age, though to Moss he looked and acted a lot older. He was a nice enough guy, but had an annoying habit of always looking down his nose at him and treating him as if he was the junior partner in the deal. As usual he looked stiff and far too serious as he addressed him from the chair at the other side of the desk. Just like the time before, and the time before that. His jacket was so tight it resembled a strait jacket last seen on an escapologist. Bentley had been in Moss's office on several previous occasions; therefore, he knew the way up, the layout and the pleasant reception he would receive.

After pouring his eyes over the summary of the case, Moss thought it was a slam dunk, or maybe a sham dump, but he didn't tell Mr. Bentley that. The claimant's business property had been torched by someone and gutted by a fire that appeared to be one hundred percent, no holds barred, plain and simple, arson. But was it?

Someone or some people had scaled a wall at the back of the premises, climbed a ladder to the roof, then let themselves in through a skylight and dropped to the floor. Maybe he or they were looking for something, couldn't find it, then started a fire that caused extensive damage to the premises. A bakery on Plashet Road in West Ham in east London.

With the claim touching £500,000 the insurance company were obliged to its shareholders to carry out a full and frank assessment of the claim, before a cheque for that amount would ever be presented to the claimant. A claim of that size would take maybe a year or two before all the investigations were fully exhausted.

Raymond Bentley, sitting in a chair in front of Moss's desk, was perusing the same file as him. He had opened a button of the jacket to reveal a flabby stomach and waistline, along with sweaty armpits. He had undoubtedly put on a few pounds since the last time he had been in this office, which was getting on for six months before.

Bentley was one of the more senior loss adjusters in the insurance company, therefore they must have attached a great deal of importance to this case. The company used Moss and several other private detectives to investigate insurance claims that were a little out of the ordinary. Clearly, Moss had been selected for this one for which he would earn £7,500 for his work.

The summary suggested it would take him a while to look through the exact facts. Maybe that was an over exaggeration. Then after considering them, let them know if he thought there was anything untoward. As he poured his eyes over the text of the summary, it didn't look likely to be the case. But it was too early to be too cocksure.

"Let's just go over the key features of the case," Moss said to his visitor. He didn't wait for Mr Bentley's okay. "On a night at the back end of November, last, six months ago, the claimant's business premises, a bakery and store on Plashet Road in West Ham, was broken into and set on fire in what looks like a clear and obvious arson attempt. The subsequent fire gutted not only the bakery but the back of the store from where the claimant, Pearce Hamill, had sold foodstuffs from sausage rolls and pork pies, to homemade bread, cakes and a wide assortment of fancies for the past thirty years."

Bentley cleared his throat. "The shop was known to all locals as the 'Gingerbread Man' because of the signature cakes they made. It was a bit of a local institution."

Moss chipped in with his two-penny worth. "His father had set up the business in the period between both war years. Hamill's shop, and bakery had been a permanent fixture on the same site since 1935. The current owner and proprietor, Pearce Hamill, took it over from his father in 1983 to the present day. The business has been closed, due to the fire, right up to the present day." He took in a deep breath. "It certainly looks like a clear and obvious case of arson," he said, while looking over the first page of the London Fire Brigade report.

"Did you ever go into the store?" Bentley asked him.

"You know I think I might have at one time in my life. I spent some time as a uniform cop in east London. I could have gone in there on duty once or twice to buy a sandwich."

"What do you remember?" Bentley asked.

"Not a lot. It was a long time ago. Just that it sold everything from bread rolls, pastries and of course the gingerbread cut into the shape of little men."

"The famous gingerbread men." Bentley added for good measure.

Moss scanned his eyes onto the salient bullet points in the fire brigade report. He chose to paraphrase what the report said: "There was evidence of a break-in at the back of the bakery. A person or persons scaled a wall, then climbed onto the roof and got in through a skylight. Possibly with the intention of robbing the place. The evidence of the use of petrol suggests that it was their intention all along to set fire to the premises." He continued. "There was no water extinguishing system, which meant that the fire quickly took hold. The oxygen coming through the open skylight fanned the flames and acted as a chimney that in turn created a funnel. The flames soon took hold and spread very rapidly."

Bentley changed his posture and turned to a side to reduce the load on his back from sitting too rigid in the seat. "A beady eyed passer-by noticed the smoke escaping out of the roof space and called the Fire Brigade. They were there in less than ten minutes after the call was made. About fifteen minutes or so after the fire had started. Their action and that of the passer-by prevented the fire from spreading and effectively destroying the entire building."

"Good job," said Moss. "Or else the claim would have been double." Bentley half smiled. "What was the damage?" Moss asked.

"The ovens and preparation areas in the bakery were destroyed. Plus, the back of the store was badly damaged and suffered peripheral smoke damage to the walls and ceiling. Fridges and other essential equipment were also badly damaged. The loss adjuster for Hamill claimed that the loss of equipment came to £120,000. Then another £260,000 damage to the integrity of the structure. Then £80,000 for the replacement of the roof and re-plastering of the walls and a new floor etcetera…etcetera. Plus, another £40,000 for the loss of stock and produce and goodwill."

"I didn't know a loss adjuster would consider such a thing," Moss remarked.

"He or she has to take everything into consideration."

"Remind me. Where was Pearce Hamill at the time of the blaze?" Moss asked.

"He was in Spain. He'd gone there for a two week break before the busy Christmas period. He was due back in the bakery on the Monday to commence work on the Christmas orders."

"So, the fire occurred on a Friday morning. Two days or thereabouts before he was due back."

"Correct."

"Who was in charge of the store when Hamill was in Spain?" Moss asked.

"His store manager. A lady called…" Bentley consulted the file… "A Mrs Fellini."

"Just like Federico. The famous Italian movie director."

"Is it?" Bentley asked.

"Eight and a Half, La Dolce Vita," said Moss, then wished he hadn't bothered.

"You sure that's not Sergio what-his-face."

"Leone?"

"Yeah."

"No, he did the spaghetti westerns."

"Oh, yeah. Of course. You're right."

"Anyway, let's get back to the file. How old is Mr Hamill?" Moss asked.

"According to our records he's touching seventy-three years of age."

"Has he never thought of retiring?"

"Not that I know of. I don't think he's got anyone to pass the business on to."

"Surely, he's got someone to hand it over to like his father did to him."

"Are you asking me or telling me?" Bentley enquired.

"Asking."

"I don't know. He never had a deputy or a son or a daughter to pass it to."

"How about selling up?"

"Not, that I know of."

"Interesting," said Moss. "Tell me this, how was the business doing in terms of profit?"

"That I don't know. Why?"

"Oh, you know. He can't compete against the big mega players. The big six supermarkets. Economies of scale and all that. Their supplier networks. The three Ps of marketing. Price, Place and Promotion. There's no way he can compete on cost and price and perhaps even quality."

"What are you suggesting?" Bentley asked.

"He decides to get out. He hires someone to break into the store to set fire to the premises, so he can claim the insurance money."

Bentley made an audible kissing sound by smacking his lips together. "Perhaps that's an angle you need to pursue," he suggested.

It was the obvious one. Moss smiled at him. "How long have you got before you need to decide one way or the other."

"What?"

"Whether you pay out the half a million quid."

"Five months. It's company policy to settle all claims within one year of the submission."

"When did he submit the claim?"

"Not long after the fire. One month or thereabouts."

"Therefore, not long after the Fire Brigade report was published?"

"That's right."

"A few days to be precise. He received the report confirming the break-in and the trace of petrol used as an accelerant."

Bentley expressed his admiration that he had read the report from the beginning to the end and recalled the exact dates in detail. "How will you approach this one?" he asked.

"I'll have a nosey around. See if anyone knows anything. There might be a few rumours doing the rounds. People, by nature, are reluctant to speak to the police if they hear anything, for fear of being found out and named. If there's anything iffy about it, I might pick up a vibe on the street. Like a word that sounds out of place or out of context."

"Such as?"

"You know. The business was doing badly in the current economic climate. People were buying less bread and cakes and what have you. The owner pays some local lads to break in while he's in Spain to burn the business to the ground in order to claim the insurance. You know. The usual thing. People tend to talk about it if they know something iffy took place."

"There's a clause in the policy which states that he must use the money to rebuild the business."

"What? He has to return to the former business come what may?"

"Yes."

"But forty grand for the loss of business is still forty grand."

"That's true," admitted Bentley.

They each took a breath, looked at each other and shared a face. They continued to chat for another five minutes then called time on their deliberations. Bentley left the office less than five minutes later. He'd been there getting on for one and a half hours.

After escorting him to the door at the bottom of the staircase, Moss went into the tiny kitchen area to fix himself a sandwich and make a cup of coffee. With all the talk about cake he considered going downstairs into the pastry shop to purchase a tart fancy, but soon decided against the idea. He was seeking to lose a few pounds from his own waistline. Too much pasta and not enough exercise.

Chapter Two

After the coffee and scanning through the file for a second time, Moss opted to take a trip out to visit the location of the place where the fire had occurred. Plashet Road in West Ham. Deep in the east-end.

West Ham had a very definite east-end melting pot feel and ambience about it. Very much a working-class area and a mixture of cultures. Down at heel, but also with a vibrant in-yer-face, happening feel. In this neck of the woods people just tended to get on with it and put any race relations issues to one side. Neither did they complain or cause hassle. People simply got along with each other.
 The streets along Plashet Road contained a large amount of social housing dating from the 1930s, to the building boom in the late 1950s and early 1960s. The stores along the roads close to the junction with Green Street contained the usual names and small business premises. Like the Indian stores in which all the members of the family took it in turn to serve the customers. An old British-Gaumont cinema building was now a second-hand used car showroom.
 The locality wasn't that busy at two-thirty in the afternoon. The only green spaces in the urban jungle were a cemetery and a children's playing field. However, West Ham park at the junction of Portway and Upton Lane was a large open area of grassland. Green Street at the eastern side of Plashet Road was a busy thoroughfare that once housed, Upton Park, the home of West Ham United, or as the locals knew it, the Boleyn Ground.
 The Gingerbread Man or Hamill's store, at the eastern end of Plashet Road, was still boarded up six months after the blaze. Notices plastered on the hardboard barrier told passers-by of the fire that had gutted the inside and advised them not to break in and enter as it was dangerous.

Moss didn't know exactly what he was likely to gain from coming here, but if he was going to discover anything he didn't already know, this was going to be the starting point. Maybe he would begin by going into a few of the stores to ask the proprietor if he or she had heard anything.

Just on the other side of the boarded-up front was a shop selling sweets, confectionary, cigarettes, newspapers, glossy magazines, and cheap booze. He ducked inside the shop and sauntered up to the counter where a chap of British-Indian heritage was standing. He eyed Moss perhaps longer than he would have done had he been a local or a regular customer. There was a good selection of chocolate bars in the sloping display to select from. A clock advertising a brand of cigarettes said the time was quarter to three.

"Hi," said Moss looking directly to the chap. "You been here long?" he asked, then quickly realised it was a nonsensical question. "I mean were you here at the time of the fire next door?"

The chap gave him a cold, suspicious look. Perhaps he didn't understand him. "What you say?" he enquired in a heavy-edged accent.

"The Gingerbread Man. Next door." Moss thrust his chin in its direction. "How long has it been closed?" he asked. He took one of the chocolate bars from out of the selection to show the fellow he was keen to purchase something.

"About six month," the chap replied. Moss raked into a trouser pocket and pulled out a handful of coins. He slowly counted out one pound and fifty pence and handed the money to the chap.

"Bad fire, wasn't it? Did it damage your place"?

"No. It not."

"Good. I bet you were pleased?"

The chap shrugged his shoulders, as if he wasn't that bothered if it had. Moss soon detected he wasn't going to get much joy from him, so he smiled, said a quick thanks then headed out of the door and back onto the road. Further along the road was a shop selling roller blinds, curtains and those fancy slatted shutters. He headed up the road, through the door and went inside. Mindful of the fact that he still had a bar of chocolate in his hand he slipped it into a jacket pocket. A very pretty, dark haired, Asian girl in her mid-twenties was sitting at a desk, on which brochures and thick bound catalogues were arranged. There were samples of curtains and blinds on display. The fixtures and fittings were neat and tidy.

She looked up at him as the bell rang and he stepped up to the desk. She gave him a kind of combined smile and frown at the same time. She was a very attractive young lady with a smart appearance, long dark hair, a dark complexion and gorgeous chocolate brown eyes.

"How can I help you?" she asked, changing her posture so she sat higher in the seat.

He was going to say just browsing then changed his mind at the ultimate moment. "To be honest, I'm more interested in knowing more about the bakery," he admitted. "The one which had the fire. Hamills or the Gingerbread Man." She looked a tad nonplussed by his admission. "I'm trying to chat to people who may have heard something about it. Like what happened?"

He had no idea if his words had any interest to her, or if they were appropriate, but it was too late to take them back.

She looked at him and lowered her chin to her chest, so she looked a paragon of seriousness. She was very attractive and perhaps she knew it. The gold jewellery on her wrist and on her fingers looked fancy and not at all cheap tat.

"The fire?" she asked.

"Yeah, the one that happened last year around the end of November."

She raised her chin off her chest and gave him a nod. "What about it?" she asked, playing silly or trying to provoke him.

"Just wondering if you've heard any rumours about how it happened?"

She gave him a mildly put-out *'what the hell'* look on her pretty face. She shook her head from side to side, so the end of her long hair bounced around her shoulders. The chain necklace around her neck with a pendant of an Indian deity on it, gently swayed from side to side.

"All I know is that it was started by some local lads breaking into the back and climbing onto the roof."

He picked up on the words *local* and *lads*. "Lads," he enquired. "More than one?"

"Boys."

"How many?"

"Three or four."

"Do they live in these parts?"

"I think they might." She had a way with words and a precise delivery.

"How do you know that?"

"I hear things."

"From who? Sorry, I mean how do you know these things?" She thought about the question or her response, but elected to keep mute. "Did you hear any names of anyone who may have been involved?" he asked.

"Why don't you ask at the West Ham Bugle?"

"The West Ham what?"

"The Bugle. It's a free newspaper. The office is down the High Street."

"Where is that?"

She told him how to find the office which wasn't that far away. Maybe five to ten minutes walking time, depending on how fast he walked. She told him to ask for Sanjeev.

"Sanjeev?" he asked.

"Yes," she confirmed.

He thanked her and told her she had been very helpful. He departed the store forthwith and followed her directions. He took the chocolate bar from his pocket, unwrapped it and took a bite.

It took him around eight minutes to come across the front of the office. There was a board over the tall double-window front saying: *The West and East Ham Bugle*, then under that: *serving the community in which we live*, though the word *live* had been made to look like *love*.

The location was across the road to the main campus headquarters of Newham College. There were long open venetian blinds over the windows. An inside light was on, as it was now becoming dim as the afternoon slipped towards late afternoon.

He opened the door and stepped inside. It was little more than a reception space with a desk at which a nice-looking dark-skinned boy, in his late teens, was sitting. He was wearing a t-shirt which had the slogan *'Buy the Bugle'*, splashed across it. The room was illuminated by the overhead ceiling lights. The walls were a creamy white shade. A couple of those pull-up displays were placed on either side of the desk. One showed an image of local kids playing in a park. The other showed a few females in school uniform holding certificates of some description and all beaming at the camera like the cats who had gotten the cream.

"Hello," said the lad in a welcoming tone of voice.

"Hi. How are you today?" Moss asked. He noticed the large square-shape glass framed photograph on the wall behind him, displaying an aerial view of the high street and the surrounding vicinity. Moss smiled.

"How can I help you?" the young chap asked, then propped himself up and got to his feet for a reason that wasn't obvious. Perhaps he was anxious that a stranger was in the office and that he was alone.

Moss elected to stay close to the door. "My name is David. I'm doing some research into the fire over in Plashet Road at the Hamill bakery. The one that gutted the place."

"Oh right," was the young man's response.

"Can I give you one of my cards?" Moss asked.

"Sure."

Moss dipped his fingers in a jacket pocket and pulled out a card. He approached the chap and handed the card to him. He took it and read the details. "Wow, a real-life private detective," he said as if in awe. "How cool is that?"

Moss felt like saying 'not very', but held back. "I understand that the newspaper may have looked into the blaze."

"Not me."

"Who?"

"Our reporter Sanjeev did."

"Is he here? Can I chat to him?"

"No. Not at the moment."

"No, I can't chat to him or he's not here?"

"He's not here."

"Would you be able to get in touch with him."

"Not at the moment. He's out covering a story."

"Okay. Perhaps you could give him my card and ask him to give me a call. I'd really appreciate it."

"I'll see that he gets it."

"You're very kind. Tell me what does the newspaper do?"

"We're a free newspaper covering the area. Local stories of local people and news items."

"Missing dogs and cats' stuff. Sporting achievements. Things like that?" Moss asked.

"Yeah. Something like that."

"Cool," said Moss getting down with the kids. "Who's Sanjeev?"

"He's the main reporter. Sanjeev Khan."

"So, he goes around looking for local stories."

"Yeah. That sort of thing."

"Did he cover the Gingerbread Man fire?"

"For sure. He's the only reporter we got."

"Where does your revenue come from?" Moss asked, but wasn't sure why.

"Advertising."

"Of course."

The young man sat down and put the card against the telephone unit. "I'll ask him to give you a call. What's best, the mobile or the other number?"

"The mobile, but if he can't get me on that the landline is just as good."

Moss thanked the young chap for his help and his welcome, then wished him farewell, left the office and headed back out onto the street. He walked onto Barking Road for a few hundred yards, found a minicab office and went inside.

He was back in his office in Soho for twenty to five.

Chapter Three.

It was quarter to six when Moss received a call to his landline phone. He put it on the loudspeaker option and sat back deep into the comfortable swivel chair. "David Moss Private Investigator. How may I help you today?" he said in a forceful, determined tone.

"This is Sanjeev Khan," came a clear and sprightly reply from out of the device.

"Is that Sanjeev from the Bugle?"

"Yes. I understand from my assistant that you came into the office this afternoon."

"I did. That's right."

"How can I be of assistance to you?" He sounded as if he was curious as to why a private detective would want to chat to him.

"I've been asked by an insurance company to investigate the fire that occurred at the Hamill's shop and bakery last November." He didn't reply. "I understand that you may have also looked at the cause of the fire and reported on it for the newspaper."

"That indeed is true," he confirmed.

"In that case. I wonder if I could meet you to have a chat about it."

"Who are you working for?" he asked.

"I'm an independent investigator. I occasionally work for insurance companies on cases. On this occasion I have been asked to carry out an investigation into the blaze. Perhaps you might have some information that could be useful to the enquiry."

There was no reply from Sanjeev for a few long moments and it all went dead-air silent. Moss was on the verge of asking him if he was still there when he said something that sent bells ringing in his head.

"Those boys who set fire to the building might have been doing it for someone."

Moss sat up and felt his grip around the phone tighten. "Who?" he asked.

"That I don't know."

"How have you come to that conclusion?"

"I've heard a few people tell me that there was something far more involved than a simple fire."

Moss felt like saying 'wow', but held back. He wondered if Sanjeev knew something that pointed to a conspiracy. "Can we meet to discuss this?" he asked.

"Yes, but there is one consideration I will insist on."

"What like?"

"I'd like you to promise to make a financial contribution to the paper."

"How much?"

"Five hundred pounds."

"In cash?"

"Yes. Cash is better."

"I think I can agree to that." said Moss swiftly. He knew that Raymond Bentley would reimburse him the money. "Can you give me a quick summary over the phone."

Khan considered the request for a few short moments. "Okay, then. Three local youths were paid to break into the bakery and to set it alight. I've got their names."

"What about the name of the person who ordered them to do it?"

"That I don't know."

"How do you know then? No, forget I asked that, slip of the tongue. I'll be very keen to meet with you face-to-face to discuss the matter. Where can we meet?"

Khan considered the question for a long moment. "Okay, but not here. Err…. How about close to here. There's an Indian buffet on Green Street in West Ham, right opposite the entrance to Upton Park underground station. It's called the 'Indian Star' I'll be in there at exactly three o'clock tomorrow afternoon.

"No problem. I'll be there."

"You'll bring the money with you."

"Yes. What do I get for my money?"

Khan chuckled to himself. "The names of the three who broke in there. And the name of the man who might have organised it."

"I thought you said you didn't have a name."

"My memory. It not so good."

"Fine. That sounds okay. Tomorrow at three. I look forward to meeting you."

"And you." Sanjeev ended the call.

The telephone number Sanjeev had called from was still highlighted in the console window. Moss quickly jotted it down onto a pad of paper. Then he checked the number of the office of the *West and East Ham Bugle*. It was the same number as the one for the office.

Rather than call Raymond Bentley to update him on the progress to date he elected to hold fire. He would speak to him after he had chatted to Sanjeev Khan. He had no idea if the information would be little more than wide speculation. Still, it was an interesting development. He turned to the window to look down to the street below. The flow of people at this time of the early evening was starting to thin out. The evening was a microcosm of the past week. Bright sunshine interspersed with cloud. He took a few moments to have a think then he decided to call Claudette at home to ask her if he could see her this evening. Since the scooter robbery, now three months before, she had revived her confidence and her outgoing personality. Their relationship was continuing to go through a hot and cold period. It was nothing new, if the truth be told.

That evening he got to her place in Bow for eight. She cooked him a spaghetti dish which they polished off with a bottle of a full-bodied red. It wasn't expensive, but it certainly hit the mark. After the meal they took a short walk to a public house in Bow. He left her place at midnight and drove home to Knightsbridge.

## Chapter Four

The following day was Thursday, Moss left his home at eight and drove the short distance into Soho. He parked his car in an NCP twenty-four-hour car park for a flat fee of £20.

When he arrived into his office, he immediately set about doing some work on another case for an hour or so, then at ten he left to take a stroll to the local branch of his bank. He withdrew £500 in cold hard cash. It came in a combination of £20s and £10s. It was surprising how small it felt, though after all, it wasn't a great deal of money.

The day had turned cold up to noon, after a pleasant morning, then it poured down for ten minutes. A typical early day in May. The damp ground soon became bone dry again as the sun reappeared and dried it. He didn't do a lot from noon up to one o'clock, other than trawl the internet for the latest news and took a couple of calls, one from a well-established client, and one from a potential new client. The case was abstract with plenty of what-ifs and maybes. He didn't know if he wanted to take it. He told the caller he would contact him before the day was out to arrange a meeting.

He was wondering where the chap who called himself Sanjeev had acquired the names of the lads who he said had broken into the bakery and set it ablaze. Along with an idea of who might have done the hiring. Though as he recalled, Sanjeev did say that he definitely wasn't sure if it was the correct name. Then he considered the possibility that the attractive young lady in the blind and curtain shop and Sanjeev were partners or connected in some way. After all, how did she know he would be worth speaking to?

It was one-forty-five when he left the office and took the walk to the car park to get his car. He was soon driving along Marylebone Road, continued on Euston Road and ventured into the east end.

It wasn't too long before he was on Mile End Road and closing in on the area around the Hams, both west and east. The time was twenty-five to three when he arrived in the locality. He parked his car on a side street close to the north end of Green Street and an expanse of Romford Road. From there he took a leisurely stroll up Green Street and was soon close to the thick block stone building that was Upton Park underground station.

Directly opposite the arched entrance to the station, across on the opposite side of the street was the 'Indian Star' *all you can eat buffet*. The surrounding residential streets were narrow, and the buildings pressed in tightly to give the vicinity a claustrophobic feel. The eatery was on the end of a row of stores and a street, so it took up a prominent position on a corner. The main entrance was on the Green Street side. The time was now close to three p.m. He stepped along the path, through the plate glass door and inside. The first thing that hit him was the aroma of food emanating from the kitchen and the trays of food placed in long rectangular-shaped trays under the glow of warm lights. The plates and eating utensils were at this end. The smell was delightful: curries, samosas, different varieties of rice, vegetables, salads, and sauces. Unlike some similar places he had been in, this place looked clean and tidy. Cards above the trays told the customers what food they contained. There were tables and bench seats in tightly arranged four-seater booths throughout the floorspace. The till was close to the entrance. Patrons were asked to pay before they took a plate. Everyone had only one hour to eat as much as they could.

He glanced around. There were a few people in at this time, but most tables were unoccupied. The majority of customers looked to be of an ethnic background. Mirrored walls gave the place that impression that it was bigger than it was, so it had a funfair arcade type of feel.

As Moss shifted his eyes to the left he put them on a single male figure sitting in one of the booths. He had a

Sanjeev Khan look about him. The light brown shade of skin and the dark brooding features. The chap had his eyes on Moss and seemed to know who he was. Moss patted the wad of money wedged in a plastic bag inside his jacket pocket. The chap must be the reporter from the *West Ham Bugle*. He was sitting upright in the booth. He was a handsome man with a cool dress sense. Diamond studs in the lobes of both ears glinted.

Moss nodded his head at him and received a similar response. He edged to the till where a young lady was sitting. It was a flat fee of £10 for one hour. He took a ten-pound note and gave her the money. In return, she handed him a ticket with two times printed on it. He had to be out by 4pm at the latest. He doubted that he would be half that time.

He stepped past the till, went to the food display, took a tray, then a plate and a knife and fork and a couple of paper napkins from a dispenser. The only thing that cost money was tea or coffee or soft drinks in cans. Tap water was free of charge. There was zero alcohol to purchase.

He headed along the food trays and helped himself to an assortment of vegetables, such as green beans, peas, cabbage and cauliflower. He didn't like the look of the meat or the pasta.

Keeping a tight hold of the tray he moved around to the booths, slid along the seat opposite the man who must have been Sanjeev Khan. His plate was nearly as barren as his.

He was a nice-looking chap with dreamy eyes, a nice mouth and slim nose. He must have been in his late twenties.

"You must be Sanjeev?"

"You must be David?"

Moss put the tray down gently, and sat down on the bench. He looked to a side to see his reflection in the mirror. He noticed how his hair was beginning to display a trace of silver- grey around the turn of his ears.

He, Sanjeev, was wearing a glistening sports watch on a thick silver metal strap around his right-hand wrist. Moss wondered if he was romantically linked to the lady in the blind shop, lucky man. Though there was no obvious signal that was the case. He was wearing a check blue jacket that had a thin black line cross pattern running through it. He reeked of a tangy aftershave or cologne.

Moss took the knife and fork and held them in the appropriate position. Sanjeev's plate contained the remains of a curry sauce and pork ribs.

"Maybe, I should have gone for a curry," said Moss as an icebreaker, while he picked at his green beans. "Anyway, nice to meet you."

"And you."

"How long have you been running the newspaper?"

"A few years," he replied in a dismissive manner.

Moss picked up on it. He didn't want to do the small talk. "The names of the youths who broke into the bakery who gave them to you?"

"I heard a rumour. Did some of my own investigation. One of them talked to a friend and you know what happens when people talk…" he chuckled out loud.

"Rumours get bounded about," said Moss finishing the sentence for him.

"Have you got the five hundred?" he asked.

Moss fished into his inside jacket pocket, took hold of the plastic bag containing the money and pulled it out. It was surprising how little five hundred pounds weighed. He placed the packet on the table top.

"Can I have a look to be sure?" said Sanjeev.

"Of course. Help yourself."

Sanjeev took the bag, opened it and peered inside at the banknotes. The scent of the notes just about trumped the scent of his body lotion.

"The names of the lads who set fire to the place, please," said Moss as he withdrew a small notebook and a pencil from his jacket pocket.

"The names are Nathan and Chris Bellamy, and Muzzy Estefan.

Moss asked him to repeat them slowly. He did as requested. Moss wrote the names into his notepad, then repeated them in a sotto voce voice to ensure he had them correct. "You said that someone had hired them to do it. Who was it?"

"A guy called Kyle Rafferty."

"Kyle Rafferty."

"That's right. Do you know him?"

"No. I don't. Who is he then?"

"He's Pearce Hamill's nephew."

"What the Gingerbread Man?" Sanjeev Khan nodded his head. "Who told you all this?"

"One of the lad's friends."

"What? One of the three lads who broke in?"

"Yes."

"Does he have a name?"

"I didn't tell you this. Justin Ali."

"Why would he tell you this?"

"Because I know him."

"Well?"

"What do you mean?"

"How well do you know him?"

"As well as anyone else."

"Why would he tell you the names?"

"One of the lads who broke in. Nathan asked Rafferty for more money."

"Blackmail?"

Sanjeev nodded. "Rafferty had three of his heavies to do him over. They put him in hospital for two weeks."

"How much did the nephew of the Gingerbread Man pay them? Do you know?"

"Three hundred pounds each."

"Is that all?"

"They all wanted more so one of them said he'd grass on Rafferty unless he agreed to pay them another three hundred each."

"Grass to who?"

"The police. I guess."

"Have you gone to the police with this?"

"No."

"Is there a reason why?"

"What will the police do?"

"Who knows."

"They'll rope me in to answer a lot of questions. Do I need that?"

Moss didn't answer the question. He took his fork and picked at the green beans. "These three youths are they local?"

"They all live around here."

"I suppose the Bellamy's are brothers."

"So, I gather."

"How does this Rafferty know them?"

"They hang around his shop. He's got a record shop on Green Street. He sells vinyl records, t-shirts and old mod culture gear. He advertises in the Bugle."

"That's how you know him then?" He didn't answer. "What does he sell?"

"Scooter bike gear?"

"What? Like a mod revival?"

Sanjeev didn't know what he was referring to, so he swerved it, but his next words were interesting. "The lads all drive scooters so they go to his place and hang out in a gang."

Moss moved on. "Why would Pearce Hamill's nephew want to burn down his uncle's business?"

"Maybe it was the result of a family dispute."

"Or maybe his uncle asked him to burn down the business while he was in Spain."

Sanjeev gave him a toothy grin of a smile that turned his face roguishly handsome.

Moss picked at his food. He drove the fork into a hard piece of cauliflower, then gave up when it fell off the end. He glanced around the interior. The smells were the same as was the level of sound. The traffic on Green Street and the number of pedestrians ambling by didn't appear to have lessened or increased. He turned back to look at Sanjeev. He didn't have much of the curry remaining on his plate. "The three heavies who beat up the Bellamy lad. Do you have their names?"

"Shaun Young, Darko Pascoe, and Brendon Towse."

Moss asked him to repeat the names for the record. He did. Moss scribed them, then looked at his plate. He had polished off the green beans and the cabbage, that left the cauliflower which didn't look all that inviting. He was done with eating. He took a second to look at the names he had scribbled onto the notepad. He didn't know if they had any credibility, though he thought Sanjeev was on the level with him.

It would appear, from what he had learned, that the Gingerbread Man's nephew had organised the arson of his uncle's business for a reason that wasn't obvious. There had to be a reason, but what was it? An insurance scam? Though it was hardly massive numbers.

There wasn't a lot more Moss could glean from the meeting. With the restaurant beginning to fill he decided this was the best time for a parting of the ways. He had to plan what to do next. There was perhaps little option but to contact DI Luke Terry to ask him if he had heard anything.

He left the food on the plate, said thanks and so long to Sanjeev Khan, then got up. He took the tray with the mostly empty plate on it and placed it on a storage rack, then stepped through the door and out onto the street. The time was approaching three-thirty. He left Sanjeev with the packet of cash. He ensured that the notepad, with the names on it was safely secure in his jacket pocket, then he walked to the end of the street where he had parked his car. All the time looking around to ensure he was safe from any sudden attack.

Chapter Five

Moss waited until well past five o'clock, and he was back in the comfort of his office in Soho, before he put in the call to his ex-serious crime squad colleague. He got through to DI Luke Terry on his private mobile phone after listening to the ringing tone for thirty seconds.

"Be quick I'm in the office," said Terry, even before Moss had chance to introduce himself.

"Take a walk outside into the corridor," he advised.

"Be quick."

"Kyle Rafferty. Have you heard the name?"

"It doesn't jump out at me. What's the angle?"

"There was an arson on a bakery over in West Ham, last November. Hamills' shop and bakery. I'm investigating it on behalf of an insurance company. I was chatting to a reporter from a small local newspaper today who had information. He confirmed that it was arson and he also gave me the names of the three who did it."

"Okay," said Terry. The nuance in his voice said he was intrigued, rather than interested. "What are the names?"

"I'll give them to you, but I need you to speak to your colleagues in the east. Can you let me know what they've got on them?"

"Okay. I'll have a word."

Moss read out the three names to him. "Nathan and Chris Bellamy, and Muzzy Estefan. The Bellamy's are brothers."

"What's the connection to the fire?" Terry asked.

"According to the source, it was Rafferty who asked three lads to break in and start the fire."

"Why?"

"That I don't know. Possibly an insurance scam. In fact, why don't you ask your colleagues to give him a pull. Tell them you've had a tip off."

"I'll pass the intel over to my colleagues in the east. Give them the name." Moss didn't reply. "What else did he give you?"

"The names of the three heavies who put a lad called Nathan Bellamy in hospital for a few weeks."

"Why did they do that."

"The kid was blackmailing Rafferty for more dough."

"Why? Was he one of the arsonists?"

"Correct."

"Give me the names of the three heavies?"

Moss thought about it for a few brief moments. He was in a win-win here. He realised the sense of giving him the names. "Shaun Young, Darko Pascoe, and Brendon Towse."

"I'll run it by east-end CID as a tip from the street."

"Good and thanks."

"Thanks for the tip. I'll give my contacts a buzz. Cheerio," said DI Terry, then swiftly terminated the call. Moss went back to wondering if he had done the right thing. He was sure he had.

Twenty-four hours went by in the blink of an eye. It was around thirty hours before DI Terry got back in touch with Moss. The information he gave him was interesting, rather than riveting. He had spoken to his colleagues in the serious crime squad in the east-end. They had, according to him, put their eyes on Kyle Rafferty. Raffety did have a sheet going back to his youth. He was now in his early forties. He had several stores selling records and other merchandise, mostly tat. One in the east end, the one on Green Street in West Ham, and one in Croydon, and one in Camden. Plus, a share of a couple of other businesses in Camden market. His shops sold vinyl records, indie books and off the wall clothing, aimed at a Mod and Punk revival, which hadn't happened yet.

"What about the Bellamy brothers?" Moss asked him.

"Nathan is doing time," he replied.

"For what?"

"He got sent down six weeks ago on a six month stretch."

"For what?"

"Carrying out robberies on a scooter."

"What muggings?"

"More like handbag snatches. Though on this occasion two of them tried to raid a petrol station in Whitechapel. They didn't get more than fifty quid when they threatened the person behind the till with a hammer. A quick-witted customer ran outside and ripped the covering off their license plates. CCTV picked them up riding away and traced them to Nathan Bellamy and another lad."

This sudden expose sent a chill through Moss. It was a very similar description to the incident involving Claudette. She had had her bag snatched in much the same way. The possibility that it was Nathan Bellamy and his brother or one of his associates flowed through his mind. He had to keep his feet on the ground. Bag snatches by youths on scooters was becoming an all-too-common occurrence throughout the city. To assume it could had been the same scrote who had attacked Claudette was perhaps stretching it a little too far. He sought to push it to the back of his mind.

"Are you guys going to interview Bellamy?" he enquired.

"We're opening an investigation led by DCI Steve Rice," he replied. "Colleagues will visit Bellamy in HMP Dartford to begin the process of getting the full SP from him. It could be a few days. Once I get some feedback, I'll let you know the outcome."

Moss thanked him for calling, then he ended the conversation. He thought about calling Ray Bentley to put him in the picture. After some thinking time he made the call. He got through to him after a delay. Moss informed him where he was placed with the investigation. It was now firmly in the hands of the local constabulary. They would look at the possibility that Kyle Rafferty had ordered the arson attack on the bakery and he had hired the three local lads to do it. If Pearce Hamill was responsible for torching his own business in order to get the insurance money, then the police would get it out of Rafferty. Moss warned him that it might not be a quick process. The police would watch them both and eavesdrop. If they thought there was something in it they would pull them in for questioning. Put the allegation to them and see how they reacted. It might take days, a week, a couple of weeks or even longer.

    In the meantime, Moss felt he would use the time to find out if there was a connection between the Bellamy brothers and the bag snatch on Claudette. Then he felt a modicum of common sense that brought him down to the ground with a bump. He had to let it go. He couldn't risk stepping on the polices' feet. His interaction may cause problems. He would let the course of justice take its path. No matter how long it took. The cogs of any investigation may turn slowly in some cases, though he did have time on his side. His client didn't have to write a cheque for another few months. By the end of one year they would be in a position to determine if there was criminal intent in the claim. He ditched the case for now and got on with something else.

## Chapter Six

A further couple of days elapsed. Moss was on the verge of calling DI Terry to ask him for an update when he received a surprise visit from DCI Steve Rice and DI Pamela Bent to his office. Their visit was as sudden as the bout of warm sunshine that had settled over the south of England. In the middle of May it was most welcome. It was FA Cup final day tomorrow. Therefore, the game might be played in eighty-degree heat which usually made for a poor spectacle.

It was the first time he had seen them since the search for Henri Barrington, when they had also paid him an unannounced visit.

Neither of them had changed that much in the gap of a year or so since he had last seen them. Pamela had changed her hairstyle and may have put on an extra pound or two. Rice was pretty much the same. Maybe his jacket was different, and his aftershave was far tangier than previously. They came up the staircase, into the office, and plumped into the armchairs. After the banalities they got down to business.

"To what do I owe the pleasure of this visit?" Moss asked them in a jocular manner.

DCI Rice cleared his voice. "We got a sniff that you've been in touch about an arson case over in West Ham."

"That's correct. It's an insurance investigation."

"Colleagues in that manor pulled in Kyle Rafferty for questioning."

"Along with his uncle Pearce Hamill," she added.

"They both denied it at first. But we've already chatted to Nathan Bellamy and got the gist of what happened from him." DCI Rice was precise in the way he spoke.

Moss forced a smile and nodded his head at the same time, something which didn't feel natural. "Who cracked first?" he asked.

"Hamill," she replied. "He admitted it was his idea to set the place on fire."

"Why?"

"He was losing money hand over fist."

"The bigger super stores were driving him underground."

"Yet another example of a small independent being driven out by the big players," quipped Moss. "It's a right shame."

"The business was haemorrhaging money, so the pair of them cooked up a half-baked plan to set it ablaze."

"More like cockeyed plan," said Moss. Rice smiled. "What did Bellamy tell you?" Moss asked.

"He admitted it all. When we presented him with our suspicions, he caved in and confirmed it all."

Moss tutted softly. "Incredible. The business has been on that site for more than seventy years. It was his father's before him. What about charges pending?"

"They've all been charged," she confirmed.

DCI Rice adjusted his posture. "This morning with various. Attempted deception, Fraud. Endangering life. Arson."

"That's just for starters," she added.

"What about the heavies who put Nathan Bellamy in hospital?"

"Rafferty denies any knowledge of that."

"What about Bellamy?"

"He denies it. Said he was jumped on by three lads outside of a kebab shop on Barking Road. It had nothing to do with any blackmail."

"So, he's decided to play possum on that one?" Moss asked.

"True," replied Rice, agreeing with him. "He's not prepared to finger them for fear of retribution."

"Quite likely," said Moss.

"We've got enough on them to ensure they'll do some jail time."

Moss thought of them doing a custodial sentence was about right. "Can you do me a favour?" he asked.

"What is it?" Rice asked.

"Check out…" Moss paused in mid-sentence. He had had a sudden change of mind…

"Check out what?" DI Bent asked.

"No, forget it."

"Okay," said Rice, glancing sideways at his female colleague.

In that split second, Moss had gone off the idea of trying to trace the scrote who had crept up behind Claudette and yanked the handbag off her shoulder.

DCI Rice and his colleague got up out of their seats. Moss escorted them onto the landing, then watched them go down the staircase to the door at the bottom. Once again, he thought he had done the right thing, but may regret it in the future and wished he had completed the sentence.

He went back into his office, stood by the window and put his eyes on the activity down below on the street. He daydreamed for a few moments, before he was pulled clear of a lot of wayward thoughts by the sound of the telephone ringing. He turned to his desk, tapped the loudspeaker button, took a deep breath and said:

"David Moss Private Investigation. How may I help you today?" he asked in a pleasant, clear and endearing voice.

## The End

About the author….

Neal Hardin lives in Hull, England. He is the author of several novels, novellas and short stories. His first published novel, 'The Go-To Guy' was published in March 2018, by Stairwell Books, based in York, England; and Norwalk, Connecticut, USA.

Before retiring in 2016, Neal worked in the Education sector for over 21 years. He enjoys travelling whenever possible. He has visited the United States and Canada on many occasions, along with Japan, China, Australia and other countries.

Despite the frustration of watching them, he follows his local football club, Hull City, home and away and enjoys most sports and working out in the gym. He continues to write and enjoys the discipline of writing and constructing great stories.

Neal Hardin is also the author of…

*Dallas After Dark*
*A Gangland Tale*
*The Four Fables*
*Moscow Calling*
*On the Edge*
*The Wish-List*
*A Titanic Story*
*The Taking of Flight 98*
*Perilous Traffic*
*Triple Intrigue*
*Soho Retro*
*A Trio of Tales*
*Saigon Boulevard*
*It's Murder in London*
*Two Steps of Intrigue*

*All these novels are available to purchase on Amazon*
See me on Twitter @HardinNealp

Printed in Great Britain
by Amazon